THE NEW YORK

MICHAEL PALMER

Author of *Silent Treatment*

SIDE EFFECTS

"HAS EVERYTHING—A TERRIFYING PLOT... BREAKNECK PACE... VIVIDLY DRAWN CHARACTERS." —John Saul

ISBN 0-553-27618-2
US $6.50 / $8.99 CAN

Michael Palmer's Bestsellers

THE SISTERHOOD

"A suspenseful page-turner . . . jolts and entertains the reader." —Mary Higgins Clark

"Terrific . . a compelling suspense tale." —Clive Cussler

FLASHBACK

"The most gripping medical thriller I've read in many years." —David Morrell

EXTREME MEASURES

"Spellbinding . . . a chillingly sinister novel made all the more frightening by [Palmer's] medical authority." —*The Denver Post*

NATURAL CAUSES

"Reinvents the medical thriller" —*Library Journal*

SILENT TREATMENT

"A *Marathon Man*–style plot loaded with innovative twists . . . extremely vivid characters." —*Kirkus Reviews*

Michael Palmer has been a practicing physician for more than twenty years, most recently as an emergency-room doctor and a specialist in the treatment of alcoholism and chemical dependency.

BANTAM BOOKS BY MICHAEL PALMER

The Sisterhood

Side Effects

Flashback

Extreme Measures

Natural Causes

Silent Treatment

SIDE EFFECTS

Michael Palmer

BANTAM BOOKS
NEW YORK • TORONTO • LONDON • SYDNEY • AUCKLAND

The characters, events, institutions, and organizations in this book are wholly fictional or are used fictitiously. Any apparent resemblance to any person alive or dead, to any actual events, and to any actual institutions or organizations, is entirely coincidental.

SIDE EFFECTS

A Bantam Book

PUBLISHING HISTORY

Bantam edition published April 1985
Bantam reissue/February 1995

ISBN 0-553-27618-2

Published simultaneously in the United States and Canada

Bantam Books are published by Bantam Books, a division of Bantam Doubleday Dell Publishing Group, Inc. Its trademark, consisting of the words "Bantam Books" and the portrayal of a rooster, is Registered in U.S. Patent and Trademark Office and in other countries. Marca Registrada. Bantam Books, 1540 Broadway, New York, New York 10036.

PRINTED IN THE UNITED STATES OF AMERICA

RAD 23 22 21 20 19 18 17 16 15

To Jane Rotrosen Berkey,
my agent, my friend, my muse;
and, of course, to Danny and Matt

Acknowledgment

A novel is hardly the sole endeavor many believe. I am both grateful and fortunate to have had Jeanne Bernkopf, my editor, and Linda Grey, editorial director at Bantam, in my writing life.

PROLOGUE

Mecklenburg, Germany
August 1944

Willi Becker leaned against the coarse wood siding of the officers' club and squinted up at the late afternoon sun, a pale disk rendered nearly impotent by the dust from a hundred allied bombings of industrial targets surrounding the Ravensbrück concentration camp for women. He closed his eyes and for an instant thought he heard the drone of enemy planes somewhere to the south.

"Not a moment too soon, Dr. Becker," he muttered. "You will be leaving this hellhole not a moment too soon." He checked the chronometer his brother, Edwin, had sent him from "a grateful patient" in the Dachau camp. Nearly fifteen-thirty. After months of the most meticulous preparations there were now only hours to go. He felt an electric excitement.

Across the dirt courtyard, clusters of prisoners, their shaved heads glistening, worked on bomb shelters, while their SS guards jockeyed for bits of shade beneath the overhangs of barracks. Becker recognized two of the women: a tall, awkward teenager named Eva and a feckless Russian who had encouraged him to call her Bunny. They were but two of the three dozen or so subjects whose examinations he was forced to omit in the interest of escape.

For a minute, Becker battled the urge to call the two scarecrow women over and tell them that fate had denied them their parts in the magnificent work that scholars and generations to come would hail as the start of the Beckerian population control. Beckerian. The word, though he spoke it daily, still had a thrilling ring. Newtonian physics, Shakespearean drama, Malthusian philosophy; upon so very few had human history bestowed such honor. In time, Becker was certain, this immortality would be his. After all, he was still six weeks shy of his thirtieth birthday, yet already acknowledged for his brilliance in the field of reproductive physiology.

Adjusting the collar on the gray-green SS uniform he was wearing for the last time, the tall, classically Nordic physician crossed the courtyard and headed toward the research buildings on the north edge of camp.

The Ravensbrück medical staff, once numbering more than fifty, had dwindled to a dozen. Himmler, bending to the cry for physicians in military hospitals, had suspended the experiments in gas gangrene and bone grafting, as well as those on battlefield cauterization of wounds using coals and acid. The doctors responsible for those programs had been transferred. Only the sterilization units remained, three of them in all, each devoted to the problem of eliminating the ability to procreate without impairing the ability to perform slave labor. Becker strode past the empty laboratories—another sign of the inevitable—and turned onto "Grünestrasse," the tarmac track on which the officials and research facilities of his Green Unit were located. To the east, he could see the camouflage-painted chimney tops of the crematorium. A gentle west wind was bearing the fetid smoke and ash away from the camp. Becker smiled thinly and nodded. The Mecklenburger Bucht, fifty kilometers of capricious Baltic Sea between Rostock and the Danish island fishing village of Gedser, would be calm. One less variable to be concerned about.

Becker was mentally working through the other incalculables when he glanced through the windows of his office. Dr. Franz Müller, his back turned, was inspecting the volumes in Becker's library. Becker tensed. A visit from Müller, the head of the Blue Unit and director of reproductive studies, was not unusual, but the man was considerate to a fault and almost always called ahead.

Was Müller's visit on this of all days a coincidence? Becker paused by the doorway to his office and prepared for the cerebral swordplay at which the older man was such a master. He congratulated himself for holding back the documentation, however scant, of Blue Unit's deception. Müller's blade might be as quick as his own, but his own had poison on its tip. Müller, he felt certain, was a sham.

The Blue Unit work concerning the effect of ovarian irradiation on fertility looked promising on paper. However, Becker had good reason to believe that not one prisoner had actually been treated with radiation. The data were being falsified by Müller and his cohort, Josef Rendl. Whether they had gone so far as to assist prisoners in escaping, Becker was unsure, but he suspected as much. His proof, though skimpy, would have been enough to discredit, if not destroy, both men. However, their destruction had never meant as much to him as their control.

In an effort to gain some tiny advantage, Becker opened the outside door silently and tiptoed up the three stairs to his office door. Not a sound. Not even the creak of a floorboard.

Becker opened the door quickly. Müller was perched on the corner of his desk, looking directly at him. "Ah, Willi, my friend. Please excuse the brazenness of my intrusion. I was just passing by and remembered your mentioning that Fruhopf's *Reproductive Physiology* was among your holdings." First exchange to the master.

"It is good to see you, Franz. My library and laboratory are always yours, as I have told you many times." A perfunctory handshake, and Becker moved to his seat behind the desk. "Did you find it?"

"Pardon?"

"The Fruhopf. Did you find it?"

"Oh. Yes. Yes, I have it right here."

"Fine. Keep it as long as you wish."

"Thank you." Müller made no move to leave. Instead, he lowered himself into the chair opposite Becker and began packing his pipe from a worn leather pouch.

Not even the formality of a request to stay. Becker's wariness grew. Hidden by the desk, his long, manicured fingers undulated nervously. "Sweet?" he asked, sliding a dish of mints across the desktop. It was Müller's show, and Müller could make the initial move.

"Thank you, no." Müller grinned and patted his belly. "You heard about Paris?"

Becker nodded. "No surprise. Except perhaps for the speed with which Patton did the job."

"I agree. The man is a devil." Müller ran his fingers through his thick, muddy blond hair. He was Becker's equal in height, perhaps an inch or so more, but he was built like a Kodiak bear. "And in the east the Russians come and come. We wipe out a division and two more take its place. I hear they are nearing the oil field at Ploesti."

"They are a barbarous people. For decades all they have done is rut about and multiply. What our armies cannot do to them, their own expanding population will eventually accomplish."

"Ah, yes," Müller said. "The theories of your sainted Thomas Malthus. Keep our panzers in abeyance, and let our enemies procreate themselves into submission."

Becker felt his hackles rise. Cynicism was the finest honed of Müller's strokes. An irritated, angry opponent left openings, made mistakes. Calm down, he urged himself. Calm down and wait until the man declares himself. Could he know about the escape? The mere thought made the Green Unit leader queasy. "Now, Franz," he said evenly, "you know how much I enjoy discussing philosophy with you, especially Malthusian philosophy, but right now we have a war to win, yes?"

Müller's eyes narrowed. "*Quatsch*," he said.

"What?"

"I said *Quatsch*, Willi. Absolute nonsense. First of all, we are not going to win any war. You know that as well as I do. Secondly, I do not believe you care. One way or the other."

Becker stiffened. The bastard had found out. Somehow he had found out. He shifted his right hand slightly on his knee and gauged the distance to the Walther revolver in his top left drawer. "How can you impugn me in this way?"

Müller smiled and sank back in his chair. "You misunderstand me, Willi. What I am saying is a compliment to you as a scientist and philosopher. *Surtout le travaille*. Above all the work. Is that not how you feel? On second thought, I will have that sweet, if you please."

Becker slid the dish across. Here he was, bewildered, apprehensive, and totally off balance, and still with no idea of the reason for Müller's visit. Inwardly, and grudgingly, he smiled. The man was slick. A total bastard, but a slick one. "I believe in my research, if that is what you mean."

"Precisely."

"And *your* research, Franz, how does *it* go?" Time for a counterthrust.

"It goes and it stops and it goes again. You know how that is."

Sure, sure, but mostly it doesn't exist, Becker wanted to say. Instead, he nodded his agreement.

"Willi, my friend, I fear the war will be over anytime now. Weeks, days, hours; no one seems to know. I have no notion of what will happen to us—to those in our laboratory—after that. Perhaps our research will be made public, perhaps not. I feel it is crucial for each unit, Blue, Green, and Brown, to know exactly the nature and status of the work being done by the others. That way, we can be as well prepared as possible for whatever the future brings." Becker's eyes widened. "I have decided to start with your Green Unit," Müller went on. "A meeting has been scheduled for twenty-one hundred hours this evening in the Blue Unit conference room. Please be prepared to present your research in detail at that time."

"What?"

"And Willi, I would like time to study your data before then. Please have them on my desk by nineteen hundred hours." Müller's eyes were flint.

Becker felt numb. His data, including the synthesis and biological properties of Estronate 250, were sealed in a dozen notebooks, hidden in the hull of a certain Rostock fishing boat. His mind raced. "My . . . my work is very fragmented, Franz. I . . . I shall need at least a day, perhaps two, to organize my data." This can't be happening, he thought. Nineteen hundred hours is too early. Even twenty-one hundred hours is too soon. "Let me show you what I have," Becker said, reaching toward the drawer with the Walther.

At that instant, Dr. Josef Rendl stepped inside the office doorway. Rendl's aide, a behemoth whom Becker knew only as Stossel, remained just outside in the hall. They had been somewhere out there all the time. Becker felt sure of it. Rendl, a former pediatrician, was a short, doughy man with a pasty complexion and a high-pitched laugh, both of which Becker found disgusting. Becker's information had it that Rendl's mother was a Jew, a fact that had been carefully concealed. For a frozen second, two, Becker sized up the situation. Müller was but two meters away, Rendl three, and the animal, Stossel, perhaps five. No real chance for three kills, even with surprise on his side, which, it seemed now, might not be the case. The battle would have to be verbal . . . at least for the moment.

Becker nodded at the newcomer. "Welcome, Josef. My, my. The entire Blue Unit brain trust. What a pleasant honor."

"Willi." Rendl smiled and returned the gesture. "Leutnant Stossel and I were just passing by and noticed the two of you in here. What do you think of the meetings? A good idea to present our work to one another, no?"

You smarmy son of a Jew whore, Becker thought. "Yes. Yes. An excellent idea," he said.

"And you will honor us by presenting the Green Unit biochemical studies tonight?" Rendl, though an oberst, exactly the same rank as Willi, often spoke with Müller's authority dusting his words.

Becker, fighting to maintain composure, sucked in an extra measure of air. "Tonight would be acceptable." Both of the other men nodded. "But," he added, "tomorrow evening would be much better." Because, he smiled to himself, I intend to be a thousand kilometers away from here by then.

"Oh?" Franz Müller propped his chin on one hand.

"Yes. I have a few final chemical tests to run on Estronate Two-fifty. Some loose ends in the initial set of experiments." As Becker scrambled through the words, searching for some kind of purchase, an idea began to take hold. "There's an extraction with ether that I was unable to complete because my supply ran out. Late yesterday, several five-gallon tins arrived. You signed for them yourself." Müller nodded. Becker's words became more confident. "Well, if you would give me tonight to complete this phase of my work, I shall gladly present what I have tomorrow. You must remember that what I have is not much. Estronate Two-fifty is far more theory than fact. A promising set of notions, with only the roughest of preliminary work on humans."

Müller pushed himself straighter in his chair and leveled his gaze across the desk. "Actually, Willi, I do not believe that what you say is true." The words, a sledgehammer, were delivered with silky calm.

"Wh . . . what are you talking about?" The question in Becker's mind was no longer whether Müller knew anything, but how much. His trump card—Blue Unit's falsified data—would have to be played. The only issue now was timing.

"What I am talking about is information that your work on Estronate Two-fifty is rather advanced."

"That's nonsense," Becker shot back.

"Further, that you are lacking only stability studies and the elimination of a troublesome side effect—some sort of bleeding tendency, is it?—before more extensive clinical testing can be done. Why, Willi, are you keeping this information from us? You have here, perhaps, the most awesome discovery—even the most awesome weapon—of our time, yet you claim to know nothing."

"Ridiculous."

"No, Willi. Not ridiculous. Information straight from a source in your laboratory. Now either we receive a full disclosure of the exact status of your work, or I shall see to it that Mengele or even Himmler receives the information we have."

"Your accusations are preposterous."

"We shall judge that after you have presented your work. Tonight, then?"

"No. Not tonight." It was time. "My work is not ready for presentation." Becker paused theatrically, drumming his fingertips on the desktop and then stroking them bowlike across one another. "Is yours?"

"What?"

Becker sensed, more than saw, Müller stiffen. "Your work. The Blue Unit radiation studies. You see, the two of you are not the only ones with—what was the word you used?—ah, yes, sources, that was it. Sources."

Rendl and Müller exchanged the fraction of a glance. The gesture was enough to dispel any doubt as to the validity of Becker's information.

"Willi, Willi," Müller said, shaking his head. "You try my patience. I shall give you until tomorrow night. Meanwhile, we shall organize our data and present them at the same time."

"Excellent," Becker said, reveling in being on the offensive at last. "And, please, do try to have some of your human subjects available for examination. It would lend so much to the understanding of your work." This time, Müller and Rendl shared a more pronounced look.

"You don't really care, Willi, do you?" Müller said suddenly.

"I . . . I'm afraid I don't know what you mean, Franz."

"You see only yourself. Your place in history. The here and now mean nothing to you. Germany, the Reich, the Jews, the Americans, the prisoners, your colleagues—all are the same to you. All are nothing."

"You have your mistresses, and I have mine," Becker said simply. "Is immortality so homely that I should throw her out of my bed? You are right, Franz. I do not concern myself with petty day-to-day issues. I have already reached planes of theory and research that few have ever even dreamed of. Should I worry about the price of eggs, or whether the Führer's hemorrhoids are inflamed, or whether the prisoners here at Ravensbrück are pathetic inside the wire or without, on top of the dirt or beneath it?"

"Willi, Willi, Willi." Müller's voice and eyes held pity rather than reproach.

Becker looked over at Rendl, and there, too, saw condescension, not ire. Don't you dare pity me, he wanted to scream. Revere me. The children of your children will prosper because of me. The *lebensraum* for which so many have fought and died will be attained not with bullets, but with my equations, my solution. Mine!

Müller broke the silence. "We are all with the same laboratory. We all stand to lose much if we fall into disfavor—either now with the Reich or soon with the Allies. I expect a full disclosure of your work with Estronate Two-fifty, Dr. Becker."

Becker nodded his acquiescence and silently prayed that his portrayal of a beaten man would be convincing.

Minutes later, the three men from the Blue Unit were gone. Becker closed his eyes and massaged the tightness at the base of his neck. Then he poured three fingers of Polish vodka from a bottle Edwin had sent him, and drank it in a single draught. The encounter with Müller and Rendl, triumphant though it had been, had left him drained. He fingered his chronometer. Was there time for a nap? No, he decided. No sleeping until this filthy camp with its petty people and skeleton prisoners was a thing of the past.

He walked briskly from his office to the low, frame, barracklike building that housed the Green Unit's biochemical research section. With glances to either side, he backed through the rear door and locked it from the inside. The wooden shutters were closed and latched, creating a darkness inside that was tangible.

The flashlight was by the door—where he had hung it that morning. Using the hooded beam, Becker counted the slate squares making up the top of his long central workbench. Reaching beneath the fifth one, he pulled. The cabinet supporting the slate slid out from the others. Beneath it, hidden from even a detailed search, was the circular mouth of a tunnel.

"And the rockets red glare, the bombs bursting in air. . . ." Alfi Runstedt sang the words as he dug, although he had no idea of their meaning. The song, he knew, was the American anthem, and this day, at least, that was all that mattered. As a child in Leipzig, he had spent hours beside his family's new Victrola memorizing selections from a thick album of anthems of the world. Even then, the American "Star Spangled Banner" had been his favorite.

Now, he would have the chance to see the country itself and, even more wonderful, to become an American.

"Oh say does that star spangled ba-a-ner-er ye-et wa-ave. . . ." With one syllable, he rammed the spade into the sandy soil. With the next, he threw the dirt up to the side of the grave. The trench, three feet deep, was better than half done. Lying on the grass to Alfi's left, two meters from him, were the corpses of the peasant woman and her son, which would be laid inside as soon as the proper depth was reached. Alfi Runstedt paid them no mind.

He was stripped to his ample waist. Dirt, mingling with sweat, was turning his arms and walrus torso into a quagmire. The thick, red hair on his chest was plastered into what looked like a fecal mat. His SS uniform pants were soaked and filthy. ". . . and the home of the brave. O-oh say can you see. . . ."

"Alfi, take a break if you need one. We cannot make any moves until dark. I told you that." From his perch atop a large boulder, Willi Becker gazed down into the narrow crypt.

Alfi stopped his digging and dragged a muddy wrist across his muddy forehead. "It is nothing, Herr Oberst. Believe me, nothing. I would dig a thousand such holes in the ground for the honor you have done me and the reward you have promised. Tell me, do you know if many American women are thin like Betty Grable? One of the men in the barracks at Friedrichshafen had her picture by his cot."

"I don't know, Alfi." Becker laughed. "Soon, you shall be able to see for yourself. If we meet the boat in Denmark and if my cousin has made all the arrangements, we should be in North America with valid papers within a few weeks."

"Big ifs, yes?"

"Not so big. The biggest if anyplace is money, and hopefully we have enough of that. We'll need some luck, but our chances of making it out undetected seem rather good."

"And you do not think me a traitor or a coward for wanting to leave with you?"

"Am I?"

"You are different, Herr Oberst. You have research to complete. Important research. I am just a junior officer in an army that is losing a war."

"Ah, but you are also my aide. My *invaluable* aide. Was it not you who informed me of the old system of drainage pipes running beneath Ravensbrück?"

"Well, it was just my fortune to have worked with the sanitation department when I was younger and—"

"And was it not you who chose to keep that information our little secret and to help me with the connecting tunnel?"

"Well, I guess—"

"So don't say you are not deserving, Unteroffizier Runstedt. Don't ever say that."

"Thank you, Oberst. Thank you." And at that moment, Alfred Runstedt, the man who had overseen or assisted in the extermination of several thousand Ravensbrück prisoners, the man who had, not an hour before, calmly strangled to death a woman, her young son, her husband, and her father, wept with joy.

Hollywood, New York, baseball, Chicago—now just words, they would soon be his life. Since the June invasion at Normandy, and even more frequently since the abortive July attempt to assassinate the Führer at Rastenburg, in eastern Prussia, he had been forced to endure the recurrent nightmare of his own capture and death. In one version of the dream, it was execution by hanging; in another, by firing squad. In still another, ghostly prisoners, totally naked, beat him to death with sticks.

Soon, the nightmares would stop.

The grave was nearly deep enough. The wooded grove which was serving as an impromptu cemetery accepted the evening more quickly than did the adjacent field and was nearly dark when Becker pushed himself off the rock. "So, just a few more spadefuls, is it?" he said.

"I think so," Alfi answered. He had donned a windbreaker against the chill of dusk. His uniform shirt, hanging on a branch, would be kept clean for a final display.

"Cigar?"

"Thank you, Herr Oberst." Alfi paused to light the narrow cheroot, one of a seemingly endless supply possessed by Becker.

"I think you are deep enough now," Becker said after a half dozen more passes. "Let me give you a hand."

Alfi scrambled from the grave. One with the arms, and one with the legs, the two men unceremoniously tossed the bodies of the woman and the boy into the pit. Alfi replaced the dirt with the spade. Becker helped, using his foot.

"Forgive me if I am out of line, Herr Oberst," Alfi said as he shoveled, "but is there any possibility of notifying my sister at the munitions plant in Schwartzheide that, contrary to the reports she will receive, I am alive and well?"

Becker chuckled and shook his head. "Alfi, Alfi. I have explained to you the need for secrecy. Why do you think I waited until only a few hours ago to tell you of my escape plan? I, myself, have been measuring every word for weeks, afraid I might give it away. For now, and for the foreseeable future both of us must remain among the lamentable casualties of the war. Even my brother, Edwin, at the camp in Dachau will not know."

"I understand," Alfi said, realizing that he did not—at least not totally.

"By the morning, you and I shall be both free and dead." Becker stamped on the topsoil of the grave and began throwing handfuls of dusty sand and pine needles over the fresh dirt.

The idea of using the bodies of the farmer and his son-in-law was sheer genius, Becker acknowledged. Originally, he had planned to have the two farmers supply him with transportation to Rostock. Their lorry would now run just as well with him at the wheel. The other refinements in his original plan were dazzling. When all was said and done, Müller and Rendl would be left to face the music with little or no suspicion that he was still alive.

". . . and the home of the brave." Becker joined the startled Runstedt in the final line.

Both Runstedt and Becker groaned repeatedly with the effort of dragging first one body and then another through the sewage pipe to the false cabinet in the biochemical research building. Intermixed with the sounds of their effort were the scratching and scraping of countless rats, scurrying about in the pitch darkness.

The young farmer was, in height and frame, a virtual twin of Becker's. The older man, like Runstedt, was heavy, but taller than Runstedt by several centimeters.

"Don't worry about the difference in your heights, Alfi," Becker had reassured him. "By the time the explosion and fire are through with these bodies, no one will want to get any closer to them than it takes to remove our watches, rings, identification medallions, and wallets."

With Becker pushing from below, Runstedt hauled the corpses through the base of the cabinet and stretched them out on the wooden floor.

"Perfect, perfect," Becker said, scrambling through the hole. "We are right on time."

"Oberst," Alfi said, "I have one question, if I may."

"Of course."

"How will we keep the tunnel from being discovered after the fire and explosion?"

"Hah! An excellent point," Becker exclaimed. "One, I might add, that I am not at all surprised to have you make. I have kept the steel plate you removed to make the opening in the pipe. It fits perfectly, and stays in place with several small hooks I have welded on. With ashes and debris piled on top, I doubt the pipe will ever be discovered."

"Brilliant. Herr Oberst, you are a truly brilliant man."

"Thank you, Unteroffizier. And now, we must check. Have you said anything to anyone which might suggest you are planning to leave tonight?"

"No, sir."

"Good. And have you told the men in your barrack that you will be working late in the laboratory with me?"

"Yes, Oberst."

"Wonderful. We are ready to arrange the ether, to set the charge and the timer, and to exchange clothes with our friends here."

"Then it is off to hot dogs and Betty Grable," Alfi said.

"Hot dogs and Betty Grable," Becker echoed. "But first a toast to our success thus far. Amaretto?"

"Cheroots! Amaretto! My God, Oberst, how do you keep coming up with these things?" Alfi took the proffered glass, inhaled the wonderful almond scent, and then drained the liqueur in a gulp. The cyanide, its deadly aroma and taste masked, took just seconds to work.

Becker was removing his uniform and jewelry as Runstedt, writhing and vomiting on the floor, breathed his last.

With some effort, Becker dressed the young farmer in his own uniform, adding a ring, billfold, identification necklace, and, finally, Edwin's watch, an elegant piece which many in the camp associated with him.

Next, he stepped back and, with the use of the hooded flashlight, surveyed the scene. Everything, everyone had to be perfectly placed.

He undressed the farmer who was to have served as Alfi's double, tossed the clothes to one side, and then dumped the naked body down the tunnel. "Now, Alfi, my most loyal of servants, we must find a place for you." He shone the torch on the contorted, violet face by his feet.

In minutes the arrangement was complete. The young farmer's body lay in the center of the laboratory, his face resting beside a laboratory timer and a five-gallon tin of ether. Several other tins were spaced throughout the dry, wooden building. Alfi's body lay near the door, as far from the explosive vapors as possible. It would be the validity of Runstedt's face which would assure acceptance of Becker's own demise.

The simple elegance of the whole plan was as pleasing as a major research success, and Becker felt ballooned with pride as he made a final survey of the scene.

He checked the small ignition charge and set the timer for ten minutes.

Willi Becker was grinning as he dropped into the tunnel and pulled the workbench cabinet back in place. He sealed the drainage pipe opening, and without a glance at the farmer's body, crawled toward the exit beyond the camp's electrified fence.

He was behind the wheel of the lorry, a quarter mile from the camp, when the peaceful night sky turned red-gold. Seconds later, he heard the muffled series of explosions.

"Good-bye, Josef Rendl," he said. "I shall enjoy reading in *The New York Times* of your trial and execution. And as for you, Dr. Müller, it is game and match between us, eh? A shame you shall never know who really won. Perhaps someday, if you survive, I will send you a postcard."

His wife and son were waiting for him in Rostock. As Becker bounced down the road, he began humming the "Star Spangled Banner."

THE PRESENT

1

Sunday 9 December

The morning was typical of December in Massachusetts. A brushed aluminum sky blended into three-day-old snow covering the cornfields along Route 127. Dulled by streaks of road salt, Jared Samuels's red MGTD roadster still sparkled like a flare against the landscape.

From the passenger seat, Kate Bennett watched her husband negotiate the country road using only the thumb and first two fingers of his left hand. His dark brown eyes, though fixed on the road, were relaxed, and he seemed to be singing to himself. Kate laughed.

"Hey, Doc," Jared asked glancing over, "just what are you laughing at?"

"You."

"Well, that's a relief. For a moment there I thought you were laughing at *me*. . . . Tell me what I was doing that was so funny, I might want to write it down."

"Not funny," Kate said. "Just nice. It makes me happy to see you happy. There's a peacefulness in you that I haven't seen since the campaign began."

"Then you should have turned on the bedroom light last night at, oh, eleven-thirty, was it?"

"You didn't just pass out after?"

"Nope. Five minutes of absolute Nirvana . . . then I

passed out." He flashed the smile that had always been reserved for her alone.

"I love you, you know," Kate said.

Jared looked at her again. It had been a while since either of them had said the words outside the bedroom. "Even though I'm not going to be the Honorable Congressman from the Sixth District?"

"Especially because you're not going to be the Honorable Congressman from the Sixth District." She checked the time. "Jared, it's only nine-thirty. Do you think we could stop at the lake for a bit? We haven't in such a long time. I brought a bag of bread just in case."

Jared slowed. "Only if you promise not to poach when goddamn Carlisle starts hitting to my backhand."

"Once. I stole a ball from you once in almost two years of playing together, and you never let me forget it."

"No poaching?"

Was he being serious? It bothered her that after almost five years of marriage she couldn't always tell. "No poaching," she vowed finally, wary of making a response that would chip the mood of the morning. Lately, it seemed, their upbeat moods were becoming less frequent and more fragile.

"The ducks bless you," Jared said in a tone which did nothing to resolve her uncertainty.

The lake, more a large pond, was a mile off 127 in the general direction of the Oceanside Racquet Club. It was surrounded by dense thickets of pine and scrub oak, separated by the backyards of a dozen or so houses—upper-class dwellings in most communities, but only average in the North Shore village of Beverly Farms. At the far end of the ice cover, hockey sticks in hand, a trio of boys chased a puck up and down a makeshift rink, their bright mufflers and caps phosphorescing against the pearl-gray morning. Nearer the road, a spillway kept the surface from freezing. Bobbing on the half-moon it created were a score of ducks. Several more rested on the surrounding ice.

The couple stood motionless by their car, transfixed by the scene.

"Currier and Ives," Kate said wistfully.

"Bonnie and Clyde," Jared responded in the same tone.

"You're so romantic, Counselor." Kate managed a two-second glare of reproach before she smiled. Jared's often black sense of humor was hit or miss—"kamikaze humor," she had labeled it. "Come on, let's duck," she called.

Her runner's legs, objects of the fantasies of more than a few of her fellow physicians at Metropolitan Hospital of Boston, brought her easily down the snowy embankment, her auburn hair bouncing on the hood of her parka.

As she approached the water, a huge gander, honking arrogantly, advanced to get his due. Kate eyed the bird and then threw a handful of bread over his head to a milling group of smaller mallards and wood ducks. A moment later, from atop the bank, Jared scaled an entire roll precisely at the feet of the gander, who snatched it up and swaggered away.

Kate turned to him, hands on hips. "Are you trying to undermine my authority?"

"Always side with the overdog. That's my motto," he said brightly. "I even voted for Mattingly in the Sixth Congressional race. I mean who would want to waste his vote on a sure loser like the other guy?"

"A two-point defeat when you started out twenty-two behind? Some loser. Slide on down here, big boy, and I'll give you our traditional Sunday morning kiss."

"We have a traditional Sunday morning kiss?"

"Not yet."

Jared surveyed the embankment and then chose a safer, albeit much longer, route than Kate had taken.

She stifled a smile. *Never lift up your left foot until your right one's firmly planted* was a favorite saying of Jared's father, and here was the scion—the disciple—embracing the philosophy in its most literal sense. Someday,

Jared, she thought, you are going to lift up both of your feet at the same time and discover you can fly.

His kiss was firm and deep, his tongue caressing the roof of her mouth, the insides of her cheeks. Kate responded in kind, sliding both her hands to his buttocks and holding him tightly.

"You kiss good, Doc," he said. "I mean *good*."

"Do you think the ducks would mind if we started making dirty snow angels?" she whispered, warming his ear with her lips.

"No, but I think the Carlisles would." Jared pulled free. "We've got to get going. I wonder why they keep inviting us to play with them when we haven't beaten them once in two years."

"They just love a challenge, I guess." Kate shrugged, tossed out the remaining bread, and followed him along the safe route to the road.

"Did someone call this morning?" he asked over his shoulder.

"Pardon?"

"While I was in the shower." Jared turned to her as he reached the MG and leaned against the perfectly maintained canvas top. "I thought I heard the phone ring."

"Oh, you did." A nugget of tension materialized beneath her breastbone. Jared hadn't missed hearing the phone after all. "It . . . it was nothing, really. Just Dr. Willoughby." Kate slid into the passenger seat. She had wanted to choose carefully the moment to discuss the pathology chief's call.

"How is Yoda?" he asked, settling behind the wheel.

"He's fine. I wish you wouldn't call him that, Jared. He's been very good to me, and it sounds so demeaning."

"It's not demeaning. Honestly." He turned the key and the engine rumbled to life. "Why, without Yoda, Luke Skywalker would never have survived the first *Star Wars* sequel. What else could I possibly call someone who's three feet tall, bald with bushy eyebrows, and lives in a swamp? Anyway, what did he want?"

Kate felt the nugget expand, and fought the sensation. "He just needed to discuss some twists and turns in the politics at the hospital," she said evenly. "I'll tell you about them later. How about we use the little time we have to plan some kind of strategic ambush for the Carlisles?"

"Don't poach. That's all the strategy we need. Now what was so important to ol' Yoda at eight-thirty on a Sunday morning?"

Although the words were spoken lightly, Kate noted that he had not yet put the car into gear. From the beginning of their relationship, he had been somehow threatened both by her career and by her unique friendship with her aging department head. It was nothing he had ever said, but the threat was there. She was certain of it. "Later?" She tried one last time.

Jared switched off the ignition.

The mood of the morning shattered like dropped crystal. Kate forced her eyes to make and maintain contact with his. "He said that tomorrow morning he was going to send letters to the medical school and to Norton Reese announcing his retirement in June or as soon as a successor can be chosen as chief of the department."

"And . . . ?"

"And I think you know already what comes next." Deep inside her, Kate felt sparks of anger begin to replace the tension. This exchange, her news, her chance to become at thirty-five the youngest department chief, to say nothing of the only woman department chief, at Metro—they should have been embraced by the marriage with the same joy as Jared's election to Congress would have been.

"Try me," Jared said, gazing off across the lake.

Kate sighed. "He wants my permission to submit my name to the faculty search committee as his personal recommendation."

"And you thanked him very much, but begged off because you and your husband agreed two years ago to start your family when the election was over, and you simply couldn't take on the responsibility and time demands of a department chairmanship—especially of a moneyless, understaffed, political football of a department like the one Yoda is scurrying away from now—right?"

"Wrong!" The snap in her voice was reflex. She cursed herself for losing control so easily, and took several seconds to calm down before continuing. "I told him I would think about it and talk it over with my husband and some of my friends at the hospital. I told him either to leave my name off his letter or wait a week before sending it."

"Have you thought what the job would take out of you? I mean Yoda's had two coronaries in the last few years, and he is certainly a lot more low key than you are."

"Dammit, Jared. Stop calling him that. And they weren't coronaries. Only angina."

"All right, angina."

"Do you suppose we could talk this over after we play? You're the one who was so worried about being late."

Jared glanced at his watch and then restarted the engine. He turned to her. There was composure in the lines of his face, but an intensity—perhaps even a fear—in his eyes. It was the same look Kate had seen in them when, before the election, he spoke of losing as "not the end of the world."

"Sure," he said. "Just answer me that one question. Do you really have a sense of what it would be like for you—for us—if you took over that department?"

"I . . . I know it wouldn't be easy. But that's not what you're really asking, is it?"

Jared shook his head and stared down at his clenched hands.

Kate knew very well what he was asking. He was thirty-nine years old and an only child. His first marriage had ended in nightmarish fashion, with his wife running off to California with their baby daughter. Even Jared's father, senior partner of one of Boston's most prestigious law firms, with all the king's horses and all the king's men at his disposal, couldn't find them. Jared wanted children. For himself and for his father he wanted them. The agreement to wait until after the election was out of deference to the pressures of a political campaign and the newness of their marriage. Now neither was a factor. Oh, yes, she knew very well what he was asking.

"The answer is," she said finally, "that if I accepted the nomination and got the appointment I would need some time to do the job right. But that is the grossest kind of projection at this point. Norton Reese has hardly been my biggest supporter since I exposed the way he was using money budgeted for the forensic pathology unit to finance new cardiac surgery equipment. I think he would cut off an arm before he would have me as a department chief in a hospital he administrated."

"How much time?" Jared's voice was chilly.

"Please, honey. I'm begging you. Let's do this when we can sit down in our own living room and discuss all the possibilities."

"How much?"

"I . . . I don't know. A year? Two?"

Jared snapped the stick shift into first gear, sending a spray of ice and snow into the air before the rear tires gained purchase. "To be continued," he said, as much to himself as to her.

"Fine," she said. Numbly, she sank back in her seat and stared unseeing out the window. Her thoughts drifted for a time and then began to focus on a face. Kate closed her eyes and tried to will the thoughts, the face, away. In moments, though, she could see Art's eyes, glazed and bloodshot; see them as clearly as she had that afternoon a dozen years before when he had raped her. She could smell the whiskey on his breath and feel the weight of his fullback's body on top of hers. Though bundled in a down parka and a warm-up suit, she began to shiver.

Jared turned onto the narrow access drive to the club. To Kate's right, the metallic surface of the Atlantic glinted through a leafless hardwood forest. She took no notice of it.

Please Art, don't, her mind begged. *You're hurting me. Please let me up. All I did was take the test. I didn't say I was going to apply.*

"Look, there are the Carlisles up ahead of us. I guess we're not late after all."

Jared's voice broke through the nightmare. Dampened by a cold sweat, she pushed herself upright. The assault had taken place the day after the second anniversary of her previous marriage, and only an hour after her husband, a failure first in a pro football tryout, then in graduate school, and finally in business, had learned that she had taken the Medical College Admission Test, and worse, that she had scored in the top five percent. His need to control her, never pleasant, had turned ugly. By the evening of that day she had moved out.

"Jared," she pleaded quietly, "we'll talk. Okay?"

"Yeah, sure," he answered. "We'll talk."

The ball rainbowed off Jared's racquet with deceptive speed. A perfect topspin lob.

From her spot by the net, Kate watched Jim and Patsy Carlisle skid to simultaneous stops and, amidst flailing arms, legs, and racquets, dash backward toward the baseline.

The shot bounced six inches inside the line and then accelerated toward the screen, the Carlisles in frantic pursuit.

"You fox," Kate whispered as Jared moved forward for the killing shot they both knew would not be necessary. "That was absolutely beautiful."

"Just keep looking sort of bland. Like we don't even know we're about to beat them for the first time ever."

Across the net, Patsy Carlisle made a fruitless lunge that sent her tumbling into the indoor court's green nylon backdrop.

Kate watched the minidrama of the woman, still seated

on the court, glaring at her husband as he stalked away from her without even the offer of a hand up. Husbands and wives mixed doubles, she thought: games within games within games. "Three match points," she said. "Maybe we should squabble more often before we play." A look at Jared's eyes told her she should have let the matter lie. "Finish 'em with the ol' high hard one," she urged as he walked back to the service line. Her enthusiasm, she knew, now sounded forced—an attempt at some kind of expiation.

Jared nodded at her and winked.

Kate crouched by the net. Eighteen feet in front of her, Jim Carlisle shifted the weight of his compact, perfectly conditioned body from one foot to another. A successful real estate developer, a yachtsman, and club champion several years running, he had never been one to take any kind of loss lightly. "You know," he had said to her on the only attempt he had ever made to start an affair between them, "there are those like you-know-who, who are content to tiptoe along in Daddy's footsteps, and those who just grab life by the throat and do it. I'm a doer."

The reference to Jared, even though prodded forth by far too many martinis, had left an aftertaste of anger that Kate knew would never totally disappear. When Carlisle sent the Samuels for Congress Committee a check for five hundred dollars, she had almost sent it back with a note telling him to go grab somebody's life by the throat. Instead, out of deference to her husband, she had invited the Carlisles over for dinner. Her hypocrisy, however honorable its purpose, continued to rankle her from time to time, especially when Carlisle, wearing his smugness like aftershave, was about to inflict yet another defeat on team Samuels/Bennett.

At last she was beating the man. Not even a disagreement with her husband could dull the luster of the moment.

Through the mirror of Jim Carlisle's stages of readiness to return serve, Kate pictured Jared's movements behind her. Feet planted: Jared had settled in at the line. Hunching over, knees bent: Jared was tapping ball against racquet, gaining his rhythm. Just before Carlisle began the quick bouncing which would signal the toss, she heard Jared's voice. "The ol' high hard one," he said.

Kate tensed, awaiting the familiar, sharp *pok* of Jared's serve and Carlisle's almost simultaneous move to return. Instead, she heard virtually nothing, and watched in horror as Carlisle, with the glee of a tomcat discovering a wounded sparrow, advanced to pounce on a woefully soft hit. The serve was deliberate—vintage Jared Samuels; his way of announcing that by no means had he forgotten their argument.

"Jared, you bastard," Kate screamed just as Carlisle exploded a shot straight at her chest from less than a dozen feet away.

An instant after the ball left Carlisle's racquet, it was on Kate's, then ricocheting into a totally unguarded corner of the court. The shot was absolute reflex, absolute luck, but perfect all the same.

"Match," Kate said simply. She shook hands with each of their opponents, giving Jim's hand an extra pump. Then, without a backward glance, she walked off the court to the locker room.

The Oceanside Racquet Club, three quarters of an acre of corrugated aluminum box, squatted gracelessly on a small rise above the Atlantic. "Facing Wimbledon," was the way the club's overstuffed director liked to describe it.

Keeping her hair dry and moving quickly enough to ensure that Jared would have to work to catch up with her, Kate showered and left the building. The rules of *their* game demanded a reaction of some sort for his behavior, and she had decided on taking the MG, perhaps stopping a mile or so down the road. As she crossed the half-filled parking lot, she began searching the pockets of her parka for her keys. Almost immediately, she remembered seeing them on the kitchen table.

"Damn!" The feeling was so familiar. She had, in the past, slept through several exams, required police assistance to locate her car in an airport parking garage, and forgotten where she had put the engagement ring Art had given her. Although she had come to accept the trait as a usually harmless annoyance, there was a time when visions of clamps left in abdomens concerned her enough to influence her decision to go into pathology rather than clinical medicine. This day, she felt no compassion whatsoever toward her shortcoming.

Testily, she strode past their car and down the road. The move was a bluff. Jared would know that as well as she. It was an eight-mile walk to their home, and the temperature was near freezing. Still, some show of indignation was called for. But not this, she realized quickly. At the moment she accepted the absurdity of her gesture and decided to turn back, she heard the distinctive rev of the MG behind her. There could be no retreat now.

It was a game between them, but not a game. Their scenarios were often carefully staged, but they were life all the same; actions and reactions, spontaneous or not, that provided the dynamics unique to their relationship. There had been no such dynamics in her first marriage. Put simply, Arthur Everett decreed and his dutiful wife Kathryn acquiesced. For two destructive years it had been that way. Her childhood programming offered no alternatives, and she had been too frightened, too insecure, to question. Even now there were times, though gradually fewer and farther between, when dreams of the farmhouse and the children, the well-stocked, sunlit kitchen and the pipe smoke wafting out from the study, dominated her thoughts. They were, she knew, nothing more than the vestiges—the reincarnations—of that childhood programming.

Unfortunately, much of Jared's programming was continually being reinforced, thanks largely to a father who remained convinced that God's plan for women was quite different from His plan for men.

"You have a wonderful behind, do you know that?" Jared's voice startled her. He was driving alongside her, studying her anatomy through a pair of binoculars.

"Yes, I know that." She stiffened enough to be sure

he could notice and walked on. Please don't get hurt, she thought. Put those silly binoculars down and watch where you're going.

"And your face. Have I told you lately about your face?"

"No, but go ahead if you must."

"It is the blue ribbon, gold medal, face-of-the-decade face, that's what."

"You tried to get me killed in there." Kate slowed, but did not stop.

"It was childish."

"And . . . ?"

"And it was dumb."

"And . . . ?"

"And it didn't work."

"Jared!"

"And I'm sorry. I really am. The devil made me do it, but I went and let 'im."

He opened the door. She stopped, hesitated the obligatory few seconds, and got in. The scenario was over. Through it, a dram of purulence had been drained from their marriage before it could fester. Energy no longer enmeshed in their anger would now be rechanneled, perhaps to a joint attack today on the pile of unsplit wood in the yard and later to a battle with the *Times* crossword puzzle. As likely as not, before the afternoon was through, they would make love.

Eyes closed, Kate settled back in her seat, savoring what she had just heard. *I'm sorry*. He had actually said it.

Apologizing has been bred out of Samuels men was yet another teaching from the philosophy of J. Winfield Samuels. Kate had suffered the pain of that one on more than one occasion. She thought about Jared's vehement reaction to the possibility of her taking over the chairmanship of her department. The morning, she had decided, had been a draw: Dad 1. Wife 1.

"Now, Dr. Engleson, you may proceed with your report."

Tom Engleson's groan was not as inaudible as he would have liked. "Your patient is still bleeding, sir. That's my report." During his year and a half of residency on the Ashburton Service at Metropolitan Hospital of Boston, Engleson had had enough dealings with D. K. Bartholomew to know that he would be lucky to escape with anything less than a fifteen-minute conversation.

Dr. Donald K. Bartholomew held the receiver in his left hand, adjusted the notepad in front of him, and straightened his posture. "And what is her blood count?"

"Twenty-five. Her crit is down to twenty-five from twenty-eight." Engleson pictured the numbers being shakily reproduced in black felt tip. "She has had a total of five units transfused in the last twenty-four hours, two of whole blood, one of packed cells, and two of fresh frozen plasma." He closed his eyes and awaited the inevitable string of questions. For a few seconds there was silence.

"How many fresh frozen did you say?"

"Two. The hematology people have been to see her again. Her blood is just not clotting normally." He had decided to keep the complicated explanation for Beverly Vitale's bleeding problem out of the conversation if at all possible. A single request from Bartholomew for specifics, and the phone call could drag on for another half hour. In fact, there was no good explanation even available. The hematologists knew *what*—two of the woman's key clotting factors were at critically low levels—but not *why*. It was a problem the surgeon should have at least identified before performing her D and C.

"Have they further tests to run?"

"No, sir. Not today, anyhow." Getting D. K. Bartholomew to come into the hospital on a Sunday morning was like getting a cat to hop into the tub. "They suggested loading her up with fresh clotting factors and perhaps doing another D and C. They're afraid she might bleed out otherwise."

"How long will it take to give her the factors?"

"We've already started, sir."

There was another pause. "Well, then," Bartholomew said at last, "I guess the patient and I have a date in the operating room."

"Would you like me to assist?" Engleson closed his eyes and prayed for an affirmative response.

"For a D and C? No, thank you, Doctor. It is a one-man procedure, and I am one man. I shall be in by twelve o'clock. Please put the OR team on notice."

"Fine," Engleson said wearily. He had already scheduled Beverly Vitale for the operating room. He hung up and checked the wall clock over the door of the cluttered resident's office. Only eight minutes. "A record," he announced sardonically to the empty room. "I may have just set a record."

Moments later, he called the operating suite. "Denise, it's Tom Engleson. You know the D and C I scheduled for Dr. Bartholomew? . . . Vitale. That's right. Well, I was wondering if you could switch it to the observation OR. I want to watch. . . . I know you're not supposed to use that room on a weekend. That's why I'm asking in such a groveling tone of voice. . . . Bartholomew doesn't want anyone assisting him, but he can't keep me from watching through the overhead. . . . I owe you one, Denise. Thanks."

Looking down from behind the thick glass observation window into the operating room, Tom Engleson exchanged worried looks with the scrub nurse assisting Dr. Donald K. Bartholomew. The dilatation of Beverly Vitale's cervix and subsequent curettage—scraping—of the inner surface of her uterus was not going well. She had gone to the emergency ward three days before because of vaginal bleeding that started with her period but would not let up. For several years, she had been receiving routine gynecologic care through the Omnicenter—the outpatient facility of the Ashburton Women's Health Service of Metropolitan Hospital. As her Omnicenter physician, D. K. Bartholomew had been called in immediately.

In his admission physical, Bartholomew had noted a number of bruises on the woman's arms and legs, but elected nevertheless to proceed with a D and C—commonly done for excessive bleeding. He did not order blood clotting studies until after his patient's bleeding worsened postoperatively. Now, with the woman loaded with fresh clotting factors, Bartholomew was repeating the curettage.

Beverly Vitale, a thin, delicate young cellist with straight jet hair and fine, artist's hands lay supine on the operating table with her eyes taped shut and her head turned ninety degrees to one side. A polystyrene tube placed through her mouth into her trachea connected her with the anesthesia machine. Her legs, draped in sterile sheets, were held aloft by cloth stirrups hooked beneath each heel. Overhead, in the observation gallery Tom Engleson watched and waited. He was dressed in standard operating room whites, with hair and shoe covers, but no mask.

As he watched the level of suctioned blood rise in the vacuum bottle on the wall, Engleson wondered if D. K. Bartholomew was considering removing the woman's uterus altogether. He cursed himself for not throwing protocol to the winds and inviting himself into the OR.

The prospect of the old surgeon moving ahead with a hysterectomy brought a ball of anger to the resident's throat. Much of his reaction, he knew, had to do with Beverly Vitale. Though he had only spoken with her a few times, Engleson had begun fantasizing about her and had become determined to see her when she was released from the hospital. Now his thoughts added, *if* she was released from the hospital. He glanced again at the vacuum bottle and then at Bartholomew. There was a flicker of confusion and uncertainty in the man's eyes.

"Her pressure is dropping a bit."

Engleson heard the anesthesiologist's voice crackle

through a barely functional speaker on the wall behind him. "Young lady, get me the freshest unit of blood we have, and see if the blood bank can send us up ten units of platelets."

"Yes, sir," the nurse said. "Dr. Bartholomew, blood loss so far is four hundred and fifty cc's."

Bartholomew did not respond immediately. He stood motionless, staring at the steady flow of crimson from Beverly Vitale's cervix.

"Let's try some pitocin. Maybe her uterus will clamp down," he said finally.

"Dr. Bartholomew," the anesthesiologist said, an even tenseness in his voice, "you've already ordered pitocin. She's been getting it. Maximum doses."

Engleson strained to see the older surgeon's face. If he rushed into the OR and the man did not need assistance, a formal complaint was sure to. . . . Before he could complete the thought, the bellboy hanging from his waistband emitted the abrasive tone signaling a transmission. "Dr. Engleson, call two eight three *stat*. Dr. Engleson, two eight three *stat*, please."

An anxious check of the scene below, and the resident rushed to the nearest phone. It was a rule of the Ashburton Service that all *stat* pages were to be answered within sixty seconds. Telephones had even been installed in the residents' bathrooms for such purposes.

The call concerned a postop patient whose temperature had risen to 103; not a life-or-death situation. By the time Engleson had listened to the nurse's report, given orders for evaluating the patient's fever and returned to the observation window, Bartholomew had begun swabbing antiseptic over Beverly Vitale's lower abdomen.

Engleson switched on the microphone by his right hand. "What's going on?" he asked. Below, no one reacted to his voice. "Can you hear me?" Again no response. Through the door to the scrub area, Engleson saw Carol Nixon, a surgical intern rotating through the Ashburton Service, beginning to scrub. Apparently Bartholomew had called her in to assist, perhaps when Engleson could not be found.

"Over my dead body," Engleson said as he raced down the hall to the stairs. "No way do you open that woman up without my being there." In less than a minute, he had joined Nixon in the scrub room.

"The nurses said Stone Hands was trying to find you," the woman said. "I was just finishing up a case down the hall when Denise grabbed me. Do I have to stay?"

"You might want to learn from the master in there," Engleson responded acidly, cleaning his fingernails with an orange stick. The intern smiled, nodded a thanks-but-no-thanks, and left him to finish his scrub.

"Order a peach and you get a pear," was Bartholomew's comment on the change in assistants. He laughed merrily at his own humor and seemed not to notice the absence of response from around the room.

With Engleson handling sponges and hemostats, Bartholomew used an electric scalpel to make an incision from just below Beverly Vitale's navel to her pubis. The scalpel, buzzing and crackling like hot bacon grease, simultaneously sliced through the skin and cauterized bleeding vessels. Next, with the voltage turned up, he cut through a thin layer of saffron-colored fat to her peritoneum, the opaque membrane covering her abdominal cavity. A few snips with a Metzenbaum scissors, and the peritoneum parted, exposing her bowel, her bladder, and beneath those, her uterus.

In a perfunctory manner, too perfunctory for Engleson's taste, the older surgeon explored the abdominal cavity with one hand. "Everything seems in order," he announced to the room. "I think we can proceed with a hysterectomy."

"No!" Engleson said sharply. The room froze. "I mean, don't you think we should at least consider the possibility of ligating her hypogastric artery?" He wanted to add his feelings about rushing ahead with a hysterectomy in a thirty-year-old woman with no children, but held back.

Also unsaid, at least for the moment, was that the hypogastric ligation, while not always successful in stopping hemorrhaging, was certainly accepted practice in a case like this. Bartholomew was still guided by the old school—the school that removed a uterus with the dispatch of a dermatologist removing a wart.

D. K. Bartholomew's pale blue eyes came up slowly and locked on Engleson's. For five seconds, ten, an eerie silence held, impinged upon only by the wheeze of air into the vacuum apparatus. The tall resident held his ground, but he also held his breath. An outburst by the older surgeon now, and there would be a confrontation that could further jeopardize the life of Beverly Vitale. Then, moment by moment, Engleson saw the blaze in Bartholomew's eyes fade.

"Thank you for the suggestion, doctor," the surgeon said distantly. "I think perhaps we should give it a try."

The relieved sighs from those in the room were muffled by their masks.

"You or me?" Engleson asked.

"It . . . it's been a while since I did this procedure," Bartholomew understated.

"Don't worry, we'll do it together."

In minutes, the ligation was complete. Almost instantly, the bleeding from within the woman's uterus began to lessen.

"While we're waiting to see if this works," Engleson said, "would you mind if I got a better look at her tubes and ovaries?"

Bartholomew shrugged and shook his head.

Engleson probed along the fallopian tubes, first to one ovary and then to the other. They did not feel at all right. Carefully, he withdrew the left ovary through the incision. It was half normal size, mottled gray, and quite firm. This time, it was his eyes that flashed. *You said everything was in order*. Bartholomew sagged. There was a bewildered, vacant air about him, as if he had opened his eyes before a mirror and seen a painful truth.

The woman's right ovary was identical to her left.

"I don't think I've ever seen anything quite like this," Engleson said. "Have you?"

"No, well, not exactly."

"Pardon?"

"I said *I* hadn't either." There was an uncertainty, a hesitation, in the older man's words. He reached over and touched the ovary.

"You sure?" Engleson prodded.

"I . . . I may have felt one once. I'm trying to remember. Do you suggest a biopsy?" Engleson nodded. "A wedge section?" Another nod. The man's confidence was obviously shaken.

By the time the wedge biopsy was taken, the bleeding had slowed dramatically. As Engleson prepared to close the abdominal incision over the uterus he had just preserved, he sensed the irony of what was happening tighten in his gut. The uterus was saved, true. A fine piece of surgery. But if the pathology in Beverly Vitale's ovaries was as extensive as it appeared, the woman would never bear children anyhow.

"Denise," he said, "could you find out who's on for surgical path this month; both the resident and the staff person, okay?"

"Right away."

Engleson glanced at the peaceful face and tousled hair of the young cellist. Some women try for years to get pregnant, never knowing whether they can or not, he thought. At least you'll know. Glumly, he began to close.

Twenty minutes later, the two surgeons shuffled into the doctor's locker room.

"Dr. Bartholomew, have you been able to remember where you might have encountered ovarian pathology like this woman's?"

"Oh, yes, well, no. I . . . what I mean is I don't think I've ever seen anything like them."

"You look as if you want to say something more."

"I may have felt something like them once. That's all."

"When? On whom?" There was some excitement in Engleson's voice.

D. K. Bartholomew, MD, Fellow of the American College of Surgeons and Diplomate of the American College of Obstetrics and Gynecology, shook his head. "I . . . I'm afraid I don't remember," he said.

"What are you talking about?"

"It was surgery for something else. Maybe removal of a fibroid tumor. The ovaries felt like this woman's did today, but there was no one around to consult, and I think I had another case or two left to do and . . ."

"So you just ignored them and closed?"

"I felt they were probably a normal variant."

"Yeah, sure. Did you mention them on your operative note?"

"I . . . I don't remember. It might have been years ago."

The wall telephone began ringing. "Dr. Bartholomew," Engleson said, allowing the jangle to continue, "I don't think you should operate anymore." With that he turned and snatched up the receiver.

"Dr. Engleson, it's Denise. I called pathology."

"Yes?"

"I couldn't find out who the resident is on surgicals, but the staff person is Dr. Bennett."

"Good."

"Excuse me?"

"I just said that's good. Thanks, Denise."

"Thank you for what you did in there, Doctor. You made my day."

Kate's back was arched over the pillows beneath her hips as Jared knelt between her legs and used her buttocks to pull himself farther inside her. Again and again he sent jets of pleasure and pain deep into her gut and up into her throat. Her climax grew like the sound of an oncoming train—first a tingle, a vibration, next a hum, then a roar. With Jared helping, her body came off the pillows until only her heels and the back of her head were touching the carpet. Her muscles tightened on him and seemed to draw him in even deeper. He dug his fingers into the small of her back and cried out in a soft, child's voice. Then he came, his erection pulsing in counterpoint to her own contractions.

"I love you," he whispered. "Oh, Katey, I love you so much." Gently, he worked his arms around her waist, and guided her onto her side, trying to stay within her as long as possible. For half an hour they lay on the soft living room carpet, their lover's sweat drying in the warmth from the nearby wood stove. From the kitchen, the aroma of percolating coffee, forgotten for over an hour, worked its way into the sweetness of the birch fire.

A cashmere blanket, one of the plethora of wedding gifts from Jared's father, lay beside them. Kate pulled it over her sleeping husband and then slipped carefully from underneath. For a time, she knelt there studying the face of the man who had, five years before, arranged to have himself and a dozen roses wheeled under a sheet into her autopsy suite in order to convince her to reconsider a rebuffed dinner invitation. Five years. Years filled with so much change—so much growth for both of them. She had been a nervous, overworked junior faculty member then, and he had been the hotshot young attorney assigned by Minton/Samuels to handle beleaguered Metropolitan Hospital. The memory of him in those days—so eager and intense—brought a faint smile.

Kate reached out and touched the fine creases that had, overnight it seemed, materialized at the corners of her husband's eyes.

"A year, Jared?" she asked silently. "Would a year make all that much difference? You understand your own needs so well. Can you understand mine?"

Almost instantly another, far more disturbing question arose in her thoughts. Did she, in fact, understand them herself?

Silently, she rose and walked to the picture window overlooking their wooded backyard. Superimposed on the smooth waves of drifted snow was the reflection of her naked body, kept thin and toned by constant dieting and almost obsessive exercise. On an impulse, she turned sideways and forced her abdomen out as far as it would go. Six months, she guessed, maybe seven. Not too bad looking for an old pregnant lady.

Fifteen minutes later, when the phone rang, Kate was ricocheting around the kitchen preparing brunch. The edge of her terry-cloth robe narrowly missed toppling a pan of sweet sausages as she leapt for the receiver, answering it before the first ring ended. Nevertheless, through the door to the living room, she saw Jared stir from the fetal tuck in which he had been sleeping and begin to stretch.

"Hello," she answered, mentally discarding the exotic plans she had made for awakening her husband.

"Dr. Bennett, it's Tom Engleson. I'm a senior resident on the Ashburton Service at Metro. Do you remember me?"

"Of course, Tom. You saw me at the Omnicenter once. Saved my life when Dr. Zimmermann was away."

"I did?" There was a hint of embarrassment in his voice. "What was the matter?"

"Well, actually, I just needed a refill of my birth control pills. But I remember you just the same. What can I do for you?" Her mental picture of Engleson was of a loose, gangly man, thirty or thirty-one, with angular features and a youthful face, slightly aged by a Teddy Roosevelt moustache.

"Please forgive me for phoning you at home on Sunday."

"Nonsense."

"Thank you. The reason I'm calling is to get your advice on handling a surgical specimen. It's one you'll be seeing tomorrow: a wedge section of a patient's left ovary, taken during a hypogastric artery ligation for menorrhagia."

"How old a woman?" Reflexively, Kate took up a pen to begin scratching data on the back of an envelope. So doing, she noticed that Jared was now huddled by the wood stove with Roscoe, their four-year-old almost-terrier and the marriage's declared neutral love object.

"Thirty," Engleson answered. "No deliveries, no pregnancies, and in fact, no ovaries."

"What?"

"Oh, they're there. But they're unlike any ovaries I've ever seen before. Dr. Bartholomew was with me—the woman is his patient—and he has never seen pathology like this either."

Kate pulled a high stool from beneath the counter and wrapped one foot around its leg. "Explain," she said.

"Well, whatever this is is uniform and symmetrical. We took a slice from the left ovary, but it could just as well have been the right. Shrunken, the consistency of . . . of a squash ball—sort of hard but rubbery. The surface is pockmarked, dimpled."

"What color?" Kate had written down almost every word.

"Gray. Grayish brown, maybe."

"Interesting," she said.

"Does what I've described ring any bells?"

"No. At least not right off. However, there are a number of possibilities. Any idea as to why this woman was having menorrhagia?"

"Two reasons. One is a platelet count of just forty-five thousand, and the other is a fibrinogen level that is fifteen percent of normal."

"An autoimmune phenomenon?" Kate searched her thoughts for a single disease entity characterized by the two blood abnormalities. An autoimmune phenomenon, the body making antibodies against certain of its own tissues, seemed likely.

"So far, that's number one on the list," Engleson said. "The hematology people have started her on steroids."

"Was she on any medications?"

"Hey, Kate." It was Jared calling from the living room. "Do you smell something burning?"

"Nothing but vitamins," Engleson answered.

Kate did not respond. Receiver tucked under her ear, she was at the oven, pulling out a tray of four blackened lumps that had once been shirred eggs—Jared's favorite.

"Shit," she said.

"What?" Both Jared and Tom Engleson said the word simultaneously.

"Oh, sorry. I wasn't talking to you." A miniature cumulonimbus cloud puffed from the oven. "Jared, it's all right," she called out, this time covering the mouthpiece. "It's just . . . our meal. That's all."

"Dr. Bennett, if you'd rather I called back . . ."

"No, Tom, no. Listen, there's a histology technician on call. The lab tech on duty knows who it is. Have whoever it is come in and begin running the specimen through the Technichron. That way it will be ready for examination tomorrow rather than Tuesday. Better still, ask them to come into the lab and call me at home. I'll give the instructions myself. Okay?"

"Sure. Thanks."

"No problem," she said, staring at the lumps. "I'll speak to you later."

"Shirred eggs?" Jared, wrapped in the cashmere blanket, leaned against the doorway. Roscoe peered at her from between his knees.

Kate nodded sheepishly. "I sort of smelled the smoke, but my one-track brain was focused on what this resident from the hospital was saying, and somehow, it dismissed the smoke as coming from the wood stove. I . . . I never was too great at doing more than one thing at once."

"Too bad you couldn't have chosen to let the resident burn to a crisp and save the eggs," he said.

"Next time."

"Good. Any possibilities for replacements?"

"Howard Johnson's?"

"Thanks, but I'll take my chances with some coffee and whatever's in that frying pan. You sure that wasn't Yoda on the phone?"

"Jared . . ."

He held up his hands against her ire. "Just checking, just checking," he said. "Come on, Roscoe. Let's go set the table."

Kate noted the absence of an apology, but decided that two in one day was too much to ask. More difficult to accept, however, was Jared's apparent lack of interest in what the call was about. It was as if by not talking about her career, her life outside of their marriage, he was somehow diminishing its importance. In public, he took special pride in her professionalism and her degree. Privately, he accepted it as long as it didn't burn his eggs. Almost against her will, she felt frustration begin to dilute the warmth and closeness generated by their lovemaking. She walked to where her clothes were piled in the living room and dressed, silently vowing to do whatever she could to avoid another blowup that day.

Minutes later, the crunch of tires on their gravel driveway heralded a test of her resolve. Roscoe heard the arrival first and bounded from his place by the stove to the front door. Jared, now in denims and a flannel work shirt, followed.

"Hey, Kate, it's Sandy," he called out, opening the inside door.

"Sandy?" Dick Sandler, Jared's roommate at Dartmouth, had been best man at their wedding. A TWA pilot, he lived on the South Shore and hadn't been in touch with them for several months. "Is Ellen with him?"

"No. He's alone." Jared opened the storm door. "Hey,

flyboy," he called in a thick Spanish accent, "welcome. I have just what you want, señor: a seexteen-year-old American virgin. Only feefty pesetas."

Sandler, a rugged Marlon Brando type, exchanged bear hugs with Jared and platonic kisses with Kate, and then scanned what there was of their brunch. "What, no bloodies?"

Kate winced before images of the two men, emboldened by a few "bloodies," exchanging off-color jokes she seldom thought were funny and singing "I Wanna Go Back to Dartmouth, to Dartmouth on the Hill." Invariably, she would end up having to decide whether to leave the house, try to shut them off, or join in. When Ellen Sandler was around, no such problem existed. A woman a few years older than Kate, and Sandy's wife since his graduation, Ellen was as charming, interesting, and full of life as anyone Kate had ever known. She was a hostess with poise and grace, the mother of three delightful girls, and even a modestly successful businesswoman, having developed an interior design consulting firm that she had run alone for several years from their home and more recently from a small studio cum office in town.

Sandy, with his flamboyance, his stature as a 747 captain, and his versatile wit, was the magnet that drew many fascinating and accomplished people into the Sandlers' social circle. Ellen, Kate believed, was the glue that kept them there.

"So, Sandy," she said, dropping a celery stick into his drink and sliding it across the table, "what brings you north of Boston? How are Ellen and the girls?" It was at that moment that she first appreciated the sadness in his eyes.

"I . . . well actually, I was just driving around and decided to cruise up here. Sort of a whim. I . . . I needed to talk to Jared . . . and to you."

"You and Ellen?" Jared's sense of his friend told him immediately what to ask.

"I . . . I'm leaving her. Moving out." Sandler stared uncomfortably into the center of his drink.

At his words, Kate felt a dreadful sinking in her gut. Ellen had stated on many occasions and in many ways the uncompromising love she bore for the man. How long had they been married, now? Eighteen years? Nineteen, maybe?

"Holy shit," Jared whispered, setting a hand on Sandler's forearm. "What's happened?"

"Nothing. I mean nothing dramatic. Somewhere along the way, we just lost one another."

"Sandy, people who have been married for almost twenty years don't just lose one another," Kate said. "Now what has happened?" There was an irritability in her voice which surprised her. Jared's expression suggested that he, too, was startled by her tone.

Sandler shrugged. "Well, between running the house and entertaining and taking the girls to one lesson or another and scouts and committees at our club and that business of hers, Ellen simply ran out of energy for me. In some areas, meals and such, she still goes through the motions, but without much spark."

"How is Ellen handling all this?" Kate asked, checking Jared's face for a sign that she might be interloping with too many questions. The message she received was noncommittal.

"She doesn't know yet."

"What?" Her exclamation this time drew a *be careful* glare.

"I just decided yesterday. But I've been thinking about it for weeks. Longer. I was hoping you two might have some suggestions as to how I should go about breaking the news to her."

"Have you been to a counsellor or a shrink or something?" Jared asked the question.

"It's too late."

"What do you mean? You just said Ellen doesn't even know what you're planning to do." Jared sounded baffled.

Across the table, Kate closed her eyes. She knew the explanation.

"There's someone else," Sandler said self-consciously. "A flight attendant. I . . . we've been seeing one another for some time."

For Kate the words were like needle stabs. Jared was pressing to get a commitment from her to alter her life along pathways Ellen Sandler could negotiate blindfolded. Yet here was Sandy, like Jared in so many ways, rejecting the woman for not devoting enough energy to him. The image of Ellen sitting there while he announced his intentions made her first queasy and then frightened. The fear, as happened more often than not, mutated into anger before it could be expressed.

"Ellen doesn't deserve this," she said, backing away from the table. " 'We just lost one another.' Sandy, don't you think that's sort of a sleazy explanation for what's really going on? How old is this woman?"

"Twenty-six. But I don't see what her . . ."

"I know you don't see. You don't see a lot of things."

Jared stood up. "Now just one second, Kate."

"And you don't see a lot of things either, dammit." There were tears streaming down her face. "You two boys work out how you're gonna break the news to Ellen that she did everything she goddamn well could in life—more than both of you put together, probably—but that it just wasn't enough. She's fired. Dismissed. Not flashy enough. Not showy enough. Her services are no longer required. Excuse me, I'm going to the bathroom to get sick. Then I'm going to my hospital. People there are grateful and appreciative for the things I do well. I like that. It helps me to get up in the morning."

Fists clenched, she turned and raced from the room. Roscoe, who had settled himself under the table, padded to the center of the room and after a brief glance at the men, followed.

◆

Ginger Rittenhouse, a first-grade teacher, had just finished her run by the ice-covered Charles River when she began to die. Like the random victim of a crazed sniper, she did not hear the sound or see the muzzle flash of the weapon that killed her. In fact, the weapon was nothing more malevolent than the corner of her bureau drawer; the shot, an accidental bump less than twenty-four hours before to a spot just above her right ear.

"That's one incredible lump!" her new roommate had exclaimed, forcing an icepack against the golfball-sized knot. The woman, a licensed practical nurse, had commented on the large bruise just below her right knee as well. Ginger was too self-conscious to mention the other, similar bruises on her lower back, buttocks, and upper arm.

Her death began with a tic—an annoying electric sensation deep behind her right eye. The wall of her right middle cerebral artery was stretching. Bruised by the shock from the bureau drawer, the vessel, narrow as a piece of twine, had developed a tiny defect along the inner lining. The platelets and fibrinogen necessary to patch the defect were present, but in insufficient amounts to do the job. Blood had begun to work its way between the layers of the vessel wall.

Squinting against the pain, she sat on a bench and looked across the river at the General Electric building in Cambridge. The outline of the building seemed blurred. From the rent in her right middle cerebral artery, blood had begun to ooze, a microdrop at a time, into the space between her skull and brain. Nerve fibers, exquisitely sensitive, detected the intrusion and began screaming their message of warning. Ginger, mindless of the huge lump over her ear, placed her hands on either side of her head and tried to squeeze the pain into submission.

Powered by the beating of her own heart, the bleeding increased. Her thoughts became disconnected snatches. The low skyline of Cambridge began to fade. Behind her, runners jogged by. A pair of lovers passed close enough to read the dial on her watch. Ginger, now paralyzed by pain that was far more than pain, was beyond calling for help.

Suddenly, a brilliant white light replaced the agony. The heat from the light bathed the inside of her eyes. Her random thoughts coalesced about woods and a stream. It was the Dingle, the secret hiding place of her childhood. She knew every tree, every rock. Home and safe at last, Ginger Rittenhouse surrendered to the light, and gently toppled forward onto the sooty snow.

2

Monday 10 December

First there was the intense, yellow-white light—the sunlight of another world. Then, subtly, colors began to appear: reds and pinks, purples and blues. Kate felt herself drifting downward, Alice drawn by her own curiosity over the edge and down the rabbit's hole. How many times had she focused her microscope in on a slide? Tens of thousands, perhaps even hundreds of thousands. Still, every journey through the yellow-white light began with the same sense of anticipation as had her first.

The colors darkened and coalesced into a mosaic of cells; the cells of Beverly Vitale's left ovary, chemically fixed to prevent decay, then embedded in a block of paraffin, cut thin as a slick of oil, and finally stained with dyes specific for coloring one or another structure within the cell. Pink for the cytoplasm; mottled violet for the nuclei; red for the cell walls.

With a deep breath calculated at once to relax herself and to heighten her concentration, she focused the lenses and her thoughts on the cells, now magnified a thousand times. Her efforts were less successful than usual. Thoughts of Sandy and Ellen, of Jared and the discussion they had had following her return from the hospital the previous night, continued to intrude.

She had come home late, almost eleven, after meeting with Tom Engleson, interviewing Beverly Vitale, examining the frozen section of her ovary, and finally spending an hour in the hospital library. Her expectations had been to find the former roommates in the den, comatose or nearly so, with the essence of a half a case of Lowenbräu permeating the room. Instead, she had found only a somber and perfectly sober Jared.

"Hi," he said simply.

"Hi, yourself." She kissed him on the forehead and then settled onto the ottoman by his chair. "When did Sandy leave?"

"A couple of hours ago. Did you get done whatever it is you wanted to?"

Kate nodded. His expression was as flat and as drained as his words. No surprise, she realized. First his wife stalks out of the house with no real explanation; then he has to listen to the agonies of the breakup of his best friend's marriage. "I . . . I guess I owe you an apology for the way I acted earlier. Some sort of explanation."

Jared shrugged. "I'll take the apology. The explanation's optional."

"I'm sorry for leaving the way I did."

"I'm sorry you left the way you did, too. I could have used some help—at least some moral support."

"Sorry again." The three feet separating them might as well have been a canyon. "Anything decided?"

"He went home to tell Ellen and to move out, I guess. It got awful quiet here after you left. Neither of us was able to open up very well. We each seemed to be wrapped up in our own bundle of problems."

"Three I'm sorries. That's my limit." She unsnapped her barrette, shook her hair free, and combed it out with her fingers. The gesture was natural enough, but at some level she knew she had done it because it was one Jared liked. "After what happened this morning—in the car, I mean—I couldn't listen to Sandy just brush off Ellen and their marriage the way he did. I mean, here I am, scrambling to do a decent job with my career and to be a reasonably satisfying friend and wife to you, and there's Ellen able to do both of those so easily and raise three beautiful, talented children to boot, and . . ."

"It's not right what you're doing, Kate."

"What's that?"

"You're comparing your insides to Ellen's outsides, that's what. She looks good. I'll give you that. But don't go and cast Sandy as the heavy just because he's the one moving out. There are things that are missing from that relationship. Maybe things too big to overcome. What's that got to do with our discussion this morning, anyway?"

"Jared, you know perfectly well what it has to do. Having children is a major responsibility. As it is, I feel like a one-armed juggler half the time. Our lives, our jobs, the things we do on our own and together . . . Toss in a baby at this point, and what guarantee is there I won't start dropping things?"

"What do you want me to say? I'm almost forty years old. I'm married. I want to have children. My wife said she wanted to have children, too. Now, all of a sudden, having children is a threat to our marriage."

"Christ, Jared, that's not what I mean . . . and you know it. I didn't say I won't have children. I didn't say it's a threat to our marriage. All I'm trying to say is there's a lot to think about—especially with the opportunities that have arisen at the hospital. It's not the idea I'm having trouble with so much as the timing. A mistake here and it's a bitter, unfulfilled woman, or a neurotic, insecure kid, or . . . or a twenty-six-year-old stewardess. Can you understand that?"

"I understand that somewhere inside you there are some issues you're not facing up to. Issues surrounding me or having children or both."

"And you've got it all together, right?" Kate struggled to stop the tears that seemed to be welling from deep within her chest.

"I know what I want."

"Well, I don't. Okay? And I'm the one who's going to have to pass up a chairmanship and go through a pregnancy and change my life so that I don't make the same horrible mistakes with our child that my mother made with us. I . . . Jared, I'm frightened." It was, she realized, the first time she had truly recognized it.

"Hi, Frightened. I'm Perplexed. How do you do?"

"You know, you could use a little better sense of timing yourself."

"Okay, folks, here we go. It's time once again to play let's-jump-all-over-everything-Jared-says. Well, please, before you get rolling, count me out. I'm going to bed."

"I'll be in in a while."

"Don't wake me."

The section from Beverly Vitale's left ovary was unlike any pathology Kate had ever encountered. The stroma—cells providing support and, according to theory, critical feminizing hormones—were perfectly normal in appearance. But the follicles—the pockets of nutrient cells surrounding the ova—were selectively and completely destroyed, replaced by the spindle-shaped, deep pink cells of sclerosis—scarring. Assuming the pattern held true throughout both ovaries—and there was no reason to assume otherwise—Beverly Vitale's reproductive potential was as close to zero as estimate would allow.

For nearly an hour, Kate sat there, scanning section after section, taking notes on a yellow legal pad. Why couldn't Jared understand what it all really meant to her? Why couldn't he see what a godsend medicine had been to a life marked by aimlessness and a self-doubt bordering on self-loathing.

"My God, woman, if I didn't know better, I'd swear you were a model the Zeiss Company had hired to plug their latest line of microscopes."

"Aha," Kate said melodramatically, her eyes still fixed

on the microscope, "a closet male chauvinist pig. I expected as much all along, Dr. Willoughby." She swung around and, as always, felt a warm jet of affection at the sight of her department head. In his early sixties, Stan Willoughby was egg bald save for a pure white monk's fringe. The pencil-thin moustache partially obscured by his bulbous nose was a similar shade. His eyes sparkled from beneath brows resembling end-stage dandelions. In all, Jared's likening him to the wise imp Yoda was, though inappropriate, not inaccurate.

Willoughby packed his pipe and straddled the stool across the table from Kate. "The young lady on Ashburton Five?" he asked. Kate nodded. "This a good time for me to take a look-see?"

Although Willoughby's primary area of interest was histochemistry, thirty-five years of experience had made him an expert in almost every phase of pathology. Every phase, that is, except how to administer a department. Willoughby was simply too passive, too nice for the dog-maim-dog world of hospital politics, especially the free-for-all for an adequate portion of a limited pool of funds.

"Stan, I swear I've never seen, or even heard of, anything like this."

The chief peered into the student eyepieces on the teaching microscope—a setup enabling two people to view the same specimen at the same time. "All right if I focus?" Kate nodded. Ritualistically, he went from low power magnification to intermediate, to high, and finally to thousand-fold oil-immersion, punctuating each maneuver with a "hmm" or an "uh huh." Through the other set of oculars, Kate followed.

They looked so innocent, those cells, so deceptively innocent, detached from their source and set out for viewing. They were in one sense a work of art, a delicate, geometrically perfect montage that was the antithesis of the huge, cluttered metal sculptures Kate had built and displayed during her troubled Mount Holyoke years. The irony in that thought was immense. Form follows function. The essential law of structural design. Yet here were cells perfect in form, produced by a biologic cataclysm tantamount to a volcano. A virus? A toxin? An antibody suddenly transformed? The art of pathology demanded that the cells and tissues, though fixed and stained, never be viewed as static.

"Did you send sections over to the electron microscopy unit?" Willoughby asked.

"Not yet, but I will."

"And the young woman is bleeding as well?"

"Platelets thirty thousand. Fibrinogen fifteen percent of normal."

"Ouch!"

"Yes, ouch. I spoke with her at some length last night. No significant family history, no serious diseases, nonsmoker, social drinker, no meds. . . ."

"None?"

"Vitamins and iron, but that's all. No operations except an abortion at the Omnicenter about five years ago." The two continued to study the cells as they talked. "She's a cellist with the Pops."

"Travel history?"

"Europe, China, Japan. None to third world spots. I told her how envious I was of people who could play music, and she just smiled this wistful smile and said that every time she picked up her cello, she felt as rich and fulfilled as she could ever want to feel. I only talked to her for half an hour or so, Stan, but I came away feeling like we were . . . I don't know, like we were friends." *Spend a day here sometime, Jared. Come to work with me and see what I do, how I do it.* "The hematology people are talking autoimmune phenomenon. They think the ovarian problem is long-standing, a coincidental finding at this point."

"Never postulate two diseases when one will explain things." Willoughby restated the maxim he had long since engrained upon her. "I suppose they're pouring in steroids."

"Stan, she's in trouble. Real trouble."

"Ah, yes. Forgive me. Sometimes I forget that there's more to this medicine business than just making a correct diagnosis. Thanks for not letting me get away with that kind of talk. Well, Doctor, I think you may really have something here. I have never encountered anything quite like it either."

"Neither had Dr. Bartholomew."

"That fossil? He probably has trouble recognizing his own shoes in the morning. Talk about a menace. All by himself he's an epidemic."

"No comment."

"Good. I have enough comments for both of us. Listen, Kate. Do you mind if I try a couple of my new silver stains on this material? The technique seems perfect for this type of pathology."

"I was about to ask if you would."

Willoughby engaged the intercom on the speakerphone system—one of the few innovations he had managed to bring into the department. "Sheila, is that you?"

"No, Doctor Willoughby, it's Jane Fonda. Of course it's me. You buzzed my office."

"Could you come into Dr. Bennett's office, please?" There was no response. "Sheila, are you still there?"

"It's not what it sounds like, Dr. Willoughby," she said finally.

"Not what *what* sounds like?"

"Sheila," Kate cut in firmly, "it's me. We're calling because we have a specimen we'd like to try the silver stain on."

For a few moments there was silence. "I . . . I'll be over shortly," the technician said.

Willoughby turned to Kate, his thick brows presaging his question. "Now what was that little ditty all about?"

"Nothing, really."

"Nothing? Kate, that woman has worked for me for fifteen years. Maybe more. She's cynical, impertinent, abrasive, aggressive, and at times as bossy as my wife, but she's also the best and brightest technician I've ever known. If there's trouble between the two of you, perhaps I'd best know about it. Is it that study of the department I commissioned you and your computer friend, Sebastian, to do?"

"It's nothing, Stan. I mean it. Like most people who are very good at what they do, Sheila has a lot of pride. Especially when it comes to her boss of fifteen years. I know it's not my place to decide, but if it's okay, I'd like the chance to work through our differences without involving you. Okay?"

Willoughby hesitated and then shrugged and nodded.

"Thanks," she said. "If I were ever to take over the chairmanship of the department, I'd like to know I had a solid relationship with my chief technician—especially if she were someone as invaluable as Sheila Pierce."

"Invaluable is right. I keep giving her raises and bonuses even though she puts a knot in my ninny just about every time she opens her mouth. Say, did I hear you just give me the green light to submit your name to Reese?"

"I said 'if' and you know it."

Willoughby grinned mischievously. "Your voice said 'if,' but your eyes . . ."

"You rang?" Sheila Pierce saved Kate from a response. Fortyish, with a trim, efficient attractiveness, she had, Kate knew, earned both bachelor's and master's degrees while working in the department. By the time Kate had begun her residence, the one-time laboratory assistant had become chief pathology technician.

"Ah, Sheila," Willoughby said. "Come in."

"Hi, Sheila." Kate hoped there was enough reassurance in her expression and her voice to keep the woman from any further outburst, at least until they had a chance to talk privately.

Their eyes locked for a fraction of a second; then, mercifully, Sheila returned the greeting. The problem between them had, as Stan Willoughby suspected, arisen during Kate's computer-aided study of the pathology department's budget and expenditures, specifically in regard to a six hundred and fifty dollar payment for an educational meeting in Miami that Sheila could not document ever having attended. Kate had decided to drop the matter without involving the department chief, but the technician was clearly unconvinced that she had done so.

"How's my new batch of silver stain coming?" Willoughby asked.

"It's much, much thicker than the old stuff," Sheila said, settling on a high stool, equidistant from the two physicians. "Fourteen hours may be too long to heat it."

"I seem to recall your warning me about that when I suggested fourteen hours in the first place. Is it a total loss?"

"Well, actually I split about half of it off and cooked that part for only seven hours."

"And . . . ?"

"And it looks fine . . . perfect, even."

Willoughby's sigh of relief was pronounced. "Do you know how much that stain costs to make? How much you just saved me by . . . ?"

"Of course I know. Who do you think ordered the material in the first place, the Ghost of Christmas Past?"

Willoughby shot Kate a what-did-I-tell-you glance; then he picked up the slides and paraffin blocks containing tissue from Beverly Vitale's ovary. "Dr. Bennett has an interesting problem here that I think might be well suited to my silver stain. Do you think you could make some sections and try it out?"

"Your command is my command," Pierce said, bowing. "Give me an hour, and your stain will be ready." She turned to Kate. "Dr. Bennett, I think you should have a little review session with our chief here on the basics of hypertension. On his desk, right next to his blood pressure pills, is a half-eaten bag of Doritos. Bye, now."

* * *

Sheila Pierce dropped off the paraffin block in histology and then returned to her office. On her desk was the stain Willoughby had referred to as "his." Pierce laughed disdainfully. If it weren't for her, the stain that was soon to be known by his name would be little more than an expensive beaker of shit. There they sat, she thought, Willoughby and that goddamn Bennett, sharing their little physician jokes and performing their physician mental masturbations and issuing orders to a woman with an IQ—a proven IQ—higher than either of theirs could possibly be. One-fifty. That's what her mother said. Genius level. One hundred and fucking fifty. So where was the MD degree that would have put her where she deserved to be?

Pierce glared at the small framed photo of her parents, carefully placed to one side of her desk. Then her expression softened. It wasn't their fault, being poor. Just their fate. They didn't want the stroke or the cancer that had forced their daughter to shelve her dreams and begin a life of taking orders from privileged brats who, more often than not, couldn't come close to her intellectual capacity. One hundred and fifty. What was Kate Bennett? One-ten? One-twenty tops. Yet there she was with the degree and the power and the future.

Listen, Sheila, you're terrific at your job. I don't see that there's anything to gain by bringing this up to Dr. Willoughby, or even by making you reimburse the department. But never again, okay?

"Patronizing bitch."

"Who's a bitch?"

Startled, Sheila whirled. Norton Reese stood propped against the doorjamb, eyeing her curiously.

"Jesus, you scared me."

"Who's a bitch?" Reese checked the corridor in both directions then stepped inside and closed the door behind him.

"Bennett, that's who."

"Ah, yes. What's our little Rebecca of Sunnybrook Farm up to now?"

"Oh, nothing new. It's that damn American Society meeting."

"Miami?"

"Yes. The time you assured me there was no way anyone would ever find out I didn't go."

"She is a resourceful cunt," Reese mumbled. "I'll say that for her."

"What?"

"Didn't she say she was going to do her Girl Scout good deed for the month and let the whole matter drop?"

"That's what she said, but she and Dr. Willoughby are like that." Sheila held up crossed fingers. "Either she's already told him or she's going to hold the thing over my head forever. Either way . . ." She shook her head angrily.

"Easy, baby, easy," Reese said, crossing to her and slipping his hands beneath her lab coat.

Sheila grimaced, but allowed herself to be embraced. Balding, moderately overweight, and wedded to three-piece suits, Reese had never held sex appeal for her in any visceral sense. Still, he was the administrator of the entire hospital complex, and time and experience had taught her that true sex appeal was based not so much on what a man could do *to* her as *for* her.

"You have the most beautiful tits of any woman I've ever known," Reese whispered. "Baby, do you know how long it's been?"

She blocked his move toward her breasts with an outstretched hand. "It's not *my* fault, Norty. I'm divorced. You're the one with all the family commitments. Remember?"

Reese gauged the determination in her eyes and decided against another advance. "So," he said, settling into the chair by her desk, "Wonder Woman has been at it again, huh? Well, believe it or not, she's the reason—one of the reasons—I came down here."

"Oh?"

"Maybe you'd better sit down." Reese motioned her to her chair and then waited until she had complied. "Did you know that old Willoughby has decided to resign?"

"No. No, I didn't, actually." She felt some hurt that Reese had been told of the decision before she was.

"He's giving health as a reason, but I think the old goat just can't cut it anymore. Never could, really."

Sheila shot him a look warning against any further deprecation of the man she had worked under for fifteen years. "That's too bad," she murmured.

"Yeah? Well, baby, hang onto your seat. You don't know what bad is. For his successor, your Willoughby wants to recommend one K. Bennett, MD."

Sheila fought a sudden urge to be sick. For years she had, in effect, run the pathology department, using Willoughby for little more than his signature on purchase orders and personnel decisions. With Bennett as chief, she would be lucky to keep her job, much less her power and influence. "You said *wants* to recommend," she managed.

"Bennett refuses to give him the go-ahead until she's talked it over with her husband."

She picked a tiny Smurf doctor doll off her desk and absently twisted its arm. "How do you feel about it?" she asked.

"After what she did last year, writing what amounted to a letter of complaint about me to the board? How do you *think* I feel?"

"So?" The blue rubber arm snapped off in Sheila's hand.

"I won't have that woman heading a department in my hospital, and that's that."

"What can you do?"

The forcefulness in Reese's voice softened. "There, at least for the moment, is the rub. I've started talking to some of the members of the board of trustees and some of the department heads. It turns out that as things stand, she would have no trouble getting approval. It seems only a few beside me—" he smiled conspiratorially, "and now you—know what an incredible pain in the ass she is."

Sheila flipped the arm and then the body of the doll into the trash. "So we both know," she said.

"Baby, I need something on her. Anything that I can use to influence some people. The prospect of dealing with Bennett's crusades month after month is more than I can take. Keep your eyes and ears open. Dig around. There's got to be something."

"If I do find something," Sheila said, "I'll expect you to be grateful."

"I'll be very grateful."

"Good," Sheila said sweetly. "Then we shall see what we shall see." She rose and kissed him on the forehead, her breasts inches from his eyes. "Very grateful," she whispered. "Now don't you forget that." She backed away at the moment Reese reached for her. "Next time, Norty. Right now I've got work to do."

The Braxton Building was more impressive as an address than it was as a structure. At one time, the twenty-eight story granite obelisk had been the centerpiece of Boston's downtown financial district. Now, surrounded by high-rise glass and steel, the building seemed somehow ill at ease. No uninformed passerby could possibly have predicted from the building's exterior the opulence of the lobby and office suites within, especially the grandeur of the twenty-eighth floor, most elegant of the three floors occupied by the law firm of Minton/Samuels.

J. Winfield Samuels selected a Havana-made panatella from a crystal humidor and offered it to his son. Jared, seated to one side of the huge, inlaid Louis Quatorze desk, groaned. "Dad, it's not even eleven o'clock. Didn't Dr. What's-his-face limit the number you're supposed to smoke in a day?"

"I pay Shrigley to fix me up so I can do whatever the hell I want to do, not to tell me how many cigars I can smoke." He snipped the tip with a bone-handled trimmer and lit it from the smokestack of a sterling silver replica of the QE II. "I swear, if Castro had found a way to keep these little beauties from making it to the States, I would have found a way to cancel the bastard's ticket years ago. Think of it. We'd probably have world peace by now because of a cigar." He took a long, loving draw, blew half of it out, inhaled the rest, and gazed out the floor-to-ceiling window at the harbor and the airport beyond.

Jared sipped at his mug of coffee and risked a glance at his watch. Win Samuels had summoned him and Win Samuels would tell him why when Win Samuels was good and ready to do so. That was the way it had always been between them and, for all Jared knew, that was the way Jared Winfield Samuels, Sr. had related to Win. The notion left a bitter aftertaste. Beyond his grandfather, the family had been traced through a dozen or more generations, three centuries, and three continents. Not that he really cared about such things. His years of rebellion in Vermont had certainly demonstrated that. But now, with the possibility that he represented the end of the line he was . . . more aware.

"So, how's Kate?" The older Samuels was still looking out the window when he spoke.

"She's okay. A little harried at work, but okay." It was unwise, Jared had learned over the years, to offer his father any more information than asked for. At seventy, the man was still as sharp as anyone in the game. What he wanted to know, he would ask.

"And how are the negotiations coming with the union people at Granfield?"

"Fine. Almost over, I think. We're meeting with them this afternoon. If that idiot shop steward can understand the pension package we've put together, the whole mess should get resolved with no more work stoppage."

"I knew you could do it. I told Toby Granfield you could do it."

"Well, like I said, it's not over yet."

"But it will be." The words were an order, not a question.

"Yes," Jared said. "It will be."

"Excellent, excellent. How about a little vacation for you and Kate when everything is signed and sealed. Goodness knows you deserve it. Those union thugs are slow, but they're tough. Bert Hodges says his place in Aruba is available the week after next. Suppose we book it for you."

"I don't . . . what I mean is I'll have to talk with Kate. She's got quite a bit going on at the hospital."

"I know." Win Samuels swung around slowly to face his son. At six feet, he was nearly as tall as Jared and no more than five pounds heavier. His rimless spectacles and discreetly darkened hair neutralized the aging effects of deep crow's feet and a slightly sallow complexion.

"What?"

"I said that I knew she was having a busy time of it at the hospital." Samuels paused, perhaps for dramatic effect. "Norton Reese called me this morning."

"Oh?" The statement was upsetting. For five years, Jared had handled all of Boston Metro's legal affairs. There was no reason for Norton Reese to be dealing directly with his father, even allowing that the two of them had known each other for years.

"He tells me the head of pathology is retiring." Jared nodded that the information was not news. "He also said that this head pathologist, Willoughby, wants Kate to take over for him."

"She mentioned that to me," Jared understated.

"Did she now? Good. I'm glad you two communicate about such minor goings on." The facetiousness in Samuels's voice was hardly subtle.

Kate's independence had been a source of discussion between them on more than one occasion. Somewhere in the drawer of that Louis Quatorze desk was a computer printout showing that while he had received forty-nine percent of the total vote cast in the congressional race, he had garnered only forty-two percent of the women's vote. To Win Samuels, the numbers meant that if Mrs. Jared Samuels had been out stumping for her husband instead of mucking about elbow deep in a bunch of cadavers, Jared would be packing to leave for Washington. Self-serving, contrary, disloyal, thoughtless—the adjectives had, from time to time, flown hot and heavy from the old man, though never in Kate's presence. Toward her, he had always been as cordial and charming as could be.

"Look, Dad," Jared said, "I've still got some preparation to do for that session at Granfield. Do you think . . ."

"Donna," Samuels said through the intercom, "could you bring in another tea for me and another coffee for my son, please?"

Jared sank back in his seat and stared helplessly at the far wall, a wall covered with photographs of politicians, athletes and other celebrities, arm in arm or hand in hand with his father. A few of them were similar shots featuring his grandfather, and one of them was an eight by ten of Jared and the President, taken at a three-minute meeting arranged by his father for just that purpose.

With a discreet knock, Samuels's sensuous receptionist entered and set their beverages and a basket of croissants on a mahogany stand near the desk. Her smile in response to Jared's "Thank you" was vacant—a subtle message that her allegiance was to the man on the power side of the Louis Quatorze.

"So," Samuels said, settling down with a mug of tea in one hand and his Havana in the other, "what do you think of this business at Metro?"

"I haven't given it much thought," Jared lied. "As far as I know, nothing formal has been done yet."

"Well, I'd suggest you start thinking about it."

"What?"

"Norton Reese doesn't want Kate to have that position and, frankly, neither do I. He thinks she's too young and too inexperienced. He tells me that if she gets the appointment, which incidentally is doubtful anyhow, she'll run herself ragged, burn out, and finally get chewed to ribbons by the politicians and the other department heads. According to him, Kate just doesn't understand the way the game is played—that there are some toes that are simply not to be stepped on."

"Like his," Jared snapped.

"Jared, you told me the two of you were planning on starting your family. Does Kate think she can do that and run a department, too? What about her obligation to you and your career? It's bad enough she's married to you and doesn't even have your name. Christ, her looks alone would be worth thousands of votes to you if she'd just plunk her face in front of a camera a few times. Add a little baby to that, and I swear you could make a run for the Senate and win."

"Kate's business is Kate's business," Jared said with neither enthusiasm nor conviction.

"Take her to the Caribbean. Have a talk with her," Samuels reasoned calmly. "Help her see that marriage is a series of . . . compromises. Give and take."

"Okay, I'll try."

"Good. Kate should see where her obligations and her loyalties lie. Ross Mattingly may be on a downhill slide, but he still managed to hang on and win the election. Don't think he's going to roll over and play dead next time. The fewer liabilities we have the better. And frankly, the way things stand, Kate is a minus. Have I made my thoughts clear?"

"Clear." Jared felt totally depleted.

"Fine. Let me know when the Granfield business is done, and also let me know the date you two decide on, so I can tell Bert Hodges." With a nod, Winfield Samuels signaled the meeting over.

◆

In his sea-green scrub suit and knee-length white coat, Tom Engleson might have been the earnest young resident on a daytime soap opera, loving his way through the nurses one moment, stamping out disease the next. But his eyes gave him away. Kate saw the immense fatigue in them the moment she entered the resident's office on the fourth floor of the building renovated by the Ashburton Foundation and renamed in memory of Sylvia Ashburton. It was a fatigue that went deeper than the circles of gray enveloping them, deeper than the fine streaks of red throughout their sclerae.

"Been to sleep at all?" Kate asked, glancing at the clock as she set two tinfoil pans of salad on the coffee table. It was twenty minutes of two.

Engleson merely shook his head and began to work off the plastic cover of his salad with a dexterity that was obviously far from what it had been when he had started his shift thirty and a half hours before. Studying the man's face, Kate wondered how residency programs could justify the ridiculous hours they required, especially of surgical trainees. It was as if one generation of doctors was saying to the next, "We had to do it this way and we came out all right, didn't we?" Meanwhile, year after year, a cardiogram was misread here, an operation fumbled there; never a rash of problems, just isolated incidents at one hospital then another, one program then another—incidents of no lasting consequence, except, of course, to the patients and families involved.

"I hope you like blue cheese," Kate said. "Gianetti's has great vinaigrette, too. I just guessed."

"It's fine, perfect, Dr. Samuels," Engleson said between bites. "I've missed a meal or two since this Vitale thing started yesterday morning."

"Eat away. You can have some of mine if you want. I'm not too hungry. And it's 'Kate.' We pathologists have a little trouble with formality."

Engleson, his mouth engaged with another forkful of salad, nodded his acknowledgment.

"Sorry I missed you when I was here last evening. The nurse said you were in the delivery room."

"A set of twins."

"How's Beverly Vitale?"

"Her blood count's down this morning. Twenty-five. She's due for a recheck in an hour or two. Any further drop, and we'll give her more blood."

"Her GI tract?" Kate asked, speculating on the site of blood loss.

"Probably. There's been some blood in every stool we've checked. She's on steroids, you know."

"I do know. Withhold steroids, and her antibodies run wild, destroying her own clotting factors; use them, and she risks developing bleeding ulcers. It's one of those situations that makes me grateful I decided on pathology. Stan Willoughby and I reviewed the ovary sections this morning. His impression is that the findings are unique. He's doing some special stains now and has sent slides to a colleague of his at Johns Hopkins, whom he says is as good as anyone in the business at diagnosing ovarian disorders. He also is calling around town to see if anything like this has turned up in another department."

"Etiology?"

"No clues, Tom. Virus, toxin, med reaction. All of the above, none of the above, A and B but not C. She told you she wasn't on any meds, right?"

"None except vitamins. The multivitamin plus iron we dispense through the Omnicenter."

"Well I'm living proof those don't cause any problems. I've taken them for a couple of years. Make frail pathologist strong like bull." Kate flexed her biceps.

"Make pathologist excellent teacher, too."

"Why, thank you." Kate's green eyes sparkled. "Thank you very much, Tom." For a moment, she saw him blush. "How about we go say hello to Beverly. I'd like to make extra sure about one or two aspects of her history. Here, you can stick this salad in that refrigerator for later."

"Provided the bacteria who call that icebox home don't eat it first," Tom said.

The two were heading down the hall toward the stairway when the overhead page snapped to life. "Code ninety-nine, Ashburton five-oh-two; code ninety-nine, Ashburton five-oh-two."

"Oh, Jesus." Tom was already racing toward the exit as he spoke. Kate was slower to react. She was almost to the stairway door before she realized that Ashburton 502 was Beverly Vitale's room.

It had been a year, perhaps two, since Kate had last observed a cardiac arrest and resuscitation attempt. She was certified in advanced cardiac life support, but training and testing then had been on Resusci-Annie, a mannequin. Her practical experience had ended years ago, along with her internship. At the moment, however, none of those considerations mattered. What mattered was the life of a young woman who loved to make music. With an athlete's quickness, Kate bolted after Tom Engleson up the stairs from Ashburton Four to Ashburton Five.

There were more than enough participants in the code. Residents, nurses, medical students, and technicians filled room 502 and overflowed into the hall. Kate worked her way to a spot by the door, from which she watched the nightmare of Beverly Vitale's final minutes of life.

It was a gastric hemorrhage, almost certainly from an ulcer eroding into an artery. The woman's relentless exsanguination was being complicated by the aspiration of vomited blood. Cloaked in abysmal helplessness, Kate witnessed Tom Engleson, desperation etched on his face, issuing orders in a deceptively composed tone; the organized chaos of the white-clad code team, pumping, injecting, monitoring, reporting, respirating, suctioning; and through the milling bodies, the expressionless, blood-smeared face of Beverly Vitale.

For nearly an hour the struggle continued, though

there was never a pulse or even an encouraging electrocardiographic pattern. In the end, there was nothing but another lesson in the relative impotence of people and medicine when matched against the capriciousness of illness and death. Tom Engleson, his eyes dark and sunken, shook his head in utter futility.

"It's over," he said softly. "Thank you all. It's over."

3

Tuesday 11 December

Simultaneously with hearing the report from the WEEI traffic helicopter of a monumental backup stemming from the Mystic/Tobin Bridge, Kate became part of it. Commuting to the city from the North Shore was an experience that she suspected ranked in pleasantness somewhere between an IRS audit and root canal work. Although Tuesday was normally a low-volume day, this morning she had encountered rain, sleet, snow, and even a bizarre stretch of sunlight during her thirty-mile drive, far too much weather for even Boston drivers to attack. With a groan, she resigned herself to being half an hour late, perhaps more, for the appointment Stan Willoughby had arranged for her at White Memorial Hospital.

The pathology chief's call had punctuated another confusing, bittersweet morning with Jared. It seemed as if the intensity and caring in their relationship was waxing and waning not only from day to day but from hour to hour or even from minute to minute. In one sentence the man was Jared Samuels, the funny, sensitive, often ingenuous fellow she had married and still loved deeply; in the next he was calculating and distant, a miniature of his father, intransigent on points they should have been working through as husband and wife. At last, after an awkward hour of lighting brush fires of dissension and then scurrying to stamp them out, Jared had suggested a week or ten days together in Aruba, away from the pressures and demands of their careers.

"What do you say, Boots?" he had asked, calling on the pet name she favored most of the four or five he used. "Aruba you all over." The expression in his eyes—urgency? fear?—belied his levity.

"Aruba you too, Jared," she had said finally.

"Then we go?"

"If Stan can give me the time off, and if you can stand the thought of trying to hang onto a woman swathed in Coppertone, we go."

At that moment, Jared looked reborn.

"Grumper-to-grumper, stall-and-crawl traffic headed in a snail trail toward the bridge, thanks to a fender bender in the left-hand lane." The Eye-in-the-Sky was sparing none of his clichés in describing the mess on Route 1 south. Kate inched her Volvo between cars, but gained little ground. Finally, resigned to the situation, she settled back, turned up the volume on the all-news station, and concentrated on ignoring the would-be Lothario who was winking and waving at her from the Trans-Am in the next lane.

The news, like Stan Willoughby's call, dealt with the sudden death of Red Sox hero Bobby Geary, a homegrown boy who had played his sandlot ball in South Boston, not a mile from the luxurious condominium where he was found by his mother following an apparent heart attack. Stan's name was mentioned several times as the medical examiner assigned to autopsy the man who had given away thousands of free tickets and had added an entire floor to Children's and Infants' Hospital in the name of "the kids of Boston."

"Kate," Willoughby had begun, "I hope I'm not interrupting anything."

"No, no. Just getting ready for work," she had said, smiling at Jared, who was nude by the bathroom door dancing a coarse hula and beckoning her to the shower with a long-handled scrub brush.

"Well, I don't want you to come to work."

"What?"

"I want you to go to White Memorial. You have an appointment in the pathology department there at eight-thirty. Leon Olesky will be waiting for you. Do you know him?"

"Only by name."

"Well, I called around town trying to see if anyone had seen a case similar to our Miss Vitale's. Initially there was nothing, but late last night Leon called me at home. From what he described, the two cases—his and ours—sound identical. I told him you'd be over to study his material."

"How old was the woman?" Kate had asked excitedly.

"I don't remember what he said. Twenty-eight, I think."

"Cause of death?"

"Ah ha! I thought you'd never ask. Cerebral hemorrhage, secondary to minor head trauma."

"Platelets? Fibrinogen?" Her hand was white around the receiver.

"Leon didn't know. The case was handled by one of his underlings. He said he'd try to find out by the time you got there."

"Can't you come?"

"Hell, no. Haven't you heard the news about Bobby Geary?"

"The ball player?"

"Heart attack late last night. Found dead in bed. I'm posting him at ten-thirty. In fact, I'd like you back here before I finish, just in case I need your help."

"You've got it. You know, you are a pretty terrific chief, Stanley. Are you sure you want to retire?"

"Yesterday, if I could arrange it, Katey-girl. You hurry on back to Metro after you see Olesky, now. No telling what this shriveled brain of mine might miss."

White Memorial Hospital, an architectural polyglot of more than a score of buildings, was the flagship of the fleet of Harvard Medical School affiliated hospitals. Overlooking the Charles River near the North End, WMH had more research facilities, professors, grants, and administrative expertise than any hospital in the area, if not the world. Metropolitan Hospital had once held sway, reportedly supplying ninety percent of all the professors of medicine at all the medical schools in the country, but that time had long since been buried beneath an avalanche of incompetent administrators, unfavorable publicity, and corrupt city politicians. Although Metro had made a resurgence of sorts under the guidance of Norton Reese, there was little likelihood of its ever recapturing the prestige, endowments, and fierce patient loyalty of the glory days, when at least one man was known to have had "Take Me To Metro" tattooed across his chest.

It had been some time since Kate had had reason to visit the pathology unit at White Memorial, and she was uncomfortably impressed with the improvements and expansion that had occurred. Equipment her department congratulated itself on acquiring, this unit possessed in duplicate or triplicate. Corridors and offices were brightly lit, with plants, paintings, and other touches that made the work environment less tedious and oppressive. Almost subconsciously, Kate found herself making mental lists of things she would press to accomplish as chief of pathology at Metro.

Leon Olesky, a mild, Lincolnesque man, brushed off her apologies for her tardiness and after exchanging compliments about Stan Willoughby, left her alone in his office with the material from the autopsy of Ginger Rittenhouse. On a pink piece of paper by his elegant microscope were the data on the woman's blood studies. Only two of many parameters measured were abnormal: fibrinogen and platelets. The levels of each were depressed enough to have been life threatening. Her hands trembling with anticipation, Kate took the first of the ovarian sections and slid it onto the stage of the microscope. A moment to flex tension from the muscles in her neck, and she leaned forward to begin another journey through the yellow-white light.

Forty-five minutes later, the one had become three. Leon Olesky hunched over one set of oculars of the teaching microscope, controlling the focus with his right hand and moving the slide with his left. Across from him, in the seat Kate had occupied, was Tom Engleson.

"You know," Olesky said, "if Stan hadn't called me about your case, the findings on our young woman would have slipped right past us. I mentioned the matter last night at our weekly department conference, but no one responded. An hour later, Dr. Hickman came to my office. Young Bruce is, perhaps, the brightest of our residents, but at times, I'm afraid, a bit too quick for his own good."

Kate sighed. Olesky's observations described many of the so-called hotshot residents she had worked with over the years. "I'll take methodical over genius any day of the week," she said.

"Both is best," Olesky responded, "but that's a rare combination, indeed. I might mention, though, that it is a combination your mentor feels he is lucky to have found in you."

"Methodical, yes," Kate allowed, "but I've yet to receive a single membership application from Mensa."

"She's only the best in the hospital," Tom interjected somewhat impetuously.

"Finish telling us about your resident." Kate withheld reaction to Engleson's enthusiasm, sensing that what she felt was, in equal parts, flattered and embarrassed.

"Well, it seems our Dr. Hickman was uncertain about the pathology he was seeing in this woman's ovaries. However, rather than think that the finding might be unique, he assumed, although he won't say so in as many words, that the condition was one he should have known about, and hence one he would look foolish asking for help with. Since the cause of death was unrelated to the ovaries, he chose to describe his findings in the autopsy report and leave it at that."

"No harm done," Kate said.

"Quite the contrary, in fact. This event may be the pinprick Hickman's ego needs so he can reach his full potential as a physician. It will make even more of an impression if, as Dr. Willoughby and now yours truly, suspect, this pathology turns out to be one never before described."

Kate and Tom exchanged excited glances. "How would you explain its showing up in two woman in the same city at about the same time?" she asked.

The professor's eyes, dark and deeply serious, met first Engleson's and then Kate's. "Considering the outcome of the illness in both individuals, I would suggest that we work diligently to find an answer to that question. At the moment, I have none."

"There must be a connection," Engleson said.

"I hope there is, young man." Olesky rose from his stool. "And I hope the two of you will be able to find it. I have a class to teach right now at the medical school. This evening, I leave for meetings in San Diego, and from there, I go to the wedding of my son in New Mexico. My office and our department are at your disposal."

"Thank you," they said.

Olesky replaced his lab coat with a well-worn mackintosh. He shook hands first with Engleson and then with Kate. A final check of his desk and he shambled from the office.

Kate waited for the door to click shut. "I'm glad you were able to get here so quickly," she said. "Did you have any trouble getting the records people to let you take Beverly's chart out of the hospital?"

"None. I just followed Engleson's first law of chutzpah. The more one looks like he should be doing what he's doing, the less anyone realizes that he shouldn't. I'll have to admit that the crooks with moving vans and uniforms who pick entire houses clean thought of the law before I did, but I was the first one I know to put it in words. Are you okay? I went to find you after the code was over yesterday, but you were gone. Before I could call, I was rushed to the OR to do an emergency C-section."

"I was okay." She paused. "Actually, I wasn't. It hurt like hell to see her lying there like that. I can't remember the last time I felt so helpless." At the thought, the mention of the word, Arthur Everett's grotesque face flashed in her mind, his reddened eyes bulging with the effort of forcing himself inside her. Yes, I do, she thought. I do remember when. "How about you?" she asked.

Engleson shrugged. "I think I'm still numb. It's like I'm afraid that if I let down and acknowledge my feelings about her and what happened, I'll never set foot in a hospital again."

Kate nodded her understanding. "You know, Tom, contrary to popular belief, being human doesn't disqualify you from being a doctor. Are you married?" Engleson shook his head. "I think it's hard to face some of the things we have to face and then have no one to talk them out with, to cry on, if necessary, when we get home." She thought about the difficult morning with Jared and smiled inwardly at the irony of her words. "Had you known Beverly outside the hospital?"

"No. I met her when she came into Metro. But I thought about trying to start up a relationship as soon as she . . ." His voice grew husky. He cleared his throat.

"I understand," Kate said. "Look, maybe we can talk about our work and our lives in medicine some day soon. Right now, we've got to start looking for some common threads between these women. I'm due back at Metro in," she checked her watch, "—shoot, I've only got about twenty minutes."

Tom was thumbing through the thin sheaf of papers dealing with Ginger Rittenhouse. "It shouldn't take long to check. They have next to no information here. Ginger

Louise Rittenhouse, twenty-eight, elementary school teacher, lived and worked in Cambridge, but she was running along the Boston side of the river when she collapsed. Apparently she lived long enough to get an emergency CAT scan, but not long enough to get to the OR."

"Married?" Kate asked.

"No. Single. That's the second time you've asked that question about someone in the last two minutes." He narrowed one eye and fingered his moustache. "You have, perhaps, a marriage fixation?"

Kate smiled. "Let's leave my fixations out of this. At least for the time being, okay? What about family? Place of birth? Next of kin? Did they document any prior medical history?"

"Hey, slow down. We obstetricians are hardly famous for our swift reading ability. No known medical history. Next of kin is a brother in Seattle. Here's his address. You know, world's greatest hospital or not, they take a pretty skimpy history."

"It doesn't look like they had time for much more," Kate said solemnly. There had to be a connection, she was thinking. The two cases were at once too remarkable and too similar. Somewhere, the lives of a teacher from Cambridge and a cellist from a suburb on the far side of Boston had crossed.

"Wait," Engleson said. "She had a roommate. It says here on the accident floor sheet. Sandra Tucker. That must be how they found out about her family."

Kate again checked her watch. "Tom, I've got to go. I promised Dr. Willoughby I'd help out with the post on Bobby Geary. Do you think you could try and get a hold of this Sandra Tucker? See if our woman has seen a doctor recently or had a blood test. Don't teachers need yearly physicals or something?"

"Not the ones I had. I think their average age was deceased."

"Are you going to call from here?" Engleson thought

for a moment and then nodded. "Fine, give me a ring when you get back to Metro. And Tom? Thanks for the compliment you paid me before." She reached out and shook his hand, firmly and in a businesslike manner. Then she left.

With the pistol-shot crack of bat against ball, thirty thousand heads snapped in horror toward the fence in right center field.

"Jesus, Katey, it's gone," was all Jared could say.

The ball, a white star, arced into the blue-black summer night sky. On the base paths, four runners dashed around toward home. There were two out in the inning, the ninth inning. The scoreboard at the base of the left-field wall in Fenway Park said that the Red Sox were ahead of the Yankees by three runs, but that lead, it appeared, had only seconds more to be.

Kate, enthralled by the lights and the colors and the precision of her first live baseball game, stood frozen with the rest, her eyes fixed on the ball, now in a lazy descent toward a spot beyond the fence. Then into the corner of her field of vision he came, running with an antelope grace that made his movements seem almost slow motion. He left the ground an improbable distance from the fence, his gloved left hand reaching, it seemed, beyond its limits, up to the top of the barrier and over it. For an instant, ball and glove disappeared beyond the fence. In the next instant, they were together, clutched to the chest of Bobby Geary as he tumbled down onto the dirt warning track to the roar of thirty thousand voices. It was a moment Kate would remember for the rest of her life.

This, too, was such a moment.

The body that had once held the spirit and abilities of Bobby Geary lay on the steel table before her, stripped of the indefinable force that had allowed it to sense and react so remarkably. To one side, in a shallow metal pan, was the athlete's heart, carefully sliced along several planes to expose the muscle of the two ventricles—the pumping chambers—and the three main coronary arteries—left, right, and circumflex. Images of that night at Fenway more than four years ago intruded on Kate's objectivity and brought with them a wistfulness that she knew had no place in this facet of her work.

"Nothing in the heart at all?" she asked for the second time.

Stan Willoughby, leprechaunish in green scrubs and a black rubber apron, shook his head. "Must a' bin somethin' he et," he said, by way of admitting that, anatomically at least, he had uncovered no explanation for the pulmonary edema, fluid that had filled Bobby Geary's lungs and, essentially, drowned him from within.

Kate, clad identically to her chief, examined the heart under a high-intensity light. "Teenage heart in a thirty-six-year-old man. I remember reading somewhere that he intended to keep playing until he was fifty. This heart says he might have made it."

"This edema says 'no way,' " Willoughby corrected. "I'm inclined to think dysrhythmia and cardiac arrest on that basis. Preliminary blood tests are all normal, so I think it possible we may never know the specific cause." There was disappointment in his voice.

"Sometimes we just don't," Kate said. The words were Willoughby's, a lesson he had repeated many times to her over the years.

Willoughby glared at her for a moment; then he laughed out loud. "You are a saucy pup, flipping my words back at me like that. Suppose you tell me what to say to the police lieutenant drinking coffee and dropping donut crumbs right now in my office, or to the gaggle of reporters in the lobby waiting for the ultimate word. Ladies and gentlemen, the ultimate word from the crack pathology department you help support with your taxes is that we are absolutely certain we have no idea why Bobby Geary went into a pulmonary edema and died."

Kate did not answer. She had grabbed a magnifying

glass and was intently examining Geary's feet, especially between his toes and along the inside of his ankles. "Stan, look," she said. "All along here. Tiny puncture marks, almost invisible. There must be a dozen of them. No, wait, there are more."

Willoughby adjusted the light and took the magnifier from her. "Holy potato," he said softly. "Bobby Geary an addict?" He stepped back from the table and looked at Kate, who could only shrug. "If he was, he was a bloomin' artist with a needle."

"A twenty-seven or twenty-nine gauge would make punctures about that size."

"And a narcotics or amphetamine overdose would explain the pulmonary edema." Kate nodded. "Holy potato," Willoughby said again. "If it's true, there must be evidence somewhere in his house."

"Unless it happened with other people around and they brought him home and put him to bed. Why don't we send some blood for a drug screen and do levels on any substance we pick up?"

Willoughby glanced around the autopsy suite. The single technician on duty was too far away to have heard any of their conversation. "What do you say we label the tube 'Smith' or 'Schultz' or something. I'm no sports fan, but I know enough to see what's at stake here. The man was a hero."

"What about the policeman?"

"His name's Detective Finn, and he *is* a fan. I think he'd prefer some kind of story about a heart attack, even if the blood test is positive."

"Schultz sounds like as good a name as any," Kate said. "Are these the tubes? Good. I'll have new labels made up."

"I'll send Finn over to the boy's place, and then I'll tell the newsnoses they will just have to wait until the microscopics are processed. Now, when can you give me a report on the goings on at the WMH?"

"Well, beyond what I've already told you, there's not

much to report. We've got some sort of ovarian microsclerosis in two women with profound deficiencies of both platelets and fibrinogen. At this point, we have no connections between the two, nothing even to tell us for sure that the ovarian and blood problems are related."

"So what's next?"

"Next? Well, Tom Engleson, the resident who was involved with Beverly Vitale, is trying to get some information from the roommate of the WMH woman."

"And thou?"

Kate held her hands to either side, palms up. "No plan. I'm on surgicals this month, so I've got a few of those to read along with a frozen or two from the OR. After that I thought I'd talk to my friend Marco Sebastian and see if that computer of his can locate data on a woman named Ginger Rittenhouse."

"Sounds good," Willoughby said. "Keep me posted." He seemed reluctant to leave.

"Is there anything else?" Kate asked finally.

"Well, actually there is one small matter."

"All right, let me have it." Kate knew what was coming.

"I . . . um . . . have a meeting scheduled with Norton Reese this afternoon. Several members of the search committee are supposed to be there and well . . . I sort of wondered if you'd had time to . . ." Willoughby allowed the rest of the thought to remain unspoken.

Kate's eyes narrowed. He had promised her a week, and it had been only a few days. She wasn't at all ready to answer. There were other factors to consider besides merely "want to" or "don't want to." Willoughby had to understand that. "I've decided that if you really think I can do it, and you can get all those who have to agree to do so, then I'll take the position," she heard her voice say.

The girl's name was Robyn Smithers. She was a high school junior, assigned by Roxbury Vocational to spend four hours each week working as an extern in the pathology department of Metropolitan Hospital. Her role was simply defined: do what she was told, and ask questions only when it was absolutely clear that she was interrupting no one. She was one of twelve such students negotiated for by Norton Reese and paid for by the Boston School Department. That these students learned little except how to run errands was of no concern to Reese, who had already purchased a new word processor for his office with the receipts from having them.

Robyn had made several passes by Sheila Pierce's open door before she stopped and knocked.

"Yes, Robyn, what can I do for you?"

"Miss Pierce, I'm sorry for botherin' you. Really I am."

"It's fine, Robyn. I was beginning to wonder what you were up to walking back and forth out there."

"Well, ma'am, it's this blood. Doctor Bennett, you know, the lady doctor?"

"Yes, I know. What about her?"

"Well, Dr. Bennett gave me this here blood to take to . . ." she consulted a scrap of paper, "Special Chemistries, only I can't find where that is. I'm sorry to bother you while you're working and all."

"Nonsense, child. Here, let me see what you've got."

Casually, Sheila glanced at the pale blue requisition form. The patient's name, John Schultz, meant nothing to her. That in itself was unusual. She made it her business to know the names of all those being autopsied in her department. However, she acknowledged, occasionally one was scheduled without her being notified. In the space marked "Patient's Hospital Number" the department's billing number was written. The request was for a screen for drugs of abuse. Penned along the margin of the requisition was the order, "STAT: Phone results to Dr. K. Bennett ASAP."

"Curiouser and curiouser," Sheila muttered.

"Pardon, ma'am?"

"Oh, nothing, dear. Listen, you've been turning the wrong way at that corridor back there. Come, I'll show you." She handed back the vials and the requisition and then guided the girl to the door of her office. "There," she said sweetly. "Just turn right there and go all the way down until you see a cloudy-glass door like mine with Special Chemistries written on it. Okay?"

"Yes. Thank you, ma'am." Robyn Smithers raced down the corridor.

"Glad to help . . . you dumb little shit."

Sheila listened until she heard the door to Special Chemistries open and close; then she went to her phone and dialed the cubicle of Marvin Grimes. Grimes was the department's deiner, the preparer of bodies for autopsy. It was a position he had held for as long as anyone could remember.

"Marvin," Sheila asked, "could you tell me the names of the cases we autopsied today?"

"Jes' two, Ms. Pierce. The old lady Partridge 'n' the ball player."

"No one named Schultz?" Sheila pictured the bottle of Wild Irish Rose Grimes kept in the lower right-hand drawer of his desk; she wondered if by the end of the day the old man would even remember talking to her.

"No siree. No Schultz today."

"Yesterday?"

"Wait, now. Let me check. Nope, only McDonald, Lacey, Briggs, and Ca . . . Capez . . . Capezio. No one named . . . what did you say the name was?"

"Never mind, Marvin. Don't worry about it."

As she replaced the receiver, Sheila tried to estimate the time it would take the technicians in Special Chemistries to complete a stat screen for drugs of abuse.

"Curiouser and curiouser and curiouser," she said.

The dozen or so buildings at Metropolitan Hospital were connected by a series of tunnels, so tortuous and poorly lit that the hospital had recommended that its employees avoid them if walking alone. Several assaults and the crash of a laundry train into a patient's stretcher only enhanced the grisly reputation of the tunnel, as did the now classic Harvard Medical School senior show, *Rats*. Kate, unmindful of the legends and tales, had used the tunnels freely since her medical student days, and except for once coming upon the hours-old corpse of a drunk, nestled peacefully in a small concrete alcove by his half-empty bottle of Thunderbird, she had encountered little to add to the lore. The single greatest threat she faced each time she traveled underground from one building to another was that of getting lost by forgetting a twist or a turn or by missing the crack shaped like Italy that signaled to her the turnoff to the administration building. At various times over the years, she had headed for the surgical building and ended up in the massive boiler room, or headed for a conference in the amphitheater, only to dead end at the huge steam pressers of the laundry building.

Concentrating on not overlooking the landmarks and grime-dimmed signs, Kate made her way through the beige-painted maze toward the computer suite and Marco Sebastian. Nurses in twos and threes passed by in each direction, heralding the approach of the three o'clock change in shift. Kate wondered how many thousands of nurses had over the years walked these tunnels on the way to their charges. The Metro tradition: nurses, professors of surgery, medical school deans, country practitioners, even Nobel laureates. Now, in her own way and through her own abilities, she was becoming part of that tradition. Jared had to know how important that was to her. She had shared with him the ugly secrets of her prior marriage and stifling, often futile life. Surely he knew what all this meant.

In typically efficient Metro fashion, the computer facilities were situated on the top floor of the pediatrics building, as far as possible from the administrative offices that used them the most. Kate paused by the elevator and thought about tackling the six flights of stairs instead. The day, not yet nearly over, had her feeling at once exhausted and exhilarated. Three difficult surgical cases had followed the Geary autopsy. Just as she was completing the last of them, a Special Chemistries technician had dropped off the results of Geary's blood test. The amphetamine level in his body was enormous, quite enough to have thrown him into pulmonary edema. Before she could call Stan Willoughby with the results, she was summoned to his office. The meeting there, with Willoughby and the detective, Martin Finn, had been brief. Evidence found on a careful search of Bobby Geary's condominium had yielded strong evidence that the man was a heavy amphetamine user. It was information known only to the three of them. Finn was adamant—barring any findings suggesting that Geary's death was not an accidental overdose, there seemed little to be gained and much to be lost by making the revelation public. The official story would be of a heart attack, secondary to an anomaly of one coronary artery.

The elevator arrived at the moment Kate had decided on the stairs. She changed her mind in time to slip between the closing doors. Marco Sebastian, expansive in his white lab coat and as jovial as ever, met her with a bear hug. She had been a favorite of his since their first meeting, nearly seven years before. In fact, he and his wife had once made a concerted effort to fix her up with his brother-in-law, a caterer from East Boston. After a rapid-fire series of questions to bring himself up to date on Jared, the job, Willoughby, and the results of their collaborative study, the engineer led her into his office and sat her down next to him, facing the terminal display screen on his desk.

"Now then, Dr. Bennett," he said in a voice with the deep smoothness of an operatic baritone, "what tidbits can I resurrect for you this time from the depths of our electronic jungle? Do you wish the hat size of our first chief of medicine? We have it. The number of syringes syringed in the last calendar year? Can do. The number of warts on the derriere of our esteemed administrator? You have merely to ask."

"Actually, Marco, I wasn't after anything nearly so exotic. Just a name."

"The first baby born here was . . ." He punched a set of keys and then another. ". . . Jessica Peerless, February eighteenth, eighteen forty-three."

"Marco, that wasn't the name I had in mind."

"How about the two hundredth appendectomy?"

"Nope."

"The twenty-eight past directors of nursing?"

"Uh-uh. I'm sorry, Marco."

"All this data, and nobody wants any of it." The man was genuinely crestfallen. "I keep telling our beloved administrator that we are being underused, but I don't think he has the imagination to know what questions to ask. Periodically, I send him tables showing that the cafeteria is overspending on pasta or that ten percent of our patients have ninety percent of our serious diseases, just to pique his interest, remind him that we're still here."

"My name?"

"Oh, yes. I'm sorry. It's been a little slow here. I guess you can tell that."

"It's Rittenhouse, Ginger Rittenhouse. Here's her address, birthplace, and birthdate. That's all I have. I need to know if she's ever been a patient of this hospital, in or out."

"Keep your eyes on the screen," Sebastian said dramatically. Thirty seconds later, he shook his head. "*Nada*. A Shirley Rittenhouse in nineteen fifty-six, but no others."

"Are you sure?"

Sebastian gave her a look that might have been anticipated from a judge who had been asked, "Do you really think your decision is fair?"

"Sorry," she said.

"Of course, she still could have been a patient of the Omnicenter."

Kate stiffened. "What do you mean?"

"Well, the Omnicenter is sort of a separate entity from the rest of Metro. This system here handles records and billing for the Ashburton inpatient service, but the Omnicenter is totally self-contained. Has been since the day they put the units in—what is it?—nine, ten years ago."

"Isn't that strange?"

"Strange is normal around this place," Sebastian said.

"Can't you even plug this system into the one over there?"

"Nope. Don't know the access codes. Carl Horner, the engineer who runs the electronics there, plays things pretty close to the vest. You know Horner?"

"No, I don't think so." Kate tried to remember if, during any of her visits to the Omnicenter as a patient, she had even seen the man. "Why do you suppose they're so secretive?"

"Not secretive so much as careful. I play around with numbers here; Horner and the Omnicenter people live and die by them. Every bit of that place is computerized: records, appointments, billing, even the prescriptions."

"I know. I go there for my own care."

"Then you can imagine what would happen if even a small fly got dropped into their ointment. Horner is a genius, let me tell you, but he is a bit eccentric. He was writing advanced programs when the rest of us were still trying to spell IBM. From what I've heard, complete independence from the rest of the system is one of the conditions he insisted upon before taking the Omnicenter job in the first place."

"So how do I find out if Ginger Rittenhouse has ever been a patient there? It's important, Marco. Maybe very important."

"Well, Paleolithic as it may sound, we call and ask."

"The phone?"

Marco Sebastian shrugged sheepishly and nodded.

* * *

DEAD END. Alone in her office, Kate doodled the words on a yellow legal pad, first in block print, then in script, and finally in a variety of calligraphies, learned through one of several "self-enrichment" courses she had taken during her two years with Art. According to Carl Horner, Marco Sebastian's counterpart at the Omnicenter, Ginger Rittenhouse had never been a patient there. Tom Engleson had succeeded in contacting the woman's roommate, but her acquaintance and living arrangement with Ginger were recent ones. Aside from a prior address, Engleson had gleaned no new information. Connections thus far between the woman and Beverly Vitale: zero.

Outside, the daylong dusting of snow had given way to thick, wet flakes that were beginning to cover. The homeward commute was going to be a bear. Kate tried to ignore the prospect and reflect instead on what her next move might be in evaluating the microsclerosis cases—perhaps an attempt to find a friend or family member who knew Ginger Rittenhouse better than her new roommate. She might present the two women's pathologies at a regional conference of some sort, hoping to luck into yet a third case. She looked at the uncompleted work on her desk. Face it, she realized, with the amount of spare time she had to run around playing epidemiologist, the mystery of the ovarian microsclerosis seemed destined to remain just that.

For a time, her dread of the drive home did battle with the need to get there in order to grocery shop and set out some sort of dinner for the two of them. Originally, they had tried to eschew traditional roles in setting up and maintaining their household, but both rapidly realized that their traditional upbringings made that arrangement impractical if not impossible. The shopping and food preparation had reverted to her, the maintenance of their physical plant to Jared. Day-to-day finances, they agreed, were beyond either of their abilities and therefore to be shared. Again she checked out the window. Then after a final hesitation, a final thought about calling home and leaving a message on their machine that she was going to work late, she pushed herself away from the desk.

As she stood up, she decided: if it was going to be dinner, then dammit, it was going to be a special dinner. In medical school and residency, she had always been able to find an extra gear, a reserve jet of energy, when she needed it. Perhaps tonight her marriage could use a romantic, gourmet dinner more than it could her moaning about the exhausting day she had endured. Spinach salad, shrimp curry, candles, Grgich Hills Chardonnay, maybe even a chocolate soufflé. She ticked off a mental shopping list as she slipped a few scientific reprints into her briefcase, bundled herself against the rush-hour snow, and hurried from her office, pleased to sense the beginnings of a surge. It was good to know she still had one.

In the quiet of his windowless office, Carl Horner spoke through his fingertips to the information storage and retrieval system in the next room. He had implicit faith in his machines, in their perfection. If there was a problem, as it now seemed there was, the source, he felt certain, was human—either himself or someone at the company. Again and again his fingers asked. Again and again the answers were the same. Finally, he turned from his console to one of two black phones on his desk. A series of seven numbers opened a connection in Buffalo, New York; four numbers more activated the line to a "dead box" in Atlanta; and a final three completed an untraceable connection to Darlington, Kentucky.

Cyrus Redding answered on the first ring.

"Carl?"

"Orange red, Cyrus." Had the colors been reversed, Redding would have been warned either that someone was monitoring Horner's call or that the possibility of a tap existed.

"I can talk," Redding said.

"Cyrus, a woman named Kate Bennett, a pathologist

at Metro, just called asking for information on two women who died from the same unusual bleeding disorder."

"Patients of ours?"

"That is affirmative, although Dr. Bennett is only aware that one of them is. Both women had autopsies that showed, in addition to the blood problems, a rare condition of their ovaries."

"Have you asked the Monkeys about them?"

"Affirmative. The Monkeys say there is no connection here."

"Does that make sense to you, Carl?"

"Negative."

"Keep looking into matters. I want a sheet about this Doctor Bennett."

"I'll learn what I can and teletype it tomorrow."

"Tonight."

"Tonight, then."

"Be well, old friend."

"And you, Cyrus. You'll hear from me later."

4

Wednesday 12 December

"Coronary Strikes Out Bobby." Kate cringed at the *Boston Herald* headline on her office desk. The story was one of the rare events that managed to make the front page in both that paper and the *Boston Globe*. Though the *Globe*'s treatment was more detailed, the lead and side articles said essentially the same thing in the two papers. Bobby Geary, beloved son of Albert and Maureen Geary, son of the city itself, had been taken without warning by a clot as thin as the stitching on a baseball. The stories, many of them by sportswriters, were the heart-rending stuff of which Pulitzers are made, the only problem being that they weren't true.

The storm, which had begun the evening before, had dumped a quick eight inches of snow on the city before skulking off over the North Atlantic. However, neither the columns of journalistic half-truths nor the painful drive into the city could dampen the warmth left by the talking and the sharing that had followed the candlelight meal Kate had prepared for her husband. For the first time in years, Jared had talked about his disastrous first marriage and the daughter he would, in all likelihood, never see again. "Gone to find something better" was all the note from his wife had said. The trail of the woman and her daughter had grown cold in New York and finally vanished in a morass of evanescent religious cults throughout southern and central California. "Gone to find something better."

Jared had cried as he spoke of the Vermont years, of his need then to break clear of his father's expectations and build a life for himself. Kate had dried his tears with her lips and listened to the confusion and pain of a marriage that was far more an act of rebellion than one of love.

Kate was finishing the last of the *Globe* stories when, with a soft knock, a ponderous woman entered carrying a paper bag. The woman's overcoat was unbuttoned, exposing a nurse's uniform, pin, and name tag. Kate read the name as the woman spoke it.

"Dr. Bennett, I'm Sandra Tucker. Ginger Rittenhouse was my roommate."

"Of course. Please sit down. Coffee?"

"No, thank you. I'm doing private-duty work, and I'm expected at my patient's house in Weston in half an hour. Dr. Engleson said that if I remembered anything or found anything that might help you understand Ginger's death I could bring it to you."

"Yes, that's true. I'm sorry about Ginger."

"Did you know her?"

"No. No, I didn't."

"We had shared the house only for a few months."

"I know."

"A week after she moved in, Ginger baked a cake and cooked up a lasagna for my birthday."

"That was very nice," Kate said, wishing she had thought twice about engaging the woman in small talk. There was a sad aura about her—a loneliness that made Kate suspect she would talk on indefinitely if given the chance, patient or no patient.

"We went to the movies together twice, and to the Pops, but we were only just getting to be friends and . . ."

"It's good of you to come all the way down here in the snow," Kate said in as gentle an interruption as she could manage.

"Oh, well, it's the least I could do. Ginger was a very nice person. Very quiet and very nice. She was thinking about trying for the marathon next spring."

"What do you have in the bag? Is that something of hers?" A frontal assault seemed the only way.

"Bag? Oh, yes. I'm sorry. Dr. Engleson, wnat a nice man he is, asked me to go through her things looking for medicines or letters or doctors' appointments or anything that might give you a clue about why she . . . why she . . ."

"I know it was a hard thing for you to do, Miss Tucker, and I'm grateful for any help."

"It's Mrs. Tucker. I'm divorced."

Kate nodded. "The bag?"

"My God, I apologize again." She passed her parcel across the desk. "Sometimes I talk too much, I'm afraid."

"Sometimes I do, too." Kate's voice trailed away as she stared at the contents of the bag.

"I found them in the top of Ginger's bureau. It's the strangest way to package pills I've ever seen. On that one sheet are nearly two months worth of them, packaged individually and labeled by day and date when to take each one. Looks sort of like it was put together by a computer."

"It was," Kate said, her thoughts swirling.

"Pardon?"

"I said it *was* put together by a computer." Her eyes came up slowly and turned toward the window. Across the street, its glass and steel facade jewellike, was the pride of Metropolitan Hospital of Boston. "The pharmacy-dispensing computer of the Omnicenter. The Omnicenter where Ginger Rittenhouse never went."

"I don't understand."

Kate rose. "Mrs. Tucker, you've been a tremendous help. I'll call if we need any further information or if we learn something that might help explain your friend's death. If you'll excuse me, there are some phone calls I must make."

The woman took Kate's hand. "Think nothing of it," she said. "Oh, I felt uncomfortable at first, rifling through her drawers, but then I said to myself, 'If you're not going to do it, then . . .' "

"Mrs. Tucker, thank you very much." One hand still locked in Sandra Tucker's, Kate used her other to take the woman by the elbow and guide her out the door.

The tablets were a medium-strength estrogen-progesterone combination, a generic birth control pill. Kate wondered if Ginger Rittenhouse had been too shy to mention to her roommate that she took them. Computer printed along the top margin of the sheet were Ginger's name, the date six weeks before when the prescription had been filled, and instructions to take one tablet daily. Also printed was advice on what to do if one dose was missed, as well as if two doses were missed. Common side effects were listed, with an asterisk beside those that should be reported immediately to Ginger's Omnicenter physician. Perforations, vertical and horizontal, enabled the patient to tear off as many pills as might be needed for time away. The setup, like everything at the Omnicenter, was slick—thoughtfully designed, considerate, and practical—further showing why there was a long list of women from every economic level waiting to become patients of the facility.

Kate ran through half a dozen possible explanations of why she had been told Ginger Rittenhouse was not a patient at the Omnicenter; then she accepted that there was only one way to find out. She answered, "Doctor Bennett," when the Omnicenter operator asked who was calling, emphasizing ever so slightly her title. Immediately, she was patched through to Dr. William Zimmermann, the director.

"Kate, this is a coincidence. I was just about to call you. How are you?" It was typical of the man, a dynamo sometimes called Rocket Bill, to forgo the redundancy of saying hello.

"I'm fine, Bill, thanks. What do you mean 'coincidence'?"

"Well, I've got a note here from our statistician, Carl Horner, along with a file on someone named Rittenhouse. Carl says he originally sent word to you that we had no such patient."

"That's right."

"Well, we do. Apparently there was a coding mistake or spelling mistake or something."

"Did he tell you why I wanted to know?"

"Only that this woman had died."

"That's right. Does your Carl Horner make mistakes often?" The idea of an error didn't jibe with Marco Sebastian's description of the man.

"Once every century or so as far as I can tell. I've been here four years now, and this is the first time I've encountered any screwup by his machines. Do you want me to send this chart over to you?"

"Can I pick it up in person, Bill? There are some other things I want to talk with you about."

"One o'clock okay with you?"

"Fine. And Bill, could you order a printout of the record of a Beverly Vitale."

"The woman who bled out on the inpatient service?"

"Yes."

"I've already reviewed it. A copy's right here on my desk."

"Excellent. One last thing."

"Yes?"

"I'd like to meet Carl Horner. Is that possible?"

"Old Carl's a bit cantankerous, but I suspect it would be okay."

"One o'clock, then?"

"One o'clock."

Ellen Sandler clutched her housecoat about her and sat on the edge of her bed staring blankly at a disheveled blackbird foraging for a bit of food on the frozen snow beyond her window. She was expected at the office in less than an hour. The house was woefully low on staples. Betsy's math teacher had set up a noontime conference to investigate her falling interest and grade in the subject. Eve needed help shopping for a dress for her piano recital. Darcy had come home an hour after weekday curfew, her clothes tinged with a musty odor that Ellen suspected was marijuana. So much to do. So much had changed, yet so little.

The silence in the house was stifling. Gradually, she focused on a few ongoing sounds: the hum of the refrigerator, the drone of the blower on the heating and air conditioning system Sandy had installed to celebrate their last anniversary, the sigh that was her own breathing.

"Get up," she told herself. "Goddamn it, get up and do what you have to do." Still, she did not move. The hurt, the oppressive, constricting ache in her chest seemed to make movement impossible. It wasn't the loneliness that pained so, although certainly that was torture. It wasn't the empty bed or the silent telephone or the lifeless eyes that stared at her from the mirror. It wasn't even the other woman, whoever she was. It was the lies—the dozens upon dozens of lies from the one person in the world she needed to trust. It was the realization that while the anguish and hurt of the broken marriage might, in time, subside, the inability to trust would likely remain part of her forever.

"Get up, dammit. Get up, get dressed, and get going."

With what seemed a major effort, she broke through the inertia of her spirit and the aching stiffness in her limbs, and stood up. The room, the house, the job, the girls—so much had changed, yet so little. She walked to the closet, wondering if perhaps something silkier and more feminine than what she usually wore to the office would buoy her. The burgundy dress she had bought for London caught her eye. Two men had made advances toward her the first day she wore it, and there had been any number of compliments on it since.

As she crossed the room, Ellen felt the morning

discomforts in her joints diminish—all, that is, except a throbbing in her left thigh that seemed to worsen with each step. She slipped off her housecoat, hung it up, and pulled her flannel nightgown off over her head. Covering much of the front of her thigh was the largest bruise she had ever seen. Gingerly, she explored it with her fingers. It was somewhat tender, but not unbearably so. She did not know how she had gotten it. She had sustained no injury that she could remember. It must, she decided, have been the way she slept on it.

She selected a blue, thin wool jumpsuit in place of the dress, which, it seemed, might not cover the bruise in every situation. She dressed, still unable to take her eyes off the grotesque discoloration. Her legs had always been one of her best features. Even after three children, she took pride that there were only a few threadlike veins visible behind her knees. Now this. For a moment, she thought about calling Kate for advice on whether or not to have a doctor check things out, but she decided that a bruise was a bruise. Besides, she had simply too much else to do.

A bit of makeup and some work on her hair, and Ellen felt as ready as she ever would to tackle the day. The face in her mirror, thin and fine featured, would probably turn some heads, but the eyes were still lifeless.

She was leaving the room when she noticed the note tacked to the doorjamb. Each day it happened like this, and each day it was like seeing the note for the first time, despite the fact that she had tacked it there more than a year before.

"Take Vit," was all it said.

Ellen went to the medicine cabinet, took the sheet of multivitamins plus iron from the shelf, punched one out, and swallowed it without water. Half consciously, she noticed that there was only a four-week supply remaining, and she made a mental note to set up an appointment with her physician at the Omnicenter.

Although she was limping slightly as she left the

house, Ellen found the tightness in her thigh bearable. In fact, compared to the other agonies in her life at the moment, the sensation was almost pleasant.

The sign, a discreet bronze plate by the electronically controlled glass doors, said, "Metropolitan Hospital of Boston; Ashburton Women's Health Omnicenter, 1975." Kate had been one of the first patients to enroll and had never regretted her decision. Gynecological care, hardly a pleasant experience, had become at least tolerable for her, as it had for the several thousand other women who were accepted before a waiting list was introduced. The inscription above the receptionist's desk said it all. "Complete Patient Care with Complete Caring Patience."

Kate stopped at the small coatroom to one side of the brightly lit foyer, and checked her parka with a blue-smocked volunteer. She could have used the tunnel from the main hospital, but she had been drawn outdoors by the prospect of a few minutes of fresh air and a fluffy western omelet sandwich, *spécialité de la maison* at Maury's Diner.

The receptionist signaled Kate's arrival by telephone and then directed her to Dr. Zimmermann's office on the third floor. The directions were not necessary. Zimmermann had been Kate's Omnicenter physician for four years, since the accidental drowning death of Dr. Harold French, his predecessor and the first head of the Omnicenter. Although she saw Zimmermann infrequently—three times a year was mandatory for women on birth control pills—Kate had developed a comfortable patient-physician relationship with him, as well as an embryonic friendship.

He was waiting by his office door as she stepped from the elevator. Even after four years, the sight of the man triggered the same impressions as had their first meeting. He was dashing. Corny as the word was, Kate could think of no better one to describe him. In his late thirties or early forties Zimmermann had a classic, chiseled handsomeness, along with an urbanity and ease of motion that Kate had originally felt might be a liability to a physician in his medical specialty. Time and the man had proven her concerns groundless. He was polite and totally professional. In a hospital rife with rumors, few had ever been circulated regarding him. Those that had gone around dealt with the usual speculations about an attractive man of his age who was not married. Active on hospital and civic committees, giving of his time to his patients and of his knowledge to his students, William Zimmermann's was a star justifiably on the rise.

"Dr. Kate." Zimmermann took both her hands in his and pumped them warmly. "Come in, come in. I have fresh coffee and . . . Have you had lunch? I could send out for something."

"I stopped at Maury's on the way over. I'm sorry for being so thoughtless. I should have brought *you* something."

"Nonsense. I only asked about lunch for your benefit. I have been skipping the meal altogether—part of a weight loss bet with my secretary."

Even if the bet were concocted on the spot, and considering the man's trim frame that was quite possible, his words were the perfect breeze to dispel Kate's embarrassment.

Zimmermann's office was the den of a scholar. Texts and bound journals filled three walls of floor-to-ceiling bookcases, and opened or marked volumes covered much of a reading table at one end of the room. On the wall behind his desk, framed photographs of European castles were interspersed with elegantly matted sayings, quotations, and homilies. "The downfall of any magician is belief in his own magic." "There are two tragedies in life: One is not to get your heart's desire; the other is to get it." And of course, "The Omnicenter: Complete patient care with complete caring patience." There were several others, most of which Kate had heard or read before. One, however, she could not recall having seen. Done in black Benedictine calligraphy, with a wonderfully ornate arabesque border, it said, "Monkey Work for the Monkeys."

Zimmermann followed her line of sight to the saying. "A gift from Carl," he explained. "His belief is that the energy of physicians and nurses should be directed as much as possible to areas utilizing their five senses and those properties unique to human beings—empathy, caring, and intuitiveness. The mechanics of our job, the paperwork, setting up of appointments, filling of prescriptions, and such, he calls 'monkey work.' His machines can do those jobs faster and more accurately than any of us ever could, and it seems Carl teaches them more almost every day."

"So," said Kate, "he's named his computers . . . the Monkeys." Zimmermann said the last two words in unison with her. Kate sensed a letup in the uneasiness she had developed toward Carl Horner and began looking forward to meeting the man.

"Now," Zimmermann asked, "can you brief me on what you have found in these two patients of ours? I have reviewed their records and found little that might be of help to you."

In the concise, stylized method of case presentation ingrained in physicians from their earliest days in medical school, Kate gave a one-minute capsule of each woman's history, physical exam, laboratory data, and hospital course. "I've brought sections from the ovaries of both patients. I think there's a decent microscope in the lab downstairs," she concluded.

Zimmermann whistled softly. "And the only link to this point is that both were patients here?" Kate nodded. "Well, I can't add much. Miss Rittenhouse had been an Omnicenter patient since nineteen seventy-nine. Nothing but routine checkups since then, except that she was within one missed appointment of being asked to go elsewhere for her gynecologic care. The contract we have our patients sign gives us that option."

"I know. I signed one," Kate said. The contract was another example of the patient-oriented philosophy of the

Omnicenter. Fees were on a yearly basis, adjusted to a patient's income. There was no profit to be made from insisting on compliance with periodic routine visits, yet insist they did. "What about Beverly Vitale?"

Zimmermann shrugged. "Six years a patient. Abortion here five years ago by suction. Had a diaphragm. Never on birth control pills or hormones of any kind. Always somewhat anemic, hematocrits in the thirty-four to thirty-six range."

"She was on iron."

"Yes. Dr. Bartholomew has had her on daily supplements since the day of her first exam."

"Who was Ginger Rittenhouse's doctor?" Kate was grasping for any connection, however remote.

"Actually, she was cared for by the residents, with the help of a faculty advisor. In this woman's case, it was me. However, there was never any need for me to be consulted. She became a patient just after I arrived. I saw her once, and she has had no trouble since." He grimaced at what he considered an inappropriate remark. "Excluding the obvious," he added.

DEAD END. Kate's mind's eye saw the words as she had written them. She glanced at her watch. There would be a surgical specimen processed as a frozen section in half an hour. Her reading would determine whether the patient underwent a limited or extensive procedure. Still, she felt reluctant to let go of the one common factor she had found. "I'm due back for a frozen in a short while, Bill. Do you think you could take me by to meet Carl Horner and his trained Monkeys?"

"Certainly," Zimmermann said. "He's expecting us. By the way, I understand congratulations are in order."

"For what?"

"Well, word has it that you are to be the next chief of pathology."

Kate laughed ruefully. "Welcome to the new game show, *I've Got No Secrets*. Actually, I don't even think my name has formally been presented for consideration yet, so you can hold the congratulations. Besides, with the financial mess the department is in, I'm not sure condolences wouldn't be a better response. You don't suppose that Ashburton Foundation of yours has a few extra hundred thousand lying around, do you?"

"I have no idea, Kate. Norton Reese handles that end of things. I am just one of the barge toters and bale lifters. You might talk to him, though. The foundation certainly has taken good care of us."

Kate stepped into the carpeted, brightly lit corridor. "I'll say they have," she said. The chance that Norton Reese would put himself out on behalf of her department was less than none.

"Monkey Work for the Monkeys." The message was displayed throughout Carl Horner's computer facility, which occupied an area at the rear of the first floor several times the size of Marco Sebastian's unit. Ensconced in the midst of millions of dollars in sophisticated electronics, Carl Horner looked to be something of an anachronism. Beneath his knee-length lab coat, he was wearing a plaid work shirt and a pair of farmer's overalls. His battered work boots might just as well have received their breaking in on a rock pile as in the climate-controlled, ultramodern suite.

Horner greeted Kate with an energetic handshake, though she could feel the bulbous changes of arthritis in every joint. Still the man, stoop shouldered and silver haired, had an ageless quality about him. It emanated, she decided, not only from his dress, but also from his eyes, which were a remarkably luminescent blue.

"Dr. Bennett, I owe you my deepest apology. The error regarding the Rittenhouse file was nothing more—nor less—than a spelling mistake on my part."

Kate smiled. "Apology accepted. Incident forgotten."

"Have you found the explanations you were looking for?"

"No. No, we haven't. Mr. Horner, could you show

me around a bit? I'm especially interested in how the machines work in the pharmacy."

"Carl," Zimmermann said, "if you and Dr. Bennett don't mind, I'm going to get back to work. Kate, I plan to review those slides later tonight and to do some reading. Together, I promise that we shall get to the bottom of all this. Meanwhile, enjoy your tour. We're certainly proud of Carl and his Monkeys."

Patiently, the old man took Kate through the filling of a prescription.

"These cards are preprinted with the patient's name and code number and included with the patient's chart when she has her appointment. The doctors tear 'em up if they're not needed. As you can see, there are twenty-five separate medications already listed here, along with the codes for dosage, amount, and instructions. The machines dispense only these medications, and then only in the form of a generic—as good as any brand-name pharmaceutical, but only a fraction of the cost. The machines automatically review the patient's record for allergies to the medication prescribed, as well as any interaction with medications she might already be taking." Horner's presentation had all the pride of a grandmother holding court at a bridge party. "If there's any problem at all, the prescription is not filled and the patient is referred to our pharmacist, who handles the matter personally."

"What if the physician wants to prescribe a medication other than the twenty-five on the card?" Kate asked.

"Our pharmacy is fully stocked. However, because of the Monkeys, we need only one pharmacist on duty, and he or she has more time to deal with problems such as drug interaction and side effects."

"Amazing," Kate said softly. "Have the Monkeys ever made an error?"

Horner's smile was for the first time somewhat patronizing. "Computers cannot make errors. There are programs backing up programs to guarantee that. Of course, human beings are a different story."

"So I've learned." Kate's cattiness was reflex. There was something about Horner's limitless confidence in the wires, chips, discs, and other paraphernalia surrounding them that she found disquieting. "Tell me, where do the generics come from that the machines dispense?"

"One of the drug houses. We hold a closed-bid auction each year, and the lowest bidder gets the contract."

"Which one has it now?" Horner's answer had been somewhat evasive, hardly in character with the man. She watched his eyes. Was there a flicker of heightened emotion in them? She couldn't tell.

"Now? Redding has it. Redding Pharmaceuticals."

"Ah, the best and the brightest." Kate was not being facetious. In an industry with a checkered past that included thalidomide and many other destroyers of human life, Redding stood alone in its reputation for product safety and the development of orphan drugs for conditions too rare for the drugs to be profitable. "Well, Mr. Horner, I thank you. Your Monkeys are truly incredible."

"My pleasure. If there's anything else I can do, let me know."

Kate turned to go, but then turned back. "Do you have a list of the companies that have held the contract in years past?"

"Since the Omnicenter opened?"

"Yes." For the second time, Kate sensed a change in the man's eyes.

"Well, it won't be much of a list. Redding's the only one."

"Eight auctions and eight Reddings, huh?"

"No bids have even been close to theirs."

"Well, thanks for your help."

"No problem."

Horner's parting handshake and smile seemed somehow more forced than had his greeting. Kate watched as he ambled off, feeling vaguely uneasy about the man, but uncertain why. She glanced at her watch. The frozen section was due in ten minutes, and the patient would be kept under anesthesia until her diagnosis was made. Aside from alerting Bill Zimmermann as to what was going on, her Omnicenter visit had accomplished essentially nothing. Still, the clinic remained the only factor common to two dead women. As she walked through the lobby to retrieve her coat, Kate ran through the possible routes by which the ovarian and blood disorders might have been acquired. Finally, with time running short, she stopped at the reception desk, and wrote a note to Zimmermann.

> Dear Bill—
>
> Thanks for the talk and the tour. No answers, but perhaps together we can find some. Meanwhile, I'm sending over some microbiology people to take cultures, viral and bacterial, if that's okay with you. They will also check on techniques of instrument sterilization—perhaps a toxin has been introduced that way.
>
> Let me know if you come up with anything. Also, check your calendar for a night you could come north and have dinner with my husband and me. I'd enjoy the chance to know you better.
>
> Kate

She sealed the note in an envelope and passed it over to the receptionist. "Could you see to it that Dr. Zimmermann gets this?" The woman smiled and nodded. Kate was halfway to the tunnel entrance when she stopped, hesitated, and then returned. She reclaimed the note, tore the envelope open, and added a PS.

> And Bill . . . could you please get me ten tablets of each of the medications dispensed by the Monkeys. Thanx.
>
> K.

"Well, what do you say, Clyde. Can I count on you or not?"

Norton Reese set aside the paper clip he was mangling and stared across his desk at the chief of cardiac surgery. Clyde Breslow was the fourth department head he had met with that day. The previous three had made no promises to help block Kate Bennett's appointment, despite delicately presented guarantees that their departments would receive much-needed new equipment as soon as her nomination was defeated. In fact, two of the men, Milner in internal medicine and Hoyt, the pediatrician, had said in as many words that they were pleased with the prospect of having her on the executive committee. "Bright new blood," Milner had called her.

Breslow, Napoleonic in size and temper, watched Reese's discomfort with some amusement. "Now jes' what is it about that little lady that bothers you so, Norton?" he asked in a thick drawl that often disappeared when he was screaming at the nurses and throwing instruments about the operating room or screaming at the medical students and throwing instruments about the dog lab. "She refuse to spread those cute little buns of hers for ya or what?"

"The bitch made me look bad in front of the board of trustees, Clyde. You should remember that. It was your fucking operating microscope that caused all the trouble. I'll be damned if I'm going to have her on my executive committee."

"Whoa, there, Norton. *Your* executive committee? Now ain't you gettin' just the slightest bit possessive about a group you don't even have a vote in?"

"Look, Clyde, I've had a bad day. Do you back me on this and talk to the surgical boys or don't you?"

"Now that jes' depends, don't it?"

"The extra resident's slot? Clyde, I can't do it. I told you that."

"Then maybe you jes' better get used to seeing that pretty little face of Katey B.'s at the meetin's every other Tuesday."

Reese snapped a pencil in half. "All right. I'll try," he said, silently cursing Kate Bennett for putting him in a position to be manipulated by a man like Breslow.

"You do that. Know what I think, Norton? I think you're scared of that woman. That's what I think. A looker with smarts is more than you kin handle."

Without warning, Reese exploded. "Look, Clyde," he said, slamming his desk chair against the wall as he stood, "you have enough fucking trouble remembering that the heart is above the belly button without taking up playing amateur shrink. Now get the hell out of here and get me some support in this thing. I'll do what I can about your goddamn resident."

With a plastic smile, Clyde Breslow backed out of the office. Reese sank into his chair. Frightened of Kate Bennett? The hell he was. He just couldn't stand a snotty, do-gooder kid going around trying to act grown up. She ought to be home keeping house and screwing that lawyer husband of hers.

"Mr. Reese, there's a call for you on two." The secretary's voice startled him, and lunging for the intercom, he spilled the dregs of a cup of coffee on his desk.

"Dammit, Betty, I told you no calls."

"I know you did, sir. I'm sorry. It's Mr. Horner from the Omnicenter. He says it's very important."

Reese sighed. "All right. Tell him to call me on three seven four four." He blotted up the coffee and waited for his private line to ring. It was unusual for Carl Horner to call at all. Omnicenter business was usually handled by Arlen Paquette, Redding's director of product safety. In the few moments before 3744 rang, he speculated on the nature of a problem that might be of such concern that Horner would call. None of his speculations prepared him for the reality.

"Mr. Reese," Horner said, "I'm calling on behalf of a mutual friend of ours." Cyrus Redding's name was one Horner would never say over the phone, but Reese had no doubt whom he meant.

"How is our friend?"

"A bit upset, Mr. Reese. One of your staff physicians has been nosing about the Omnicenter, asking questions about our pharmacy and requesting Dr. Zimmermann to send her samples of the medications we dispense."

The word "her" brought Reese a bone-deep chill. "Who is it?" he asked, already knowing the answer.

"It's the pathologist, Dr. Bennett. She's investigating the deaths of two women who were patients of ours."

"Damn her," Reese said too softly to be heard. "Horner, are you . . . I mean, is the Omnicenter responsible for the deaths?"

"That appears to be negative."

"What do you mean appears to be? Do you know what's at stake? Paquette promised me nothing like this would happen." Reese began feeling a tightness in his chest and dropped a nitroglycerine tablet under his tongue, vowing that if this discomfort was the start of the big one, his last act on earth would be to shoot Kate Bennett between the eyes.

"Our friend says for you to remain cool and not to worry. However, he would like you to find some effective way of . . . diverting Dr. Bennett's interest away from the Omnicenter until we can fix up a few things and do a little more investigating into the two deaths in question."

"What am I supposed to do?"

"That, Mr. Reese, I do not know. Our friend suggests firing the woman."

"I can't do that. I don't hire and fire doctors, for Christ's sake."

"Our friend would like something done as soon as possible. He has asked me to remind you that certain contracts are up for renewal in less than a month."

"Fuck him."

"Pardon?"

"I said, all right. I'll think of something." Suddenly, he brightened. "In fact," he said, reaching into his desk drawer, "I think I already have."

"Fine," Carl Horner said. "All of us involved appreciate your efforts. I'm sure our friend will be extremely beholden when you succeed."

Reese noted the use of 'when' instead of 'if,' but it no longer mattered. "I'll be in touch," he said. Replacing the receiver, he extracted a folder marked "Schultz/Geary." Inside were a number of newspaper articles; the official autopsy report, signed by Stanley Willoughby and Kathryn Bennett, MDs; and an explanatory note from Sheila Pierce. Also in the folder were a number of laboratory tests on a man named John Schultz—a patient who, as far as he or Sheila could tell, never existed in Metropolitan Hospital. While the chances of some kind of coverup weren't a hundred percent, they certainly seemed close to that.

Sheila, he thought as he readied a piece of paper in his typewriter, if this works out, I'm going to see to it that you get at least an extra night or two each month. "To Charles C. Estep, Editor, *The Boston Globe*." Reese whispered the words as he typed them. He paused and checked the hour. By the time he was done with a rough draft, the pathology unit would be empty. A sheet of Kate Bennett's stationery and a sample of her signature would then be all he needed to solve any number of problems. The woman would be out of his hair, perhaps permanently, and Cryus Redding would be—how had Horner put it?—extremely beholden.

"Dear Mr. Estep . . ."

As Norton Reese typed, he began humming "There Is Nothing Like a Dame."

5

Thursday 13 December

"Do you think God is a man or a woman, Daddy?"

Suzy Paquette sat cross-legged on the passenger seat of her father's new Mercedes 450 SL, parked by the pump at Bowen's Texaco.

Behind the wheel, Arlen Paquette watched the mid-morning traffic glide by along Main Street, his thoughts neither on the traffic nor on the question he had just been asked.

"Well, Daddy?"

"Well what, sugar?" The attendant rapped twice on the trunk that he was done. "Company account, Harley," Paquette called out as he pulled away.

"Which is it, man or woman?"

"Which is what, darlin'?"

"God! Daddy, you're not even listening to me at all." She was seven years old with sorrel hair pulled back in two ponytails and a China doll face that was, at that moment, trying to pout.

Paquette swung into a space in front of Darlington Army/Navy and stopped. Never totally calm, he was, he knew, unusually tense and distracted this morning. Still, it was Second Thursday and that gave him the right to be inattentive or cross, as he had been earlier with his wife. He turned to his daughter. She had mastered the expression she wanted and now sat pressed against the car door displaying it, her arms folded tightly across her chest. In that instant, Paquette knew that she was the most beautiful child on earth. He reached across and took her in his arms. The girl stiffened momentarily, then relaxed and returned the embrace.

"I'm sorry, sugar," Paquette said. "I wasn't listening. I'm sorry and I love you and I think God is a woman if you're a woman and a man to someone who's a man and probably a puppy dog to the puppy dogs."

"I love you too, Daddy. And I still don't know why I should have to pray to Our Father when God might be Our Mother."

"You know, you're right. I think that from now on we should say . . . 'Our Buddy who art in Heaven.'"

"Oh, Daddy."

Paquette checked the time. "Listen, sugar, my meeting is in half an hour. I've got to get going. You be brave, now."

She flashed a heart-melting smile. "I don't have to be brave, Daddy. It's only a cleaning."

"Well then, you be . . . clean. Mommy will be by in just a little while. You wait if she's not here by the time you're done." He watched as she ran up the stairs next to the Army/Navy and waited until she waved to him from behind the picture window painted *Dr. Richard Philips*, DDS. Then he eased the Mercedes away from the curb, and headed toward the south end of town and his eleven o'clock Second Thursday meeting with Cyrus Redding, president and chairman of the board of perhaps the largest pharmaceutical house in the world. The meeting would start at exactly eleven and end at precisely ten minutes to noon. For seven years, as long as Paquette had been with the company, it had been like that, and like that it would remain as long as Cyrus Redding was alive and in charge. Nine o'clock, labor relations; ten o'clock, public relations; eleven, product safety; an hour and ten minutes for lunch, then research and development, sales and production, and finally from three to three-fifty, legislative liaison: department heads meeting with Cyrus Redding, one on one, the second Thursday of each month. The times and the order of Second Thursday were immutable. Vacations were to be worked around the day, illnesses to be treated and tolerated unless hospitalization was necessary. Even then, on more than one occasion, Redding had moved the meeting to a hospital room. Second Thursday: raises, new projects, criticisms, termination—all, whenever possible, on that day.

The factory covered most of a thirty-acre site bordered to the south and west by pine-covered hills and to the east by Pinkham's Creek. Double fences, nine feet high with barbed wire outcroppings at the top, encircled the entire facility. The inner of the two barriers was electrified—stunning voltage during the day, lethal voltage at night and on weekends. The only approach, paralleling the new railbed from the north, was tree lined and immaculately maintained. Two hundred yards from the outer fence, a V in the roadway directed employees and shippers to the right and all others to the left. A rainbow sign, spanning the approach at that point announced:

REDDING PHARMACEUTICALS, INCORPORATED
DARLINGTON, KENTUCKY
1899
"The Most Good for the Most People at the Least Cost"

Paquette bore to the right beneath the sign and stopped by a brightly painted guardhouse, the first of a series of security measures. He found himself wondering, as he did on almost every Second Thursday, if knowing what he knew now, he would have left his university research position in Connecticut to become director of product safety. The question was a purely hypothetical one. He had taken the job. He had agreed to play Cyrus Redding's game by Cyrus Redding's rules. Now, like it or not, he was Cyrus Redding's man. Of course an annual salary that, with benefits, exceeded four hundred thousand dollars went far toward easing pangs of conscience. Suzy was the youngest of three children, all of whom would one day be in college at the same time. He stopped at the final pass gate, handed the trunk key to the guard, and drummed nervously on the wheel while the man completed his inspection. It hardly paid to be late for a Second Thursday appointment.

Over the hundred and eighty years since Gault Darling led a band of renegades, moonshiners, and other social outcasts to a verdant spot in the foothills of the Cumberlands, and then killed two men for the right to have the new town named after himself, Darlington, Kentucky, had undergone any number of near deaths and subsequent resurgences. Disease, soldiers, Cherokees, floods, fires, and even a tornado had at one time or another brought the town to its knees. Always, though, a vestige survived, and always Darlington regrew.

In 1858, the Lexington-Knoxville Railway passed close enough to Darlington to send off a spur, the primary purpose of which was the transport of coal from the rich Juniper mines. By the end of the century, however, output from the Junipers had fallen to a trickle, and the railbed was left to rot. Darlington was once again in danger of becoming a ghost town. Shops closed. The schoolhouse and Baptist church burned down and were not rebuilt. Town government dwindled and then disappeared. In the end, where once there had been well over a thousand, only a handful remained. Fortunately for the town, one of those was Elton Darling, self-proclaimed descendant of Gault.

In 1897, Darling engineered a massive hoax utilizing three pouches of low-grade gold ore, two confederates, and a remarkable ability to seem totally inebriated when stone sober. Rumors of the "Darlington Lode" spread quickly through cities from Chicago to Atlanta, and Darlington acquired an instant citizenry, many of whom stayed on, either out of love for the beauty of the area or out of lack of resources to move elsewhere.

Having single-handedly repopulated his town, Elton Darling set about giving it an industry, making use of the area's only readily available resource, the sulfur-rich water of Pinkham's Creek, a tributary of the Cumberland River. In less than a year, with some food coloring, smoky-glassed bottles, an attractive label, and an aggressive sales force, the vile water of Pinkham's Creek, uninhabitable by even the hardiest fish, had become Darling's Astounding Rejuvenator and Purgator, an elixir alleged effective against conditions ranging from dropsy to baldness.

Over the years before his death in 1939, Elton Darling made such changes in his product as the market and times demanded. He also made a modest fortune. By the time his son, Tyrone, took control of the family enterprises, the rejuvenator had been replaced by a variety of vitamin and mineral supplements, and Darlington Pharmaceuticals was being traded, though lightly, on the American Stock Exchange.

Far from being the visionary and businessman his father was, Tyrone Darling spent much of his time, and most of his money, on a string of unsuccessful thoroughbreds and a succession of city women, each of whom was more adept at consuming money than he was at making it. Darling's solution to his diminishing cash reserves was simple: issue more stock and sell off some of his own. In the fall of 1947, at the annual Darlington stockholders meeting, the ax fell. Intermediaries for a man spoken of only as Mr. Redding produced proof of ownership of more than fifty-three percent of Darlington Pharmaceuticals and in a matter of less than a day, took over the company on behalf of Mr. Cyrus Redding of New York, New York. Stripped of influence, as well as of a source of income, Darling tried to negotiate. To the best of anyone's knowledge, he had not succeeded even in meeting with the man who had replaced him when, on the following

New Year's Eve, he and a woman named Densmore were shot to death by the woman's husband.

Thus it was that the fortunes of Darlington, Kentucky became tied to a reclusive genius named Cyrus Redding and to the pharmaceutical house that now bore his name. In the years to follow, there were a number of minor successes: Terranyd, a concentrated tetracycline; Rebac, an over-the-counter antacid: and several cold preparations. Redding Pharmaceuticals doubled in size, and the population of Darlington grew proportionally. Then, in the early 1960s, Redding obtained exclusive U.S. patents to several successful European products, including the tranquilizer that was, following a blitzkrieg promotional campaign, to become one of the most prescribed pharmaceuticals in the world. A year after release of the drug, Darlington was selected an All-American City, and shortly after that, the Darlington Dukes minor league baseball franchise was established.

Marilyn Wyman sipped at a cup of tea and risked a minute glance at her gold Rolex. Ten minutes to go and another Second Thursday would be over for Redding's director of public relations. From across his enormous desk, Cyrus Redding appraised her through his Coke-bottle spectacles.

"There are exactly eight minutes and thirty seconds to go, Marilyn," he said. "Does that help?"

"I'm sorry, sir." Wyman, in her midfifties, had been with the company longer than had any other department head. Still, no one had ever heard her refer to her employer as anything other than Mr. Redding or, to his face, sir. She had close-cut gray-brown hair and a sophisticated sensuality that she used with consummate skill in dealing with media representatives of both sexes.

"We have one final piece of business. No small piece, either. It's Arthgard."

"I thought it had been taken off the market."

"In England it has, but not yet here. It has been only eight weeks since we released it and already it is in the top forty in volume and the top twenty-five in actual dollar return."

"That's a shame. The feedback I've gotten from pharmacists and patients has been excellent, too. Still, the British have proven it responsible for how many deaths so far, sixty?"

"Eighty-five, actually."

"Eighty-five." Reflexively, Wyman shuddered. Arthgard had been released to the American market almost immediately after the patent had been acquired by Redding. Though she had no way of knowing how it had been accomplished, the FDA-required testing periods, both laboratory and clinical, seemed to have been circumvented. It was not her place to ask about such things. Testing was the provinoe of Arlen Paquette, and the exchange of information between department heads was not only frowned upon by Redding but, in most cases, forbidden. "Well, we still have Lapsol and Carmalon," she said. "The figures I looked at yesterday showed them both in the top ten of antiarthritic preparations. I'll write a press release announcing the suspension of our Arthgard production and then see what I can do to remind the public about both of those other products."

"You will do no such thing, Marilyn."

"Pardon?"

Redding pulled a computer printout from a file on his desk. "Do you have any idea how many millions it cost us to buy the Arthgard patent, test the product, go into production, advertise, get samples out to physicians, and finally distribute the product to pharmacies and hospitals? Correction, Miss Wyman. Not how many millions—how many tens of millions?" Marilyn Wyman shook her head. Redding continued. "The projections I have here say that, at our present rate of increase in sales, the product would have to stay on the market for another ten weeks just for us to break even. That is where you will be concentrating your efforts."

"But. . . ." Redding's icy look made it clear that there was to be no dialogue on the matter. She stared down at the toes of her two-hundred-dollar Ferragamo pumps. "Yes, sir."

"I've got some preliminary data from that survey firm you contracted with showing that less than forty percent of physicians and less than ten percent of consumers are even aware of what's going on in England. I want those numbers to stay in that ball park for the next ten weeks."

"But. . . ."

"Dammit, I am not looking for buts. I am looking for ten weeks of sales so that we can get our ass out of this product without having it burned off. Our legislative liaison will do his job with the FDA. Now if you want to give me 'buts,' I'll find a PR person who does her job. And need I remind you that her first job will be to do something creative with that M. Wyman file I have locked away?"

Wyman bit at her lower lip and nodded. It had been several years since Redding had mentioned the collection of photographs, telephone conversations, and recordings from the company hotel suite she had vacationed in at Acapulco. Beneath her expertly applied makeup, she was ashen.

Redding, seeing the capitulation in her eyes, softened. "Marilyn, listen. You do your part. I promise that if there's any trouble on this side of the Atlantic with Arthgard, we'll pull it immediately. Okay? Good. Now tell me, how's that little buggy of yours riding?"

"The Alpha? Fine, thank you. Needs a tune-up. That's all."

"Well, don't bother. Just bring it over to Buddy Michaels at Darlington Sport. He's got a spanking new Lotus just arrived and itching for you to show it the beauty of the Kentucky countryside." He checked the slim digital timepiece built into his desk. "Eight minutes of eleven.

It's been a good meeting, Marilyn. As usual, you're doing an excellent job. Why don't you stop by next week and give me a progress report. I also want to hear how that new Lotus of yours handles the downgrade on the back side of Black Mountain." With a smile, a nod, and the smallest gesture of one hand, Marilyn Wyman was dismissed.

Arlen Paquette was drinking coffee in the sumptuous sitting room outside of Redding's office when Wyman emerged. Though they had worked for the same company for years, they seldom met in situations other than Second Thursday. Still, the greeting between them was warm, both sensing that in another place and at another time, they might well have become friends.

At precisely eleven o'clock, Marilyn Wyman exited through the door to the reception area and Paquette crossed to Redding's door, knocked once, and entered. Hour three of Second Thursday had begun.

Redding greeted Paquette with a handshake across his desk. On occasion, usually when their agenda was small, the man would guide his motorized wheelchair to a spot by the coffee table at one end of his huge office and motion Paquette to the maroon Chesterfield sofa opposite him. This day, however, there was no such gesture.

"I've sent for lunch, Arlen. We may run over."

Paquette tensed. In seven years, his eleven o'clock visit had never run over. "I'm all yours," he said, realizing, as he was sure the old man across from him did, that the words were more than a polite figure of speech.

"Have you any problem areas you wish to discuss with me before we start?"

Paquette shook his head. He knew Cyrus Redding abhorred what he called "surprises." If Paquette encountered major problems in the course of his work, a call and immediate discussion with Redding were in order.

"Fine," Redding said, adjusting his tie and then combing his gray crew cut back with his fingers. "I have two situations that we must ponder together. The first concerns Arthgard. Do you have your file handy?"

"I have my files on everything that is current," Paquette said, rummaging through his large, well-worn briefcase.

"Is our testing on Arthgard current?" Redding's tone suggested that he would consider an affirmative response a "surprise."

"Yes and no, sir. The formal testing was completed several months ago. You have my report."

"Yes, I remember."

"However," Paquette continued, "I began reading about the problems in the UK, and decided to continue dispensing the drug to some of the test subjects at the Women's Health Center in Denver."

"Excellent thinking, Arlen. Excellent. Have there been any side effects so far?"

"Minor ones only. Breast engorgement and pain, stomach upsets, diarrhea, hair loss in half a dozen, loss of libido, rashes, and palpitations. Nothing serious or life threatening."

Serious or life threatening. Even after seven years, Paquette's inner feelings were belied by the callousness of his words. Still, he was Redding's man, and Redding was concerned only with those side effects that would be severe enough, consistently enough to cause trouble for the company. Only those were deemed reason to delay or cancel the quick release of a new product into the marketplace. In a business where a week often translated into millions of dollars, and a jump on the competition into tens of millions, Redding had set his priorities.

"How many subjects were involved in the Arthgard testing?"

"Counting those at the Denver facility and at the Omnicenter, in Boston, there were almost a thousand." He checked his notes. "Nine hundred and seventy."

"And no one from the Omnicenter is receiving Arthgard right now?"

"The testing there was stopped months ago. There

were too many other products that we had to work into the system."

Paquette knew that the Arthgard recall in Great Britain was going to prove a fiasco, if not a disaster, for Redding Pharmaceuticals, a company that had not suffered a product recall or even an FDA probe since the man in the wheelchair had taken over. Testing of pharmaceuticals in Europe seldom met FDA standards. Still, the UK had a decent safety record, and the Boston and Denver testing facilities served as a double check on all foreign-developed products, as well as on drugs invented in Redding Labs. Problems inherent in various products—at least by Cyrus Redding's definition of problems—had always been identified before any major commitment by the company was undertaken . . . always, until now.

"Tell me, Arlen," Redding said, drawing a cup of coffee from a spigot built into his desk and lacing it with a splash from a small decanter, "what do you think happened? How did this get past us?"

Paquette searched for any tension, any note of condemnation in the man's words. There was none that he could tell. "Well," he said, "basically, it boils down to a matter of numbers." He paused, deciding how scientific to make his explanation. He knew nothing of Cyrus Redding's background, but he was certain from past discussions that there was science in it somewhere. Straightforward and not condescending—that was how he would play it. "The Arthgard side effect—the cardiac toxicity that is being blamed for the deaths in England—seems to be part allergy and part dose related."

"In other words," Redding said, "first the patient has to be sensitive to the drug and then he has to get enough of it."

"Exactly. And statistically, that combination doesn't come up too often. Arthgard has been so effective, though, and so well marketed, that literally millions of prescriptions have been written in the six years since it was first released in the United Kingdom. A death here, a death there. Weeks or months and miles in between. No way to connect them to the drug. Finally, a number of problems show up at just about the same time in just about the same place, and one doc in one hospital in one town in the corner of Sussex puts it all together. A little publicity, and suddenly reports begin pouring in from all over the British world."

"Do you have any idea how many hundreds of thousands of arthritis patients have had their suffering relieved by Arthgard?"

"I can guess. And I understand what you're saying. Risk-benefit ratio. That's all people in our industry, or any health provider for that matter, have to go by."

"I've decided to keep Arthgard on the American market for ten more weeks." Redding dropped the bomb quietly and simply; then he sat back and watched Paquette's reaction. Noticeably, at least, there was none.

"Fine," Paquette said. "Would you like me to continue the Denver testing? We have about an eighteen-month head start on the overall marketplace."

"By all means, Arlen."

Paquette nodded, scratched a note on the Arthgard file, and slid it back in his briefcase, struggling to maintain his composure. There was little to be gained by revealing his true feelings about what Redding was doing, and much—oh, so much—to lose. His involvement in the testing centers alone—involvement of which Redding possessed detailed documentation—was enough to send him to prison. In fact, he suspected that Redding could claim no knowledge of either facility and make that claim stick. Even if no confrontation occurred, the chances were that he would be fired or demoted . . . or worse. Several years before, a department head had been openly critical of Redding and his methods, to the point of discussing his feelings with the editor of the Darlington *Clarion Journal*. Not a week later, the man, a superb horseman, had his neck broken in a riding accident and died within hours of reaching Darlington Regional Hospital.

"Have you the product test reports for this month?"

"Yes, sir. I took them off the computer yesterday evening."

Paquette was rummaging through his briefcase for the progress reports on the fourteen medications currently being investigated when he heard the soft hum of Redding's wheelchair.

"Just leave the reports on my desk, Arlen," Redding said, gliding to the center of the room. "I'll review them later. Could you bring my coffee over to the table, please? I want to apprise you of a potential problem at the Omnicenter, and I could use a break from talking across this desk."

Paquette did as he was asked, keeping his eyes averted from Redding as much as possible, lest the man, a warlock when it came to reading the thoughts of others, realized how distasteful the Arthgard decision was to him. On the day of their first interview, over eight years ago, he had sensed that uncanny ability in the aging invalid. It was as if all the power that would have gone into locomotion had simply been transferred to another function.

"Arlen, the Omnicenter was already operational when you joined us, yes?"

"Sort of, sir." Paquette settled into the Chesterfield and took a long draught of the coffee he had surreptitiously augmented with cognac while Redding was motoring across the room. "The computers were in, our people were in place, and the finances had been worked out, but no formal testing programs had been started."

"Yes, of course. I remember now. You should go easy on that cognac so early in the day, my friend. It's terrible on the digestion. In the course of your dealings in Boston, did you by chance run into a woman pathologist named Bennett, first name Kathryn, or Kate?"

Paquette shook his head. He had set his coffee aside, no longer finding reassurance in the warm, velvety swallows. "Reese keeps me away from as many people as possible." He smiled and whispered, "I think he's ashamed of me."

Redding enjoyed the humor. "Such a reaction would be typical of the man, wouldn't it. He lacks the highly advanced abilities to appreciate and respect. With him, a person is to be either controlled or feared—none of the subtleties in between."

"Exactly." Paquette was impressed, but not surprised, by the insight. As far as he knew, Redding had had but one direct contact with the Metropolitan Hospital administrator, but for the Warlock, one was usually enough. "What about this Dr. Bennett?"

"She has begun investigating the Omnicenter in connection with two unusual deaths she has autopsied. The women in question had similar blood and reproductive organ disease, and both were Omnicenter patients."

"So are a fair percentage of all the women in Boston," Paquette said. "Have you talked to our people?"

"Carl called me. Both women have participated at various times in our work, but never with the same product. The Omnicenter connection appears to be a red herring."

"Unfortunately, we have other herrings in that building which are not so red."

"That is precisely my concern," Redding said, "and now yours. I have sent instructions to Reese that he is to find a way to divert young Dr. Bennett's interest away from our facility. He seems to think he can do so. However, I have had my sources do some checking on this woman, and I tell you, Norton Reese is no match for her, intellectually or in strength of character."

"He would be the last to admit that."

"I agree." Redding opened a manila folder he had apparently placed on the coffee table prior to Paquette's arrival. "Here are copies for you of all the information we have obtained thus far on the woman. I want you to go to Boston and keep tabs on things. Do not show yourself in any way without checking with me first. Meet with our Omnicenter people only if absolutely necessary."

"Yes, sir."

"There is a small item in that report which may be of

some help to us. Bennett's father-in-law heads the law firm that handles the Metropolitan Hospital account, as well as some of the Northeast business of the Tiny Tummies line of breakfast cereals. Although the connection is not generally known, Tiny Foods is a subsidiary of ours. The man's name is Winfield Samuels. From all I can tell, he's a businessman."

Paquette nodded. Coming from Cyrus Redding, the appellation "businessman" was the highest praise. It meant the man was, like Redding himself, a pragmatist who would not allow emotions to cloud his handling of an issue. "Do you have any idea of what Reese has in mind to deal with the doctor?"

"No, except that Carl Horner says he seems quite sure of himself."

"If that's the case," Paquette said, "I should be back in just a few days."

Redding smiled benignly. "I told you how I perceive the Bennett-Reese matchup, Arlen," he said. "I've had reservations made for you at the Ritz. Open-ended reservations."

◆

METRO DOC LABELS BOBBY JUNKIE.

The layout editor of the *Herald* had, it seemed, dusted off type that had not been used since D-Day. The paper lay on the living room floor, along with the *Globe* and Roscoe, who was keeping an equal distance between himself and both his masters. It was still afternoon, but the mood and the dense overcast outside made the hour feel much later.

The calls had begun at two that morning and had continued until Jared unplugged their phones at four-thirty. Letters, typed on Kathryn Bennett's stationery and signed by her, had been dropped off at both Boston dailies and all three major television stations sometime during the previous night. The gist of the letters was that, driven by conscience and a sense of duty to the people of Boston, Kate had decided to tell the truth about Bobby Geary. Stan Willoughby, who was mentioned in the letter, and Norton Reese, as Metro administrator, were called immediately by reporters. The pathology chief, not as sharp as he might have been had he not been woken from a sound sleep, confirmed the story, adding that Kate was an honest and highly competent pathologist whom, he was sure, had good reason for doing what she had done. It was not until an hour after speaking with the first newsman that he thought to call her. By then, Kate's line was so busy that it took him almost another hour to get through. Meanwhile, Norton Reese, aided by Marco Sebastian and an emergency session with the hospital computers, had confirmed that there was, in fact, no patient named John Schultz ever treated or tested at Metropolitan Hospital. Reese was careful to add that he knew absolutely nothing of the allegations lodged by Dr. Bennett, whom he described as a brilliant woman with a tendency at times to rebel against traditional modes of conduct. Questioned for details, he refused further comment.

The house was like a mausoleum. Both Kate and Jared had attempted to go to work for business as usual, but both had been forced by harassing reporters to return home. Over the hours that followed, they sat, drapes closed, ignoring the periodic ring of the front doorbell. The telephones remained disconnected. There was a silence between them chilly enough to offset even the warmth from the wood stove.

"Jared, do you want a cup of coffee?"

"Thanks, but no. Three in an hour and a half is a little over my limit." He leaned forward from his easy chair and plucked the *Herald* from beside Roscoe's nose. Beneath the headline were insert photos of Bobby Geary's parents, along with a quotation from each about Kate, neither the least bit complimentary. "Goddamn tabloid really knows how to slobber it on," he said, unable to mask the irritation in his voice.

"Honey, you do believe what I said about not knowing anything about those letters, don't you?"

"Of course I believe you. Why would you think otherwise?"

"No reason, I guess." The anger she had felt earlier in the day had been greatly muted by frustration and the growing realization that beyond a simple denial and the call for a handwriting analysis of her signature, she had absolutely no cards to play. Even the signature was of doubtful assistance to her claims of innocence. No one had yet come forward with the original letter, and on the photostat she had seen, the signature appeared quite accurate.

"Why would somebody do this? Why?" Jared seemed to be talking as much to himself as to her, but it was clear that in his mind, confusion and doubt remained. "You say that Yoda and this Detective Finn were the only two besides you who knew about the amphetamines?"

"I said as far as I knew they were. Reese has it in for me, and he has his finger in just about every pie in Metro. He could have found out somehow, and. . . ." She shrugged and shook her head. "I don't think much of the man, but I can't imagine him doing a thing like this."

"You know, Kate, you could have told me you were going to fake Geary's autopsy report. I mean, I am your husband."

Kate glared at him. "Jared, the three of us decided that nobody else should know. Call Mrs. Willoughby or Mrs. Finn and ask if their husbands told them. Do you share all the inner secrets of your work with me?"

"You never ask."

"Give me a break, will you? Listen, I know you're upset. You are a public figure, and directly or indirectly, you're getting negative press. But don't go blaming me, Jared. I didn't do anything."

Jared rose, shuffled to the stove, and began stoking embers that were already burning quite nicely. "I spoke with my father this morning," he said over his shoulder.

"My God, Winfield must be absolutely fried over all this. Do you think it would help matters if I called him?"

"He thinks you should call a press conference and admit that you sent the letters."

"What?"

"It's his feeling that as things stand, it looks like you performed an act of conscience, and then *I* talked you out of owning up to it."

"So my father-in-law wants me to lie in public to keep his protegé from losing any votes."

Jared slammed the poker against the stove door. "Dammit, you already did lie. That's what caused all this trouble in the first place."

Kate felt herself about to cry. "I did what I thought was the kindest and fairest thing I could do for that boy and his family."

"Well, now you're going to have to think about what's kind and fair to *this* boy and *his* family."

"So you think that's what I should do, too?"

A loud pounding on the front door precluded Jared's response.

"Police. Open up."

Kate opened the door a slit and peered out, expecting to see another overly resourceful reporter. Instead, she saw Detective Lieutenant Martin Finn. Any lingering doubt they might have had about whether or not the policeman was responsible for the letters evaporated with the man's first words.

"You really fucked me, Dr. Bennett. Do you know that?"

"I'm sorry, but I didn't send those letters," she said with exaggerated calm. "Would you like to sit down? Can I get you some coffee?"

Finn ignored her questions, and instead, remained in the center of the room, pacing out a miniature circle on the rug. "I went along with this because I'm Irish and a fan, and look what it gets me. I was up for a promotion. Maybe captain. Now, thanks to you and your fucking grandstand play, I'm going to be lucky I don't get busted to dogcatcher."

"Went along with it?" Kate was incredulous. "Lieutenant Finn, it was your suggestion in the first place. For the kids of Boston. Don't you remember saying all that?" Her voice cracked. The day had been punishing enough without this.

Suddenly, Jared pushed past her and confronted the man. Though he was taller than Finn, the policeman was far stockier. "Finn, if you've said what you came to say, I want you and your foul mouth out of here. If not, say it. Then leave."

"I'll leave when I'm fucking ready."

"Get out."

Jared stepped forward, his fists clenched in front of him. It was only then that Kate sensed how heavily Finn had been drinking. She moved toward them, but not quickly enough. With no warning or windup, Finn sank a vicious uppercut into Jared's solar plexus. A guttural grunt accompanied the explosion of air from his lungs, as he doubled over and dropped to his knees.

Kate knelt beside her husband. "You damn animal," she screamed at Finn.

"I wish it had been you, lady," Finn said as he turned and walked clumsily from the house. The antique vase Kate threw shattered against the door as it closed behind him.

Jared remained doubled over, but his breathing was deepening. "You okay?" she said softly.

"Never laid a glove on me," he responded with no little effort. "Could you bring over the wastebasket, please? Just in case."

"You poor darling. Can I do anything else? Get you anything?"

Slowly, Jared sat back and straightened up. His eyes were glazed. "Just remind me again what I told that minister."

"For better or for worse. That's what you told him.

Jared, I don't want to sound corny, but that was a pretty wonderful thing you did standing up to that animal."

"For better or for worse? You sure that was it?"

"Uh-huh."

"Katey, I don't know how to tell you this, but in some perverse way getting hit the way I just did felt good."

"I don't understand."

"Right before Finn came in I was ready to tell you that I agreed with my father in thinking everything would be simpler and look better for all of us if you would just admit to writing the letter. Then that asshole started in. All of a sudden, I realized how wrong I was . . . and I'm sorry. I couldn't stand hearing him talk to you that way. Katey, please just try to remember that there's a lot going on that's confusing to me. Sometimes I feel that living with you is like trying to ride a cyclone. Sometimes I feel like a slab of luncheon meat between one slice of Winfield and one slice of Kate. Sometimes I . . ." He whirled to the wastebasket and threw up.

Sheila Pierce stared past Norton Reese's sweat-dampened pate at the stucco ceiling of their room in the Mid City Motel and reminded herself to continue the groans that the man found so exciting.

Careful not to disrupt his rhythm, she reached up and reassured herself that her new diamond studs hadn't come dislodged.

"Oh, baby," she murmured. "Oh, baby, you're so good. So good."

She wished she could have seen Kate Bennett's face when the reporters started calling. Reese was hardly a Valentino for her, but she had to give credit where credit was due, and Reese deserved what she was giving him for what he had given Bennett.

"Oh, baby, come to me. Come to me," she moaned.

It had been a thrill just to watch: Kathryn Bennett, MD, Miss Perfect, confused and irritable, suddenly not in control of every little thing. How good at last to be the one pulling the strings. Too bad there was no way for Bennett ever to know.

"Don't stop, Norty. Oh, yes, baby, yes. Don't stop."

6

Friday 14 December

Compared with the conference rooms of other departments in Metropolitan Hospital of Boston, the one belonging to the pathology unit was spartan. French Impressionist prints mounted on poster board hung on stark, beige walls. Below them, metal, government-surplus bookcases were half filled with worn, dog-eared texts and journals. The meager decor, plus a large, gouged oak table and two dozen variegated folding chairs did little to obscure the fact that prior to a modest departmentwide renovation in 1965, the room had been the hospital morgue. Some among the twenty-nine assembled for the hastily called meeting still sensed the auras of the thousands of bodies that had temporarily rested there.

Kate, Stan Willoughby seated to her right, stood at one end of the table and surveyed the room. There were six pathologists besides the two of them, some residents, and a number of lab technicians. It bothered her terribly to think that one—or more—of them might be capable of an act as malicious as the Bobby Geary letter. Those in the room were, in a sense, her family—people she spent as many waking hours with each week as she did with her husband. It had always been her way to deal with them in a straightforward manner, respectfully, and with no hidden agendas. There were only two characteristics that they knew she would not tolerate—laziness and dishonesty. However, to the best of her knowledge, none in the room could be accused of either.

The closest had been the business of Sheila Pierce's claiming she had misplaced the required vouchers and certification for her Miami trip, and even then, Kate had no proof of her suspicions. Besides, the matter had been settled between them with little disagreement.

John Gilson, the unit's electron microscopist; Liu Huang, a meticulous pathologist, whom Kate tutored in English; Marvin Grimes, the always pleasantly inebriated deiner; Sheila, herself, so very bright, so dedicated to the department; momentarily, Kate's eyes met each of theirs.

"I want to thank you all for taking the time out of your schedules to hear me out," she began. "I know the last day and a half have been . . . how should I say, a bit disrupted around here." There was a murmur of laughter at the understatement. "Well, I'm here to tell you that compared to what you all have been through, my life has been absolutely nuked. At three o'clock this morning, my husband and I caught a reporter trying to sneak out of our bedroom in time to make the morning edition. He had disguised himself as our antique brass coatrack." Laughter this time was more spontaneous and animated. Kate smiled thinly. "Norton Reese has set up a news conference for me in about an hour. He wants me to state my position on the Bobby Geary business once and for all. Well, before I tell those vultures, I wanted to tell you.

"What the press has been saying about Bobby Geary is true. From all we were able to tell at post, he had been a longtime user of intravenous amphetamines. How he could do what he did to his body and still play ball the way he did is a mystery to me, but the chronic scarring we found along certain veins makes the truth clear. Sad for Bobby's family, sad for the baseball fans and the kids, and, I'm sure, a nightmare for Bobby. The decision to withhold our findings from the press was as much mine as Dr. Willoughby's or Detective Finn's." A jet of acid singed her throat at the mention of the man. "I have trouble with deceit in any form, but every sense I have of what is decent says that our decision was the right one. Now someone is doing his best to make me pay for that decision. I did not write the letter, and I have no idea who did, why they did it, how they got the information on Bobby Geary's post, or how they obtained my stationery. The possibility exists that it was someone from this department. I very much hope not—all of you are very important to me. I feel like we're a team, and that helps me show up every day ready to try and practice decent pathology in this dinosaur of a hospital.

"But what's done is done. I've agonized as much as I'm going to, and after the little Q-and-A session in Reese's office, I intend to begin stuffing this whole business into the barrel I use to dispose of the garbage in my life. If any of you have any questions, I'll be happy to answer them as best I can."

Stan Willoughby rose and put his arm around her shoulders. "No questions from me, Kate. Just a statement for everybody. I have submitted this woman's name to the search committee as my personal recommendation to succeed me as department chief. It's possible this whole business is someone's way of trying to sabotage that appointment. I want you all to know that I am more committed than ever to seeing that she gets it."

For a moment there was silence. Then diminutive Liu Huang stood and began applauding. Another joined in and then another. Soon all but one were demonstrating their support.

"We're behind you, Doc," a technician called out.

The reaction was as enthusiastic and sustained as it was spontaneous. In the back of the room, the lone hold-out smiled around clenched teeth and then stiffly joined in the applause.

"That was pretty special, wasn't it," Willoughby said to Kate as the room emptied out. "Little Looie Huang standing there in his formal, inscrutable way, leading the cheers. I just love 'im. Are you all right?"

"If you mean am I about to come apart and start bawling like a baby, the answer is yes."

"So bawl," Willoughby said, taking her by the arm as they followed the last of the meeting-goers from the room.

"You know, Stan. I don't understand it. I don't think I ever will."

"What's that?" Willoughby bent over the bubbler he had tried for years to get replaced, and sucked vigorously for a sip of tepid water.

"People, I guess." She shrugged. "You know, you wake up in the morning, you get dressed, you march off for another encounter in the battle of life—all you want to do is grow a little, try your best, and grab some little morsel of peace and contentment along the way. No big deal. Every day you do that, and every day you think that everyone else is doing the same thing, trying for that same smidgen of happiness. It makes so much sense that way."

"Ah, yes, my child, but therein lies the rub. You see, what makes sense and what is are seldom the same thing. The stew you propose cooking up would taste just fine, but it's a bit short on the condiments of reality—greed, envy, bigotry, insecurity, to say nothing of that ol' standby, just plain craziness. No matter who you are, no matter how hard you try to tend your own little garden, no matter how kind you try to be to your fellow man, there's always gonna be someone, somewhere tryin' to stick it to you. You can count on it."

"Terrific."

"It all boils down to priorities."

"What do you mean?"

"Well, I know I have the reputation around here for being too passive. My door is always open. Bring in your troubles and problems whenever you want . . . as long as you bring in the solutions to them at the same time. I wasn't always like that, Kate. There was a time when I would have gone to the mat with the toughest of them.

And I did. Many times in the early days before you came on board. Then I started getting the pains beneath the ol' sternum, and I started visiting all those eager young cardiologists. Gradually, my priorities began to shift away from playing with the stick-it-to-you fanatics. I went back to basics. My wife, my children, my grandchildren, my health—physical and mental. I couldn't see how a new microscope or an extra technician or a refurnished room could measure up against any of them."

"But Stan, your work is important. It's your job to fight for the department. Don't you agree?"

"Yes."

"Well then, how do you resolve that fact with what you just said?"

Stanley Willoughby leaned over and kissed her gently on the forehead. "I can't, Kate. Don't you see? That's why I'm stepping down. See you at the conference." With a smile that held more wistfulness and sadness than mirth, he turned and entered the office that, if he had his way, Kate would occupy within a few months.

Kate's office, half the size of her chief's, was on a side corridor next to the autopsy suite. There was room only for a desk and chair, a file cabinet, a small microscope bench, and two high stools. On one of the stools sat Jared.

"Well, hi," she said, crossing to kiss him.

"Hi, yourself."

His response was chilly, perfunctory.

"How's your belly?"

"As long as I don't try to sit down, get up, or walk, it's only painful as hell," he said. "But not nearly as painful as this." He slid a handbill across to her. "Copies of this have been circulating all over South Boston and are beginning to work their way up into the city."

"Damn," she whispered, staring at tne paper in disbelief. "Jared, I'm sorry. I really am." The flyer, printed on an orange stock bright enough to offend even the least political Irish Catholic, was headlined PARTNERS IN COMPASSION. Beneath the words were Kate and Jared arm in arm in a photograph she could not remember ever having posed for. It was labeled "Atty. J. Samuels and Dr. K. Bennett." At the bottom of the page was a photograph of Bobby Geary in the midst of his picture-perfect swing. It was captioned simply "Bobby, R.I.P."

"Finn?" she ventured.

"Maybe. Maybe not. He's hardly the only Irish Catholic around who'd like to firebomb us. The name Bobby Geary seems set to take its place right next to Chappaquiddick and Watergate in the list of political death knells. For all I know, Mattingly or his sleazy campaign manager decided to make sure I was no problem for them in the next election."

"I'm sorry."

"You already said that."

Kate sighed and sank down on her desk chair. "Jared, things aren't really going very well for me right now. Do you have to make them worse?"

"Things aren't going well for *you*? Is that all you can think of?"

"Please, honey. I've got this damn news conference in half an hour; I've got a biopsy due from the OR. Don't you remember saying yesterday how you were going to try to be more understanding?" She clenched her teeth against any further outburst.

"I remember getting laid out by a policeman I'd never seen before that moment. That's what I remember. My father tells me that Martin Finn is *numero uno* in power and influence in certain quarters of the BPD. With him for an enemy, it's possible that I might end up having my car towed while it's stopped for a red light."

Kate's eyes narrowed. Suddenly, Jared's appearance in her office made sense. Win Samuels. One of the man's countless sensors, scattered about the city and throughout the media, must have reported that his daughter-in-law was scheduled to meet the press. "Jared, did your father tell you to come here this morning to make sure I didn't disgrace anyone at the news conference?"

"We're just trying to avoid any more of this stuff." He held up the orange handbill.

Kate glared at her husband for a moment; then her expression softened. "You know, when you are yourself, you are the funniest, nicest, gentlest, handsomest man I have ever known. I swear you are. Given a build-it-myself husband erector set, I don't think I could have done any better. But when you start operating with that man in the Braxton Building, I swear. . . ."

"Look, let's leave my father out of this, shall we? I'm the one who's watching a political career go down the toilet, not him."

"I'm not so sure."

"What?"

"Nothing, Jared. Look, I've got some work to finish, and any moment I have to diagnose the biopsy of a woman's thyroid gland that one of the other pathologists is having trouble with. I can't talk about this any more right now."

"How about you just . . ."

His outburst was cut short by the arrival of a technician carrying a stainless steel specimen tray and cardboard slide holder, which she set on the microscope bench.

"Please tell Dr. Huang I'll call him in a few minutes with my diagnosis," Kate said.

Jared watched the young woman leave and then checked his watch.

"Look," he said coolly, "I've got to go. I have an appointment with Norton Reese in two minutes."

"What for?"

"Apparently he's been contacted by a lawyer friend of the Gearys. They're thinking of some kind of action against the hospital based on invasion of privacy."

"Jesus," Kate said, pressing her fingertips against the fatigue burning in her eyes.

Jared stood to go. "Don't forget about the Carlisles' cocktail party tonight." Kate groaned. "I guess you already have, huh?"

"I'm sorry. What time?"

"Seven-thirty."

"Okay, Jared, I. . . ."

"Yes?"

She shook her head. "Never mind." It wasn't, she decided, the moment to tell him that she felt she was losing her mind. Please hold me, Jared, she wanted to say. Come over here and hold me and tell me everything's going to be all right. Instead, she waved weakly and turned to the slide and tissue in the specimen dish.

Before Jared had crossed to the door, the telephone began ringing. Reflexively, he turned back.

"Hello? . . . Oh, hi," Kate said. "How're you holding up? . . . How long? . . . Have you tried pressure? . . . Ice? . . . Ellen, please. Just calm down and get a hold of yourself. Have you ever had any trouble like this before? . . . Any bruising you can't explain? . . . Your whole thigh? . . . Why didn't you call me? . . . Ellen, a few years ago, I helped get you accepted into the Omnicenter. Are you still going there? . . . All right. Now listen carefully. I want you to come up to the emergency ward here, but I don't want you to drive. Can you get someone to bring you? . . . Fine. Pack an overnight bag and ask your sister or someone to cover the girls, just in case. . . . Ellen, relax. Now I mean it. Coming apart will only make things worse. Besides, it raises havoc with your mascara. . . . That's better. Now, maintain pressure as best you can, and come on up here. I'll have the best people waiting to see you. You'll probably be home in a couple of hours. . . . Good. And Ellen, bring your medicines, too. . . . I know they're only vitamins. Bring them anyway."

"Ellen Sandler?" Jared asked as she hung up.

Kate nodded, her face ashen. "Her nose has been bleeding steadily for over two hours. Do you know where Sandy is, by any chance?"

"Europe, I think."

Kate stared down at the specimen tray and thought about the woman on the operating table, waiting word on whether the lump in her neck was cancerous or not.

Chances were that the initial biopsy had been done under local, so the woman would be fully awake, frightened. "Jared, there is something you can tell Norton Reese for me. Tell him that I won't be able to make his news conference. Tell him that I didn't do anything and didn't write anything, so I really don't have anything to say anyway."

"But . . ."

"Tell him that as my husband for almost five years, you know that whatever I say is the truth, and that if anyone wants to get at me, they'll have to go through you. Just like last evening. Okay?" She placed a slide under her microscope, and prepared for an encounter with the yellow-white light.

Jared moved to respond, but then stopped himself, walked to the door, and finally turned back. "I hope Ellen's all right," he said softly.

Kate looked up. Every muscle in her body seemed to have tensed at the prospect of what the blood studies on her friend might reveal. "So do I, Jared," she said. "So do I."

Relax. Concentrate. Focus in. Center your mind. Center it. It took a minute or two longer than usual, but in the end, the process worked. It always did. Extraneous thoughts and worries lifted from her like a fog until finally all that remained in her world were the cells.

Arlen Paquette sat by the window of his suite in the Ritz, watching the slow passage of pedestrians along the snow-covered walks of the Public Gardens. His schooling had been at Harvard and MIT, and no matter how long he lived in Kentucky, coming to Boston always felt like coming home. Watching the students and lovers, the vagrants and executives, Paquette found himself longing for the more sheltered, if much more improverished, life in a university. Over the seven years with Redding, he had gained much. The land, the house, the tennis court and pool, to say nothing of the opportunities for his children and lifetime security for himself and his wife. Only now was he beginning to appreciate fully the price he had paid. More and more, especially since the Arthgard recall, he avoided looking at himself in mirrors. More and more, as his self-respect dwindled, his effectiveness as a lover also declined. And now, a thousand miles from his exquisitely manicured lawn and the country club he was about to direct, two women had bled to death. As he looked out on the gray New England afternoon, Paquette prayed that the connection of the dead women to the Omnicenter was mere coincidence.

At precisely three o'clock, a messenger arrived with the large manila envelope he had been expecting. Paquette tipped the man and then spread the contents on the coffee table next to the dossier he had brought with him from Darlington. The thoroughness with which Cyrus Redding approached a potential adversary surprised him not in the least. The Warlock kept his edge, honed his remarkable intuitiveness, through facts—countless snatches of data that taken individually might seem irrelevant, but which, like single jigsaw-puzzle pieces, helped construct the truth; in this case, the truth that was Kathryn Bennett Samuels, MD.

Paquette found the volume of information amassed over just a few days both impressive and frightening. Biographical data, academic publications, medical history from a life insurance application, even grades and a yearbook picture from Mount Holyoke. There were, in addition to the photostats and computer printouts, a dozen black-and-white photographs—five-by-seven blowups of shots obviously taken with a telephoto lens. Instinctively, the chemist glanced out the window of his eighth-floor suite, wondering if there were a spot from which someone might be taking photographs of him.

One at a time, Paquette studied the carefully labeled photographs. "K.B. and husband, Jared Samuels." "K.B. and pathologist Stanley Willoughby. (See p. 4B.)" "Samuels/Bennett residence, Salt Marsh Road, Essex." "K.B. jogging near home." The woman had a remarkable face, vibrant and expressive, with the well-defined features that translated into photogenicity. Her beauty was at once unobtrusive and unquestionable, and as he scanned the photos, Arlen Paquette felt the beginning pangs of loneliness for his wife.

"Pay special attention to Dr. Stein's report," Redding had instructed him. "The man has done this sort of thing for me before, on even shorter notice and with even less data than he has had to work with here. If you have questions, let me know and I'll have Stein get in touch with you."

The report was typed on stationery embossed "Stephen Stein, PhD; Clinical Psychologist." There was no address or telephone number. Paquette mixed himself a weak Dewar's and water and settled onto the brocaded sofa with the three, single-spaced pages.

Much of the report was a condensation of the data from the rest of the dossier. Paquette read through that portion, underlining the few facts he hadn't encountered before. Actually, he was familiar with Stein's work. Nearly seven years before, he had studied a similar document dealing with Norton Reese. He had wondered then, as he did again this day, if somewhere in the hundreds of manila folders locked in Cyrus Redding's files was one containing a Stein study of Arlen Paquette.

Two older brothers . . . high-school cheerleader . . . ribbon-winning equestrian . . . art department award for sculpture, Mt. Holyoke College . . . one piece, *Search #3*, still on display on campus grounds . . . fourteen-day hospitalization for depression, junior year. . . . Paquette added the information to what he already knew of the woman.

"In conclusion," Stein wrote, "it would appear that in Dr. Bennett we have a woman of some discipline and uncommon tenacity who would make a valuable ally or a dangerous foe under any circumstances. Her principles appear solidly grounded, and I would doubt seriously that she can be bought off a cause in which she believes.

Intellectually, I have no reason to believe her abilities have declined from the days when she scored very high marks in the Medical College Admission Test (see p. 1C) and National Medical Boards (also 1C). Her friends, as far as we have been able to determine, are loyal to her and trusting in her loyalty to them. (Statements summarized pp. 2C and 3C.)

"She does, however, have some problem areas that we shall continue to explore and that might yield avenues for controlling her actions. She likely has a deep-seated insecurity and confusion regarding her roles as a wife and a professional. A threat against her husband may prove more effective in directing her actions than a threat against herself. Faced with a challenge, it is likely that she would fight rather than back away or seek assistance.

"The possibility of influence through blackmail (areas for this being investigated) or extortion seems remote at this time.

"Follow-up report in one week or as significant information is obtained.

"Estimate of potential for control on Redding index is two or three."

Paquette set the report aside and tried to remember what Norton Reese had been graded on Redding's scale. An eight? And what about himself?

"A ten," he muttered. "Move over Bo Derek. Here comes Arlen Paquette, an absolute ten." He poured a second drink, this one pure Dewar's, and buried it.

In minutes, the amber softness had calmed him enough for him to begin some assessment of the situation. Bennett had sent specialists to the Omnicenter to take cultures. No problem. If they were negative, as he suspected they would be, the clinic had gotten a free, comprehensive microbiology check. If they were positive, investigation would move away from the pharmacy anyhow. She had asked for, and received, samples of the pharmaceuticals dispensed by Horner's Monkeys. No problem. The samples would prove to be clean. Horner had seen to that.

Would she press her investigation further? Stein's report and what he knew of the woman said yes. However, that was before she had become mired down in the baseball player mess. The more he thought about the situation, the more convinced Paquette became that there was no avenue through which Kate Bennett could penetrate the secret of the Omnicenter, especially since all product testing had been suspended. Tenacity or no tenacity, the woman could not keep him away from home for more than a few days.

As he mixed another drink, Paquette realized that there was, in fact, a way. It was a twisting, rocky footpath rather than an avenue, but it was a way nonetheless. After a moment of hesitation, he placed a call to the 202 area.

"Good afternoon. Ashburton Foundation."

"Estelle?"

"Yes."

"It's Dr. Thompson."

"Oh. Hi, Doctor. Long time no hear."

"Only a week, Estelle. Everything okay?"

"Fine."

"Any calls?"

"Just this one. I almost jumped out of my skin when the phone rang. I mean days of doing nothing but my nails, I . . ."

"Any mail?"

"Just the two pieces from Denver I forwarded to you a while ago."

"I got them. Listen, if any calls come in, I don't want you to wait until I check in. Call me through the numbers on the sheet in the desk. The message will get to me, and I'll call you immediately."

"Okay, but . . ."

"Thank you, Estelle. Have a good day."

"Good-bye, Dr. Thompson."

To Kate Bennett the scene in Room 6 of the Metropolitan Hospital emergency ward was surreal. Off to one side, two earnest hematology fellows were making blood smears and chatting in inappropriately loud tones. To the other side, Tom Engleson leaned against the wall in grim silence, flanked by a nurse and a junior resident. Kate stood alone by the doorway, alternating her gaze from the crimson-spattered suction bottle on the wall to the activity beneath the bright overhead light in the center of the room.

Pete Colangelo, chief of otorhinolaryngology, hunched in front of Ellen Sandler, peering through the center hole of his head mirror at a hyperilluminated spot far within her left nostril.

"It's high. Oh, yes, it's high," he murmured to himself as he strove to cauterize the hemorrhaging vessel that because of its location, was dripping blood out of Ellen's nose and down the back of her throat.

Kate looked at her friend's sheet-covered legs and thought about the bruise, the enormous bruise, which had been a harbinger of troubles to come. *Don't let it be serious. Please, if you are anything like a God, please don't let her tests come back abnormal.*

In the special operating chair, Ellen sat motionless as marble, but her hands, Kate observed, were whitened from her grip on the armrest. *Please . . .*

"Could you check her pressure?" Colangelo asked. He was a thin, minute man, but his hands were remarkable, especially in the fine, plastic work from which surgical legends were born. Kate was grateful beyond words that she had found him available. Still, she knew that the real danger lay not so much in what was happening as in why. Gruesome images of Beverly Vitale and Ginger Rittenhouse churned in her thoughts. At that moment, in the hematology lab, machines and technicians were measuring the clotting factors in a woman who was no more than a name and hospital number to them. *Please . . .*

Colangelo's assistant reported Ellen's pressure at one-forty over sixty. No danger there. The jets of blood into the suction bottle seemed to be lessening, and for the first time Kate sensed a slight letup in the tension around the room.

"Come to papa," Colangelo cooed to the bleeding arteriole. "That's the little fellow. Come to papa, now."

"What do you think?"

Kate spun to her left.

Tom Engleson had moved next to her. "Sorry," he whispered. "I didn't mean to startle you." The concern she was feeling was mirrored in his face. His brown eyes, dulled somewhat by the continued pressures of his job, were nonetheless wonderfully expressive.

"I think Pete is winning," she said, "if that's what you're asking."

"It isn't."

"In that case, I don't have an answer. At least not yet. Not until the hematology report comes back." She continued speaking, but turned her gaze back to the center of the room. "If her counts are normal, and you have the time, we can celebrate. I'll buy you a coffee. If they're low, I'd like to—wait, make that need to—talk with you anyhow. Besides Stan Willoughby, you are the only one who knows as much as I do, and I think these past two days Stan has been battered enough by his association with me."

"I'm free for the rest of the day," Tom said. "If you like, maybe we could have dinner together." The moment the words were out, he regretted saying them. Impetuous, inappropriate, tactless, dumb.

Kate responded with a fractional look—far too little for him to get a fix on. "I think Pete's done it," she said, making no reference to his invitation.

Moments later, Colangelo confirmed her impression. "We've got it, Mrs. Sandler. You just stay relaxed the way you have been, and we should be in good shape. You are a wonderful patient, believe me you are. I love caring for people who help me to do my best work." He took a step back and waited, the reflected light from his head mirror illuminating the blood-smeared lower half of Ellen's face. Then he turned to Kate, his lips parted in a hopeful half-smile.

"Good job, Pete," she whispered. "Damn good."

Colangelo nodded and then turned back to his patient. "Mrs. Sandler, I think it best for you to stay overnight here. There are some lab studies that haven't come back yet, and I would also like to be sure that vessel stays cauterized."

"No," Ellen said. "I mean, I can't. I mean I don't want to if I don't have to. Kate, tell Dr. Colangelo all the things I have to do, and how responsible I am, and how I'll do exactly what he tells me to do if I can go home. Please, Kate. No offense, but I hate hospitals. Hate them. I almost had Betsy in a roadside park because I wanted to wait until the last minute."

Kate crossed to her friend and wiped the dried blood from her face with damp gauze. "Let's see," she said finally. "As I see it, you want me to arbitrate a disagreement in medical philosophy between the chief of ENT surgery, who also happens to be a professor at Harvard, and the chief of E. Sandler Interior Designs, Inc. . . ."

"Kate, please."

Ellen's grip on Kate's hand and the quaver in her voice reflected a fear far more primal than Kate had realized. Kate turned to the surgeon. "Pete?"

Colangelo shrugged. "I get paid to do surgery and give advice," he said. "If you're asking me whether I think admission is one hundred percent necessary, the answer is no. However, as I said, I get paid to give advice, and observation in the hospital is my advice."

Before Kate could respond, a white-coated technician from the hematology service entered and handed her three lab slips, two pink and one pale green. She studied the numbers and felt a grinding fear and anger rise in her throat. "Lady," she said, struggling to mask the tension in her voice, "I'm going to cast in with Dr. Colangelo. I think you ought to stay."

Ellen's grip tightened. "Kate, what do the tests show? Is it bad?"

"No, El. A couple of the numbers are off a bit and should be rechecked, but it's not bad or dangerous at this point." Silently, she prayed that her judgment of the woman's strength was correct, and that she had done the right thing in not lying. Ellen studied her eyes.

"Not bad or dangerous *at this point*, but it could be. Is that what you're saying?" Kate hesitated and then nodded. Ellen sighed. "Then I guess I stay," she said.

"You shouldn't be here long, and you'll have the very best people taking care of you. I'll help you make arrangements for the girls, and I'll also let them know what's going on."

"Thank you."

"I know it sounds foolish to say don't worry, but try your best not to. We'll keep an eye on your nose and recheck the blood tests in the morning. Most likely you'll be home by the end of the weekend." Kate fought to maintain an even eye contact, but somewhere inside she knew that her friend didn't believe the hopeful statement any more than she did.

"It's the Omnicenter. Somehow I just know it is."

Kate grimaced at the coffee she had just brewed, and lightened it with half-and-half ferreted out from among the chemicals in her office refrigerator.

"The Omnicenter is just that pile of glass and stone across the street. Every one of these reports is negative. Bacteriology, chemistry, epidemiology. All negative. Where's the connection?" Tom Engleson flipped through a sheaf of reports from the studies Kate had ordered. There was nothing in any of them so far to implicate the outpatient center.

"I don't know," Kate responded, settling in across the work bench from him. He was dressed in jeans and a bulky, ivory fisherman's sweater. It was the first time she had seen the man wearing anything but resident's whites.

The change was a positive one. The marvelous Irish knit added a rugged edge to his asthenic good looks. "I think it's a virus or some sort of toxin . . . or a contaminant in the pharmacy. Whatever it is is in there." She jabbed a thumb in the general direction of the Omnicenter.

"The pharmacy? These reports say that the analyses of Ginger Rittenhouse's medications and of the ones Zimmermann sent you were all perfectly normal. Not a bad apple in the bunch."

"I know."

"So . . .?"

"So, I don't know. Look, my friend has whatever this thing is that has killed two women. Platelets seventy thousand, fibrinogen seventy-five percent of normal. You saw the report. Not as bad as either of the other two, at least not yet, but sure headed in the wrong direction." Her words came faster and her voice grew more strident. "I don't really need you to come down here and point out the obvious. For that I can go get Gus from the newsstand outside. I need some thoughts on what *might* be the explanation, not on what *can't* be." Suddenly she stopped. "Jesus, I'm sorry, Tom. I really am. Between political nonsense here at the hospital, the mess with Bobby Geary and his damn amphetamine addiction, two young women dying like ours did, the everyday tensions of just trying to do this job right, and now Ellen, I'm feeling like someone has plunked me inside a blender and thrown the switch. You don't deserve this."

"It's okay. I'm sorry for not being more helpful." He was unable to completely expunge the hurt from his voice, and Kate reminded herself that while the five or so years difference in their ages meant little in most areas, hypersensitivity might not be one of them. "If you think it's the pharmacy," he said, "maybe you should call the FDA."

"One jot of evidence, and I would. I'm the one who talked her into going to the Omnicenter in the first place." Absently, she slipped her hands into her lab coat pockets. In the right one, folded back and again on itself, was the cardboard and plastic card containing what remained of Ellen's Omnicenter vitamins plus iron. She set them on the bench. "No luck finding any of Beverly Vitale's vitamins?" she asked.

"None."

Kate crossed to her desk, returned with a medication card similar to Ellen's, and slapped it down next to the other. "I think we should try one last time with our friends at the toxicology lab and their magic spectrophotometer. Ellen's vitamins and these. If the reports come back negative, I shall put all my suspicions in the witch-hunt file and turn my attention to other pursuits—like trying to regain some of the respect that was snatched away in the Bobby Geary disaster."

"Don't worry," Tom said, "you still have respect, admiration, and caring in a lot of places . . . especially right here." He tapped himself on the breastbone with one finger.

"Thank you for saying that."

"Whose pills are those other ones?" he asked.

"Huh?"

"The other card of pills, whose are they?"

"Oh. They're mine."

7

Friday 14 December

There was an air of excitement and anticipation throughout the usually staid medical suite of Vernon Drexler, MD. The matronly receptionist bustled about the empty waiting room, straightening the magazines and taking pains to see that the six-month-old issue of *Practical Medical Science* with Drexler's picture on the cover was displayed prominently enough to be impossible for Cyrus Redding to miss, even if he were ushered directly into the doctor's office.

In the small laboratory, the young technician replaced the spool of paper in the cardiograph machine and realigned the tubes, needle, and plastic sleeve she would use to draw blood from the arm of the man Drexler had described as one of the most influential if not one of the wealthiest in the country.

Behind her desk, Lurleen Fiske, the intense, severe office manager, phoned the last of their patients and rescheduled him for another day. She had been with Drexler in 1967, when Cyrus Redding had made his first trip up from Kentucky. *Nineteen sixty-seven*. Fiske smiled wistfully. Their office in the Back Bay section of Boston had been little more than two large closets then, one for the doctor and one for herself. Now, Drexler owned the entire building.

It was twelve-thirty. Redding's private 727 had probably touched down at Logan already. In precisely an hour, the woman knew, his limousine would glide to a stop in front of their brownstone. Redding, on foot if he could manage it, in his wheelchair if he could not, would be helped up the walk and before entering the building, would squint up at their office window, smile, and wave. His aide, for the last five or six years a silent, hard-looking man named Nunes, would be carrying a leather tote bag containing Redding's medicines and, invariably, a special, personal gift for each of those working in the office. On Redding's last visit, nearly a year before, his gift to her had been the diamond pendant—almost half a carat—now resting proudly on her chest. Of course, she realized, this day could prove an exception. Some sort of pressing situation had arisen requiring Redding to fly to Boston. He had called the office late on the previous afternoon inquiring as to whether, as long as he had to be in the city, he might be able to work in his annual checkup.

"Mrs. Fiske," Drexler called from his office, "I can't remember. Did you say Dr. Ferguson would be coming in with Mr. Redding, or did you say he wouldn't be?"

"I said 'might,' Doctor. Mr. Redding wasn't sure." The woman smiled lovingly and shook her head. Vernon Drexler may have been a renowned endocrinologist, and a leading expert on the neuromuscular disease myasthenia gravis, but for matters other than medicine, his mind was a sieve. She and his wife had spent many amusing evenings over the years imagining the Keystone Comedy that would result were they not available to orchestrate his movements from appointment to appointment, lecture to lecture.

The thought of Dr. Ferguson sent the office manager hurrying to the small, fire-resistant room housing their medical records; she returned to her desk with the man's file. John Ferguson, MD, afflicted, as was Cyrus Redding, with myasthenia, was a close friend of the tycoon. The two men usually arranged to have their checkups on the same day, and then for an hour or so they would meet with Dr. Drexler. Lurleen Fiske suspected, though Drexler had never made her party to their business, that the two men were in some way supporting his myasthenia research laboratory at the medical school.

"Mrs. Fiske," Drexler called out again, "perhaps you'd better get Dr. Ferguson's chart just in case."

"Yes, Doctor, I'll get it right away," she said, already flipping through the lengthy record to ensure that the laboratory reports and notes from his last visit were in place. Drexler was nervous. She could tell from his voice. He was conducting himself with proper decorum and professional detachment, but she could tell nonetheless. Once, years before, he had been ferried by helicopter to Onassis's yacht for a consultation on the man's already lost battle against myasthenia. That morning, he had calmly bid the office staff good day and then had strode out minus his medical bag, journal articles, and sport coat.

Redding's limousine, slowed by the snow-covered streets, arrived five minutes late. Lurleen Fiske joined the two other employees at the window. Across the room, Drexler, a tall, gaunt man in his midfifties, watched his staff pridefully.

"Look, look. There he is," the receptionist twittered.

"Is he walking?" Drexler wanted to see for himself, but was reluctant to disrupt the ritual that had developed over the years.

Lurleen Fiske craned her neck. "His wheelchair is out," she said, "but yes . . . yes, he's taking a few steps on his own. Another year, Dr. Drexler. You've done it again." There was no mistaking the reverence in her voice.

In spite of himself, Drexler, too, was impressed. In sixty-seven he had predicted three years for Redding, four at the most. Now, after more than fifteen, the man was as strong as he had been at the start, if not stronger. *You've done it again*. Mrs. Fiske's praise echoed painfully in his thoughts. Myasthenia gravis, a progressive deterioration of the neuromuscular system. Cause: unknown. Prognosis:

progressive weakness—especially with exertion—fatigue, difficulty in chewing, difficulty in breathing, and eventually, death from infection or respiratory failure. Treatment: stopgap even at its most sophisticated. Yet here were two men, Redding and John Ferguson, who had, in essence, arrested or at least markedly slowed the progress of their disease. And they had performed the minor miracles on their own. Though his staff thought otherwise, and neither patient would ever suggest so, they had received only peripheral, supportive help from him. They were certainly a pair of triumphs, but triumphs that continually underscored the futility of his own life's work.

From the hallway, Drexler heard the elevator clank open. For years, his two prize patients had been treating themselves with upwards of a dozen medications at once, most of them still untested outside the laboratory. For years he had dedicated his work to trying to ascertain which drug or combination of drugs was responsible for their remarkable results. The answer would likely provide a breakthrough of historic proportions. Perhaps this would be his year.

Redding, seated in an unmotorized wheelchair, waved his aide on ahead and then wheeled himself to the doorway. Using the man's arm for some support, he pulled himself upright and took several rickety steps into the office.

"Thank you for seeing me on such short notice, Vernon," he said, extending his hand to give Drexler's a single, vigorous pump. "Mr. Nunes?" The aide, a sullen, swarthy man with the physique of an Olympic oarsman, slid the wheelchair into place for Redding to sit back down. Across the waiting room, Lurleen Fiske and the two other women beamed like proud grandmothers.

"You look wonderful, Cyrus," Drexler said. "Absolutely wonderful. Come on into my office."

"In a moment. First, I should like to wish your staff an early Merry Christmas. Mr. Nunes?"

The expressionless Nunes produced three gifts of varying sizes from the leather bag slung over his shoulder, and

Redding presented them, one at a time, to the women, who shook his hand self-consciously. Lurleen Fiske squeezed his shoulders and kissed him on the cheek.

"My limousine will go for Dr. Ferguson," Redding said, as he was wheeled into Drexler's office. "He will be here to share notes with the two of us, but not to be examined. He would rather keep the appointment he has for next month, if that is agreeable to you."

"Fine, fine," Drexler said.

The two men, Ferguson and Redding, had met perhaps a dozen years before in his waiting room and had developed an instant rapport. By their next appointment, Redding had asked that a half day be set aside for just the two of them. The request, supported as it was by the promise of substantial research funds, was, of course, granted.

Redding's bodyguard wheeled him into Drexler's office, set the bag of medications on the desk, and left to accompany the limousine to John Ferguson's house. Carefully, Redding arranged the vials and plastic containers on the blotter before Drexler. There were, all told, thirteen different preparations.

"Well, Doctor," he said, "here they are. Most of them you already know we have been taking. A couple of them you don't."

"Dr. Ferguson continues to follow exactly the same regimen as you?"

"As far as I know."

The endocrinologist made notes concerning each nedication. There were two highly experimental drugs—still far from human testing—that he himself had only learned of in the past six or seven months. He bit back the urge, once again, to warn against the dangers of taking pharmaceuticals before they could be properly investigated, and simply recorded the chemical names and dosages. Somehow, the two men were screening the drugs for side effects. They had let him know that much and no more. As far as Vernon Drexler, MD, was concerned, with a goodly proportion of his own research at stake, there was no point in pushing the matter.

"This one?" Drexler held up a half-filled bottle of clear, powder-filled gelatin capsules.

"From Podgorny, at the Institute for Metabolic Research, in Leningrad," Redding said simply. "He believes the theory behind the compound to be quite sound."

"Amazing," Drexler muttered. "Absolutely amazing." Rudy Podgorny was a giant in the field, but so inaccessible that it had been two years since he had met with him face to face. Redding's resourcefulness, the power of his money, was mind-boggling. "Well," he said when he had finished his tabulations, "these two preparations have finally had clinical evaluations. Both of them have been shown to be without significant effect. We can discuss my thoughts when Dr. Ferguson arrives, but I feel the data now are strong enough to recommend stopping them."

Redding fingered the bottles. "One of these was your baby, yes?"

The physician shrugged helplessly and nodded. "Yes," he said, "I am afraid I have hitched my wagon to a falling star." He failed in his attempt to keep an optimistic tone in his voice. Four years of work had, in essence, gone down the drain.

"Then you must strike out in other directions, eh?"

Just tell me, Drexler thought, *tell me how in the hell you know the medications you are taking won't just kill you on the spot?*

"Yes," he said, through a tight smile, "I suppose I must."

The sleek, stretch limousine moved like a serpent through the light midafternoon traffic on the Southeast Expressway. In the front seat, Redding's portly driver chattered at the taciturn Nunes, whose contribution to the conversation was an occasional nod or monosyllable. In the rear, seated across from one another, surrounded on all sides by smoked glass, Redding and John Ferguson sipped brandy and reviewed the session they had just completed with Vernon Drexler.

"I am sorry things have not been going well with you, John," Redding said. "Perhaps we should have stayed and let Drexler examine you."

"Nonsense. I have an appointment next month, and that will be quite time enough."

"Yes, I suppose so." There was little question in Redding's mind that Ferguson, perhaps eight years his senior, was failing. The man, never robust, had lost strength and weight. He could shuffle only a few dozen steps without exhaustion. His face was drawn and sallow, dominated by a mouth of full, perfect teeth that gave his every expression a cadaverous cast. Only his eyes, sparkling from within deep hollows like chips of aquamarine, reflected the immense drive and intellectual power that had marked the man's life.

Their collaboration, for that is what it quickly became, had begun on the day of their first meeting in Drexler's office. Ferguson, though still ambulatory with a cane, had the more advanced disease of the two. He was employed at the time as medical director of a state hospital outside of the city and was already taking two experimental drugs after testing them for a time on the patients of his facility.

Within a year, Redding had begun locating new preparations, while Ferguson expanded his testing program to include them. Quickly, though, both men came to appreciate the need for a larger number of test subjects than could be supplied by Ferguson's hospital. Establishment of the Total Care Women's Health Center in Denver and, soon after, the Omnicenter in Boston, was the upshot of that need. Vernon Drexler continued as their physician, monitoring their progress and watching over their general states of health.

Redding's driver, still prattling cheerfully at Nunes, swung onto 95 North. Although they would eventually end up at John Ferguson's Newton home, his only other instruction had been for a steady one-hour drive.

"John," Redding said, setting his half-filled snifter in its holder on the bar, "how long has it been since you were at the Omnicenter?"

Ferguson laughed ruefully. "How long since I've been anyplace would be a better question. Two years, perhaps. Maybe longer. It's just too difficult for me to get around."

"I understand."

"I take it from our conversation yesterday evening that there's been some kind of problem. Zimmermann?"

This time it was Redding who laughed. "No, no," he said. "From all I can tell, Zimmermann was the perfect choice for the job. You were absolutely right in recommending him. A harmless fop with the intelligence to implement and monitor our testing program without getting in the way. No, not Zimmermann."

"Well, then?"

"Actually, there may not even be a problem. When you were working with Dr. French to set up the Omnicenter, did you ever run into a Dr. Kathryn Bennett?" Ferguson thought for a moment and then shook his head. "I suspected you wouldn't have," Redding said.

It took only a few minutes for Redding to review the events leading to Kate Bennett's inspection of the Omnicenter.

Ferguson listened with the dispassion of a scientist, his silence punctuated only by occasional gestures that he was following the account.

"Carl Horner assures me," Redding concluded, "that none of the pharmaceuticals we are studying could have been responsible for the problems young Dr. Bennett is investigating."

"But you are not so sure."

"John, you've worked with Carl. You know that being wrong is not something he does very often. The man's mind is as much a computer as any of his machines."

"But you think two such distinctive cases, and now possibly a third, are too many to explain by coincidence?"

Redding stared out the window; he removed his glasses

and cleaned them with a towel from the bar. "To tell you the truth, John, I don't know what to think. The facts say one thing, my instincts another. You know the Omnicenter better than I do. Could anyone be fooling around with some drug or other kind of agent behind our backs?"

"I hope not."

"John, mull over what I've told you. See if you can come up with any theories that might explain why all three women with this bleeding problem, and two of them with the same ovary problem, were all patients of the Omnicenter." He flipped the intercom switch. "Mr. Crosscup, you may drive us to Dr. Ferguson's house," he said.

"I will think it over," Ferguson said, "but my impression is that this once at least, your instincts should yield to the facts."

"A week."

"Excuse me?"

"A week, John," Redding said. "I should like to hear something from you about this matter in a week."

Ferguson probed the younger man's eyes. "You seem to be implying that I am holding something back."

"I imply nothing of the kind." He smiled enigmatically. "I am only asking for your help."

The limousine pulled into the snow-banked drive of John Ferguson's house, a trim white colonial on perhaps an acre of land. Redding engaged the intercom. "Mr. Nunes," he said, "our business has been concluded. Kindly assist our guest to his home."

The men shook hands and Redding watched as Nunes aided an obviously exhausted John Ferguson up the walk to the front door. The old man was many things, Redding acknowledged, a brilliant physician and administrator, an exceptional judge of human nature and predictor of human behavior, a gifted philosopher. What he was not, Redding had known since the early days of their association, was John Ferguson. Redding's investigators had been able to learn that much, but no more. There had been a John

Ferguson with an educational background identical to this man's, but that John Ferguson had died in the bombing of a field hospital in Bataan. Originally, Redding's instincts had argued against a confrontation with his new associate over what, exactly, the man was hiding from. That decision had proved prudent—at least until now.

Ferguson bid a final good-bye with a weak wave and entered his home.

Behind the smoked glass of the limousine, Cyrus Redding was placing a phone call through the mobile operator. "Dr. Stein, please," Redding said. "Hello, Doctor, this is your friend from Darlington. The man, John Ferguson, of whom I spoke last night: I should like the reinvestigation and close observation instituted at once. Keep me informed personally of your progress. He seems to have materialized shortly after World War Two, so perhaps that is a period to reinvestigate first. Thank you."

All right, my friend, he thought. For fifteen years, I have allowed you your deception. Let us hope that courtesy was not misplaced.

Kate Bennett set her dictaphone headpiece in its cradle and stared across the street at the darkened Omnicenter. Reflections from the headlights of passing cars sparkling off its six-foot windows lent an eerie animation to the structure, which stood out against its dark brick surroundings like a spaceship. Kate knew it was her never-timid imagination at work, knew it was the phone call she was expecting, but she still could not rationalize away her sense of the building as something ominous, something virulent.

The message had been on her desk when she returned from the Friday meeting of the hospital Infection Control Committee, which she had chaired for almost a year.

"Ian Toole at State Toxicology Lab called," the department secretary's note said. "One spec you sent normal, one spec contaminated. Please await phone call with details between six and seven tonight."

Contaminated.

"It's you. I know it is." Her mind spoke the words to the gleaming five stories. "Something inside you, inside your precious Monkeys, has gone haywire. Something inside you is killing people, and you don't even know it."

The ringing of the telephone startled her. "Kate Bennett," she answered excitedly.

"Kate Bennett's husband," Jared said flatly.

"Oh, hi. You surprised me. I was expecting a call from Ian Toole in the toxicology lab and . . . never mind that. Where are you? Is everything all right?"

"At home, where you're supposed to be, and no."

Kate glanced at the clock on her desk and groaned. "Oh, damn. Jared, I forgot about the Carlisles. I'm sorry."

"Apology not accepted," he said with no hint of humor.

Kate sank in her chair, resigned to the outburst she knew was about to ensue, and knowing that it was justified. "I'm sorry anyhow," she said softly.

"You're always sorry, aren't you?" Jared said. "You're so wrapped up in Kate's job and Kate's world and Kate's problems that you seem to forget that there are any other jobs or worlds or problems around. My father and several big-money people are going to be at that party tonight. What kind of an impression is it going to make when I show up without my wife?"

"Jared, you don't understand. Something is going on here. People are dying."

"People like Bobby Geary?"

Kate glanced at the clock. It was five minutes to seven. "Look," she said, "I'm waiting for a call that could help solve this mystery. I can call you back or I can get home as soon as possible, change, and make it over to the Carlisles by eight-thirty or nine."

"Don't bother."

"Jared, what do you want me to do?"

Jared's sigh was audible over the phone. "I want you

to do whatever it is you feel you have to do," he said. "I'll go to the Carlisles and make do. We can talk later tonight or tomorrow. Okay?"

"All right," she said, taken somewhat aback by his reasonableness.

"How's Ellen?"

"Pardon?" It was one minute to seven.

"Ellen. You remember, our friend Ellen. How is she?"

"She's in the hospital, Jared. Listen, I really am sorry, and I really am in the middle, or at least on the fringes of something strange. Ellen's life may be at stake in what I'm doing."

"Sounds pretty melodramatic to me," Jared said, "but then again, I'm just a poor ol' country lawyer. We'll talk later."

"Thank you, Jared. I love you."

"See you later, Kate."

Ian Toole's call came at precisely seven-fifteen.

"These are some little pills you sent me here, Dr. Bennett," he said. "My assistant, Millicent, and I have been running them most of the afternoon, and we still don't have a final word for you."

"But you said Ellen's pills were contaminated."

"Ellen Sandler's? Hardly. I think your secretary mixed up my message. Probably went to the same school as ours."

"What do you mean?"

"Ellen Sandler's vitamins are a pretty run-of-the-mill, low-potency preparation. B complex, a little C, a little iron, a splash of zinc. It's yours that are weird."

"Mine?" Kate's throat grew dry and tight.

"Uh-huh. You're not only taking the same vitamins as Ellen Sandler, but you're also taking a fairly sizable jolt every day of some kind of anthranilic acid."

"Anthranilic acid?"

"Millicent and I are trying to work out the side chains, but that's the basic molecule."

Kate felt sick. "Mr. Toole, what is it?"

"I'm a chemist, not a doctor, but as far as I've been able to determine, you're taking a painkiller of some sort. Nonnarcotic. Some kind of nonsteroidal anti-inflammatory drug. The basic molecule is listed in our manuals, but I don't think we're going to find the exact side chains. Whatever it is, it's not a commercially available drug in this country. If it were, we'd have it in the book. I'll check out the European manuals as soon as we know the full structure."

"Let me know?" Kate had written out the word "anthranilic" and begun a calligraphic version.

"Of course. Probably won't be until next week, though. I had to promise Millicent a bottle of wine to get her to put off her date with her boyfriend even this long."

"Mr. Toole, is it dangerous?"

"What?"

"Anthranilic acid."

"Like I said, I'm not a doctor. It's not poisonous, if that's what you mean, but it's not vitamins either. Any drug can do you dirt if you're unusually sensitive or allergic to it."

"Thanks," Kate said numbly. "And thanks to Millicent, too."

"No problem," Ian Toole said.

It was a hot, sultry day at Fenway Park when Kate, seated in a box next to Jared, began to bleed to death. Silently, painlessly, thick drops of crimson fell from her nose, landing like tiny artillery bursts on the surface of the beer she was holding, turning the gold to pink.

She squeezed her nose with a napkin, but almost instantly tasted the sticky sweetness flowing down the back of her throat. Jared, unaware of what was happening, sipped at his beer, his attention riveted on the field. Help me. Please, Jared, help me, I'm dying. The words were in her mind, but somehow inaccessible to her voice. Help me, please. Suddenly she felt a warm moistness inside her jeans, and knew that she was bleeding there as well. Help me.

In the box to her right, Winfield Samuels looked her way, smiled emptily as if she weren't even there, and then turned back to the field and genteelly applauded a good play by the shortstop.

The players and the grass, the spectators and the huge green left-field wall—all had a reddish cast. Kate rubbed a hand across one eye and realized she was also bleeding from there.

Giddy with fear, she stood and turned to run. Sitting in the row behind her chatting amiably and smiling as blandly as Jared's father had, were Norton Reese and a man with the overalls and gray hair of Carl Horner but the grotesque face of a monkey.

"I see you're bleeding to death," Reese said pleasantly. "I'm so sorry. Carl, aren't you sorry?"

Jared, please help me. Help me. Help me.

The words faded like an echo into eternity. Kate became aware of a gentle hand on her shoulder.

"Dr. Bennett, are you all right?"

Kate lifted her head and blearily met the eyes of night watchman Walter MacFarlane. She was at a table, alone in the hospital library, surrounded by dozens of books and journals dealing with bleeding disorders, ovarian disease, and pharmacology.

"Oh, yes, Walter," she said, "I'm fine, thank you. Really." Her blouse was uncomfortably damp, and the taste in her mouth most unpleasant.

"Just checking," the man said. "It's getting pretty late. Or should I say early." He tapped a finger on the face of his large gold pocket watch and held it around for her to see.

Twenty after two.

Kate smiled weakly and began gathering her notes together.

"I'll see you to your car if you want, Doctor."

"Thanks, Walter, I'll meet you by the main entrance in five minutes."

She watched as the man shuffled from the library. Then she discarded the notion of calling Jared, knowing that she would just be adding insult to injury by waking him up, and finished packing her briefcase. As she neared the doorway, she glanced out the window. Across the street, the winter night reflected obscenely in its dark glass, stood the Omnicenter.

8

Sunday 16 December

The night was heavy and raw. Crunching through slush that had begun to gel and shielding her face from blowgun darts of sleet, Kate crossed Commercial Street and plowed along Hanover into the North End. Traffic and the weather had made her twenty minutes late, but Bill Zimmermann was not the irritable, impatient type, and she anticipated a quick absolution. Demarsco's, the restaurant they had agreed upon, was a small, family-owned operation where parking was as difficult to find as an unexceptional item on the menu.

Initially, when Kate had called and asked to meet with him, Zimmermann had proposed his office at the Omnicenter. It was, perhaps, among the last structures on earth she felt like entering on that night. Unfortunately if there were a list of such things, Demarsco's, his other suggestion, might also have been on it. Demarsco's was one of her and Jared's favorite spots.

And now Jared was gone.

"A sort of separation, but not a separation," he had called it in the note she had found waiting for her at three o'clock on Saturday morning. He had taken some things and gone to his father's, where he would stay until leaving for business in San Diego on Monday.

"A sort of separation, but not a separation."

There was no lengthy explanation. No apology. Not even any anger. But the hurt and confusion were there in every word. It was as if he had just discovered that his wife was having an affair—an up-and-down, intense, emotionally draining affair—not with another man, but with her job, her career. "Space for both of us to sort out the tensions and pressures on our lives without adding new ones," he had written. "Space for each of us to take a hard look at our priorities."

Kate wondered if, standing in the center of his fine, paneled study, his elegant mistress awaiting him on his black satin sheets, Winfield Samuels, Jr., had raised a glass to toast his victory over Kate and the return of his son and to plan how to make a temporary situation permanent. It was a distressing picture and probably not that far from reality.

However, as distressing to her as the image of a gloating Win Samuels, was the realization that her incongruous emotion, at least at that moment and over the hour or so that followed before sleep took her, was relief. Relief at being spared a confrontation. Relief at being alone to think.

Someone was trying to sabotage her reputation and perhaps her career. Her close friend was lying in a hospital bed bleeding from a disorder that had killed at least two other women—a disorder that had no definite cause, let alone a cure. And now, there was the discovery that she herself had been exposed to contaminated vitamins, that her own body might be a time bomb, waiting to go off—perhaps to bleed, perhaps to die.

Priorities. Why couldn't Jared see their marriage as a blanket on which all the other priorities in their lives could be laid out and dealt with together? Why couldn't he see that their relationship needn't be an endless series of either-ors? Why couldn't he see that she could love him and still have a life of her own?

Demarsco's was on the first floor of a narrow brownstone. There were a dozen tables covered with red-and-white checkered tablecloths and adorned with candle-dripped Chianti bottles—a decor that might have been tacky, but in Demarsco's simply wasn't. Bill Zimmermann, seated at a small table to the rear, rose and waved as she entered. He wore a dark sport jacket over a gray turtleneck and looked to her like a mix of the best of Gary Cooper and Montgomery Clift. A maternal waitress, perhaps the matriarch of the Demarsco clan, took her coat and ushered her to Zimmermann with a look that said she approved of the woman for whom the tall dashing man at the rear table had been waiting.

"They have a wonderful soave," Kate answered, settling into her seat, "but you'll have to drink most of it. I haven't been getting much sleep lately, and when I'm tired, more than one glass of wine is usually enough to cross my eyes."

"I have no such problem, unfortunately," he said, nodding that the ample waitress could fill his earlier order. "Sometimes, I fear that my liver will desert me before my brain even knows I have been drinking. It is one of the curses of being European. I stopped by the hospital earlier to see your friend Mrs. Sandler."

"I know. I was with her just before I came here. She was grateful for your visit. Whatever you said had a markedly reassuring effect." Kate smiled inwardly, remembering the girlish exchange she and Ellen had had regarding the Omnicenter director's uncommon good looks and marital status.

"Maybe I could rent him for a night," Ellen had said, "just to parade past Sandy a time or two."

Zimmermann tapped his fingertips together. "The lab reports show very little change."

"I know," Kate said. "If anything, they're worse. Unless there are several days in a row of improvement, or at least stability, I don't think her hematologist will send her home." She felt a heaviness in her chest as her mind replayed the gruesome scene on Ashburton Five during Beverly Vitale's last minutes. Ellen's counts were not yet down to critical levels, but there were so many unknowns. A sudden, precipitous fall seemed quite possible. The stream of thoughts flowed into the question of whether with Ian Toole's findings, Kate herself should have some clotting measurements done. She discarded the notion almost as quickly as she recognized it.

"I hope as you do that there will be improvement," Zimmermann said. He paused and then scanned the menu. "What will it be for you?" he asked finally.

"I'm not too hungry. How about an antipasto, some garlic bread . . . and a side order of peace of mind?"

Zimmermann's blue-gray eyes, still fixed on the leather-enclosed menu, narrowed a fraction. "That bad?"

Kate chewed at her lower lip and nodded, suddenly very glad she had gone the route of calling him. If, as seemed possible, a confrontation with Redding Pharmaceuticals was to happen, it would be good to have an ally with Bill Zimmermann's composure and assuredness, especially considering the fragility of her own self-confidence.

"In that case, perhaps I had best eat light also." Zimmermann called the waitress over with a microscopic nod and ordered identical meals.

"I want to thank you for coming out on such a grisly night," Kate began. "There have been some new developments in my efforts to make sense out of the three bleeding cases, and I wanted to share them with you."

"Oh?" Zimmermann's expression grew more attentive.

"You know I've had sample after sample of medications from the Omnicenter analyzed at the State Toxicology Lab."

"Yes, of course. But I thought the results had all been unremarkable."

"They were . . . until late Friday afternoon. One of the vitamin samples I had analyzed contained a painkiller called anthranilic acid. The basic chemical structure of the drug is contained in several commercial products—Bymid, from Sampson Pharmaceuticals, and Levonide, from Freeman-Gannett, to name two. However, the form contaminating the vitamins is something new—at least in this country. Ian Toole at the state lab is going to check the European manuals and call me tomorrow."

"Is he sure of the results?"

"He seemed to be. I don't know the man personally, but he has a reputation for thoroughness."

"What do you think happened?"

"Contamination." Kate shrugged that there was no other explanation that made any sense. "Either at Redding Pharmaceuticals or perhaps at one of the suppliers of the vitamin components, although I would suspect that a company as large as Redding can do all the manufacturing themselves."

"Yes. I agree. Do you think this anthranilic acid has caused the bleeding disorders in our three women?"

"Bleeding *and* ovarian disorders," Kate added, "at least ovarian in two of the women. We don't know about Ellen. The answer to your question is I don't know and I certainly hope not."

"Why?"

"Because, Bill, the vitamins that were finally positive for something were mine. Ones you prescribed for me."

Zimmermann paled. The waitress arrived with their antipasto, but he did not so much as glance up at her. "Jesus," he said softly. It was the first time Kate had ever heard him use invective of any kind. "Are you sure this Toole couldn't have made a mistake? You said yourself there were any number of samples that were negative."

"Anything's possible," she said. "I suppose Ian Toole and his spectrophotometer are no more exempt from error than . . . Redding Pharmaceuticals."

"Do you have more of a sample? Can we have the findings rechecked at another lab?"

Kate shook her head. "It was an old prescription. There were only half a dozen left. I think he used them all."

Zimmermann tried picking at his meal but quickly gave up. "I don't mean to sound doubtful about what you are saying, Kate. But you see what's at stake here, don't you?"

"Of course I do. And I understand your skepticism. If I were in your position and the Omnicenter were my baby, I'd want to be sure, too. But Bill, the situation is desperate. Two women have died. My friend is lying up there bleeding, and I have been unknowingly taking a medication that was never prescribed for me. Someone in or around Redding's generic drug department has made an error, and I think we should file a report with the FDA as quickly as possible. I spoke to the head pharmacist at Metro about how one goes about reporting problems with a drug."

"Did you mention the Omnicenter specifically?" Zimmermann asked.

"I may be nervous and frightened about all this, Bill, but I'm neither dumb nor insensitive. No. Everything I asked him was hypothetical."

"Thank you."

"Nonsense. Grandstand plays aren't my style." She smiled. "Despite what the papers and all those angry Red Sox fans think. Any decisions concerning the Omnicenter we make together." Kate nibbled on the edge of a piece of garlic bread and suddenly realized that for the first time since returning home to Jared's note, she had an appetite. Perhaps, after the incredible frustrations of the week past, she was feeling the effects of finally doing something. She passed the basket across to Zimmermann. "Here," she offered, "have a piece of this before it gets cold."

Zimmermann accepted the offering, but deep concern continued to darken his face. "What did the pharmacist tell you?"

"There's an agency called the U.S. Pharmacopia, independent of both the FDA and the drug industry, but in close touch with both. They run a drug-problem reporting program. Fill out a form and send it to them, and they send a copy to the FDA and to the company involved."

"Do you know what happens then?"

"Not really. I assume an investigator from the FDA is assigned to look into matters."

"And the great bureaucratic dragon rears its ugly head."

"What?"

"Have you had many dealings with the FDA? Speed and efficiency are hardly their most important products. No one's fault, really. The FDA has some pretty sharp people—only not nearly enough of them."

"What else can we do?" Absently, Kate rolled a black olive off its lettuce hillock and ate it along with several thin strips of prosciutto. "I need help. As it is, I'm spending every spare moment in the library. I've even asked the National Institutes of Health library to run a computer cross on blood and ovarian disorders. They should be sending me a bibliography tomorrow. I've sent our slides to four other pathologists to see if anyone can make a connection. The FDA seems like the only remaining move."

"The FDA may be a necessary move, but it is hardly our only one. First of all I want to speak with Carl Horner and our pharmacist and see to it that the use of any Redding products by our facility will be suspended until we have some answers."

"Excellent. Will you have to bring in extra pharmacists?"

"Yes, but we've had contingency plans in place in case of some kind of computer failure since . . . well, since even before I took over as director. We'll manage as long as necessary."

"Let's hope it won't be too long," Kate said, again thinking of Beverly Vitale's lifeless, blood-smeared face.

"If we go right to the FDA it might be."

"Pardon?"

"Kate, I think our first move should be to contact Redding Pharmaceuticals directly. I think the company deserves that kind of consideration for the way they've stood up for orphan drugs and for all the other things they've done to help the medical community and society as a whole. Besides, in any contest between the bureaucratic dragon and private industry, my money is on industry every time. I think it's only fair to the Omnicenter and our patients to get to the bottom of matters as quickly as possible."

Kate sipped pensively at her wine. "I see what you mean . . . sort of," she said. "Couldn't we do both? I mean contact Redding and notify the FDA?"

"We could, but then we lose our stick, our prod, if you will. The folks at Redding will probably bend over backward to avoid the black eye of an FDA probe. I know they will. I've had experience with other pharmaceutical houses—ones not as responsive and responsible as Redding. They would go to almost any length to identify and correct problems within their company without outside intervention."

"That makes sense, I guess," she said.

"You sound uncertain, Kate. Listen, whatever we do, we should do together. You said that yourself. I've given you reasons for my point of view, but I'm by no means inflexible." Zimmermann drained the last half of his glass and refilled it.

Kate hesitated and then said, "I have this thing about the pharmaceutical industry. It's a problem in trust. They spend millions and millions of dollars on giveaways to medical students and physicians. They support dozens upon dozens of throwaway journals and magazines with their ads. I get fifty publications a month I never ordered. And I don't even write prescriptions. I can imagine how many you get." Zimmermann nodded that he understood. "In addition, I have serious questions about their priorities—you know, who comes first in any conflict between profit and people."

"What do you mean?"

"Well, look at Valium. Roche introduces the drug and markets it well, and the public literally eats it up. It's a tranquilizer, a downer, yet in no time at all it becomes the most prescribed and taken drug in the country. Unfortunately, it turns out to be more addicting than most physicians appreciated at first, and lives begin to get ruined. Meanwhile, a dozen or so other drug houses put out a dozen or so versions of Valium, each with its own name and its own claim. Slower acting. Faster acting. Lasts all night. Removed more rapidly. Some busy physicians get so lost in the advertising and promises that they actually end up prescribing two of these variants to the same patient at the same time. Others think they're doing their patients a big favor by switching. Some favor."

"Pardon me for saying it, Kate, but you sound a little less than objective."

"I'm afraid you hear right," she said. "I had some emotional stresses back in college, and the old country doctor who served the school put me on Valium. It took a whole team of specialists to realize how much my life came to revolve around those little yellow discs. Finally, I had to be hospitalized and detoxed. So I just have this nagging feeling that the drug companies can't be trusted. That's all."

Zimmermann leaned back, rubbed his chin, and sighed. "I don't know what to say. If speed is essential in solving this problem, as we both think it is, then the route to go is the company. I'm sure of that." He paused. "Tell you what. Let's give them this coming week to straighten out matters to our satisfaction. If they haven't done so by Friday, we call in the FDA. Sound fair?"

Kate hesitated, but then nodded. "Yes," she said finally. "It sounds fair and it sounds right. Do you want to call them?"

Zimmermann shrugged. "Sure," he said, "I'll do it first thing tomorrow. They'll probably be contacting you by the end of the day."

"The sooner the better. Meanwhile, do you think you could talk to some of your Omnicenter patients and get me a list of women who would be willing to be contacted by me about having their medications analyzed?"

"I certainly can try."

"Excellent. It's about time things started moving in a positive direction. You know, there's not much good I can say about all that's been happening, except that I'm glad our relationship has moved out of the doctor-patient and doctor-doctor cubbyholes into the person-person. Right now I'm the one who needs the help, but please know that if it's ever you, you've got a friend you can count on."

Zimmermann smiled a Cary Grant smile. "That kind of friend is hard to come by," he said. "Thank you."

"Thank you. Except for Tom Engleson, I've felt pretty much alone in all this. Now we're a team." She motioned the waitress over.

"Coffee?" the woman asked.

"None for me, thanks. Bill?" Zimmermann shook his head. "In that case could I have the check, please?"

"Nonsense," Zimmermann said, "I won't . . ."—the reproving look in Kate's eyes stopped him in mid-sentence—". . . allow you to do this too many times without reciprocating."

Kate beamed at the man's insight. "Deal," she said, smiling broadly.

"Deal," Zimmermann echoed.

The two shook hands warmly and, after Kate had settled their bill, walked together into the winter night.

Numb with exhaustion, John Ferguson squinted at the luminescent green print on the screen of his word processor. His back ached from hunching over the keyboard for the better part of two full days. His hands, feeling the effects of his disease more acutely than at any time in months, groped for words one careful letter at a time. It had been an agonizing effort, condensing forty years of complex research into thirty pages or so of scholarly dissertation, but a sentence at a time, a word at a time, he was making progress.

To one side of his desk were a dozen internationally read medical journals. Ferguson had given thought to submitting his completed manuscript to all of them, but then had reconsidered. The honor of publishing his work would go only to *The New England Journal of Medicine*, most prestigious and widely read of them all.

The New England Journal of Medicine. Ferguson tapped out a recall code, and in seconds, the title page of his article was displayed on the screen.

STUDIES IN ESTRONATE 250
A Synthetic Estrogen Congener and
Antifertility Hormone
John N. Ferguson, MD

It would almost certainly be the first time in the long, distinguished publication of the journal that an entire issue would be devoted to a single article. But they would agree to do that or find the historic studies and comment in *Lancet* or *The American Journal of Medicine*. Ferguson smiled. Once *The New England Journal*'s editors had reviewed his data and his slides, he doubted there would be much resistance to honoring his request. For a time he studied the page. Then, electronically, he erased the name of the author. There might be trouble for him down the road for what he was about to do, but he suspected not. He was too old and too sick even for the fanatic Simon Weisenthal to bother with.

With a deliberateness that helped him savor the act, he typed Wilhelm W. Becker, MD, PhD where Ferguson's name had been. Perhaps, he thought with a smile, some sort of brief funeral was in order for Ferguson. He had, after all, died twice—once in Bataan, forty years ago, and a second time this night.

With the consummate discipline that had marked his life, Willi Becker cut short the pleasurable interlude and advanced the text to the spot at which he had left off. Because of a pathologist named Bennett, Cyrus Redding had picked up the scent of his work at the Omnicenter. Knowing the man as well as Becker did, he felt certain the tycoon would now track the matter relentlessly. There was still time to put the work on paper and mail it off, but no way of knowing how much. He had to push. He had to fight the fatigue and the aching in his muscles and push, at least for another hour or two. The onset of his scientific immortality was at hand.

Furtively, he glanced at the small bottle of amphetamines on the table. It had been only three hours. Much too soon, especially with the irregular heartbeats he had been having. Still, he needed to push. It would only be a few more days, perhaps less. Barely able to grip the top of the small vial, Becker set one of the black, coated tablets on his tongue, and swallowed it without water. In minutes, the warm rush would begin, and he would have the drive, however artificial and short lived, to overcome the inertia of his myasthenia.

"You really shouldn't take those, you know, father. Especially with your cardiac history."

Becker spun around to face his son, cursing the diminution in his hearing that enabled such surprises. "I take them because I need them," he said sharply. "What are you doing sneaking up on me like that? What do you think doorbells are for?"

"Such a greeting. And here I have driven out of my way to stop by and be certain you are all right."

Three blocks, Becker thought. Some hardship. "You startled me. That's all. I'm sorry for reacting the way I did."

"In that case, father, it is I who should be sorry."

Was there sarcasm in his son's voice? It bothered Becker that he had never been able to read the man. Theirs was a relationship based on filial obligation and respect, but little if any love. For the greater portion of his son's years, they had lived apart: Becker in a small cottage on the hospital grounds where he worked, and his wife and son in an apartment twenty miles away. It was as necessary an arrangement as it was painful. Becker and his wife had tried for years to make their son understand that.

There were those, they tried to explain, who would arrest Becker in a moment on a series of unjust charges, put him in prison, and possibly even put him to death. In the hysteria following the war, he had been marked simply because he was German, nothing more than that. For their own safety, it was necessary for the boy and his mother to keep their address and even their name separate from his. Although Becker would provide for them and would visit as much as he could, no one would ever know his true relationship to the woman, Anna Zimmermann, and the boy, William.

"So," Becker said. "Now that we have apologized profusely to one another, come in, sit down, pour yourself a drink."

William Zimmermann nodded his thanks, poured an inch of Wild Turkey into a heavy glass, and settled into an easy chair opposite his father.

"I see you've started putting your data together," he said. "Why now?"

"Well, I . . . no special reason, really. It would seem that the modifications I made have greatly, if not completely, eliminated the bleeding problems we were experiencing with the Estronate. So what else is there to wait for?"

"Which journal will you approach?"

"I think *The New England Journal of Medicine*. I plan to submit the data and discussion but to withhold several key steps in the synthesis until a commission of the journal's choosing can take charge of my formulas and decide how society can best benefit from them."

"Sounds fine to me," Zimmermann said. "With all that's been happening this last week, the sooner I see the last of Estronate Two-fifty, the better."

"Have any further bleeding cases turned up?"

Zimmermann shook his head. "Just the Sandler woman I told you about. The one who's the friend of Dr. Bennett's. She was treated over eighteen months ago, in the July/August group, the last group to receive the unmodified Estronate."

"How is she doing?"

"I think she is going to end up like the other two."

"Couldn't you find some way of suggesting that they try a course of massive doses of delta amino caproic acid and nicotinic acid on her?"

"Not without risking a lot of questions I'd rather not answer. I mean I am a gynecologist, not a hematologist. Besides, you told me that that therapy was only sixty percent effective in such advanced states."

Becker shrugged. "Sixty percent is sixty percent."

"And my career is my career. No, father, I have far too much to lose. I am afraid Mrs. Sandler will just have to make it on her own."

"Perhaps you are right," Becker said.

The men shook hands formally, and William Zimmermann let himself out. Twelve miles away, on the fourth floor of the Berenson Building of Metropolitan Hospital of Boston, in Room 421, Ellen Sandler's nose had again begun to bleed.

9

Monday 17 December

"Now, Suzy, promise Daddy that you will mind what Mommy tells you and that you will never, never do that to the cat again. . . . Good. . . . I have to go now, sugar. You better get ready for your piano lesson. . . .I know what I said, but my work here isn't done yet, and I have to stay until it's finished. . . . I don't know. Two, maybe three more days. . . . Suzy, stop that. You're not a baby. I love you very much and I'll see you very soon. Now, tell Daddy you love him and go practice that new piece of yours. . . . Suzy? . . ."

"Damn." Arlen Paquette slammed the receiver down. He had protested to Redding the futility of remaining in Boston over the weekend, but the man had insisted he stay close to the situation and the Omnicenter. As usual, events had proven Redding right. Paquette stuffed some notes in his briefcase and pulled on his suitcoat. Right for Redding Pharmaceuticals, but not for Suzy Paquette, who was justifiably smarting over her father's absence from her school track meet earlier in the day. How could he explain to a seven-year-old that the very thing that was keeping him away from home was also the sole reason she could attend a school like Hightower Academy? He straightened his tie and combed his thinning hair with his fingers. How could he explain it to her when he was having trouble justifying it to himself? Still, for what he and his family were gaining from his association with Redding, the dues were not excessive. He glanced down at the photographs of Kate Bennett piled on the coffee table. At least, he thought, not yet.

The cab ride from the Ritz to Metropolitan Hospital took fifteen minutes. Paquette entered the main lobby through newly installed gliding electronic doors and headed directly for Norton Reese's office, half expecting to have the woman whose life and face he had studied in such detail stroll out from a side corridor and bump into him.

"Arlen, it's good to see you. You're looking well." Norton Reese maneuvered free of his desk chair and met Paquette halfway with an ill-defined handshake. Theirs was more an unspoken truce than a relationship, and no amount of time would compensate for the lack of trust and respect each bore the other. However, Paquette was the envoy of Cyrus Redding and the several millions of Redding dollars that had sparked Reese's rise to prominence. Although it was Reese's court, it was the younger man's ball.

"You're looking fit yourself, Norton," Paquette replied. "Our mutual friend sends his respects and regards."

"Did you tell him about our speed freak outfielder and the letters to the press and TV?"

"I did. I even sent a packet of the articles and editorials to him by messenger. He commends your ingenuity. So, incidentally, do I." Try as he might, he could put no emotion behind the compliment.

Still, Reese's moon face bunched in a grin. "It's been beautiful, Arlen," he gushed. "Just beautiful. I tell you, ever since that story broke, Kathryn Bennett, MD, has been racing all over trying to stick her fingers in the holes that are popping open in her reputation. By now I doubt if she would know whether she had lost a horse or found a rope."

"You did fine, Norton. Just fine. Only, for our purposes, not enough."

"What?" Reese began to shift uneasily. "A diversion. That's what Horner asked me for, and by God, that's what I laid on that woman. A goddamn avalanche of diversion."

"You did fine, Norton. I just told you that."

"Why, she's had so much negative publicity it's a wonder she hasn't quit or been fired by the medical school." Reese chattered on as if he hadn't heard a word. "In fact, I hear the Medical School Ethics Committee is planning some kind of an inquiry."

Paquette silenced him with raised hands. "Easy, Norton, please," he said evenly. "I'm going to say it one more time. What you did, the letter and all, was exactly what we asked of you. Our mutual friend is pleased. He asked that I convey to you the Ashburton Foundation's intention to endow the cardiac surgical residency you wrote him about."

"Well, then, why was what I did not enough?" Reese realized that in his haste to defend himself, he had forgotten to acknowledge Redding's generosity. Before he could remedy the oversight, Paquette spoke.

"I'll convey your thanks when I return to Darlington," he said, a note of irritation in his words. "Norton, do you know what has been going on here?"

"Not . . . not exactly," he said, nonplussed.

Paquette nodded indulgently. "Dr. Bennett, in her search to identify the cause of an unusual bleeding problem in several women, has zeroed in on the Omnicenter. Although the women were Omnicenter patients, we see no other connection among them."

"The . . . the work you're doing . . . I mean none of the women got . . ." After years of scrupulously avoiding the Omnicenter and the people involved in its operation, Reese was uncertain of how, even, to discuss the place.

Paquette spared him further stammering. "From time to time, each of the women was involved in the evaluation of one or more products," he said. "However, Carl Horner assures me that there have been no products common to the three of them. Whatever the cause of their problem, it is not the Omnicenter."

"That's a relief," Reese said.

"Not really," Paquette said, his expression belying his impatience. "You see, our Dr. Bennett has been most persistent, despite the pressures brought about by your letter."

"She's a royal pain in the ass. I'll grant you that," Reese interjected.

"She has tested several Omnicenter products at the State Toxicology Lab, charging the analyses, I might add, to your hospital."

"Damn her. She didn't find anything, did she? Horner assured me that there was nothing to worry about."

Paquette's patience continued to fray. "Of course she found something, Norton. That's why I'm here. She even had Dr. Zimmermann phone the company to tell us about it."

"Oh. Sorry."

"Our friend in Kentucky has asked that we step up our efforts to discredit Dr. Bennett and to add, what was the word you used? distraction? . . . no, diversion, that was it—diversion to her life. We have taken steps to obscure, if not neutralize, her findings to date, but there is evidence in dozens of medicine cabinets out there of what we have been doing. If Dr. Bennett is persistent enough, she will find it. I am completely convinced of that, and so is our friend. Dr. Bennett has given us one week to determine how a certain experimental painkiller came to be in a set of vitamins dispensed at the Omnicenter. If we do not furnish her with a satisfactory explanation by that time, she intends to file a report with the US Pharmacopeia and the FDA."

"Damn her," Norton Reese said again. "What are we going to do?"

"Not we, you. Dr. Bennett's credibility must be reduced to the point where no amount of evidence will be enough for authorities to take her word over ours. The letter you wrote was a start, but, as I said, not enough."

Once again, Reese began to feel ill at ease. Paquette was not making a request, he was giving an order—an order from the man who, Reese knew, could squash him with nothing more than the eraser on his pencil. He unbuttoned his vest against the uncomfortable moistness between the folds of his skin.

"Look," he pleaded, "I really don't know what I can do. I'll try, but I don't know. You've got to understand, Arlen; you've got to make him understand. Bennett works in my hospital, but she doesn't work for me." There was understanding in Paquette's face, but not sympathy. Reese continued his increasingly nervous rambling. "Besides, the woman's got friends around here. I don't know why, but she does. Even after that letter, she's got supporters. Shit, I'd kill to make sure she didn't. . . ." His voice trailed away. His eyes narrowed.

Paquette followed the man's train of thought. "The answer is no, Norton," he said. "Absolutely not. We wish her discredited, not eliminated, for God's sake. We want people to lose interest in her, not to canonize her. She has already involved Dr. Zimmermann, a chemist at the state lab, and a resident here named Engleson. There may be others, but as far as we can tell, the situation is not yet out of control. We are doing what we can do to ensure it remains that way. Dr. Bennett's father-in-law does some business with our company. I believe our friend has already called him and enlisted his aid. There are other steps being taken as well." He rose and reached across the desk to shake Reese's hand. "I know we can count on you. If you need advice or a sounding board, you can reach me at the Ritz."

"Thank you," Reese said numbly. His bulk seemed melted into his chair.

Paquette walked slowly to the door, then turned. "Our friend has suggested Thursday as a time by which he wants something to have been done."

"Thursday?" Reese croaked.

Paquette nodded, smiled blankly, and was gone.

Half an hour later, his shirt changed and his composure nearly regained, Reese sat opposite Sheila Pierce, straightening one paper clip after another and thinking much more than he wanted to at that particular moment of the chief technician's breasts.

"How're things going down there in pathology?" he asked, wondering if she would take off her lab coat and then reminding himself to concentrate on business. The woman was going to require delicate handling if she was going to put her neck on the line to save his ass.

"You mean with Bennett?" Sheila shrugged. "She's getting some letters and a few crank phone calls every day, but otherwise things seem pretty much back to normal. It's been . . . amusing."

"Well," Reese said, "I know for a fact that the Bobby Geary business is hardly a dead issue."

"Oh?"

"I've heard the matter's going to the Medical School Ethics Committee."

"Good," Sheila said. "That will serve her right, going to the newspapers about that poor boy the way she did." They laughed. "Do you think," she went on, "that it will be enough to keep her from becoming chief of our department?"

Inwardly, Reese smiled. The question was just the opening he needed. "Doubtful," he said grimly. "Very doubtful."

"Too bad."

"You don't know the half of it."

"What do you mean?"

"Well . . ." He tapped a pencil eraser on his desk. He closed his eyes and massaged the bridge of his nose. He chewed at his lower lip. "I got a call this morning from Dr. Willoughby. He requested a meeting with the finance and budget committee of the board, at which time he and

Kate Bennett are going to present the results of a computer study she's just completed. They plan to ask for six months worth of emergency funding until a sweeping departmental reorganization can be completed."

Sheila Pierce paled. "Sweeping departmental reorganization?"

"That's what the man said."

"Did he say anything about . . . you know."

Reese sighed. "As a matter of fact, baby, he did. He said that by the time of the meeting next week, Bennett will have presented him with a complete list of lost revenues, including the misappropriation of funds by several department members."

"But she promised."

"I guess a few brownie points with the boss and the board of trustees outweigh her promise to a plain old technician."

"*Chief* technician," she corrected. "Damn her. Did it seem as if she had already said something about me to Willoughby?"

The bait taken, Reese set the hook. "Definitely not. I probed as much as I could about you without making Willoughby suspicious. She hasn't told him anything specific . . . yet."

"Norty, we've got to stop her. I can't afford to lose my job. Dammit, I've been here longer than she has. Much longer." Her hands were clenched white, her jaw set in anger and frustration.

"Well," Reese said with exaggerated reason, "we've got two days, three at the most. Any ideas?"

"Ideas?"

"I don't work with the woman, baby, you do. Doesn't she ever fuck up? Blow a case? Christ, the rest of the MD's in this place do it all the time."

"She's a pathologist, Norty. Her cases are all dead to begin with. There's nothing for her to blow except . . ." She stopped in midsentence and pulled a typed sheet from her lab coat pocket.

"What is it?"

"It's the surgical path schedule for tomorrow. Bennett and Dr. Huang are doing frozen sections this month." She scanned the entries.

"Well?"

Sheila hesitated, uncertainty darkening her eyes. "Are you sure she's going to report me to Willoughby?"

"Baby, all I can say is that Dr. Willoughby asked me for a copy of the union contract, expressly for the part dealing with justifiable causes for termination."

"She has no right to do that to me after she promised not to."

"You know about people with MD degrees, Sheila. They think they're better and smarter than the rest of us. They think they can just walk all over people." Sheila's eyes told him that the battle—this phase of it at any rate—was won.

"We'll see who's smarter," she muttered, tapping the schedule thoughtfully. "Maybe it's time Bennett found out that there are a few people with brains around who couldn't go to medical school."

"Make it good, baby," Reese urged, "because if she's in, you're out."

"No way," she said. "There's no way I'm going to let that happen. Here, look at this."

"What?"

"Well, you can see it's a pretty busy schedule. There's a lung biopsy, a thyroid biopsy, a colon, and two breast biopsies. Bennett will be working almost all day in the small cryostat lab next to the operating rooms. Usually, she goes into the OR, picks up a specimen, freezes it in the cryostat, sections it, stains it, and reads it, all without leaving the surgical suite."

"And?"

"Well, there are a lot of ifs," Sheila said in an even, almost singsong voice. "But if we could disable the surgical cryostat and force Bennett to use the backup unit down in the histology lab, I might be able somehow to switch a specimen. All I would need is about three or four minutes."

"What would that do?"

Sheila smiled the smile of a child. "Well, with any luck, depending on the actual pathology, we can have the great Dr. Bennett read a benign condition as a malignancy. Then, when the whole specimen is taken and examined the next day, her mistake will become apparent."

"Would a pathologist make a mistake like that?" Reese asked.

Again Sheila smiled. "Only once," she said serenely. "Only once."

Louisburg Square, a score of tall, brick townhouses surrounding a raggedy, wrought-iron-fenced green on the west side of Beacon Hill, had been *the* address in Boston for generations. Levi Morton lived there after his four years as vice president under Benjamin Harrison. Jennie Lind was married there in 1852. Cabots and Saltonstalls, Lodges and Alcotts—all had drawn from and given to the mystique of Louisburg Square.

Kate had the cab drop her off at the foot of Mount Vernon Street; she used the steep two-block walk to Louisburg Square to stretch her legs and clear her thoughts of what had been a long and trying day at the hospital. Two committee meetings, several surgical specimens, and a lecture at the medical school, combined with half a dozen malicious phone calls and an equal number of hate letters, all relating to her callous treatment of Bobby Geary and his family.

Ellen's nose had begun bleeding again—just a slow trickle from one nostril, but enough to require Pete Colangelo to recauterize it. Her clotting parameters were continuing to take a significant drop each day, and the unencouraging news was beginning to take a toll on her spirit. Late that afternoon, the National Institutes of Health library computer search had arrived. There were many articles listed in the bibliography dealing with sclerosing diseases of the ovaries, and a goodly number on clotting disorders similar to the Boston cases. There were none, however, describing their coexistence in a single patient. Expecting little, Kate had begun the tedious process of locating each article, photocopying it, and finally studying it. The project would take days to complete, if not longer, but there was a chance at least that something, anything, might turn up that could help Ellen.

At the turnoff from Mount Vernon Street, Kate propped herself against a gaslight lamp post and through the mist of her own breath, reflected on the marvelous Christmas card that was Louisburg Square. Single, orange-bulbed candles glowed from nearly every townhouse window. Tasteful wreaths marked each door. Christmas trees had been carefully placed to augment the scene without intruding on it.

Having, season after season, observed the stolid elegance of Louisburg Square, Kate had no difficulty understanding why, shortly after the death of his agrarian wife, Winfield Samuels had sold their gentleman's farm and stables in Sudbury and had bought there. The two—the address and the man—were made for one another. Somewhat reluctantly, she mounted the granite steps of her father-in-law's home, eschewed the enormous brass knocker, and pressed the bell.

In seconds, the door was opened by a trim, extremely attractive brunette, no more than two or three years Kate's senior. Dressed in a gold blouse and dark straight skirt, she looked every bit the part of the executive secretary, which, in fact, she had at one time been.

"Kate, welcome," she said warmly. "Come in. Let me take your coat."

"I've got it, thanks. You look terrific, Jocelyn. Is that a new hairstyle?"

"A few months old. Thanks for noticing. You're looking well yourself."

Kate wondered if perhaps she and Jocelyn Trent could

collaborate on a chapter for Amy Vanderbilt or Emily Post: "Proper Conversation Between a Daughter-in-law and her Father-in-law's Mistress When the Father-in-law in Question Refuses to Acknowledge the Woman as Anything Other Than a Housekeeper."

"Mr. Samuels will be down in a few minutes," Jocelyn said. "There's a nice fire going in the study. He'll meet you there. Dinner will be in half an hour. Can I fix you a drink?"

Mr. Samuels. The inappropriate formality made Kate queasy. At seven o'clock, the woman would serve to Mr. Samuels and his guest the gourmet dinner she had prepared; then she would go and eat in the kitchen. At eleven or twelve o'clock, after the house was quiet and dark, she would slip into his room and stay as long as she was asked, always careful to return to her own quarters before any houseguest awoke. Mr. Samuels, indeed.

"Sure," said Kate, following the woman to the study. "Better make it something stiff. As you can tell from your houseguest the last few days, things have not been going too well in my world."

Jocelyn smiled understandingly. "For what it's worth," she said, "I don't think Jared is very pleased with the arrangement either."

"I appreciate hearing that, Jocelyn. Thank you. I'll tell you, on any given Sunday in any given ballpark, marriage can trounce any team in the league." When she could detach the woman from her position, Kate liked her very much and enjoyed the occasional one-to-one conversations they were able to share.

"I know," Jocelyn said. "I tried it once, myself. For me it was all of the responsibility, none of the pleasure."

The words were said lightly, but Kate heard in them perhaps an explanation of sorts, a plea for understanding and acceptance. Better to be owned than to be used.

Kate took the bourbon and water and watched as Jocelyn Trent returned to the kitchen. The woman had, she knew, a wardrobe several times the size of her own, a remarkable silver fox coat, and a stylish Alfa coupé. If this be slavery, she thought with a smile, then give me slavery.

It was, as promised, several minutes before Winfield Samuels made his entrance. Kate waited by the deep, well-used fireplace, rearranging the fringe on the Persian rug with the toe of her shoe and trying to avoid eye contact with any of the big-game heads mounted on the wall. Samuels had sent Jared away on business—purposely, he made it sound—so that he and Kate could spend some time alone together talking over "issues of mutual concern." Before her marriage, they had met on several occasions for such talks, but since, their time together had always included Jared. Samuels had given no hint over the phone as to what the "issues" this time might be, but the separation—causes and cures—was sure to be high on the list. Kate was reading a citation of commendation and gratitude from the governor when the recipient entered the room.

"Kate, welcome," Win Samuels said. "I'm so glad you could make it on such short notice." They embraced with hands on shoulders and exchanged air kisses. "Sit down, please. We have," he consulted his watch, "twenty-three minutes before dinner."

Twenty-three minutes. Kate had to hand it to the man. Dinner at seven did not mean dinner at seven-oh-three. It was expected that the stunning cook cum housekeeper cum mistress would be right on time. "Thank you," she said. "It's good to see you again. You look great." The compliment was not exaggeration. In his twill smoking jacket and white silk scarf, Samuels looked like most men nearing seventy could only dream of looking.

"Rejuvenate that drink?" Samuels asked, motioning her to one of a pair of matched leather easy chairs by the hearth.

"Only if you're prepared to resuscitate me."

Samuels laughed and drew himself a bourbon and soda. "You're quite a woman, Kate," he said, settling in across from her. "Jared is lucky to have nabbed you."

"Actually, I did most of the nabbing."

"This . . . this little disagreement you two are having. It will blow over before you know it. Probably has already."

"The empty half of my bed wouldn't attest to that," Kate said.

Samuels slid a cigar from a humidor by his chair, considered it for a moment, and then returned it. "Bad for the taste buds this close to dinner, particularly with Jocelyn's duck à l'orange on the menu."

"She's a very nice woman," Kate ventured.

Samuels nodded. "Does a good job around here," he said in an absurdly businesslike tone. "Damn good job." He paused. "I'm a direct man, Kate. Some people say too direct, but I don't give a tinker's damn about them. Suppose I get right to the business at hand."

"You mean this wasn't just a social invitation?"

Samuels was leaping to equivocate when he saw the smile in her eyes and at the corners of her mouth. "Do you zing Jared like this, too?" he asked. Kate smiled proudly and nodded.

They laughed, but Kate felt no letup in the tension between them.

"Kate," he continued, "I've accomplished the things I've accomplished, gained the things I've gained, because I was brought up to believe that we are never given a wish or a dream without also being given the wherewithal to make that dream, that wish, a reality. Do you share that belief?"

Kate shrugged. "I believe there are times when it's okay to wish and try and fail."

"Perhaps," he said thoughtfully. "Perhaps there are. Anyhow, at this stage in my life, I have two overriding dreams. Both of them involve my son and, therefore, by extension, you."

"Go on."

"Kate, I want a grandchild, hopefully more than one, and I want my son to serve in the United States Congress.

Those are my dreams, and I am willing to do anything within my power to help them come to pass."

"Why?" Kate asked.

"Why?"

"Yes. I understand the grandchild wish. Continuation of the family, stability for Jared's home life, new blood and new energy, that sort of thing, but why the other one?"

"Because I feel Jared would be a credit to himself, to the state, and to the country."

"So do I."

"And I think it would be a fulfilling experience for him."

"Perhaps."

Samuels hesitated before adding, "And, finally, it is a goal I held for myself and never could achieve. Do you think me horrid for wanting my son to have what I could not?"

"No," Kate responded. "Provided it is something Jared wants, too, for reasons independent of yours."

"The time in life when a father no longer knows what is best for his son is certainly moot, isn't it?"

"Win, what you want for Jared, what you want for me, too, will always matter. But the hardest part about loving someone is letting him figure out what's best for himself, especially when you already know—or at least think you know."

"And you think I'm forcing my will on Jared?"

"You have a tremendous amount of influence on him," she replied. "I don't think I'm giving away any great secrets by saying that."

Samuels nodded thoughtfully. "Kate," he said finally, "humor this old man and let me change the subject a bit, okay?"

Old man. Give me a break, counselor, she wanted to snap. Instead she sat forward, smiled, and simply said, "Sure."

"Why do you want to be the chief of pathology at Metro?"

Kate met his gaze levelly and said silent thanks for the hours she had spent answering that question for herself. "Because it would be a fascinating experience. Because I think I could do a credible job. Because my work—and my department—mean a great deal to me. Because I feel a person either grows or dies."

"Jared tells me you feel accepting the position will delay your being able to start your family for at least two years."

"Actually, I said one or two years, but two seems a reasonable guess."

Samuels rose slowly and walked to the window and then back to the fire. If he was preparing to say something dramatic, she acknowledged, he was doing a laudable job of setting it up.

"Kate," he said, still staring at the fire, "when I phoned, I invited you to stay the night if you could. Are you going to be able to do that?"

"I had planned on it, yes." Actually, the invitation had been worded in a way that would have made it nearly impossible for her to refuse.

"Good. I'd like to take you for a ride after dinner. A ride and a visit. I . . . I know I sound mysterious, but for the moment you'll have to indulge me. This is something I never thought I would be doing."

There was a huskiness, an emotion to the man's voice that Kate had never heard before. Was he near crying? For half a minute there was silence, save for the low hiss of the fire. But when her father-in-law turned to her, his composure had returned.

"Kate," he said, as if the moment by the fire had never happened, "do you think that you are ready to handle the responsibilities of a whole department?"

She thought for a moment. "This may sound funny, but in a way it doesn't matter what I think. You see, Dr. Willoughby, the only person who knows both me and the job, thinks I can handle it. It's like becoming a doctor—or, for that matter, a lawyer. You only decide you *want* to do it. They—the bar or the medical examiners—decide whether or not you can and should. From then on, your only obligation is to do your best." She paused. "Does that sound smug?"

"Not really."

"I hope not, Win. Because actually I'm scared stiff about a lot of things. I'm frightened of taking the job and I'm frightened of not taking it. I'm frightened of having children and I'm frightened of not having them. And most of all, I am frightened of having to face the dilemma of either losing my husband or losing myself."

"There *are* other possibilities," Samuels said.

"I know that, but I'm not sure Jared does, and to be perfectly honest, until this moment, I wasn't sure you did, either."

"There are *always* other possibilities," he said with a tone that suggested he had voiced that belief before. "Kate, you know hospital politics are no different from any other kind of politics. There's power involved and there's money involved, and that means there are things like this handbill involved."

He took the garish orange flyer from his desk drawer and held it up for her to see. Kate shuddered at the sight of it. "Do you think that brilliant effort was aimed at me or at Jared?" she asked.

"The truth is it makes no difference. Politics is politics. The minute you start playing the game you have enemies. If they happen to be better at the game than you are, you get buried. It's that simple." He held up the flyer again. "My sense of this whole business—assuming, of course, that you didn't send Bobby Geary's autopsy report to the papers—is that someone is determined to keep you from becoming head of your department. If they have any kind of power, or access to power, your department could suffer dearly."

"My department?"

"Certainly. Your people end up overworked because of staffing cutbacks and outmoded equipment. Turnover is high, morale low. Quality of work drops. Sooner or later there's a mistake. You may be the best pathologist in the world, Kate, and the best-intentioned administrator, but unless you play the politics game and get past the competition to people like the Ashburton Foundation, you will end up an unhappy, harried, unfulfilled failure. And take it from me, winning that game means plenty of sacrifice. It means that if you know the competition is getting up at six, you damn well better be up at five-thirty."

"I appreciate your thoughts," she said. "I really do. All I can say is that the final decision hasn't been made yet, and that I was hoping to work the whole thing out with Jared."

"But you have okayed submission of your name."

"Yes," she said, averting her gaze for the first time. "Yes, I have." Samuels turned and walked again toward the window. For a time, there was only the fire. "Say, Win," she said, hoping to lead them in other directions, "how much do you know about the Ashburton Foundation?"

He turned back to her. "I really don't know anything. In the early days of their involvement here, my firm handled some of their correspondence with the hospital. But I haven't dealt with them in years. Why?"

"Just some research I've been doing at work. Nothing, really. Do you by any chance have their address?"

"I don't know," Samuels said, somewhat distractedly. "In the Rolodex over there on my desk, perhaps. I really don't know. Kate, you know it is my way to reason, not to beg. But for the sake of my son and myself, if not for yourself, I'm begging you to put the chairmanship on the back burner and devote yourself for a few years to your family and to helping Jared get his foot in the political door."

At that instant, a chime sounded from the kitchen. Kate glanced instinctively at her watch, but she knew that it was exactly seven o'clock. She rose. "When is Jared due back?" she asked.

"Wednesday or Thursday, I suspect."

"Win, I have no response to what you just asked. You know that, don't you?"

"Perhaps before too much longer you might. Let us eat. After our meal, there is a trip we must take."

With a faint smile, Samuels nodded Kate toward the dining room and then took her elbow and guided her through the door.

The IV nurse, a square-shouldered woman overweight by at least thirty pounds, rubbed alcohol on the back of Ellen Sandler's left hand, slapped the area a dozen times, and then swabbed it again.

"Now, Ellen," she said in the patronizing, demeaning tone Ellen had come to label *hospitalese*, "you've got to relax. Your veins are in spasm. If you don't relax, it will take all night for me to get this IV in."

Relax? Ellen glared at the woman, who was hunched over her hand. *Can't you tell I'm frightened? Can't you see I'm scared out of my wits by all that's happening to me? Take a minute, just a minute, and talk to me. Ask me, and I'll try to explain. I'll tell you how it feels to be seven years old and to learn that your father, who entered the hospital for a "little operation," has been taken to a funeral home in a long box with handles. Relax? Why not ask me to float off this bed? Or better still, just demand that I make the blood in my body start clotting, so you'll be spared the inconvenience of having to plunge that needle into the back of my hand. Relax?* "I . . . I'm trying," she said meekly.

"Good. Now you're going to feel a little stick."

Ellen grabbed the bedrail with her free hand as electric pain from the "little stick" shot up her arm.

"Got it," the nurse said excitedly. "Now don't move. Don't move until I get it taped down, okay? You know," she continued as she taped the plastic catheter in place, "you've got the toughest veins I've seen in a long time."

Ellen didn't answer. Instead, she stared at the ceiling,

tasting the salt of the tears running over her cheeks and into the corners of her mouth, and wondering where it was all going to end. Apparently, blood had begun appearing in her bowel movements. The intravenous line was, according to the resident who announced she was going to have it, merely a precaution. He had neglected to tell her what it was a precaution against.

"Okay, Ellen, we're all set," the nurse announced, stepping back to admire her handiwork. "Just don't use that hand too much. All right?"

Ellen pushed the tears off her cheeks with the back of her right hand. "Sure," she said.

The woman managed an uncomfortable smile and backed from the room.

It isn't fair. With no little disgust, Ellen examined the IV dripping saline into her hand. Then she shut off the overhead light and lay in the semidarkness, listening to the sighs of her own breathing and the still alien sounds of the hospital at night. *It isn't fair*. Over and over her mind repeated the impotent protest until she was forced to laugh at it in spite of herself.

Betsy, Eve, Darcy, Sandy, the business, her health. Why had she never appreciated how fragile it all was? Had she taken too much for granted? asked too few questions? Dammit, there were no answers, anyhow. What else could she do? What else could anyone do? Here she was, almost forty, lying in a hospital bed, possibly bleeding to death, with no real sense of why she had been alive, let alone why she should have been singled out to die. It just wasn't fair.

A soft tap from the doorway intruded on her painful reverie. Standing there, silhouetted by the light from the hall, was Sandy. He was holding his uniform hat in one hand and a huge bouquet in the other.

"Permission to come aboard," he said.

Ellen could feel, more than see or hear, his discomfiture. "Come on in," she said.

"Want the light on?"

"I don't think so. On second thought, I'd like to see the flowers."

Sandy flipped on the light and brought them to her. Then he bent over and kissed her on the forehead. Ellen stiffened for an instant and then relaxed to his gentle hug.

"How're you doing?" he asked.

"On which level?"

"Any."

"The flowers are beautiful. Thank you. If you set them over by the sink, I'll have the nurse get a vase for them later on."

"Not so great, huh." He did as she asked with the bouquet, then pulled a green vinyl chair to the bedside and sat down.

Ellen switched off the overhead light. "You look nice in your uniform. Have you been home yet?"

"Just long enough to drop off my things and look in on the girls."

"How do they seem to you?"

"Concerned, confused, a little frightened maybe, but they're okay. I think it helped when your sister brought them up to see you yesterday. I've moved back into the house until you're better."

"You may be there a long time."

"That bad?"

"Kate says no, but her eyes, and now this"—she held up her left hand—"say something else."

"But they don't really know, do they?"

"No. No, I guess not."

"Well, then, you just gotta hang in there a day or an hour or if necessary a minute at a time and believe that everything's going to be all right. I've taken an LOA from the air line to be with the girls, so you don't have anything to worry about on that account. I'll see to it that they get up here every day."

"Thanks. I . . . I'm grateful you're here."

"Nonsense. We've been through a lot these nineteen years. We'll make it through this."

Softly, Ellen began to cry. "Sandy, I feel like such a . . . a clod, an oaf. I know it's dumb, but that's how I feel. Not angry, not even sick, just helpless and clumsy."

"Well, you're neither, and no one knows that better than I do. Hey, that's the second time you've yawned since I got here. Are you tired, or just bored?"

She smiled weakly. "Not bored. A little tired, I guess. It turns out that lying in bed all day doing nothing is exhausting."

"Then how about you don't pay any attention to me and just go to sleep. If it's okay with you, I'll sit here for a while."

"Thanks, Sandy."

"It's going to be okay, you know."

"I know."

He took her hand. "Kate's watching out for you, right?"

"She's in twice a day, and she's doing everything she can to find out why I'm bleeding." Her voice drifted off. Her eyes closed. "Don't be afraid."

"I'm not," he said. "I'm not afraid. . . .It's going to be okay.

The ride in Win Samuels's gray Seville took most of an hour along a network of dark country roads heading south and east from the city. They rode largely in silence, Samuels seeming to need total concentration to negotiate the narrow turns, and Kate staring out her window at dark pastures and even darker woods, at times wondering about the purpose of their journey and at times allowing disconnected thoughts to careen through her mind. Jared . . . Stan Willoughby . . . Bobby Geary . . . Roscoe . . . Ellen . . . Tom . . . even Rosa Beekes, her elementary school principal—each made an appearance and then quickly faded and was replaced by the image of another.

"We're here," Samuels said at last, turning onto a gravel drive.

"Stonefield School." Kate read the name from a discreet sign illuminated only by the headlights of their car. "What town is this?"

"No town, really. We're either in southernmost Massachusetts or northwestern Rhode Island, depending on whose survey you use. The school has been here for nearly fifty years, but it was rebuilt about twenty-five years ago, primarily with money from a fund my firm established."

The school was a low, plain brick structure with a small, well-kept lawn and a fenced-in play area to one side. To the other side, a wing of unadorned red brick stretched towards the woods. They entered the sparsely furnished lobby and were immediately met by a stout, matronly woman wearing a navy skirt, dull cardigan, and an excessive number of gold bracelets and rings.

"Mr. Samuels," she said, "it's good to see you again. Thank you for calling ahead." She turned to Kate. "Dr. Bennett, I'm Sally Bicknell, supervisor for the evening shift. Welcome to Stonefield."

"Thank you," Kate said uncertainly. "I'm not exactly sure where I am or why we're here, but thank you, anyway."

Sally Bicknell smiled knowingly, took Kate by the arm, and led her down the hall to a large, blue velvet curtain. "This is our playroom," she said, drawing the curtain with some flair to reveal the smoky glass of a one-way mirror. The room beyond was large, well lit, and carpeted. There were two tumbling mats, a number of inflatable vinyl punching dummies, and a stack of large building blocks. To one corner, her back toward them, a chunky girl with close-cropped sandy hair hunched over a row of large cloth dolls.

"She's never in bed much before two or three in the morning," Sally Bicknell explained.

"Kate," Samuels said. "I brought you here because I thought that seeing this might help you understand some of my urgency as regards your moving forward with starting your family. Mrs. Bicknell."

The evening shift supervisor rapped loudly on the glass three times, then three times again. The girl in the playroom cocked her head to one side and then slowly turned around.

"Kate, meet your sister-in-law, Lindsey."

The girl was, physically, a monster. Her eyes were lowset and narrow, her facial features thick and coarse, with heavy lips and twisted yellow teeth. What little there was of her neck forced her head to the right at an unnatural angle. Her barrel chest merged with her abdomen, and her legs were piteously bowed.

"That can't be," Kate said softly, her attention transfixed by the grotesquery. "Jared's sister Lindsey . . ."

"Died when she was a child," Samuels finished the sentence for her. "I'm afraid his mother and I chose not to tell him the truth. It seemed like the best idea at the time, considering that we were assured Lindsey would live only a few years. She has Hunter's Syndrome. You are familiar with that, yes?" Kate nodded. "Severe mental retardation and any number of other defects. Her mother, my wife, was nearly forty when she gave birth."

Kate continued staring through the glass as the gargoylelike child—no, woman, for she had to be in her thirties—lumbered aimlessly about the playroom. Reflected in the window, Kate saw the faces of Sally Bicknell and her father-in-law, watching for her reaction. *You are the monster, Win Samuels, not that poor thing,* her thoughts screamed. *What do you think I am, a piece worker in a factory? Did you think this . . . this demonstration would frighten me? Do you think I know nothing of amniocentesis and prenatal diagnosis and counseling? Did you think I would just brush off the enormous lie you have been telling my husband for the past thirty years? Why? Why have you brought me here? Why haven't you included Jared?*

"Take me home," she ordered softly. "Take me home now."

The antique clock on Win Samuels's huge desk said two-fifty. It had been nearly two hours since Kate had abandoned her efforts to sleep and wandered into the study searching for reading matter distracting enough to close her mind to the events of the evening. Something was wrong. Something did not sit right in the bizarre scenario to which her father-in-law had treated her. But what?

On the ride home from Stonefield, Samuels had quietly assailed her with statistics relating maternal age to infertility, fetal death, chromosome abnormalities, genetic mutation, spontaneous abortions, and mental retardation. He had, over many years apparently, done his homework well. The few arguments she had managed to give him on the accuracy of intrauterine diagnosis were countered with more facts and more statistics. Still, nothing the man said could dispel her gut feeling that something was not right. At one time during his presentation—for that is what it was—she came close to crying out that their whole discussion was quite possibly a futile exercise, because a production error at Redding Pharmaceuticals might have already cost her any chance of seeing her forties, let alone conceiving in them.

From the direction of Samuels's room on the second floor, she heard a door open and then close softly. Seconds later, the sound was repeated further down the hall. Jocelyn Trent had returned to her room.

The study, now divested of its fire, was chilly and damp. Kate shuddered and tightened the robe Jocelyn had given her. It was only around midnight in San Diego. Jared wouldn't mind a call, she thought, before realizing that she had forgotten to ask Win at which hotel he was staying. As she reached for a pad and pen to write herself a reminder, she noticed Samuels's Rolodex file. She spun it to "A." The man was right about having a card for the

Ashburton Foundation. On it were an address and a number that had been crossed out. A second, apparently newer, address and number were written in below.

Kate copied the new address and added a note to check in the morning on Jared's hotel. She glanced at the clock. Three-fifteen. How many surgicals were scheduled for the day? Five? Six? Too many. Desperate for sleep, she took her note and an anthology of Emily Dickinson and padded up two flights of stairs to her room.

Forty-five minutes of reading were necessary before Kate trusted the heaviness in her eyes and the impotence in her concentration enough to flip off the light. The realization that her drowsiness was continuing to deepen brought a relieved, contented smile. Then, in her final moments of consciousness, she sensed a troublesome notion. It appeared, then vanished, then appeared again like a faint neon sign. It was not the trip or the school or even the girl. No, it was the address—the address of the Ashburton Foundation; not the newer Washington, DC, address, but the one that was crossed out. With each flash, the neon grew dimmer, the thoughts less distinct. There was something, she thought at the moment of darkness, something special about Darlington, Kentucky. Something.

10

Tuesday 18 December

Soundlessly, Kate unlocked the heavy oak door and slipped out of her father-in-law's home into the gray glare of morning. The deserted streets, sidewalks, and stone steps were covered with an immaculate dusting of white. Over the three days past, a blizzard had crushed the midwest and moved, unabated, into the mid-Atlantic states. Stepping gingerly down Beacon Hill toward Charles Street, Kate wondered if the feathery snow was, perhaps, the harbinger of that storm.

She had slept far too little. Her eyes were dry and irritated, her temples constricted by the ache of exhaustion—an ache she had not experienced so acutely since her days as a medical student and intern. She thought about the surgicals scheduled to begin at ten o'clock and run through most of the rest of the day. With tensions thrusting at her life from one direction after another like the spears in some medieval torture, she debated asking one of the others to take over for her. No way, she decided quickly. As it was, the members of her department were stretched beyond their limits. Stan Willoughby's repeated requests for an additional pathologist had been laughed at. No, she was expected to do her part, and she would find whatever concentration it took to do it right.

As she made her way toward the cab stand near

White Memorial, Kate began her morning ritual of mentally ticking off the events and responsibilities of her day. The cab was halfway to Metro when she ended the ritual, as she inevitably did, by scrambling through her purse for her daily calendar, certain that she had forgotten something crucial. Her schedule was abbreviated, due largely to a block of time marked simply "surgicals." Penciled in at the bottom was the one item she had forgotten, "Drinks with Tom." The three words triggered a surprising rush of feelings, beginning with the reflex notion to call and cancel, and ending with the sense of what her return home to an empty house would be like. Scattered in between were any number of images of the intense, gangly resident who had been her staunchest supporter during the difficult days that had followed the biopsy of Beverly Vitale. Tom Engleson was a man and a youth, enthusiastic at times even to exuberance, yet sensitive about people, about medicine, and especially about what her career involved and meant to her. The prospect of an hour or two together in the corner of some dark, leather and wood lounge might be just the carrot to get her through the day.

"Dammit, Jared," she muttered as the cab rolled to a stop in front of her hospital. "I need you."

She began her day as she had each of the last several working days, with a visit to Room 421 of the Berenson Building.

Ellen was lying on her back, staring at the wall. Her breakfast was untouched on the formica stand by her bed. Suspended from a ceiling hook, a plastic bag drained saline into her arm.

"Hi," Kate said.

"Hi, yourself." Ellen's eyes were shadowed. Her skin seemed lacking in color and turgor. Bruises, large and small, lined both arms. There was packing in one side of her nose.

Kate set the *Cosmopolitan* and morning *Globe* she had brought on the stand next to the breakfast tray.

"Something new's been added, huh?" She nodded toward the IV.

"Last night. A little while after you left."

Kate raised Ellen to a sitting position and then settled onto the bed by her knee. "They say why?"

"All they'll tell me is that it's a precautionary measure."

"Have you had some new bleeding?"

"In my bowel movements, and I guess in my urine, too." She took a glass of orange juice from her tray and sipped at it absently.

"That's probably why the IV," Kate said. "In case they have to inject any X-ray dye or give you any blood." *How much do you want to hear, El? Give me a sign. Do you want to know about sudden massive hemorrhage? About circulatory collapse sudden and severe enough to make emergency insertion of an intravenous line extremely difficult? Do you want to know about Beverly Vitale?*

"Listen, Kate. As long as you're on top of what's going on, I'm satisfied."

"Good." *Thank you, my friend. Thank you for making it a little easier.*

"Sandy's back. He flew in late last night and then moved into the house to look after the girls."

Kate motioned to a vase of flowers by the window. "From him?"

"Uh-huh."

"So?"

Ellen shrugged. "No significance. He's still on his way out, I think."

"I hope not."

"Am I?"

"Are you what?"

"On my way out."

"Jesus, Sandler, of course not."

Ellen took her hand. "Don't let me die, Katey, okay?"

"Count on it," Kate said, having to work to keep from breaking down in front of her friend. Silently, she vowed to place her efforts on Ellen's behalf ahead of every other task, every other pressure in her life. Somewhere, there was an answer, and somehow she would find it. "Listen, I've got to go and get ready for some biopsies. I'll check on your lab tests and speak with you later this afternoon. Okay?"

"Okay." The word was spiritless.

"Anything I can bring you?"

"A cure?"

Kate smiled weakly. "Coming right up," she said.

The flowers, in a metallic gray box with a red bow, were on her desk when Kate returned from the Berenson Building. First a huge bouquet for Ellen from Sandy and now flowers from Jared. The former Dartmouth roommates had come through in the clutch.

"I knew you guys must have learned something at that school besides how to tap a keg," she said, excitedly opening the box.

They were long-stem roses, eleven red and one yellow—the red for love and the yellow for friendship, she had once been told. She scurried about her office, opening and closing doors and drawers until she found a heavy, green-glass vase. It was not until the roses were arranged to her satisfaction and set on the corner of her desk that she remembered the card taped to the box. It would say something at once both witty and tender. That was Jared's style—his way.

"To a not so unexceptional pathologist, from a not so secret admirer. Tom."

Kate groaned and sank to her desk chair, feeling angry and a little foolish. Try as she might, she could not dispel the irrational reaction that Jared had somehow let her down.

Call Tom. She wrote the reminder on a scrap of paper and taped it in a high-visibility spot on the shade of her desk lamp. Still, she knew from experience that even a location only inches from her eyes gave her at best only a fifty-fifty chance of remembering. Perhaps now was the time to call. It was almost nine. If Tom wasn't in the OR, a page would reach him. Things were beginning to get out of hand, and at this point, meeting Tom for a drink hardly seemed fair.

Kate was reaching for the phone when it rang.

"Hello. Kate Bennett," she said.

"Dr. Bennett, how do you do? My name is Arlen Paquette, *Doctor* Arlen Paquette, if you count a PhD in chemistry. I'm the director of product safety for Redding Pharmaceuticals. If this is an inopportune time for you, please tell me. If it is not, I would like to speak with you for a few minutes about the report Dr. William Zimmermann phoned in to us yesterday."

"I have a few minutes," Kate said, retaping the Tom note to her lampshade.

"Fine. Thank you. Dr. Bennett, I spent a fair amount of time taking information from Dr. Zimmermann. However, since you seem to have done most of the legwork, as it were, I had hoped you might go over exactly what it was that led you to the conclusion there was a problem with one of our Redding generics."

"I'd be happy to, Dr. Paquette."

It was obvious from the few questions Paquette asked during her three-minute summary that Zimmermann's account to him had been a complete one and, further, that the director of product safety had studied the data well.

"So," the caller said when she had finished, "as I see it, your initial suspicions of trouble at the Omnicenter were based on a coincidence of symptoms in three patients of the thousands treated there. Correct?"

"Not exactly," Kate said, suddenly perturbed by the tone of the man's voice.

"Please," he said, "bear with me a moment longer. You then decided to focus your investigation on the pharmaceuticals provided for the Omnicenter by my company, and . . ."

"Dr. Paquette, I don't think it's at all fair to suggest that I jumped to the conclusion that the drugs were at fault. Even now I am not at all sure that is the case. However, of all the factors I checked—sterilization techniques, microbiology, and all others common to my three patients—the contaminated vitamins were the only finding out of the ordinary."

"Ah, yes," Paquette said. "The vitamins. Several dozen samples analyzed, yet only one containing a painkiller. Correct?"

"Dr. Paquette," Kate said somewhat angrily, "I have a busy schedule today, and I've told you about all there is to tell. You are sounding more and more like a lawyer and less and less like a man concerned with correcting a problem in his company's product. Now, I don't know whether Dr. Zimmermann told you or not, but I feel that the need to get to the bottom of all this is urgent, critical. A woman who happens to be a dear friend of mine is in the hospital right now, with her life quite possibly at stake, and for all I know, there may be others. I shall give you two more days to come up with a satisfactory explanation. If you don't have one, I am going to get the chemist from the state toxicology lab, and together we will march straight down to the FDA."

"By chemist, I assume you mean Mr. Ian Toole?"

"Yes, that's exactly who I mean."

"Well, Doctor, I'm a little confused. You see, I have in front of me a notarized letter, copies of which I have just put in the mail to you and Dr. Zimmermann. It is a letter from Mr. Ian Toole stating categorically that in none of his investigations on your behalf did he find *any* contamination in *any* product dispensed at the Omnicenter."

"What?" Kate's incredulity was almost instantly replaced by a numbing fear. "That's not true," she said weakly.

"Shall I read you the letter?"

"You bought him off."

"I beg your pardon."

"I gave you the courtesy of reporting this to your

company instead of going to the FDA, and you bought off my chemist."

"Dr. Bennett, I would caution you against carelessly tossing accusations about," Paquette said. "The statement in front of me is, as I have said, notarized."

"We'll see about that," she said with little force. The vitamins she had sent to Toole were all she had. In a corner of her mind, she wondered if Arlen Paquette knew that.

"I would like to confirm my company's sincere desire to correct any shortcomings in its products, and to thank you for allowing us to investigate the situation at your hospital." Paquette sounded as if he was reading the statement from a card.

"You may think this is the end of things, Dr. Paquette," Kate said, "but you don't know me. Please be prepared to hear from the FDA."

"We each must do what we must do, Doctor."

Kate had begun to seethe. "Furthermore, you had better hope that whatever you paid Ian Toole was enough, because that man is going to be made to visit a certain hospital bed to see first hand the woman he may be helping to kill." She slammed the receiver to its cradle.

Seated in his suite at the Ritz, Arlen Paquette hung up gently. He was shaking.

You don't know me.

Paquette snorted at the irony of Kate Bennett's words, splashed some scotch over two ice cubes, drank it before it had begun to chill, and then set the glass down on the photographs of the woman he had just helped nail to a cross of incompetence, mental imbalance, and dishonesty. Cyrus Redding had decreed that she be discredited, and discredited she would be. Kate Bennett had only herself and a few shaky allies. Cyrus Redding had an unlimited supply of Norton Reeses, Winfield Samuelses, Ian Tooles, and, yes, Arlen Paquettes.

He glanced down at the pad where he had written the words he had rehearsed and then used when talking to the woman, and he wondered if he could have come off so self-assured in a face-to-face confrontation. Doubtful, he acknowledged. Extremely doubtful. Their conversation had lasted just a few minutes, with all of the surprises coming from his end. Yet here he was, soaked with sweat and still trembling. He'd take a dozen in-person encounters with Norton Reese over the one phone call he had just finished. Water. That was it, he needed some water. No more goddamn scotch.

He snatched his empty glass from the coffee table. Beneath it was one of the five-by-seven blowups of Kate Bennett, this one of her bundled in a sweatsuit, scarf, and watch cap, jogging with her dog along a snowbanked road. Paquette turned and unsteadily made his way to the bathroom.

"You bastard," he said to the thin, drawn face staring at him from the mirror. "You weak little fucking bastard."

He hurled the glass with all his strength, shattering it and the mirror. Then he dropped to his knees amidst the shards and, clutching the ornate toilet, retched until he felt his insides were tearing in two.

"Don't you see, Bill? Someone at Redding Pharmaceuticals, maybe this . . . this Paquette, bought off Ian Toole. Damn, I knew I was right not to trust them. I knew it. I knew it." Kate, still breathless from her run across the snowy street and up three flights of stairs, screamed at herself to calm down.

William Zimmermann, as relaxed as Kate was intense, rose from behind his desk and crossed to the automatic coffee maker on a low table by his office door. His knee-length clinic coat was perfectly creased and spotless, his demeanor as immaculate as his dress. "How about a few deep breaths and a cup of coffee?"

"Coffee's about the last thing I need in my state,

thanks, but I will try the deep breaths. Vacation. Can you believe it? One day the man is at his little spectrophotometer running tests, and the next he's off on vacation and nobody knows when he'll be back. Now if that isn't a payoff, I don't know what is. Next thing you know, Ian Toole's name will be on a lab door somewhere in Redding Pharmaceuticals."

"The deep breaths?" Zimmermann asked, returning to his desk.

"Oh, yes. I'm sorry, Bill. But you don't blame me, do you?"

"No, I don't blame you." He paused, obviously searching for words. "Kate," he said finally, "I want to be as tactful as possible in what I have to ask, and if I'm not, please excuse me, but . . ."

"Go on."

"Well, since you brought the subject up at our dinner the other night, I feel I must ask. Just how badly do you have it in for the pharmaceutical industry?"

The question startled her. Then she understood. "What you're saying is that without Ian Toole, it becomes a matter of my word against theirs. Is that it?"

"If I'm out of line, Kate, I'm sorry. But remember, there is a lot at stake here—for me and my clinic, and as far as I know, this whole matter was between you and your Mr. Toole. I mean I called in the report because it was our facility, but the hard data are strictly . . ."

"Wait," Kate interrupted excitedly. "There is someone else. I just remembered."

"Who?"

"Her name's Millicent. She's Toole's assistant, and I remember him telling me she was put out about having to work late on the stuff I sent him."

"Do you have a last name?"

"No, but how many Millicents can there be at the State Toxicology Lab?" She was already reaching for the phone and her address book. "You don't know me, Dr.

Paquette," she murmured as she dialed. "Oh, no, you don't know me at all."

The call lasted less than a minute.

"Millicent Hall is no longer in the employ of the state lab," Kate said as she hung up, her expression and tone an equal mix of embarrassment, dejection, and anger. "They wouldn't give out any further information."

This time it was Zimmermann who took a deep breath. "First the baseball player and now this," he said. "You certainly aren't having a very easy time of it."

Kate's eyes narrowed. An emptiness began to build inside her. "You're having trouble believing me, aren't you?"

Zimmermann met her gaze and held it. "Kate, what I can say in all honesty is that at this moment I believe that you believe." He saw her about to protest, and held up his hands. "And at this moment," he added reassuringly, "that is enough. There is too much at stake for me to make any hasty moves. I shall await Redding's formal response to my report, meanwhile keeping our pharmacy on backup. No Redding generics until then. However, if there have been no further cases or further developments in, say, a week, I plan to reinstate our automated system."

"With Redding products?"

"We have a contract."

"But they . . ."

"Facts, Kate. We need substantiated facts."

Kate sighed and sank back in her seat, deflated. It was nearly ten and she had done nothing to prepare for the day's surgicals. "Have you started working on that list of patients who might be willing to allow me to have their medications analyzed?"

Zimmermann smiled patiently. "You can see how that might be a bit tricky to explain to a patient, can't you?" He handed her a brief list and five Omnicenter medication cards. "These belong to long-term patients of mine, who agreed to exchange them as part of what I said was a routine quality-control check."

"It is," Kate said. "Thanks, Bill. I know this isn't easy for you and I'm grateful."

"I'll try and get you some more today."

"Thanks. You're being more than fair. I know I'm right, and sooner or later I'm going to prove it." She stood to go.

"You know," Zimmermann said, "even if you find there was a manufacturing error at Redding, you have no way of tying it in with the cases you are following."

The faces of three women—two dead and one her friend—flashed in her thoughts. "I know," she said grimly. "But it's all I . . . it's all *we* have. Say, before I forget. Have you got the purchase invoices for the Redding generics that I asked you about?"

Zimmermann opened his file cabinet. "Carl Horner does the ordering. He gave me these and asked that I convey his desire to cooperate with you as fully as possible. He also asked that you return these as soon as you're done."

"Of course," Kate said, glancing at the pile of yellow invoice carbons. Redding Pharmaceuticals, Inc.; Darlington, Kentucky. The words sputtered and sparked in her mind. Then they exploded.

"Kate, are you all right?" Zimmermann asked.

"Huh? Oh, yes, I'm fine. Bill, something very strange is going on here. I mean *very strange*." Zimmermann looked at her quizzically. "I don't know how long ago they moved, but at one time, the Ashburton Foundation was located in Darlington, Kentucky."

"How do you know?"

"I found their old address in my father-in-law's Rolodex."

"So?"

Kate held up an invoice for him to see. "Darlington. That's where Redding Pharmaceuticals is headquartered."

For the first time, William Zimmermann seemed perturbed. "I still don't see what point you're trying to make."

Kate heard the irritation in the man's voice and, recalling his oblique reference to the Bobby Geary letter, cautioned herself to tread gently. Her supporters, even skeptical ones, were few and far between. "I . . . I guess I overreacted a little," she said with a sheepishness she was not really feeling. "Ellen's being in the middle of all this has me grasping at straws, I guess." She glanced at her watch. "Look, I've got to get over to the OR. Thanks for these. If I come up with any facts," she corrected herself with a raised finger, "make that substantiated facts, I'll give you a call."

"Fine," Zimmermann said. "Let me know if there's any further way I can help."

Kate hurried outside and across the street, mindless of the wind and snow. Ashburton and Redding—once both in Darlington, and now both at the Omnicenter. A coincidence? Not likely, she thought. No, not likely at all. The lobby clock read two minutes to ten as she sped toward the surgical suite and the small frozen-section lab. The room was dark. Taped to the door was a carefully printed note.

OR CRYOSTAT INOPERATIVE. BRING
BIOPSY SPECS
TO PATH DEPARTMENT CRYOSTAT FOR
PROCESSING

"Ten seconds to ignition. Nine. Eight. Seven. Six. Five. Four. Three. Two. One. Ignition." Tom Engleson struck the wooden match against the edge of an iron trivet and touched the brandy-soaked mound of French vanilla ice cream. "Voilà!" he cried.

"Bravo!" Kate cheered.

Tom filled two shallow dishes and set Kate's in front of her with a flourish.

The evening had been a low-key delight: drinks at the Hole in the Wall Pub, dinner at the Moon Villa, in

Chinatown, and finally dessert in Tom's apartment, twenty stories above Boston Harbor. She had forgotten to break their date, and for once her poor memory had proven an asset. Twenty minutes into their conversation at the Hole in the Wall, Kate had given up trying to sort out what she wanted from the evening and the man and had begun to relax and enjoy both. Still, she knew, thoughts of Jared were never far from the surface; nor were thoughts of Redding Pharmaceuticals and the Ashburton Foundation.

"Okay," Tom said as he poured two cups of coffee and settled into the chair next to her, "now that my brain is through crying for food and drink and such, it's ready to try again to understand. There is no Ashburton Foundation?"

"No, there's something *called* the Ashburton Foundation, but I'm not at all certain it's anything other than a laundry for money."

"Pharmaceutical company money."

"Right. I called the number I got from my father-in-law's Rolodex and got a receptionist of some sort. She referred every question, even what street they were located on in DC, to someone named Dr. Thompson, apparently the director of the so-called foundation."

"But Dr. Thompson was out of the office and never called you back."

"Exactly. I tried calling the receptionist again, and this time she said that Thompson was gone for the day and would contact me in the morning. It was weird, I tell you, weird. The woman, supposedly working for this big foundation, didn't have the vaguest idea of how to handle my call."

"Did you ask Reese about all this?"

"He was gone for the day by the time I called, but tomorrow after I see Ellen, I intend to camp out on his doorstep."

"But why? What does Redding Pharmaceuticals get out of funneling all this money into our hospital?"

Kate shrugged. "That, Thomas, is the sixty-four dollar question. At the moment, every shred of woman's intuition in my body is screaming that the tie-in has something to do with the contaminated vitamins our friend Dr. Paquette has gone to such lengths to cover up."

"Incredible."

"Incredible, maybe. Impossible?" She took a folded copy of an article from her purse and passed it over. "I came across this yesterday during one of my sessions in the library. It's part of a whole book about a drug called MER/29, originally developed and marketed by Merrell Pharmaceuticals."

"That's a big company," Tom said, flipping through the pages.

"Not as big as Redding, but big enough. This MER/29 was supposed to lower cholesterol and thereby prevent heart disease. Only trouble was that other companies were racing to complete work on other products designed to do the same thing. The good folks at Merrell estimated a potential yearly profit in the billions at just one twenty-cent capsule a day for each person over thirty-five. However, they also knew that the lion's share of that profit would go to the first company whose product could get cleared by the FDA and launched into the marketplace."

"I'm not going to want to hear the rest of this, am I," Tom said.

"Not if you have much trust in the pharmaceutical industry. Remember, the FDA doesn't evaluate products; the pharmaceutical companies do. The FDA only evaluates the evaluations. In its haste to get MER/29 into the bodies of the pharmaceutical-buying public, Merrell cut corner after corner in their laboratory and clinical testing. But since none of the shortcuts was evident in the massive reports they submitted to the FDA, in 1961, MER/29 was approved by the FDA and launched by Merrell. Two years later, almost by accident, the FDA discovered what the company had done and ordered the drug removed. By that time, a large number of people had gone blind or developed hideous, irreversible skin conditions or lost all their hair."

Tom whistled.

"Kids with no arms because their mothers took a sleeping pill called thalidomide. Kids with irreparably yellow teeth because tetracycline was rushed into the marketplace before all its side effects were known. The list goes on and on."

"You sound a little angry," Tom said, taking her hand and guiding her to the couch across the room.

"They paid off my chemist, Tom," she said. "They've made me look like a fool, or worse, a liar. You're damn right I'm angry." She sighed and leaned back, still holding his hand. "Forgive me for popping off like that, but I guess I needed to."

Tom slipped his free arm around her shoulders and drew her close. Together they sat, watching fat, wind-whipped flakes of snow tumble about over the harbor and melt against the huge picture window.

"Thank you," she whispered. "Thank you for understanding."

Again and again they kissed. First her blouse, then her bra, then Tom's shirt dropped to the carpet, as he bore her gently down on the couch. His lips, brushing across the hollow of her neck and over the rise of her breasts, felt wonderful. His hand, caressing the smooth inside of her thigh was warm and knowing and patient. She felt as excited, as frightened, as she had during her earliest teenage encounters. But even as she sensed her body respond to his hunger, even as her nipples grew hard against his darting tongue, she sensed her mind begin to pull back.

"Kate. Oh, Kate," Tom whispered, the words vibrating gently against the skin of her breast.

"Tom?" The word was a soft plea, almost a whimper.

"Hold me, Kate. Please don't stop."

She took his face in her hands. "Tom," she said huskily. "I . . . just can't."

Her emotions swirling like the snow on the interstate, Kate took most of an hour and a half to make the drive from Boston to Essex. Tom had been hurt and frustrated by her sudden change in attitude, but in the end he had done his best to understand and accept.

"I only hope Jared knows how goddamn lucky he is," he had snapped as she was dressing. Later, he had insisted on driving her back to Metro and her car, where they had shared a quasi-platonic good-bye kiss.

The phone was ringing as she opened the door from the garage to her house. Roscoe, who had spent most of the past two days at a sleepover with neighbors and their golden retriever, bounded down the hall, accepted a quick greeting, and then followed her to the den.

It was Jared. "Hi," he said. "I called the house at three A.M. and no one was home. Are you okay?"

"I'm fine, Jared. I spent the night at your father's. Didn't he tell you he had invited me?"

"No." There was no mistaking the curiosity in Jared's voice. "Did you get my letter?"

Kate thumbed through the pile of bills and throw-away journals she had carried in with her. Jared's letter was sandwiched between the magazines *Aches and Pains* and *Pathologist on the Go*.

"I just brought it in," she said. "If you want to wait, I'll read it right now."

"No need, Kate. I've got it memorized." Kate opened the letter and read along as he said the words. "It says 'I love you, I miss you, and I don't want to not live with you anymore. Jared.' "

Kate's heart was pounding so much she could barely respond. "I love you too, Jared. Very, very much. When are you coming home?"

"Day after tomorrow, unless you want me to hitch home now."

"Thursday's fine, honey. Just fine. I'll pick you up at the airport."

"Seven P.M. United."

"Perfect. I have a lot to tell you about. Maybe we'll

take a ride in the country. There's someone you should visit."

"Who?"

"You'll see. Let me leave it at that until Thursday. Okay?"

"Okay, but . . ."

"I love you."

"I love you, Boots. Sometimes I don't know who the heck you are or where Jared Samuels is on your list of priorities, but I love you and I want to ride it all out with you as long as I can hang on."

"We'll do just fine, honey. Everything is going to be all right."

As she hung up, Kate realized that for the first time in weeks she believed that.

11

Wednesday 19 December

Arlen Paquette, stiff and sore from lack of sleep, cruised along the tree-lined drive toward Redding Pharmaceuticals. Paralleling the icy roadway were the vestiges of the first December snow in Darlington in eleven years. His homecoming the evening before had been a fiasco, marked by several fights with the children, too much to drink before, during, and after dinner, and finally, impotence and discord in bed—problems he and his wife had never encountered before.

He adjusted the rearview mirror to examine his face and plucked off the half dozen tissue-paper patches on the shaving nicks caused by his unsteady hand. Even without the patches he looked like hell. It was the job, the job he couldn't quit. Bribery, payoffs, deceptions, threats, ruined lives. Suddenly he was no longer a chemist. Suddenly he was no longer even an administrator. He was a lieutenant, a platoon leader in Cyrus Redding's army. It was an army of specialists, held together by coercion, blackmail, and enormous amounts of money—poised to strike at anything or anyone who threatened Cyrus Redding or the corporation he had built.

The guard greeted him warmly and performed a perfunctory search of the Mercedes. Paquette had once asked the man exactly what it was he was checking for. His polite, but quite disconcerting, reply was, "Anything Mr. Redding doesn't want to be there."

The executive offices, including Cyrus Redding's, were at the hub of the wagon wheel of six long, low structures that made up the manufacturing and packaging plants. Research and other laboratory facilities occupied an underground annex, joined to the main structure by tunnels, escalators, and moving walkways. Paquette parked in the space marked with his name, stopped at his office to leave his coat, and then headed directly for Redding's suite. He was ushered in immediately.

"Arlen, Arlen," Redding said warmly, "welcome home." He was in his wheelchair behind his desk and was dressed in the only outfit Paquette could remember him wearing at work, a lightweight blue-gray suit, white shirt, and string tie, fastened with a turquoise thunderbird ring.

"So," Redding said, when they had moved to the sitting area with coffee and a sugary pastry, "you look a bit drawn. This Boston business has not been so easy, has it?"

"You told me it might not be," Paquette said. "Do you remember when we decided to move the mailing address of the Ashburton Foundation?"

"Of course. A few months after you started working here. Six, no, seven years ago, right?" Paquette nodded. "It was an excellent suggestion and the first time I fully appreciated what a winning decision it was to hire you."

Paquette smiled a weak thank you. "Well," he said, "it was my feeling at that time that with the foundation registered as a tax-exempt philanthropic organization and located in DC, there was no way Redding Pharmaceuticals could ever be connected to it."

"And yet our tenacious friend Dr. Bennett has done so."

"Yes, although as I told you last night, I'm not certain she has put it all together."

"But she will," the Warlock said with certainty.

"She called twice yesterday trying to reach me—that is, trying to reach Dr. Thompson, the foundation director.

I couldn't even call her back for fear of having her recognize my voice."

"It was a wise decision not to."

"She's got to hear from someone today."

"She will," Redding said. He glanced at his watch. "At this moment, our persuasive legislative liaison, Charlie Wilson, is on his way to the foundation office to become Dr. James Thompson."

"Office?"

"Of course. We wouldn't want Dr. Bennett to try and locate the Ashburton Foundation only to find a desk, phone and secretary, would we?" Paquette shook his head. The man was absolutely incredible, and efficient in a way that he found quite frightening. "By eleven o'clock this morning, the office, its staff, photographic essays describing its good works, testimonial letters, and a decade or so of documented service will be in place, along with Charlie Wilson, who is, I think you'll agree, as smooth and self-confident as they come."

"Amazing," Paquette said.

"Are you feeling a bit more relaxed about things now?"

"Yes, Mr. Redding. Yes, I am."

"Good. You'll be pleased to know that the company will be taking care of that mirror at the Ritz."

Paquette froze. He had gone to great pains to pay for the damage himself and to insure that in no way would Redding find out about what had happened. Instability under fire was hardly the sort of trait the man rewarded in his platoon leaders. "I . . . I'm sorry about that, sir. I really am."

Redding gestured to the coffee table before them. Sealed under thick glass was the emblem of Redding Pharmaceuticals: a sky-blue background with white hands opening to release a pure, white dove. Below the dove was the name of the company; above it, in a rainbow arc, the motto: *The Greatest Good for the Most People at the Least Cost*. "Arlen, ever since the day I took over this company, I have tried to chart a course that would lead to exactly what this motto says. In this business—in any business—there are always choices to be made, always decisions that cannot be avoided. In the thirty-five years since I first came to Darlington, I've made more gut-wrenching decisions and smashed more glasses and more mirrors in anguish than I care to count. But always, when I needed direction, when I needed advice or council, it was right in front of me." He tapped the motto with his finger. "The legislators, state and federal, the competition, and especially the goddamn FDA are all doing their best to cloud the issue, but in the end it always boils down to this." Again, he tapped the glass.

If the pep talk was meant to buoy Paquette's flagging morale, it failed miserably. The greatest good for the most people at the highest profit was all he could think of. The shortcuts and the human testing, the clinics in Denver and Boston, the bribery and extortion involving FDA officials—all had been tolerable for him because all were abstractions. Kate Bennett was flesh and blood, a voice, a face, a reality; and worse than that, a reality he was growing to admire. Paquette snapped out of his reverie, wondering how long it had lasted. A second? A minute? Then he realized that Redding's eyes were fixed on him.

"I understand, sir," he said, clearing away the phlegm in his throat, "and I assure you, you have nothing to worry about." How did the man know about the stinking mirror? Spies in Boston? A bug in the room? Damn him, Paquette thought viciously. Damn him to hell.

"Fine, Arlen," Redding said. "Now, you have a flight back to Boston this afternoon?"

"Two o'clock."

"I suspect that our meddlesome pathologist is on the ropes. However, her father-in-law assures me that she is far from out on her feet. Her discovery regarding the Ashburton Foundation suggests that he is quite correct."

"I believe Norton Reese is arranging a surprise for her that may help," Paquette said, vividly recalling the glee in Reese's voice as he announced that something was set to fall heavily on Kate Bennett.

"Excellent," Redding said. "Her father-in-law has promised to do what he can to help us as well. One final thing."

"Yes?"

"Has anything further surfaced on the cause of the ovary and blood problems in those three women?" Paquette shook his head. "Strange," Redding said, more to himself than to the other man. "Very strange . . ." For several seconds, he remained lost in thought, his eyes closed, his head turning from side to side as if he were internally speedreading a page. "Well, Arlen," he said suddenly, opening his eyes, "thank you for the excellent job you are doing. I know at times your duties are not easy for you, but continue to carry them out the way you have, and your rewards will be great."

"Yes, sir," Paquette said. He sat for nearly half a minute before realizing that the Warlock had said all he was going to. Sheepishly, he rose and hurried from the room.

Cyrus Redding studied the man as he left. The Boston business seemed to be having some untoward effects on him, particularly in the area of his drinking. As he motored from the sitting area to his desk, Redding made a mental note to arrange a vacation of some sort for Paquette and his wife as soon as Boston was over. That done, he put the issue and the man out of his head. There was more important business needing attention.

Stephen Stein, the enigmatic, remarkably resourceful investigator, had made a discovery that he suspected would unlock the mystery of John Ferguson.

"Mr. Nunes," Redding said through the intercom of his desk, "would you bring that package to me now."

At the far end of the office, a perfectly camouflaged panel and one-way mirror slid open. The man Nunes emerged from the small, soundproof room from which he kept vigil, revolver at hand, whenever Redding was not alone in his office. The package, containing a book, several typewritten pages, and an explanatory letter from Stein, had arrived by messenger only minutes before Arlen Paquette.

"If you have errands to run, Mr. Nunes, this would be a good time. When you return in, say, an hour, we could well have a new slant on our friend, Dr. Ferguson." He smiled, nearly beside himself at the prospect. "I think this occasion might call for a pint of that mint chip ice cream I have forbidden you to let me talk you into buying."

The taciturn bodyguard nodded. "I can't let you talk me into it," he said, "but perhaps I could purchase some on my own."

Redding waited until his office door had clicked shut; then he locked it electronically and spread the contents of the package on his desk.

"My apologies," Stein wrote, "for missing this volume during the course of earlier efforts to tie our mysterious Dr. Ferguson's background in with the war. I borrowed it from the Holocaust Library at the university here with assurances of its return, along with some token of our gratitude. Its title, according to the German professor who did the enclosed translation for us, is *Doctors of the Reich; The Story of Hitler's Monster Kings*. The work is the product of painstaking research and countless interviews by a Jewish journalist named Sachs, himself a death camp survivor, and is believed by my source to be accurate within the limits of the author's prejudices. Only the chapters dealing with the experiments at the Ravensbrück concentration camp for women have been translated. The photographs on pages three sixty-seven and three sixty-eight will, I believe, be of special interest to you."

For most of the next hour, Cyrus Redding sat transfixed, moving only to turn the pages of the translation or to refer to specific photographs in the worn, yellowed text. John Ferguson was a physician and scientist named Dr. Wilhelm Becker. The photographs, though slightly blurred and taken nearly forty years before, left no doubt whatsoever.

"Amazing," Redding murmured as he read and reread the biography of his associate. "Absolutely amazing."

There were two snapshots of Wilhelm Becker, one a full-face identification photo and one a group shot with other physicians at the Ravensbrück Camp. There was also a shot of what remained of the laboratory in which Becker was purported to have died, with the bodies of the man and his staff sergeant still curled amidst the debris on the floor. Redding withdrew a large, ivory-handled magnifying glass from his desk and for several minutes studied the detail of the scene. The body identified as Willi Becker was little more than an ill-defined, charred lump.

"Nicely done, my friend," Redding said softly. "Nicely done."

Familiar now with the man and with his spurious death, Redding turned to the page and a half dealing with Becker's research, specifically, with his research on a substance called Estronate 250. Much of the information presented was gleaned from transcripts of the war-crimes trial of a physician named Müller and another named Rendl, both of whom were sentenced to Nuremberg Prison in large measure because of their association with the supposedly late Wilhelm Becker. Redding found the men in the Ravensbrück group photo. Müller had served five years at hard labor before certain Ravensbrück survivors were able to document his acts of heroism on their behalf and get his sentence commuted. For Rendl, the revelations of his humanitarianism came too late. Three years after his incarceration, he hanged himself in his cell.

Redding read the Estronate material word by word, taking careful notes. By the time he had finished, he was absolutely certain that neither Wilhelm Becker nor the notebook containing his work on the hormone had perished in the Ravensbrück fire.

A substance, harmless in every other way, that could render a woman sterile without her knowledge. Redding was staggered by the potential of such a drug. China, India, the African nations, the Arabs. What would governments be willing to pay for a secret that might selectively thin their populations and thereby solve so many of their economic and political woes? What would certain governments pay for a weapon which, if delivered properly, could decimate their enemies in a single generation without the violent loss of one life?

Redding's thoughts were soaring through the possibilities of Estronate 250 when, with a soft knock, Nunes entered the office, set a package on the desk, and retired to his observation room. For another hour, Redding sat alone, savoring his mint chip ice cream and deciding how he might best break the news to Dr. John Ferguson that their fifteen-year-old collaboration was about to take on a new dimension.

"I love you, I miss you, and I don't want to not live with you anymore."

Kate read Jared's note again and then again, drawing strength and confidence from it each time. She had returned to her office following two distressing and frightening visits. One was to Ellen, who was, for the first time, receiving a transfusion of packed red blood cells. The second was to Norton Reese. If the connection between Metropolitan Hospital of Boston, the Ashburton Foundation, and Redding Pharmaceuticals was as intimate as Reese's clumsy evasions were leading her to believe, she would need all the strength and confidence she could muster. Thank you, Jared, she thought. Thank you for pulling me out from under the biggest pressure of all.

Her meeting with Reese had started off cordially enough. In fact, the man had seemed at times to be inappropriately jovial and at ease. Ever since their confrontation before the board of trustees over his diversion of budgeted pathology department funds to the cardiac surgical program, Reese had dealt with her with the gingerliness of an apprentice handling high explosives. Now, suddenly, he was all smiles. His congeniality lasted through several minutes of conversation about her department and Stan Willoughby's recommendation that she succeed him as chief, and ended abruptly with mention of the Ashburton Foundation. Whatever fortes the man might have, Kate mused at that moment, they certainly did not include poker faces. His eyes narrowed fractionally, but enough to deepen the fleshy crow's feet at their corners. His lips whitened, as did the tips of his fingers where they were touching one another.

"I'm afraid I'm not at liberty to open the Ashburton Foundation files to you," he had said, his eyes struggling to maintain contact with hers and failing. "However, I shall be happy to answer what questions I can."

"Okay," Kate said, shrugging. "My first question is why aren't you at liberty to open the Ashburton Foundation files to me?"

"It's . . . it's part of the agreement we signed when we accepted a grant from them." It was bizarre. In a very literal sense, the man was squirming in his seat.

"Well, suppose I wanted to apply for a grant for my department. How would I go about contacting them?"

"I'll have Gina give you the address on your way out. You can write them yourself."

"I already have a post office box number in Washington, DC. Is that it?"

"Yes. I mean, probably."

"Well, suppose I wanted to visit their offices in person. Could you ask Gina to give me a street address as well?"

Reese continued to fidget. "Look," he said, "I'll give you their mailing address and phone number. I'm sorry, but that's all I can do. Why do you want to know about the Ashburton Foundation anyway?" he managed.

"Mr. Reese," Kate said calmly, "If I answer that question, will you open their files to me?"

"Not without written permission from the Ashburton Foundation."

"Well then, it appears we've got a Mexican standoff, doesn't it? I'll tell you this much," her voice grew cold.

"Two women have died and a third may be dying. If I find out the Ashburton Foundation is connected in any way with what has happened to them, and you have kept significant information from me, I promise that I won't rest until everyone who matters knows what you have done. Is that clear?" Her uncharacteristic anger had, she knew, been prodded by the sight of Ellen Sandler mutely watching the plastic bag dripping blood into her arm and by the knowledge that this was, in all likelihood, just the first of many transfusions to come.

Reese checked his watch in a manner that was as inappropriate as it was unsubtle. It was as if he had left a message to be called at precisely nine-twelve and was wondering why the phone hadn't rung.

"Mr. Reese?"

The administrator shifted his gaze back to her. His face was pinched and gray with anger—no, she realized, it was something deeper than anger. Hatred? Did the poor man actually hate her?

"You really think you're something, don't you," he rasped in a strained, muddy voice.

"I beg your pardon?"

"Who made you the crusader? Do you think that just because you have an MD degree and all that old family money you can ride all over people?"

"What? Mr. Reese, I nev—"

"Well, let me tell you something. You don't intimidate me like you do some around here. No, sir, not one bit. So you just ride off on that high horse of yours and let me and the department heads—the *official* department heads—worry about grants and foundations and such."

Kate watched as the man sat there, panting from the exertion of his outburst. For five seconds, ten, her green eyes fixed on him. Then she rose from her chair and left, unwilling to dignify Reese's eruption with a response.

Now, alone in her office, Kate sat, trying to crystallize her thoughts and doodling a calligraphic montage of the words "Reese" and "Asshole." After finishing four versions of each, she began adding "Ashburton" and "Paquette." First there was the bribery of Ian Toole, an act which seemed to her equivalent to shooting a chipmunk with an elephant gun. She would have been quite satisfied with an admission by Redding Pharmaceuticals that they had somehow allowed a batch of their generic vitamins to become contaminated and would gladly recall and replace them. Their illogically excessive response had to have been born out of either arrogance or fear. But fear of what? "Omnicenter" made its first appearance in the montage.

The Ashburton Foundation had endowed an entire ob-gyn department and subsidized a massive, modern women's health center. Philanthropic acts? Perhaps, she thought. But both of her calls to the foundation had gone unanswered by Dr. Thompson, the director, and her efforts, though modest, had failed to come up with an address for the place. Then there was Reese's refusal to discuss the organization that had been, at least in part, responsible for the resurgence of his hospital. At that moment, almost subconsciously, she began adding another name to the paper. Again and again she wrote it, first in the calligraphic forms she knew, then in several she made up on the spot. "Horner." Somehow the cantankerous, eccentric computer genius was involved in what was going on. The notion fit too well, made too much sense. But how? There really was only one person who could help her find out. Another minute of speculation, and she called William Zimmermann.

Fifteen minutes later, she was on her way through the tunnel to the Omnicenter when Tom Engleson entered from the cutoff to the surgical building.

"Hi," she said, searching his face for a clue as to how he was handling the abortive end to their evening together.

"H'lo," his voice was flat.

She slowed, but continued walking. "Going to the Omnicenter?"

Tom nodded. "I have a clinic in twenty minutes."

"You all right?"

"Yeah, sure. Great."

"Tom, I—"

"Look, Kate, it's my problem, not yours."

"Dr. Engleson, you weren't exactly alone on the couch last night," she whispered, glancing about to ensure that none of the tunnel traffic was too close. "I feel awful about giving out such mixed messages. But you are an incredibly comfortable and understanding man. With all the trouble at the hospital I'm afraid I just allowed myself to hide out in your arms. It was wrong and unfair—more so because I really care very much for you. I'm sorry, Tom."

They reached the stairwell leading up to the Omnicenter.

"Wait," Tom said. "Please." He guided her to a small alcove opposite the staircase.

"You know, considering the nature of the Metro grapevine, we'll probably be an item by . . ." Two nurses chattered past them and up the stairs. "Hell," she said, following them with her eyes, "we most likely are already."

"Do you really mean that, about caring for me?"

"Tom, I love my husband very much. We've had some trouble getting our lives back in sync since the election, but my feelings for him haven't changed. Still, you're very special to me. Believe me, if my home situation, my marriage, were any different, we would have been lovers last night."

"Yeah?" The muscles in his face relaxed, and some measure of energy returned to his voice.

"Yes," she said. Tom Engleson might have been nine years Jared's junior, but they still had much in common, including, it now appeared, the need for strong reassurance about such things.

"I said it last night, and I'll say it again. Jared is a very lucky man." Acceptance had replaced the strain in Tom's voice.

"I know," Kate said. "Tom, seriously, thank you for not making it any harder for me. Between the wretched business with Bobby Geary, the disappearance of my chemist, and some incredible crap from Norton Reese, I feel like I need all the friends—all the help—I can get." She glanced at her watch. "Say, do you have a few minutes?"

"Sure, why?"

"I'm going to see Bill Zimmermann to discuss the Ashburton Foundation. I'd love to have you come along if you can."

"Rocket Bill? I do have a little time if you think he wouldn't mind."

"Hardly," Kate said. "He knows how much help you've been to me through all this. Okay?"

During the four-flight climb, Tom reviewed for her the protocols for patient care in the Omnicenter. On arrival, both new and returning patients met with a specially trained female intake worker, who blackened in the appropriate spaces in a detailed computer-readable history sheet. Medications, menstrual history, new complaints, and side effects of any treatment were carefully recorded. The worker then slid the history sheet into a computer terminal on her desk, and in thirty seconds or less, instructions as to where the patient was to go next would appear on the screen along with, if necessary, what laboratory tests were to be ordered.

"Do you feel the system is a bit impersonal?" Kate asked.

"You're a patient here. Do you?"

"No, not really, I guess," she said. "I can remember when a visit to the gynecologist consisted of sitting for an hour in a ten-foot-square waiting room with a dozen other women, having my name called out, stripping in a tiny examining room, and finally having the doctor rush in, thumbing through my chart for my name, and then as often as not telling me to put my heels in the stirrups before he even asked why I was there."

"See," Tom laughed, "no system is perfect. But seriously, the one here is damn good. It frees me up to do a careful exam and to answer as many questions as my patients have."

The system might be great, Kate thought, but something, somewhere inside it, was rotten. Something was killing people.

Large, colored numbers marked each floor. The 3, filling half a wall at the third-floor landing, was an iridescent orange. Kate reached for the handle of the door to the corridor, but then stopped, turned to Tom, and kissed him gently on the cheek.

"Thank you for last night, my friend," she said.

Tom accepted the kiss and then squeezed her hand and smiled. "If you need anything at all, and I can do it or get it, you've got it," he said.

William Zimmermann greeted Kate warmly and Tom with some surprise. It was clear from his expression and manner that he was concerned about anything that might affect the reputation of the Omnicenter, including involvement of one of the Ashburton Service senior residents.

Kate sought immediately to reassure him. "Bill, as you know, Dr. Engleson's been an enormous help to me in sorting all this out. He knows, as do I, the importance of absolute discretion in discussing these matters with anyone."

"You've spoken to no one at all about this?" Zimmermann asked Tom.

"No, sir. Only K . . . only Dr. Bennett."

"Good. Well, sit down, sit down both of you."

"I'll try not to take up too much of your time," Kate began, "but I want to keep you abreast of what has been happening since we talked yesterday."

"You were concerned about the Ashburton Foundation."

"Exactly. You know how upset I was with Redding Pharmaceuticals after they bribed my chemist. Well—"

Zimmermann stopped her with a raised hand. "Kate, please," he said, with an edge of irritation she had never heard before. "I told you how I felt about the situation with the chemist. I believe that you believe, but no more than that." He turned to Tom. "Do you have any personal knowledge of this chemist, Toole?"

Tom thought for a moment and then shook his head. "No, not really."

"All right, then," Zimmermann said. "Substantiated facts."

Kate took a breath, nodded, and settled herself down by smoothing out a pleat in her charcoal gray skirt. "Sorry, Bill. Okay, here's a substantiated fact." She passed a telephone number across to him. "It's the number of the Ashburton Foundation in Washington, DC. At one time, maybe seven or eight years ago, the foundation was located in Darlington, Kentucky, the same town as Redding Pharmaceuticals. I tried calling them yesterday, several times, but all I got was a stammering receptionist who promised I would hear from a Dr. James Thompson, the director, as soon as he returned to the office. I never heard. Then this morning, I went to see Norton Reese and asked to see the Ashburton Foundation files. You would have thought I asked to read his diary. He refused and then exploded at me."

"Did he give any reason for refusing?" Tom asked.

Kate shook her head. "Not really. He seemed frightened of me. Scared stiff."

"Kate," Zimmermann asked, fingering the paper she had given him, "just what is it you're driving at?" The edge was still in his voice.

Even before she spoke, she sensed her theory would not sit well with the Omnicenter director. Still, there was no way to back off. "Well, I think Redding Pharmaceuticals may be investing money in hospitals—or at least this hospital—and using the Ashburton Foundation as some kind of front, sort of a middle man."

Zimmermann's pale eyes widened. "That's absurd," he said, "absolutely absurd. What would they have to gain?"

"I'm not certain. I have an idea, but I'm not certain. Furthermore, I think Norton Reese knows the truth."

"Well?"

Substantiated facts. Suddenly, Kate wished she had taken more time, prepared herself more thoughtfully. Then she remembered Ellen. Time was, she felt certain, running out for her friend. With that reality, nothing else really mattered. She girded herself for whatever Zimmermann's response was to be and pushed on.

"I don't think the anthranilic acid in my vitamins was an accidental contaminant," she said, forcing a levelness into her voice though she was shaking inside. "I think it was being tested on me, and probably on others as well; not tested to see whether or not it worked, because I didn't have any symptoms, but rather for adverse reactions, for side effects, if you will."

Zimmermann was incredulous. "Dr. Bennett, if such a thing were going on in the Omnicenter, in *my* facility, don't you think I would know about it?"

"Not really," Kate said. "It was starting to come together for me, but Tom's description of how the intake process works made it all fit. It's Carl Horner, downstairs. Horner and his Monkeys. You and the other docs here just go on prescribing his medications and then recording his data for him. There's no reason you have to know anything, as long as the computers know."

"And you think the Ashburton Foundation is bankrolling his work?" Kate nodded. "This is getting out of control." He turned to Tom. "Do you follow what she is saying?" Reluctantly, Tom nodded. "And do you believe it?"

"I . . . I don't know what to believe."

"Well, I think it's time I checked on some of these things for myself," Zimmermann said, snatching up the telephone and setting the Ashburton number on his desk. "Dr. William Zimmermann, access number three-oh-eight-three," he told the operator, as Kate looked on excitedly, "I'd like a Watts line, please."

Only a few more minutes, Kate told herself. Only a few more minutes, a few words from the confused, stammering receptionist, and Zimmermann would at least realize that something was not right at the Ashburton Foundation. For the moment, that would be enough. Measured against the fiascoes surrounding Bobby Geary and Ian Toole, the planting of even a small seed of doubt in the man's mind would be a major victory.

"Yes, good morning," she heard Zimmermann say. "I am Dr. William Zimmermann, from Boston. I should like to speak with the director. . . . Yes, exactly. Dr. Thompson." Kate turned to Tom and gave him a conspiratorial smile. Suddenly, she realized that Zimmermann was waving to get her attention and pointing to the extension phone on the conference table. She came on the line just as did Dr. James Thompson.

"This is Dr. Thompson," the man said.

"Dr. Thompson, I'm sorry to disturb you. My name is Zimmermann. I'm the director of the Omnicenter here in Boston."

"Oh, yes, Dr. Zimmermann, I know of you," Thompson said. "You took over for poor Dr. French, what was it, four years ago?"

"Five."

"Tragic accident, tragic, as I recall."

"Yes, he drowned," Zimmermann said, now looking directly at Kate, who was beginning to feel sick.

"What can I do for you, sir?" Thompson had a deep, genteel voice.

"I'm here with Dr. Kate Bennett, one of our physicians."

"Ah, yes. Her name is right in front of me here on my desk. Twice, in fact. She phoned here yesterday and was told I would return her call. However, my secretary had no way of knowing that my son, Craig, had fallen at school and broken his wrist and that I was going to be tied up in the emergency room for hours."

"He's all right, I hope?"

Thompson laughed. "Never better. That plaster makes him the center of attention. Now, what can I do for you and Dr. Bennett?"

"Nothing for me, actually, but Dr. Bennett has a question or two for you. One moment."

"Certainly."

Zimmerman, his expression saying, "Well, you asked for it, now here it is," motioned for her to go ahead.

Kate felt as if she were being bludgeoned. She had been sure, so sure, and now. . . . "Dr. Thompson," she managed, "my apologies for not being more patient." She glanced over at Tom, who shrugged helplessly. "I . . . I was calling to find out if there was any connection between the Ashburton Foundation and Redding Pharmaceuticals." There was no sense in trying anything other than a direct approach. She was beaten, humiliated again, and she knew it.

"Connection?"

"Yes, sir. Isn't it true that the foundation was once located in Darlington, Kentucky, the same town as Redding?"

"As a matter of fact, it was. John and Sylvia Ashburton, whose estate established the foundation, were from Lexington. Their son, John, Jr., ran one of their horse farms, Darlington Stables. For two years after his parents died, John stayed at the farm, tidying up affairs and setting up the mechanics of the foundation. I was hired in, let me see, seventy-nine, but by then, the center of operations had already been moved to Washington. I'm afraid that as far as Redding Pharmaceuticals goes, the geographical connection was pure coincidence."

"Thank you," Kate said meekly. "That certainly helps clear up my confusion." Another glance at Tom, and she grasped at one final straw. "Dr. Thompson, I was trying to find out the street address of your office, but there's no Ashburton Foundation listed in the DC directory."

"By design, Dr. Bennett, quite by design. You see, where there is grant money involved, there are bound to be, how should I say it, somewhat less than fully qualified applicants contacting us. We prefer to do our own preliminary research and then to encourage only appropriate institutions and agencies to apply. Our offices are at 238 K Street, Northwest, on the seventh floor. Please feel free to visit any time you are in Washington. Perhaps your pathology department would be interested in applying for a capital equipment grant."

"Perhaps," Kate said distractedly.

William Zimmermann had heard enough. "Dr. Thompson," he said, "I want to thank you for helping to clear up the confusion here, and also for the wonderful support your agency has given my Omnicenter."

"Our pleasure, sir," Dr. James Thompson said.

"Well?" Zimmermann asked after he had hung up.

"Something's not right," she said.

"What?"

"He mentioned my pathology department. How did he know I was a pathologist?"

"I told him you were at the very start of the call."

"I'm not trying to be difficult, Bill—really, I'm not—but you referred to me as a physician, not a pathologist. You remember, Tom, don't you?" A look at the uncertainty in Tom's eyes, and she began having doubts herself. "Well?"

"I . . . I'm not sure," was all the resident could say.

Kate stood to go. "Bill, I may seem pigheaded to you, or even confused, but I tell you, something still doesn't feel right to me. I just have a sense that Dr. Thompson knew exactly who I was and what I wanted before you ever called."

"You must admit, Kate," Zimmermann said clinically, "that when one looks first at the business with the baseball player, then at the conflict over whether or not a chemist actually performed tests he swears he never ran, and now at what seem to be groundless concerns on your part regarding the Ashburton Foundation and my long-standing computer engineer, it becomes somewhat difficult to get overly enthusiastic about your hunches and senses and theories. Now, if you've nothing further, I must get back to work."

"No," Kate said, smarting from the outburst by the usually cordial man. "Nothing, really, except the promise that no matter how long it takes, I will find out who, or what, is responsible for Ellen's bleeding disorder. Thanks for coming, Tom. I'm sorry it worked out this way." With a nod to both men, she left, fingers of self-doubt tightening their grip in her gut.

She bundled her clinic coat against the wind and snow and pushed head down out of the Omnicenter and onto the street. What if she were wrong, totally wrong about Redding and Horner, about the Omnicenter and Ellen's bleeding, about Reese? Perhaps, despite the critical situation in Berenson 421, despite the nagging fears about her own body, she should back off and let things simmer down. Perhaps she should listen to the advice of her father-in-law and reorder her priorities away from Metropolitan Hospital.

They were waiting for her in her office: Stan Willoughby, Liu Huang, and Rod Green, the flamboyant, black general surgeon who was, it was rumored, being groomed for a Harvard professorship.

"Kate," Willoughby said. "I was just writing you a note." He held the paper up for her to see.

Kate greeted the other two men and then turned back to Willoughby. He was tight. His stance and the strain in his smile said so. "Well?" she asked.

"Pardon?"

"The note, Stan. What would it have said?"

"Oh, I'm sorry. My mind is racing." He cleared his throat. "Kate, we need to talk with you."

"Well, sit down then, please." She felt her heart respond to her sudden apprehension. "A problem?"

Willoughby was totally ill at ease. "I . . . um . . . Kate, yesterday you did a frozen section of a needle biopsy on one of Dr. Green's patients."

"Yes, a breast. It was an intraductal adenocarcinoma. I reported the results to Dr. Green myself." Her pulse quickened another notch.

"Was there, um . . . any question in your mind of the—"

"What Dr. Willoughby is trying to say," Rod Green cut in, "is that I did a masectomy on a woman who, it appears, has benign breast disease." The man's dark eyes flashed.

"That's impossible." Kate looked first to Willoughby and then to Liu Huang for support, but saw only the tightlipped confirmation of the surgeon's allegation. "Liu?"

"I have examined specimen in great detail," the little man said carefully. "Track of biopsy needle enters benign adenoma. No cancer there or in any part of breast."

"Are . . . are you sure?" She could barely speak.

"Kate," Willoughby said, "I reviewed the slides myself. There's no cancer."

"But, there was. I swear there was."

"There was no cancer in my patient," Green said. "None." His fury at her was clearly under the most marginal control. "You have made a mistake. A terrible, terrible mistake."

Kate stared wide-eyed at the three men. It was a dream, a grotesque nightmare from which she would awake at any moment. Their stone faces blurred in and out of focus as her mind struggled to remember the cells. There were three breast biopsies, no, two, there were two. Green's patient was the first. The pathology was a bit tricky, but it was nothing she would ever miss in even one case out of a thousand, unless. . . .She remembered the fatigue and the strain of the previous morning, the stress of Jared's being away, the crank phone calls, and the disappearance of Ian Toole. No, her thoughts screamed, she couldn't have made such a mistake. It wasn't as if they were saying she had missed something, although even that kind of error would have been hard to believe, they were claiming she had read a condition that wasn't there. It was . . . impossible. There was just no other word.

"Did you check the slides from yesterday?" she managed. "The frozens?"

Willoughby nodded grimly. "Benign adenoma. The exact same pathology as in the main specimen." He handed her a plastic box of slides.

Green stood up, fists clenched. "I have heard enough. Dr. Bennett, thanks to you, a woman who came to me in trust has had her breast removed unnecessarily. When she sues, even though I will in all likelihood be one of the defendants, I shall also be her best witness." He started to leave and then turned back to her. "You know," he said, "that letter you sent to the papers about Bobby Geary was a pretty rotten thing to do." He slammed the door hard enough to shake the vase of roses on the corner of her desk.

Kate could barely hold the slide as she set it on the stage of her microscope. This time, the yellow-white light held no excitement, no adventure for her. She knew, even before she had completed focusing down, that the specimen was benign. It was that clear-cut. Her mistaking the pattern for a cancer would have been as likely as an Olympic diver springing off the wrong end of the board.

"Something's wrong," she said, her eye still fixed on the cells. The words reverberated in her mind. Something's wrong. She had said that to Bill Zimmermann not half an hour ago.

"Kate," Willoughby said gently, "I'm sorry."

Only after she looked up from the microscope did she realize she was crying. "Stan, I swear this is not the slide I read yesterday. It can't be." But even as she said the words, she admitted to herself that, as in the situation with Bobby Geary, her only defense was a protestation of innocence.

"You've been under a great deal of stress lately, Kate. Do you suppose that—"

"No!" She forced herself to lower her voice. "I remember the biopsy I saw yesterday. It was cancer. I didn't make a mistake."

"Look," Willoughby said, "I want you to take a few days off. Rest. After this coming weekend we can talk."

"But—"

"Kate, I'm taking you off the schedule for a while. Now I don't want you coming back into work until after we've had a chance to discuss things next week. Okay?" There was uncharacteristic firmness in the man's voice.

Meekly, she nodded. "Okay, but—"

"No buts. Kate, it's for your own good. I'll call you at home and check on how you're doing. Now off you go."

Kate watched her colleagues leave: Stan Willoughby, head down, shuffling a few feet ahead of Liu Huang, who turned for a moment and gave her a timid, but hopeful, thumbs-up sign. Then they were gone.

For a time she sat, uncertainly, isolation and self-doubt constricting every muscle in her body, making it difficult to move or even to breathe. With great effort, she pulled the telephone over and lifted the receiver. "I want to place a long-distance call, please," she heard her voice say. "It's personal, so charge it to my home phone. . . . I'm calling San Diego."

12

Thursday 20 December

It had taken narcotic painkillers and amphetamines along with his usual pharmacopoeia, but in the end, Becker had prevailed. Now he ached for sleep. He could not remember his last meal. Catnaps at his desk, cool showers every six or seven hours, bars of chocolate, cups of thick coffee for four days, or was it five? These had been his only succor.

Still, he had endured. In the morning, a messenger would hand deliver his manuscript and box of slides to the editor in chief of *The New England Journal of Medicine*. The letter accompanying the manuscript would give the man ten days to agree to publish the Estronate studies in their entirety within four months and to oversee the appointment of an international commission to assume responsibility for the initiation of Beckerian population control.

The study was in a shambles, with reference books, scrap paper, coffee cups, discarded drafts, candy-bar wrappers, and dirty glasses covering the furniture and much of the floor. Like a prizefighter at the moment of triumph, Willi Becker, more skeleton than man, stood in the midst of the debris and pumped his fists in the air. After forty years and through hardship almost unimaginable, he had finished. Now there was only the matter of gaining acceptance.

It was ironic, he acknowledged, that decades of the most meticulous research had come down to a few frenetic days, but that was the way it had to be. With the pathologist Bennett snooping about the Omnicenter and Cyrus Redding's antennae up, time had become a luxury he could no longer afford.

Studies in Estronate 250. Becker cleared off his easy chair, settled down, and indulged in thoughts of the accolades, honors, and other tributes to his genius and dedication certain to result from the publication and implementation of his work. He was nearing receipt of a Nobel Prize when the phone began ringing. It took half a dozen rings to break through his reverie and another four to locate the phone beneath a pile of journals.

"Hello?"

"John? Redding here."

The voice brought a painful emptiness to Becker's chest. For several seconds, he could not speak.

"John?"

Becker cleared his throat. "Yes, yes, Cyrus. I'm here."

"Good. Fine. Well, I hope I'm not disturbing anything important for you."

"Not at all. I was just . . . doing a little reading before bed." Did his voice sound as strained, as strangled, as it felt? "What can I do for you?" Please, he thought, let it be some problem related to their myasthenia. Let it be anything but . . .

"Well, John, I wanted to speak with you a bit about that business at the Omnicenter." Becker's heart sank. "You know," Redding continued, "the situation with these women having severe scarring of their ovaries and then bleeding to death."

"Yes, what about it?"

"Have you learned anything new about the situation since we spoke last?"

"No. Not really." Becker sensed that he was being toyed with.

"Well, John, you know that the whole matter has

piqued my curiosity, as well as my concern for the safety of our testing programs. Too many coincidences. Too much smoke for there not to be a fire someplace."

"Perhaps," Becker said, hanging onto the thread of hope that the man, a master at such maneuvers, was shooting in the dark. For a time, there was silence from Redding's end. Becker shifted nervously in his chair. "Cyrus?" he asked finally.

"I'm here."

"Was there . . . anything else?"

"John, I won't bandy words with you. We've been through too much together, accomplished too many remarkable things for me to try and humiliate you by letting you trip over one after another of your own lies."

"I . . . I don't understand."

"Of course you understand, John." He paused. "I know who you are. That is the gist of what I am calling to say. I know about Wilhelm Becker, and even more importantly, I know about Estronate Two-fifty."

Becker glanced over at his manuscript, stacked neatly atop the printer of his word processor, and forced himself to calm down. There was little he could think of that Redding could do to hurt him at this stage of the game. Still, Cyrus Redding was Cyrus Redding, and no amount of caution was too much. *Stay calm but don't underestimate*. "Your resourcefulness is quite impressive," he said.

"John, tell me truly, it was Estronate Two-fifty that caused the problems at the Omnicenter, wasn't it?"

"It was."

"The hemorrhaging is an undesirable side effect?"

Becker was about to explain that the problem had been overcome and that his hormone was, to all intents, perfected. He stopped himself at the last moment. "Yes," he said. "A most unfortunate bug that I have not been able to get out of the system."

"You should have told me, John," Redding said. "You should have trusted me."

"What do you want?"

"John, come now. It is bad enough you didn't respect me enough to take me into your confidence. It is bad enough your uncondoned experiments have put my entire company in jeopardy. Do not try to demean my intelligence. I want to extend our partnership to include that remarkable hormone of yours. After all, it was tested at a facility that I fund."

"Work is not complete. There are problems. Serious problems."

"Then we shall overcome them. You know the potential of this Estronate of yours as well as I do. I am prepared to make you an on-the-spot offer of, say, half a million dollars now and a similar amount when your work is completed to the satisfaction of my biochemists. And of course, there would be a percentage of all sales."

Sales. Becker realized that his worst possible scenario was being enacted. Redding understood not only the chemical nature of Estronate, but also its limitless value to certain governments. How? How in hell's name had the man learned so much so quickly? "I . . . I was planning eventually on submitting my work for publication," he offered.

Redding laughed. "That would be bad business, John. Very bad business. The value of our product would surely plummet if its existence and unique properties became general knowledge. Suppose you oversee the scientific end and let me deal with the proprietary."

"If I refuse," Becker said, "will you kill me?"

Again Redding laughed. "Perhaps. Perhaps I will. However, there are those, I am sure, who would pay dearly for information on the physician whom the Ravensbrück prisoners called the Serpent."

For a time there was silence. "How did you learn of all this?" Becker asked finally.

"Why don't we save explanations, Dr. Becker, for a time after our new business arrangement has been consummated."

"I need time to think."

"Take it. Take as much as you need up to, say, twenty-four hours."

"The intrinsic problems of the hormone may be insurmountable."

"A chance I will take. You owe me this. For the troubles you have caused at our testing facility, you owe me. In fact, there is something else you owe me as well."

"Oh?"

"I wish to know the individual at the Omnicenter who has been helping you with your work."

Becker started to protest that there was no such person, but decided against testing the man's patience. In less than twelve hours a messenger would deliver the Estronate paper and slides to *The New England Journal of Medicine*, making the hormone, in essence, public domain. He had already decided that exposure of his true identity and the risk of spending what little was left of his life in prison was a small price to pay for immortality. "Forty-eight hours," he said.

Redding hesitated. "Very well, then," he said finally. "Forty-eight hours it will be. You have the number. I shall expect to hear from you within two days. The Estronate work and the name of your associate. Good-bye." He hung up.

"Good-bye," Becker said to the dial tone. As he drew the receiver from his ear, he heard a faint but definite click. The sound sent fear stabbing beneath his breastbone. Someone, almost certainly William, was on the downstairs extension. How long? How long had he been there?

In the cluttered semidarkness of his study, Willi Becker strained his compromised hearing. For a time, there was only silence. Perhaps, he thought, there hadn't been a click at all. Then he heard the unmistakable tread of footsteps on the stairs.

"William?" Again there was silence. "William?"

"Yes, Father, it is." Zimmermann appeared suddenly in the doorway and stood, arms folded, looking placidly across at him.

"You . . . ah . . . you surprised me. How long have you been in the house?"

"Long enough." Zimmermann strode to the bookcase and poured himself a drink. He was, as usual, immaculately dressed. Light from the gooseneck reading lamp sparked off the heavy diamond ring on the small finger of his left hand and highlighted the sheen on his black Italian-cut loafers.

"You were listening in on my conversation, weren't you?"

"Oh, perhaps." Zimmermann snapped a wooden swizzle stick in two and used one edge to clean beneath his nails.

"Listening was a rude thing to do."

"Me, rude? Why, Father . . ."

"Well, if you heard, you heard. It really makes no difference."

"Oh?"

"Just how long *were* you listening in?"

Zimmermann didn't answer. Instead, he walked to the printer, picked up the Estronate manuscript, and turned it from one side to the other, appraisingly. "A half million dollars and then some. It would seem there is some truth about good things coming in small packages."

"Give me that." Becker was too weak, too depleted by the drugs, even to rise.

Zimmermann ignored him. "Wilhelm W. Becker, MD, PhD," he read. "So that's who my father is."

"Please, William."

"How good it is to learn that the man John Ferguson, who so ignored and abused my mother all those years, was not my father. The Serpent of Ravensbrück. That's my real father."

"I never abused her. I did what I had to do."

"Father, please. She knew that you could have come home much more often and didn't. She knew about your women, your countless women. She knew that neither of us would ever mean anything to you compared to your precious research."

Becker stared at his son with wide, bloodshot eyes. "You hate me, don't you?" There was incredulity in his voice.

"Not really. The truth is, I don't feel much for you one way or the other."

"But I was behind you all the way. My money sent you through school. Your position at the Omnicenter, how do you think that came about? Do you think Harold French just happened to drown accidentally at the moment you were experienced enough to take over for him? It was me!" Becker's hoarse, muddy voice had become barely audible. "If you care so little about me, William, then why have you helped me in my work all these years? Why?"

Zimmermann gazed blandly at his father. "Because of your connections, of course. Your friend Redding triples what the hospital pays me. You suggested my name, and he arranged for me to get my professorship. I know he did."

"He got you the position on my say-so, and he can have it taken from you the same way."

"Can he, now." Zimmermann held up the Estronate manuscript. "You lied to him. You told him there were still flaws in the work. Why? Are you thinking that once he finds out you have sent this off for publication, he will just walk away and leave us alone? Do you think he won't find out who I am? What I have been helping you do behind his back? Do you?" He was screaming. "Well, I tell you right here and now, Father, this is mine. I have paid for it over the years with countless humiliations. Cyrus Redding will have his Estronate, and I shall have my proper legacy."

"No!" Even as he shouted the word, Willi Becker felt the tearing pain in his left chest. His heart, weakened by disease, and sorely compromised by amphetamines, pounded mercilessly and irregularly. "My oxygen," he rasped. "In the bedroom. Oxygen and nitroglycerine." The study was beginning a nauseating spin.

For the first time, William Zimmermann smiled. "I'm afraid I can't hear you, Father," he said, benevolently. "Could you please speak up a bit?"

"Will . . . iam . . . please . . ." Becker's final words were muffled by the gurgle of fluid bubbling up from his lungs, and vomitus welling from his stomach. He clawed impotently in the direction of his son and then toppled over onto the rug, his face awash in the products of his own death.

Stepping carefully around his father's corpse, Zimmermann slipped the Estronate paper into a large envelope; then he removed the disc from the word processor and dropped it in as well. Next he copied a number from the leather-bound address book buried under some papers on one corner of the desk. Finally, he stacked the three worn looseleaf notebooks containing the Estronate data and tucked them under his arm. He would phone Cyrus Redding from the extension downstairs.

The pharmaceutical magnate evinced little surprise at Zimmermann's call or at the rapid turn of events in Newton. Instead, he listened patiently to the details of Willi Becker's life as the man's son knew them.

"Dr. Zimmermann," he said finally, "let us stop here to be certain I fully understand. Your father, when he was supervising construction of the Omnicenter, secretly had a laboratory built for himself in the subbasement?"

"Correct," Zimmermann said. "On the blueprints it is drawn as some sort of dead storage area, I think."

"And the only way to get into the laboratory is through an electronic security system?"

"The lock is hidden and coded electronically. The door is concealed behind a set of shelves."

"Does anyone besides you have the combination?"

"No. At least not as far as I know."

"Remarkable. Dr. Zimmermann, your father was a most brilliant man."

"My father is dead," Zimmermann said coolly.

"Yes," Redding said. "Yes, he is. Tell me, this bleeding problem, it *has* been eliminated?"

"Father modified his synthesis over a year ago. It was taking from six to eighteen months after treatment for the bleeding problem to develop. The three patients you know about were all treated a year ago last July. There have, to our knowledge, been no new cases since. Keep in mind, too, that there weren't that many to begin with. And most of those were mild."

"Yes, I understand. It is remarkable to me that you were able to insert your testing program into Carl Horner's computer system without his ever knowing."

"As you said, Mr. Redding, my father was a brilliant man."

"Yes. Well, then, I suppose we two should explore the possibility of a new partnership."

"The terms you laid out for my father are quite acceptable to me. I have the manuscript and the notebooks. Since the work is already completed, I would be willing to turn them over to you, no further questions asked, for the amount you promised him."

"That is a lot of money, Doctor."

"The amazing thing is that until I overheard your conversation with my father, I had not fully appreciated the valuable potential of the hormone." Zimmermann could barely keep from laughing out loud at his good fortune.

"Are you a biochemist, Doctor?"

"No. Not really."

"In that case, I should like to reserve my final offer until my own biochemist has had the chance to review the material, to see the laboratory, and to take himself through the process of synthesizing the hormone."

"When?"

"Why not tomorrow? Dr. Paquette, whom you know, will meet you at your office at, say, seven o'clock tomorrow night. My man Nunes will accompany him and will have the authority and the money to consummate our agreement if Dr. Paquette is totally satisfied with what he sees."

"Sounds fine. I'll make certain the side door to the Omnicenter is left open."

"That won't be necessary, Dr. Zimmermann. Paquette has keys."

"All right, then, seven o'clock. . . . Was there something else?"

"As a matter of fact, Dr. Zimmermann, there is. It's this whole business with the Omnicenter and that pathologist."

"You mean Bennett?"

"She has proven a very resilient young woman. Do you believe she was convinced by her conversation with our man at the Ashburton Foundation?"

"No. Not completely. She said she was going to continue investigating. The woman currently hospitalized here with complications from Estronate treatment is a close friend of hers."

"I see. You know, Doctor, none of this would have happened if you and your father hadn't conducted your work so recklessly and independently." His voice had a chilling edge. "Don't you feel a responsibility to this company for what you have done?"

"Responsibility?"

"If we are to have a partnership, I should like to know that the millions I have spent on the Omnicenter will not be lost because we were unable to neutralize one woman."

"But she has been neutralized. A serious mistake on a pathology specimen. She's been put on leave by her department head. Isn't that enough to discredit her?"

"I am no longer speaking of discrediting her, my friend. I am speaking of stopping her. You heard my conversation with your father. You know the importance of keeping Estronate a secret. It has been bad enough that Dr. Bennett is threatening, by her doggedness, to bring the Omnicenter tumbling down about our ears. If she uncovers Estronate, we stand to lose much, much more."

"I'll see to it that won't happen."

"Excellent. But remember, I don't handle disappointment well. Until tomorrow, then, Doctor."

"Yes, tomorrow."

William Zimmermann made a final inspection of the house, taking pains to wipe off anything he had touched. The precaution was, in all likelihood, unnecessary. The houseboy was due in at eight in the morning, and the death he would discover upstairs would certainly appear due to natural causes.

As he slipped out the back door of his father's house, a fortune in notebooks and computer printouts under his arm, Zimmermann was thinking about Kate Bennett.

The nightmare was a juggernaut, more pervasive, more oppressive it seemed with each passing hour. Its setting had changed from the clutter of her office to the deep-piled, fire-warmed opulence of Win Samuels's study, but for Kate Bennett, the change meant only more confusion, more humiliation, more doubt.

I know what it looks like. I know what it sounds like. But it isn't true. . . . I don't know who did it. . . . I don't know. . . . Dammit all, I just don't know.

Jared's return earlier in the evening had started on a positive note—an emotional hug and their first kiss in nearly a week. For a time, as they weaved their way through the crowds to the baggage area, he seemed unable to keep his hands or his lips off her. It seemed he was reveling in the freedom of at last truly acknowledging his love for her. *I accept you, regardless of what you are involved in, regardless of what the impact might be on me. I accept you because I believe in you. I accept you because I love you.*

But as she shared her nightmare with him, she could feel him pulling back, sense his enthusiasm erode. It showed first in his eyes, then in his voice, and finally in his touch. He was trying, Kate knew, perhaps even trying his best. But she also knew that confusion and doubt were taking their toll. Why would a company as large as Redding Pharmaceuticals do the things of which she was accusing them? The Ashburton Foundation had an impeccable reputation. What evidence was there that they were frauds? Why would anyone do something as horrible as switching biopsies? How did they do it? Weren't there any records of the tests she had run at the state lab? How did the letter about Bobby Geary fit in with all this?

I know what it looks like. I know what it sounds like. But it isn't true.

With each *why*, with each *I don't know*, Kate felt Jared drifting further and further into her nightmare. By the time the subject of his father and sister came up, she was feeling isolated, as stifled as before, perhaps more so. They were nearly halfway home to Essex.

"That is absolutely incredible," Jared had said, swinging sharply into the breakdown lane and jamming to a stop. "I . . . I don't believe it." It was the first time since his return that he had said those words. "After all these years, why wouldn't he tell me my sister was alive?"

"I don't know." The phrase reverberated in her mind. "Perhaps he was trying to spare you the ugliness."

"That makes no sense. You say he took you to this institution to convince you to turn down the position at Metro and concentrate on having babies?"

"That's what he said."

Jared shook his head. "Let me be sure I have this straight. My father, who has never communicated all that well with my wife to begin with, sends me out of town so that he can take her to an institution in the middle of nowhere and introduce her to the sister he had led me to believe died thirty-odd years ago. Does that make sense to you?"

"Jared," she said, her voice beginning to quaver, "nothing has made sense to me for days. All I can do is tell the truth."

"Well, if that's the case," he said finally, "I think I'd like to find out first hand why my father has been holding out on me."

"Couldn't we at least wait until—"

"No! I can't think of a damn thing to do about Bobby Geary or the Omnicenter or the Ashburton Foundation or the runaway technician or the goddamn breast biopsies, but I sure as hell can do something about my father."

Without waiting for a reply, he had swung off and under the highway and had screeched back onto the southbound lane, headed for Boston.

Now, in the uncomfortably warm study, Kate sat by a hundred-and-thirty-year-old leaded glass window, watching the fairyland Christmas lights of Louisburg Square and listening to her husband and her father-in-law argue over whether she was a liar, a woman in desperate need of professional help, or some combination of the two. Jared, in all fairness, was doing his best to give her the benefit of the doubt, but it had, purely and simply, come down to her word against his father's. When taken with the other issues, the other confusions she had regaled him with since his landing at Logan, it was not hard to understand why he was having difficulty taking her side.

"Once again, Jared," Win Samuels said with authoritative calm, "we dined together—Jocelyn's special duck. After dinner we talked. Then we went for a long drive in the country. I hadn't been out of the house all day and was getting a severe case of cabin fever. We did stop at the Stonefield School; I'm on the board of trustees there. But I assure you, Son, our visit was quite spur of the moment. We were only a few miles from the school when I remembered a set of papers in the back seat that I was planning on mailing off tomorrow to Gus Leggatt, the school administrator. While we were there, we did look in on some of the children. Largely because of our visit, on the way home I was able to share my fears with Kate about what happens to the rate of birth defects in children of older mothers. Kate explained the advances in amniocentesis to me; facts, I might add, that I found quite reassuring. I mentioned your sister, certainly, but I never implied she was alive. I'm sorry, Jared. And I am sorry for you, too, Kate." He looked at her levelly. "You've been under a great deal of pressure. Perhaps . . . a rest, some time off."

Time off. Kate sighed. Winfield had no way of knowing Stan Willoughby had already seen to that. She rose slowly, and crossed to Jared. "Stonefield School is listed in information," she said wearily. "Broderick, Massachusetts. If the snow doesn't get any worse, I can drive us there in forty-five minutes to an hour. That should settle this once and for all."

"Do you want to come with us, Dad?" Jared asked.

"There is no reason to go *anyplace*," Win Samuels said simply. "Kate, Jared's sister had severe birth defects and died exactly when he thinks she did, thirty years ago. Perhaps you had a dream of some sort. Strands of fantasy woven into reality. It happens, especially when one has been under an inordinate amount of stress such as you—"

"It is not stress! It is not stress, it is not a dream, it is not the desperate lie of a desperate woman, it is not . . . insanity." She confronted him, her eyes locked on his. Samuels held his ground, his face an expressionless mask. "It is the truth. The truth! I don't know why you are doing this, I don't know what you hope to accomplish. But I do know one thing. I'm not going to break. You manipulate the people in your life like they were pieces on some some enormous game board. Jocelyn to king's knight four, Jared to queen three. Not your turn? Well you'll just throw in a few thousand dollars and make it your turn."

Samuels moved to speak, but Kate stopped him with raised hands. "I'm not through. I want to tell you something, Win. You've underestimated me. Badly. I've made it through a childhood of total loneliness, an education of total aimlessness, and a marriage to an alcoholic madman who insisted on picking out my pantyhose for me. I've survived and grown in a profession where I am patronized, and discriminated against. I've dealt with men who couldn't bring their eyes, let along their minds, above my breasts. I've dealt with them and I've succeeded.

"It's been hard. At times, it's been downright horrible. But for the last five years, I've had a secret weapon. He's right there, Win. Right over there." She nodded toward Jared. "When I forget that I'm okay, he reminds me. When I have to face the Norton Reeses and the Arlen Paquettes and, yes, the Winfield Samuelses of this world, he gives me strength. I love him and I have faith in him. Sooner or later, he's going to see the way you toy with the lives of those around you. Sooner or later, you'll go to move him, and he won't be there."

"Are you done?" Samuels said.

"Yes, I'm done. And I don't want to hear any more from you unless it's an apology and the truth about the other night. How could you think I wouldn't tell Jared? How could you think I wouldn't remember where we went, what we did? Please, Jared, let's get going. It's late, and we have quite a drive ahead of us."

At that moment, there was a noise, the clearing of a throat, from the doorway. The three of them turned to the sound. Jocelyn Trent stood holding a silver tray with coffee and tea.

"How long have you been there?" Samuels demanded. The woman did not answer. "Well?"

She hesitated; then she set the tray on the nearest table and ran from the room.

"Stonefield School," Kate said. "See, I told you I could find it. Only two wrong turns." She swung into the driveway, past the small sign, and up to the front door. "This is almost the exact hour we were here the other night. With any luck, the nurse who was on duty then will be on again. Her name was Bicknell, Sally Bicknell; something like that. I'll recognize her. She wore about eighty gold bracelets and had rings on three or four fingers of each hand. What a character!"

Her chatter was, she knew, somewhat nervous. Jared

had said little during their drive. His pensiveness was certainly understandable, but she found herself wishing he could recapture at least some of the emotion he had shown at the airport. No matter, she consoled herself. Two minutes at Stonehill, and he would know that, in this arena, at least, she was telling the truth. How foolish of Win to think things would not develop the way they had. How unlike the man to miss predicting a person's actions as badly as he had missed hers.

The nurse, Bicknell, was working at her desk in a small office just off the lobby. Her hair was pulled back in a tight bun, and she was wearing only a single gold chain on one wrist. Hardly the flamboyant eccentric Kate had depicted. It was an observation, Kate noted uneasily, that was not overlooked by her husband.

"Are you sure it's the same woman?" he whispered, as they crossed the lobby.

"It's her. Hi, Miss Bicknell. Remember me?"

The woman took only a second. "Of course. You were with Mr. Samuels four—no, no,—three nights ago. Right?"

"Exactly. You have an excellent memory."

"An elephant," Sally Bicknell said, tapping one finger against her temple.

"This is my husband, Jared, Miss Bicknell. Mr. Samuels's son."

"Pleased to meet you." The woman took the hand Jared offered. "We don't get too many evening visitors here at Stonefield. In fact, we don't get too many visitors at other times, either." She looked around. "Sort of a forgotten land, I guess."

"Miss Bicknell, we came to see my husband's sister."

The woman's expression clouded. "I . . . I'm afraid I don't understand."

Kate felt an ugly apprehension set in. "Lindsey Samuels," she said, a note of irritation—or was it panic?—in her voice, "the girl we saw Monday night right over there." She pointed to the blue velvet curtain.

Sally Bicknell looked at her queerly and then ushered

them over and drew back the curtain. "Her?" The girl was there, lumbering about exactly as she had been before.

"Yes, exactly," Kate said. "That's her, Jared. That's Lindsey."

"I'm sorry, Mrs. Samuels, but you're mistaken. That girl's name is Rochelle Coombs. She is sixteen years old and has a genetic disease called Hunter's Syndrome."

Kate stopped herself at the last possible moment from calling the woman a liar. "Could I see her medical records, please?"

The nurse snapped the curtain shut. "Her medical records are confidential. But I assure you, her name is Rochelle Coombs, not—what did you say?"

"Lindsey," Jared said, "Lindsey Samuels." It was, Kate realized, the first time he had spoken since just after their arrival.

"It is not Lindsey Samuels." Sally Bicknell completed her sentence.

In that moment, Kate realized what had bothered her so about the girl the first time she had observed her. She was too young to have been Jared's sister. Far too young. Her thick features and other physical distortions added some years, but not twenty of them. The girl's grotesqueness had made her too uncomfortable to look very closely. Had Win Samuels counted on that? Silently, she cursed her own stupidity. Helpless and beaten, she could only shrug and shake her head.

"Will there be anything else?" Bicknell asked.

Kate looked over at Jared, who shook his head. "No," she said huskily. "We're . . . we're sorry for the intrusion."

"In that case," the woman said, "I have rounds to make." She turned and, without showing them out, walked away.

Kate felt far more ill than angry. As they approached the car, she handed Jared the keys. "You drive, please. I'm not up to it. Your father told me it was Lindsey, Jared. I swear he did. And that woman was right there when he said it."

There was, she realized, no sense in discussing the matter further. Win Samuels had set up a no-lose situation for himself. Either she would be impressed by his demonstration, in which case she might have agreed to back off at the hospital and, as he wished, turn her attention to domestic issues; or she would be angered enough to do exactly what she had done. His son, already in doubt about her, would be drawn further away from their marriage and toward a political future, unencumbered by a wife whose priorities and mental state were so disordered. All that for only the price of a tankful of gas and whatever it cost to buy off Sally Bicknell. Nice going, Win, she thought. Nice goddamn going. She sank into her seat and stared sightlessly into the night.

13

Friday 21 December

"She's out, suspended, finished. I did it," Norton Reese boasted exultantly. "Yesterday afternoon. I tried to call you then, but there was no answer."

Still in his bed at the Ritz, Arlen Paquette squinted at his watch, trying to get the numbers in focus. Seven-thirty? Was that right? Was goddamn Reese waking him up at seven-thirty in the morning? He fumbled for the bed-side lamp, wincing at the shellburst in his temples. Some-where in the past four hours, he had passed from being drunk to being hung over. His mouth tasted like sewage, and his muscles felt as if he had lost a gang fight.

"Norton, just a second here while I wake up a little bit." He worked a cigarette from a wrinkled packet and lit it on the third try. Over the past week, his smoking had gone from his usual four or five cigarettes a day to three packs. For a moment, he eyed the half-empty quart of Dewar's on the bureau. "No, goddamn it," he muttered, "At least not yet." It took two hands to hold the phone steady against his ear. "Now, sir, just how did you go about accomplishing this remarkable feat of yours?"

Paquette listened to Reese's excited recap of the events leading to the unofficial suspension of Kate Bennett by her chief, Stan Willoughby. By the time the administrator had finished, Paquette had made his way across to the scotch and buried half a water glass full. The story was disgusting. A woman had lost her breast unnecessarily, and another had been professionally destroyed, and he, as much as the idiot on the other end of the phone, was responsible. As he listened to Reese's crowing, a resolve began to grow within him. He picked up a picture of Kate Bennett from the floor by his bed, wondering briefly how it had gotten there.

"Norton," he said cheerfully, "you've done one hell of a job there. Our friend's gonna be pleased when I tell him. Real pleased. Say, listen. Are you going to be at your office for a while . . . Good. I'd like to stop by and get some of the details in person. Probably be nine-thirty or so . . . Great. See you then."

He hung up and studied the picture in his hand. The scotch had stilled the shakes and begun to alleviate the pounding in his head. "I think you've taken enough shit from us, Dr. Bennett," he said. "It's time someone helped you fight back."

A glance at his watch, and he called Darlington. His wife answered on the second ring. "Honey, have the kids left for school yet? . . . Good. They're not going. I want you to pack them up and drive to your mother's house. . . . Honey, I know where your mother lives. If you step on it, you can be there by dinner time. There've been some problems here with old Cyrus, and I just want to be sure you and the kids are safe. . . . Maybe a few days, maybe a week. I don't know. Please, honey. Trust me on this one for a little while. I'll explain everything. And listen, I love you. I'm sorry about the other night and I love you. Not a word to anyone, now. Just get out and go to your mother's."

Paquette showered and then shaved, taking greater pains than usual not to nick himself. He dressed in a suit he had just bought, eschewing the vest in favor of a light brown cashmere sweater. Some Visine, another shot of scotch, some breath mints, and he was ready. On his way to the hospital, he would attend to one final item of business, stopping at an electronics store to purchase a miniature tape recorder.

"Okay, Doctor," he said to Kate's picture, "let's go get us some evidence." He glanced at the mirror. For the first time in nearly two weeks he liked what he saw.

Nothing to do. Nowhere to go. No one to hold. The thoughts, the futility, kept intruding on Kate's efforts to wring another hour, even another half hour, of sleep from the morning. They had spent the night—what was left of it after their return from Stonehill—in separate beds. Or perhaps Jared hadn't slept at all. She had offered him food, then company, and then sex, but his only request had been to be left alone. After an hour or so of staring at the darkened ceiling over their bed, she had tiptoed down the hall and peeked into the living room. He was right where she had left him, on the couch, chewing on his lower lip, and studying the creases in his palm. Her immediate impulse was to go to him, to beg him to believe her, to plead for his faith. The feeling disappeared as quickly as it had arisen. If their marriage had come down to begging, she was beaten. Aching with thoughts of what he was going through, at the choices he was trying to make, she had crept quietly back to bed, hoping that before long, she would feel him nudging his way under the covers.

Nothing to do. Nowhere to go. No one to hold. The ringing of the phone interrupted the litany. Kate glanced at the clock. Eight-thirty. Not too bad. The last time she had looked it was only six.

"Hello?"

"Kate?" It was Ellen.

"Hi. How're you feeling?"

"I got concerned when you didn't stop by this morning, and I called your office." Her voice was quite hoarse, her speech distorted. "When you didn't answer I rang the department secretary. Kate, what's the matter? Are you sick?"

"Hey, wait a minute, now. Let us not forget who is the patient here, and who is the doctor, okay?"

"Kate, be serious. She said she didn't know what day you'd be back. I . . . I got frightened. They're giving me more blood, and now I have a tube down my nose. I think the inside of my stomach has started bleeding."

"Shit," Kate said softly.

"What?"

"I said 'shit.' "

"Oh. Well, *are* you all right?"

Kate pulled a lie back at the last possible instant. "Actually, no," she said. "Physically I'm fine, but there's been trouble at work and here at home. I've been asked to take some time off while my department head sorts through some problems with a biopsy."

"Oh, Kate. And here I am all wrapped up in my own problems. I'm sorry. I know it sounds foolish coming from where I'm lying, but is there anything I can do?"

"No, El, just be strong and get well, that's all."

"Don't talk to *me*, Katey. Talk to these little platelets or whatever they're called. They're the ones who are screwing up. You said trouble at home, too. Jared?"

Stop asking about me, dammit. You're bleeding to death! "I'm afraid Jared's wife and his father in all their infinite wisdom have put him in a position where he's going to have to choose between them." At that moment, she began wondering where he was. Upstairs in the guestroom, perhaps? Maybe still on the couch. She listened for a telltale sound, but there was only heavy silence.

"You versus Win?" Ellen said. "No contest. Thank goodness. I thought it was something serious." Her cheer was undermined by the weakness in her voice.

"Listen, my friend," Kate said. "I'll see you later today. I may be shut out of the pathology department, but I'm not shut out of the library. There are two Australian journals I'm expecting in from the NIH. Together, we're going to beat this. I promise you."

"I believe you," Ellen said. "I really do. See you later, Doc."

Kate set the receiver down gently, then slipped into a blue flannel nightshirt, a gift from Jared, and walked to the living room. Roscoe, who had materialized from under the bed, padded along beside her. She glanced through the doorway and then systematically checked the rest of the house. She had, as she feared, read the silence well. Jared had left.

"Well, old shoe," she said, scratching her dog behind one ear, "it looks like you and me. How about a run together and then some shirred eggs for breakfast. Later, maybe we'll make love."

The letter, in Jared's careful printing, was on the kitchen table. He had taken their wedding picture from the mantel, and used it as a weight to keep the single sheet in place. Kate moved the photograph enough to read his words, but left it touching the page.

> It sounds so easy, so obvious, that I'm not sure I even listened when the minister said the words. "For better or for worse." It all sounds so easy until one day you stop and ask yourself, For whose better? For whose worse? What do I do when her better seems like my worse? Dammit, Kate, I'm forty years old and I feel like such a child. Do you know that in all the time she was alive, I never once heard my mother say no to my father? Some role model, huh? Next came Lisa—bright, beautiful, and imbued with absolutely no ambition or direction. I thought she would make a perfect wife. She cooked the soup and pinched back the coleus, and I kept her pipe filled with good dope and decided when we could afford to do what, and that was that. I still don't know why she ran off the way she did, and if

another Lisa had come along, I probably would have married her in a snap. But another Lisa didn't. You did.

Almost before I knew it, I had fallen in love with and married a woman who had as rich and interesting and complicated a life outside of our marriage as I did. Probably, more so. After first mother and then Lisa, it was like moving to a foreign country for me. New customs. New mores. What do you mean I was wrong to assume we'd have the same last name? What do you mean I was wrong to assume that you would be free to attend three rallies and a campaign dinner with me? What do you mean I should have asked first? What do you mean you've been involved in trouble at your job that might affect my career? I could go on all night listing my misguided assumptions in this marriage. It's as though I don't have the programming to adapt.

Well, I may not have the programming, but I do have the desire. It's taken most of the night sitting here to feel sure of that. If what you've said is all true, I want to do whatever I can to help straighten it out. If what you've told me is not true, then I also want to face that issue and my commitment to you, and we'll get whatever kind of help is necessary. If we don't make it, it won't be because I ran away.

I've gone to speak to my father and then, who knows, perhaps a chat with Norton Reese. Bear with me, Kate. It may say five years on the calendar, but this marriage business is still new stuff for me. I love you. I really do.

Jared

Kate reread the letter, laughing and crying at once. Jared's words, she knew, meant no more than a temporary reprieve, a respite from the nightmare. Still, he had given her the one thing she needed most next to answers: time. Time to work through the events that were steamrolling her life.

"We're going to find out, Rosc," she said grimly. "We're going to find out who, and we're going to find out why."

A sharp bark sounded from the living room, and Kate realized that she had been talking to herself. Through the doorway, she could see Roscoe prancing uncomfortably by the door to the rear deck.

"Oh, poor baby," she laughed. "I'm sorry." Focused on letting the dog out, she missed the slight movement outside the kitchen window and failed to sense the eyes watching her. She pulled open the slider, and Roscoe dashed out into a most incredible morning. The temperature, according to the thermometer by the door, was exactly freezing. Fat, lazy flakes, falling from a glaring, silver-white sky vanished into a ground fog that was as dense as any Kate could remember. Roscoe dashed across the deck, and completely disappeared into the shroud halfway down the steps to the yard.

Kate estimated the height of the fog at three or four feet. Much of it, she guessed, was arising off the surface of nearby Green Pond, a small lake that because of warm underground feeders, was always late to freeze and early to thaw. Winter fog was not uncommon on the North Shore, especially around Essex, but this was spectacular. It was a morning just begging to be run through.

She dressed and then stretched, sorting out the route they would run, mixing low spots and high hills and straightaways along five miles of back roads. Wearing a gold watch cap and a high-visibility red sweatsuit, she trotted out the front door and whistled for Roscoe. He was almost at her side before she could see him.

"A fiver this morning, dog," she said, as they moved up the sloping driveway and out of the fog. "Think you're mutt enough to handle it?"

At the end of the drive, she turned right. Had she

mapped their route to the left, she might have wondered about the BMW, parked not particularly near anyone's house, and perhaps even noticed the blue Metropolitan Hospital parking sticker on the rear window.

It was near perfect air for running, cold and still. To either side of the narrow roadway, the fog covered the forest floor like cotton batting.

"Race pace, today, Rosc," she said. "Eight-minute miles or less. And I'm not waiting for you, so keep up." In reality, she knew Roscoe could maintain her pace all day, and still stop from time to time to sniff out a shrub or two. After a quarter of a mile, they left the pavement and turned onto a plowed dirt road meandering along an active stream named on the maps as Martha's Brook. Kate loved crossing the picturesque, low-walled fieldstone bridges that spanned the water; in part, she had chosen this route because of them.

By the end of the first mile, her thoughts had begun to separate themselves from the run. For the next two or three miles, she knew, her ideas would flow more freely, her imagination more clearly, than in any other situation. Following a kaleidoscope of notions, a kind of sorting-out process, her mind settled on the breast biopsy. Perhaps under the stress of exhaustion, Ellen's deteriorating condition, and the rest of the chaos in her life, she actually *had* made a mistake. For a time, the grisly thought held sway, bringing with it a most unpleasant tightness in her gut. Gradually, though, the truth reappeared, emerging like a phoenix from the ashes of her self-doubt. The cells she had read had been, she was certain, cancerous. But if they had been, then somewhere a switch had been made and later reversed. But how? who? The broken cryostat was, she decided, part of the puzzle. Sheila? Possible. But why? The images led into those of other tissues, other cells—the ovaries of Beverly Vitale and Ginger Rittenhouse. Ever since the discovery of anthranilic acid in her own vitamins, Kate had, several times a day, been checking herself for bruises and wondering if pockets of scar tissue in her ovaries had already made a mockery of their discussions about having children. She had to find out. The answer, almost certainly, lay in the Omnicenter, and more specifically, in the data banks of Carl Horner's Monkeys.

Kate was heading down a steep grade toward the first of the fieldstone overpasses when the blue BMW crested the hill behind her and accelerated. Immersed in the run and her thoughts, she lost several precious seconds after hearing the engine before she turned to it. The speeding automobile made a sharp, unmistakably deliberate swing to the right and headed straight for her. There was no time to think. There was only time to react. The waist-high wall of the bridge was only a few feet away. A single step, and she dove for the top of it. She was in midair when the BMW hit her just below her right knee. The impact spun her in a horizontal pinwheel. She struck the edge of the wall midthigh and then tumbled over it. As she fell, she heard the crunch of metal against stone and the agonizing cry of her dog.

The fall, twelve feet from the top of the wall, was over before she could make any physical adjustment whatsoever. She landed on her back in a drift of half-frozen snow; air exploded from her lungs, and a branch from a rotting log tore through her sweatshirt and her right side, just below her ribs. Desperately, she tried to draw in a breath. For five seconds, ten, nothing would move. Finally, she felt a whisper of air, first in the back of her throat and then in her chest. She tried to deepen her effort, but a searing pain from her side cut her short. She touched the pain and then checked the fingertips of her tan woolen gloves. They were soaked with blood.

Frantically, she tried to sort out what had happened. She had been hit. Roscoe had been hit, too. Possibly killed. It had not been an accident. Whoever was driving had tried to run them down. Gingerly, she tested her hands and then her legs. Her right leg throbbed, and her right foot, which was dangling in the icy water of the brook, seemed twisted at an odd angle. *Please, God, don't let it be broken*. There was pain, but, gratefully, there was full movement as well.

At that moment, overhead, a car door opened and closed. She turned toward the noise, but could see nothing. It took several seconds to realize why. She was quite literally buried in the fog. From somewhere above and to her left, a branch snapped; then another. The driver of the car was making his way down the steep embankment, more than likely to check the completeness of his work. Could he see where she was? Possibly not. The fog might well be concealing her, at least from farther away than ten feet or so. Carefully, she slipped off her gold cap and stuffed it into the snow. The burning rent in her side was making it hard to concentrate. Should she try crawling away beneath the fog? Would her battered legs even hold weight? Her back was hurting. Should she test it, roll to one side? Could she?

From farther to her left, she heard still another snap and then a soft splash and a groan. Her pursuer had stepped or slipped into the brook. It was definitely a man, or perhaps there were two. She thought about Roscoe. Was he still alive? Was he helpless? in pain? The images sickened her.

For a time, there was silence. Kate peered into the mist, but could see nothing. The pain in her legs, back, and side sent chilly tears down her cheeks. Then she heard it, a soft crunch, still downstream from where she was lying, but almost certainly moving in her direction. She swept her hand over the snow, searching for a rock or a stick of some sort. Her fingers touched and then curled about a dead branch, perhaps an inch and a half in diameter. She drew it toward her. Was it too long, too unwieldy, to use? She would get one swing, if that, and no more. Again, she jiggled the branch. It seemed unentangled, but she would not know for sure until she made her move.

Suddenly, she saw movement to her left, the legs and gloved hand of a man, not ten feet away. Dangling from his hand, swinging loosely back and forth, was a tire wrench.

Kate drew in a breath, held it, and tensed. At any moment she would be seen. The legs were just turning toward her when she lunged, rising painfully to her knees and swinging the branch in the same motion. Her weapon, three feet long with several protruding wooden spikes, came free of the snow and connected with the side of the man's knee. He dropped instantly to the water, as much from the surprise and location of the blow as from its force.

Ignoring the pain in her legs and side, Kate stood up, readying the branch for another swing. It was then she saw her attacker's face.

"Bill!" she cried, staring at the wild-eyed apparition. Her hesitation was costly. Zimmermann lashed out with his feet, sweeping her legs out from under her and sending her down heavily against the rocks and into the shallow, icy water. The wrench lay in the snow, just to his right. Zimmermann grabbed at it and still on his knees in the brook, swung wildly. Sparks showered from a small boulder, inches from Kate's hip. She rolled to her left as he swung again, the blow glancing off her thigh. Another spin and she was free of the water, scrambling for footing on the icy rocks and snow. Zimmermann, still clutching the wrench, crawled from the brook and dove at her ankles. He grabbed the leg of her sweatpants, but she was on her feet with enough leverage to jerk away. Before he could make another lunge, she was off, stumbling along the bank and then under the fieldstone bridge.

The ground fog, once her shield, was now her enemy. Again and again, she slipped on rocks she could not see and tripped over fallen logs. From the grunts and cries behind her, though, she could tell that Zimmermann was encountering similar difficulties. Still, the man was coming. She had been so stupid not to have considered that he might be involved in the evil at the Omnicenter, so foolish to think that he didn't know what was going on.

She glanced over her shoulder. Zimmermann, visible from the chest up, was bobbing along not thirty yards behind her. He was over six feet tall, and the deep snow was, she feared, more difficult for her to negotiate than it was for him. In addition, she was hobbled by the tightness and pain in her leg where the fender of Zimmermann's car had struck. She had only two advantages: her conditioning and her knowledge of the area. If the man caught up with her, she knew neither would matter. She risked another check behind her. He was closer, unquestionably closer. The snow was slowing her down too much. She cut to her left and into the brook. There, at least, Zimmermann's longer legs would be no advantage, possibly even a hindrance. The frigid, ankle-high water sloshed in her running shoes and bathed her lower legs in pain. Could she outrun or at least outlast him? It was possible, but one slip, one misplaced branch, and it would be over for her. She had to get back to the road. Either back to the road or . . . or hide.

She slowed, casting about for familiar landmarks. Somewhere nearby was a culvert, a steel tube, perhaps three feet across, running fifty or so feet through the high embankment on which the road had been built. If she could find it, and if it were not blocked, she could crawl inside, hoping that Zimmermann would not see her or, even if he did, would be too broad across the shoulders to follow.

She glanced downstream just as the man fell. In seconds, however, he was on his feet and, arms flailing for balance, was again beginning to close on her. If she was to do something, anything, it had to be soon. At that moment, she saw what she had been seeking. It was a huge old elm, sheared in two by lightning, its upper half forming a natural bridge across Martha's Brook. Fifty yards beyond it, if her memory hadn't failed her, the stream would bend sharply to the left, and just beyond the bend, at about knee level, would be the culvert that Roscoe had discovered two or three years before.

She ducked beneath the elm and ran low to the water, her eyes barely above the fog. At the bend, she dropped to all fours, and began crawling along the icy embankment. *Please, be there. Be there.* Frozen chunks of snow scraped her face, and rocks tore away the knees of her sweatpants. She felt a fullness in her throat and coughed, spattering the snow beneath her with blood, more than likely, she knew, from a punctured lung.

She crawled ahead, sliding one hand along the slope at the height where she remembered the culvert. Her hopes had begun to fade when she saw it. The diameter was even less than she had thought, nearer two feet than three, but it was still wide enough for her to fit. A fine trickle of water suggested that the small pond on the other side of the embankment was lower than her exit point. From somewhere in the fog, not far back, came a splash. Zimmermann was close. Kate ducked into the dank, rusty pipe; inches at a time, she began to pull herself toward the faint, silver-gray light at the other end.

The culvert, coarse and corroded, was painfully cold. With the exertion of her run now past, Kate was beginning to freeze. Her feet, especially her toes, throbbed, and the sound of her teeth chattering like castanets was resonating through the metal tube. Again she coughed. Again there was the spattering of blood. She was, perhaps, a third of the way along when she heard him, crunching about in the snow behind her. Fearing the noise her movement was making, she stopped, biting down on the collar of her sweatshirt to stop the chattering.

"Kate, I know you're hurt," he called out. "I want to help you. No more violence. We can work things out."

Did he know where she was? Dammit, why couldn't she stop shaking?

"Kate, you want to know about the drugs, about whether or not you are sterile, about how you can stop your friend's bleeding. I can answer all your questions. I can get you someplace warm."

Frightened of the bleeding in her chest and numb in those areas of her body that weren't in merciless pain, Kate found herself actually considering the man's offer. Warm. He had promised she would be warm. Warmth and answers. Maybe she *should* try and reason with him. She forced her mind to focus on the wrench and bit down on her sweatshirt all the harder.

"You know," Zimmermann called out, "even if you make it back, no one is going to believe your story. I have my whereabouts at this moment completely vouched for. You're crazy and a pathological liar. Everyone knows that. You're the talk of the hospital. Half the people think you're on drugs, and the other half think you're just plain sick. I'm the only person who can help you, Kate. I'm the only one who can save your friend. I'm the only one who can get you warm. Now come on over here, and let's talk."

Twenty feet away from where Zimmermann stood, Kate buried her face in the crook of her arm and struggled against the insanity that was telling her the man meant what he was saying about no violence.

"Suit yourself," she heard him say. "It's your funeral. Yours and your friend's."

Steaming coffee. Crackling, golden fire. Sunshine. White beach. Flannel. Down comforter. Fur slippers. Stifling her sobs in the sleeve of her sweatshirt, Kate fought the fear and the pain and the cold with images of anything that was warm. Cocoa. Wood stove. Jacuzzi. Tea. Quartz heater. Electric blanket. Soup. Behind her now, there was only silence. Had he left? She strained to hear the engine of his car. Had he found the culvert and crossed over the road to wait by the far end? Her legs and arms were leadened by the cold. Could she even make it out? *Damn him,* she thought, forcing herself ahead an inch. He knew how to save Ellen. *Damn him.* Another inch. He even knew whether she herself had been sterilized or not. *Damn him. Damn him. Damn him.* The silver-gray hole grew fainter. Her eyes closed. Her other senses clouded. Seconds later, what little consciousness remained slipped away.

◆

It was as if a decade had melted away. Jared faced his father as he had so many times during the confused years of Lisa and Vermont, struggling to remain reasonably calm and maintain eye contact.

"Kate is sick, son. Very sick," Samuels said. "I would suggest we make arrangements for her hospitalization as soon as possible, and as soon as that is done, you should begin to separate your career from her. She will bring you down. I promise you that. Martha Mitchell did it to her husband, and I assure you, Kate will do it to you—if she hasn't already. I've contacted Sol Creighton at Laurel Hill. He has a bed waiting for her, and he says we have grounds for commitment if necessary. With some time, and perhaps some medication, he assures me that even the worst sociopathic personality can be helped."

"Dad, stop using that word. You have no right to diagnose her."

"Jared, face the facts. Kate is a lovely woman. I care for her very much. But she is a liar, and quite possibly a liar who completely believes her own fabrications. I know she looks perfectly fine and sounds logical, but the hallmark of a sociopath is exactly that physical and verbal glibness. The only way to realize what one is dealing with is to catch her in lie after lie."

"But—"

"Do you really think someone other than Kate sent that letter to the papers about Bobby Geary?"

"I don't know."

"And the chemist, and the Ashburton Foundation, and the nurse at Stonefield. Do you think they were all lying?"

"I don't—"

"And what about the biopsy? You tell me everyone in Kate's department says she made a mistake. The truth is right there in the slides. Yet there is Kate, insisting she did nothing wrong."

Samuels withdrew a cigar from his humidor, tested

the aroma along its full length, and then clipped and lit it. He motioned for Jared to have one if he wished.

Jared glanced at his watch, made an expression of distaste, and shook his head. "Christ, Dad, it's only eight-thirty in the morning."

Samuels shrugged. "It's my morning and it's my cigar."

Jared looked across the desk at his father, trim and confident, wearing the trappings of success and power as comfortably as he wore his slippers. Unable to speak, Jared stared down at the gilded feet of his father's desk, resting on the exquisite oriental carpet. A secret weapon, that's what Kate had called him. A source of strength for her. She had spoken the words to his father, but they were really meant for him. With tremendous effort, he brought his eyes up.

"I hear what you are saying, Dad. And I understand what you want."

"And?"

"I can't go along with it. Kate says she's innocent of any lying, and I believe her."

"You what?"

Jared felt himself wither before the man's glare. "I believe her. And I'm going to do what I can to help clear her." There was a strength in his words that surprised him. He stood up. "I'll tell you something else, Dad. If I find that she's telling the truth, you're going to have a hell of a lot of explaining to do."

Samuels rose, anger sparking from his eyes. "I seem to recall a conversation similar to this. We were in that matchbox office of yours in Vermont. I warned you not to marry that rootless hippie you were living with. I told you there was nothing to her. You stood before me then just as you are now and as much as threw me out of your office. Two years later your wife and daughter were gone, and you were crawling to me for help. Have you forgotten?"

"Dad, that was then. This is—"

"Have you forgotten?"

"No, I haven't."

"Have you forgotten the money and the time I spent trying to find that woman despite my own personal feelings about her?"

"Look, I don't want to fight."

"Get out," Samuels said evenly. "When you come to your senses, when you discover once again that I was right, call me."

"Dad, I—"

"I said get out." Samuels turned his back and stared out the window.

As Jared opened the door, he nearly collided with Jocelyn Trent, who was standing up and backing away at the same time. Quickly, he closed the door behind him.

"What were you doing there?" he asked.

"Jared, please, don't make me explain." She took him by the arm, led him to the hall closet, and began helping him on with his coat. "Meet me in ten minutes," she whispered in his ear. "The little variety store on the corner of Charles and Mount Vernon. I have something important for you, for Kate actually."

The study door opened just as she was letting Jared out. Winfield Samuels stood, arms folded tightly across his chest, and watched him go.

Even dressed down, in pants and a plain wool overcoat, Jocelyn Trent turned heads. Jared stood by the variety store and watched several drivers slow as they passed where she was waiting to cross Charles Street. He left the shelter of the recessed doorway and met her at the corner. Their relationship, while cordial, had never approached a friendship in any sense. His father had taken some pains to keep the interaction between them superficial, and neither had ever been inclined to push matters further.

"Thank you for meeting me like this," she said, guiding him back to the shadow of the doorway. "I don't have much time, so I'll say what I have to say and go."

"Fair enough."

"Jared, I'm leaving your father. I intend to tell him this afternoon."

"I'm sorry," he said. "I know how much he cares for you."

"Does he? I think you know as well as I do that caring isn't one of Win Samuels's strong suits. It's too bad, too, because strange as it might sound, I think I might actually love him."

"Then why—"

"Please, Jared. I really don't have much time, and what I'm doing is very hard for me. Just know that I have my reasons—for leaving him and for giving you this." She handed him a sealed envelope. "Kate's a wonderful woman. She doesn't deserve the treatment he's giving her. I've been completely loyal to your father. That is until now. I know how hard it is to stand up to him. Lord knows I've wanted to enough. I think you did the right thing back there."

"Jocelyn, do you know if my father is lying or not? It's very important."

She smiled. "I'm aware of how important it is. I was listening at the door, remember? The answer is that I don't know, at least not for sure. There's a phone number in that envelope, Jared. Go someplace quiet and dial it. If my suspicions about that number are correct, you should be able to decide for yourself which of the two, Kate or your father, is telling the truth."

"I don't understand," he said. "What is this number? Where did you get it?"

"Please, I don't want to say any more because there's a small chance I might be wrong. Let's just leave it that the number is one your father has called from time to time since I've known him. I handle all of the household bills, including the phone bill, so I know. A year or two ago I accidentally overheard part of a conversation he was having. Some of what I heard disturbed me, so I noted down the exact time of the call. That's how I learned this number. I don't want to say any more. Okay?"

"Okay, but—"

"I wish you well, Jared. Both of you. The things I overheard Kate say last night have really helped me make some decisions I should have made a long time ago. I hope that what I've done will help her." She took his hand, squeezed it for a moment, and was gone.

Jared watched her hurry up Mt. Vernon Street; then he tore open the plain envelope. The phone number, printed on a three-by-five card, was in the 213 area. Los Angeles.

He drove to his office, trying to imagine what the number might be. Once at his desk, he sat for nearly a minute staring at the card before he finally dialed.

A woman, clearly awakened by the call, answered on the third ring. "Hello?" she said.

Jared struggled for a breath and pressed the receiver so tightly against his ear that it hurt.

"Hello?" the woman said again. "Is anybody there?"

Even after so many years he knew. "Lisa?" He could barely say the word.

"Yes. Who is this? Who is this, please?"

Slowly, Jared set the receiver back in its cradle.

14

Friday 21 December

It was pressure pain from the pipe more than cold that tugged Kate free of a sleep that was deeper than sleep. In the twilight moment before she was fully conscious, she imagined herself buried alive, the victim of some twisted, vicious kidnapper. In just a few hours she would suffocate or freeze to death. Jared had that little time to raise her ransom, and the only one he could turn to, she knew, was his father. The sound of Win Samuels's laughter echoed in her tomb, growing louder and louder until with a scream she came fully awake.

She was on her back. Her lips and cheeks were caked with dried and frozen blood. Dim light from the ends of the culvert barely defined the corroding metal, just a foot or so from her face. *Lie still*, she thought. *Just don't move. Sleep until Jared comes. Close your eyes again and sleep.* The thoughts were so comforting, so reassuring, that she had to struggle to remember that they were no more than the cold, lying to her, paralyzing her from within. For a time, all she could think about was sleep, sleep and Zimmermann's taunting warning that even if she survived, no one would believe her story. Sick, crazy, drugged up, that's what they all believed. It was hopeless for her. Zimmermann said it, and he was right. Over and over again, in a voice as soothing as a warm tub, the cold spoke to her of hopelessness and sleep.

Kate flexed her hands and her feet, struggling against the downy comfort of the lies and the inertia. *Remain still and you will die. Surrender to the cold and you will never see Jared again; never get the chance to tell him how much his letter and his decision mean to you.*

She tried pushing herself along with her feet, but could not bend her knees enough to get leverage. She had to see him. She had to tell him that she, too, was ready to make choices. Aroused by the aching in her legs and the far deeper pain in her side, she twisted and wriggled onto her belly. She had been wrong to allow Willoughby to nominate her without trying harder to see things from Jared's perspective. She had been wrong. Now she could only admit that and hope Jared believed it had been he, and not the devastating events, who had helped her see the true order of her priorities.

She was less than halfway from the far end of the pipe. The fog seemed to have lifted. She could now make out the silhouettes of trees against the white sky. A few more feet and there was enough light to read the numbers on her watch. Eleven fifteen. She had been entombed for over an hour. *Was Zimmermann still out there? Could he possibly have stayed around in the snow and the cold for over an hour?*

Driven by the need to see Jared again, to set matters straight, she worked herself arm over arm along the icy metal. A foot from the edge she stopped and listened. Beyond the soft wisp of her own breathing, there was nothing. Had an hour been long enough? Wouldn't Zimmermann have left, concerned about having his car attract attention? Finally, she abandoned her attempts at reasoning through the situation. If he was out there, waiting, there was little she would be able to do. If he wasn't, she would overcome whatever pain and cold she had to and make it home. There were amends to be made.

With a muted cry of pain, she curled her fingers around the edge of the culvert and pulled.

"We're sorry, but we are unavailable to take your call right now. Please wait for the tone, leave your name, number, and the time, and Kate or Jared will get back to you as soon as possible."

"Kate, it's just me again. Ignore the previous two messages. I'm not going to stay at the office, and I'm not going to speak with Reese. I'm coming home. Please don't go anywhere. Thanks. I love you."

Something was wrong. In almost five years of marriage, Jared had never felt so intense a connection to his wife. With that heightened sensitivity and three unanswered calls home had come a foreboding that weighed on his chest like an anvil. The feeling was irrational he told himself over and again, groundless and foolish. She was at a neighbor's or on a run. With his MG still in the office garage, where it had been all week, he had taken her Volvo; but still, there were plenty of places to which she could have walked.

He left the city and crossed the Mystic River Bridge, the rational part of him struggling to keep the Volvo under seventy. She was fine. There was some perfectly logical explanation why she hadn't answered his calls the past hour and a half. He just hadn't hit on it. Certainly, his concentration and powers of reason were not all they could be. It had been one hell of a morning.

The call to California, the sound of Lisa's voice, had left him at once elated and sickened. His father had lied. He had lied about Lisa and possibly about Stonefield as well. Jared cringed at the thought of how close he had come to siding with the man. Silently, he gave thanks that he had made his decision, set down on paper his commitment to Kate, before he had learned the truth about his father. The man had been paying Lisa off all those years. That conclusion was as inescapable as it was disgusting.

They were some pair, his ex-wife and Winfield. One totally vapid, one totally evil. Some goddamn pair.

Then there was Stacy. As he weaved along past Route 1's abysmal stretch of fast-food huts, factory outlets, budget motels, garish restaurants, and raunchy nightclubs, Jared ached with thoughts of her. What did she believe had become of her father? Would there ever be a way he could reenter her life without destroying whatever respect she had for her mother, possibly thereby destroying the girl herself? Kate would have a sense of what was right to do. Together they could decide. Damn, but he had come close, so close, to blowing it all.

The house was deserted. Kate's running gear was gone, and so was Roscoe. It had been several hours since his first call—far too long. He checked the area around the house and yard. Nothing. There were but two choices: wait some more or call the police. The heavy sense of apprehension, so ill-defined while he was in Boston, seemed more acute. There was no sense in waiting.

As he walked to the phone in the kitchen, he glanced out the front window. Three neighborhood children, all around eight, were trudging up the driveway pulling a sled. On the sled was a cardboard carton. The path to the front door, only as wide as a shovel, was too narrow for the sled. Two youngsters stayed behind, kneeling by the box, while the third ran up the walk. Jared met her at the door.

"Mr. Samuels, it's Roscoe," she panted. "We found him in the snow."

Jared, a dreadful emptiness in his gut, raced past the girl to the sled. Roscoe, packed in blankets, looked up and made a weak attempt to rise. His tail wagged free of the cover and slapped excitedly against the cardboard.

"His leg is broke," one of the other children, a boy, said simply.

Jared held the dog down and pulled back the blanket. Roscoe's right leg was fractured, the bone protruding from a gash just above the knee. "Come kids," he said, scooping up the box. "Come inside, please, and we'll take care of Rosc. Do you think you can take me to where you found him?"

"Yes, I know," the little girl said. "We have teacher's conference today, so no school. We were sledding down the hill to the bridge, and there he was, just lying in the snow. My mom gave us the blankets and the box."

"It looks like he's been hit by a car," Jared said. "Kids, this is important. Did any of you see Kate—you know, my wife?" The children shook their heads. He reached down and stroked the dog's forehead. Blood trickled from the corner of his mouth where his teeth had torn through. "Well, let's get some help for Roscoe; then we'll go back to the spot where you found him." He felt consumed by feelings of panic and dread, and struggled to keep a note of calm in his voice. Frightened, confused children would be no asset to him—or to Kate.

Minutes later three of them, Jared and two of the youngsters, were in the car. The third had been left behind to keep the dog still and await the arrival of the veterinarian.

"Okay, kids," Jared said, "you said you were sledding near a bridge. The stone bridge over the little stream?" Both nodded enthusiastically. "Good. I know just where that is."

The short drive over the narrow, snowy road seemed endless. Finally, Jared parked the Volvo at the top of the hill and then half ran, half slid to the indentation in the snow where the children assured him they had found Roscoe. He had thought to take his parka but had not changed his slacks or loafers, and the trek from the spot into the surrounding woods was both awkward and cold. The snow around him was, save for his own footprints, smooth and unbroken. After a scanning search, he made his way back to the road and started down the hill. At his request, the children followed, one on each side of the road, checking to be sure he had not missed anything.

At the stone bridge, he stopped. There was evidence of some sort of collision at the base of the wall. A piece of granite had been sheared off, and a gouge, perhaps two feet long, extended along the wall from that point. He searched the roadway and then looked over the wall. The snow on one side of the shallow brook seemed disrupted. In the very center of the area, he saw a flash of bright yellow, partially buried in the snow.

Ordering the children to remain where they were, he raced down the steep embankment to the water. It was Kate's cap, quite deliberately, it seemed, wedged into the snow. Then, only a few feet from the cap, he saw a swatch of another color. It was blood, almost certainly, dried blood smeared across a small stretch of packed snow. There had been some kind of struggle. The marks around him made that clear. Had Kate been dragged off somewhere? He looked for signs of that, but instead noticed footprints paralleling the stream just beyond the bridge. Slipping in and out of the water, he ran to the spot. There were, he was certain, two sets. He looked overhead. The children, following his progress, had crossed the road and were peering down at him from atop the wall. The girl, he knew, lived just past the end of the road, half a mile, perhaps a bit more, away.

"Crystal," he called out, "is your mommy still home?"

"Yes."

"Can you two make it back home to her?"

"Yes."

"Please do that, then. Tell her Kate is lost and may be hurt. Ask if she can drive out here and help look for her. Okay?"

"Okay."

"And Crystal, you all did a fine job bringing Roscoe in the way you did. Hurry on home, now."

Jared stayed where he was until the crunch of the children's boots had completely vanished. Then he closed his eyes and listened within the silence for a sound, any kind of sign. He heard nothing. Increasingly aware of the cold in his feet and legs, he stepped in the deep tracks, fearing the worst, and expecting, with each stride, to have his fears become reality. A hundred yards from the bridge, the tracks turned sharply to the left and vanished into the stream.

"Kate?" He called her name once and then again. His voice was instantly swallowed by the forest and the snow. "Kate, it's me. It's Jared." There was a heaviness, a fastness, to the place and a silence that was hypnotic. As he trudged along the side of the stream looking for renewed signs, he felt the silence deepen.

Then suddenly, he knew. He felt it as surely as he felt the cold. Kate was somewhere nearby. She was nearby, and she was still. He called to her every few feet, as he ducked under a huge fallen tree and followed the stream bed in a sharp bend to the left. Then he stopped. There was something different about this place. Far to his right, embedded in the steep slope that he guessed led up to the road, was a drainage pipe. At the base of the pipe were footprints.

"Kate?" He closed his eyes and almost immediately felt a strange sense of detachment. She was not far, and she was alive. He felt it clearly. It was as if their lives, their energies, were joined by a thin, silken strand of awareness.

"Jared?" It was a word, but not a word; a sound, but not a sound. His eyes still closed, he exhaled slowly and then listened. "Jared, help me." Her voice, it seemed, was more within him than without. He worked his way along the embankment, calling her name. Then he shouted it several times into the long, empty culvert. Finally, hoping for a better vantage point, he hauled himself up to the road.

She was there, face down, a third of the way down the slope on the far side, still clawing, though feebly, at the snow. Jared leapt over the edge, sliding and tumbling down to her. Gently, he turned her onto his lap. Her hair was matted and frozen, her face spattered with blood. Her warm-up suit, shredded in spots, was stiffened with ice. Her eyes were closed.

"Katey, it's me," he said. "I've got you. You're going to be all right."

He worked her hair free from where it had frozen to her face. Her breathing was shallow, each expiration accompanied by a soft whimper of pain.

"Honey, can you hear me?"

Her eyes opened and then slowly focused on his face. "Oh, Jared . . . please . . . Roscoe . . ."

He kissed her. "He's hurt, but he's okay. Dr. Finnerty's coming to get him. What about you? Have you broken anything?"

"Ribs," she managed in a voice that was half groan, half cough. "Lung . . . may . . . be . . . punctured."

"Jesus. Kate, I'm going to lift you up. I'll try not to hurt you, but we've got to get up to the road."

With strength enhanced by the urgency of the moment, he had no trouble lifting her. Negotiating the steep, icy slope, however, was another matter. Footing was treacherous, and every two or three baby steps upward, he was forced to set her down in order to regain purchase. Inches at a time, they moved ahead. When he finally heaved over the top of the slope onto the roadside, Jared fell to his knees, clutching her to his chest and gasping for air.

Helplessly, he sat there, warming her face with his breath and watching the minute but steady rise and fall of her chest. Then through the silence surrounding their breathing, he heard the soft hum of an approaching car. Moments later, a beige station wagon rounded the bend ahead of them. In the front seat were a woman and two very excited children.

"Way to go, Crystal," Jared whispered. He put his lips by Kate's ear. "Help is here, honey. Just hang in there. Help is here."

Her eyes opened momentarily. Her lips tightened in a grim attempt at a smile. "Zimmermann did this," she said.

◆

Jared paced from the small, well-appointed quiet room out to the hall and back. Mary T. Henderson Hospital was reputed to be among the best community hospitals in the state, but it was still a community hospital, only a fraction of the size of the Boston teaching facilities.

Nearly three hours had passed since the surgeon, Lee Jordan, had taken Kate into the operating room. Jordan was, according to the emergency room physician, the finest surgeon on the hospital staff. Jared had to laugh at his total surprise when the distinguished, gray-templed man his mind had projected as Lee Jordan turned out, in fact, to be a slender, extremely attractive woman in her midforties. Would he ever truly overcome all the years of programming?

Kate's wound was a bad one. The gash, Jordan had explained, required debridement in the operating room, and in all likelihood, an open-chest procedure would be needed to repair the laceration to her lung.

Jared had been allowed to see Kate briefly during the wait for the OR team to arrive, but there had been no real chance to discuss any details of William Zimmermann's attempt on her life. An officer from the Essex Police Department had come, taken what little information was available from him, and left with promises of state police involvement as soon as Kate could assist them with a statement. Meanwhile, it was doubtful that Jared's word would be enough to issue an arrest warrant.

Jared was studying the small plaque proclaiming that the quiet room was the gift of a couple named Berman when Lee Jordan emerged through the glass doors to the surgical suite. Her face, which had been fresh and alert on her arrival in the emergency ward four hours before, was gray and drawn, and for a moment, he feared the worst.

"Your wife's okay," Jordan said as soon as she was close enough to speak without raising her voice. She appraised him. "Are you?"

"I . . . yes, I'm okay." He braced himself against the

wall. "It's just that for a moment there I was frightened that . . ."

Jordan patted him on the shoulder. "You married one tough lady, my friend," she said. "There's frostbite on the tips of her toes, ears, and nose, but it looks like she came in from the cold in time to save everything. The tear in her lung wasn't too, too big. I sewed it up and then fixed that gash in her side. She's in for a few pretty achy days, but I hope nothing worse than that. You'll be able to see her in half an hour or so. I've asked the nurses to come and get you."

"Thank you. Thank you very much."

"I'm glad she's all right," Dr. Lee Jordan said.

It was after five by the time Jared arrived home. Medicated and obviously affected by her anesthesia, Kate had managed only to squeeze his hand and acknowledge that she knew he was in her hospital room. Even so, Dr. Jordan had warned him that she would, in all likelihood, remember nothing of the first five or six hours postop.

Roscoe was another story. As soon as Jared arrived at the veterinarian's, the dog was up and hopping about his cage, mindless of his plaster cast and showing no residual effects from the anesthesia that had allowed a metal plate to be screwed in place across the fracture in his leg. After seeing Kate with half a dozen tubes running into and out of her body, the sight of the battered and broken animal was the last straw. Zimmermann would pay. Whatever it took, Jared vowed, the man would pay dearly.

Exhausted from the day and, in fact, from almost thirty-six hours without sleep, Jared brought a bottle of Lowenbräu Dark to the bedroom, finished half of it in two long draughts, and then stripped to his underwear and stretched out on the bed. There was little sense, the nurses had told him, in returning to the hospital before morning. So be it. He would rest and read and say a dozen prayers of thanks for Kate's life and for Roscoe's, and for Jocelyn Trent, and for being allowed to learn the sad truth about his father before it was too late.

He had bunched up two pillows and was looking through the magazines on the bedside table when he noticed their telephone answering machine. It had been on since Kate left for her run, and there were a number of messages. The first three were from Jared himself, another was from Ellen, and still another was from one of the firm's VIP clients, who had apparently been assured that Winfield's son wouldn't mind in the least being called at home. The final message was for Kate from a man named Arlen Paquette.

"Kate Bennett, this is Arlen Paquette from Redding," the man said in a rushed, anxious tone. "I won't be alone for more than a few seconds. I have answers for you. Many answers. Come to the subbasement of the Omnicenter at precisely eight-thirty tonight. Bring help. There may be trouble. Please, trust me. I know what we've done to you, but please trust me. He's coming. I've got to go. Good-bye."

Jared raced for pen and paper; then he played the message over and wrote it down verbatim. Answers. At last someone was promising answers. He scrambled into a pair of jeans, a work shirt, and a sweater. It was already after seven. There would barely be time to get to Metro by eight-thirty, let alone to try and pick up police help on the way. He would have to hurry to the subbasement of the Omnicenter and rely on himself. *The Omnicenter*. He threw on his parka and rushed to Kate's Volvo. That was Zimmermann's place. The man would be there. He felt certain of it.

"I'm coming for you, you fucker," he panted as he skidded out of the drive and down Salt Marsh Road.

15

Friday 21 December

Like so many works of greatness, the formulas derived by William Zimmermann's father were elegant in their simplicity. Even without Zimmermann's help in translating the explanatory notes from the German, Arlen Paquette suspected he would have been able to follow the steps involved in the synthesis of the hormone Estronate 250—especially in the subbasement Omnicenter laboratory, which was specifically equipped for the job.

The message to call Cyrus Redding had been waiting at the front desk when Paquette returned to the Ritz from surreptitiously recording a conversation with Norton Reese during which the gloating administrator had incriminated himself and a technician named Pierce a number of times. The compact recorder still hooked to his belt, Paquette had entered the elevator to his floor.

"I was beginning to think you had run away," a man's voice said from behind.

Startled, the chemist whirled. It was Redding's bodyguard, a wiry, seemingly emotionless man whom Paquette had never heard called any name other than Nunes.

"Why, hello," Paquette said, wishing he had stayed at the tavern on the way back for a third drink. "I just picked up a message from Mr. Redding, but it says to call him at the Darlington number. Is he—?"

"He's there," Nunes said, showing nothing to dispel Paquette's image of a gunman whose loyalty to the pharmaceutical magnate had no limits. "He's waiting for your call."

From that moment on, Paquette had barely been out of Nunes's sight.

Now, in the bright fluorescence of the subbasement laboratory, Paquette glanced first at Zimmermann and then at Nunes and prayed that the forty-five minutes until eight-thirty would pass without incident. A deal had been struck between Redding and Zimmermann—money in exchange for a set of formulas. Redding had let him in on that much. However, the presence of the taciturn thug suggested that Redding anticipated trouble, or perhaps he had no intention of honoring his end of the bargain—quite possibly both.

"Okay, that's seven minutes," Zimmermann said, seconds before the mechanical timer rang out. "There's a shortcut my father used at this juncture, but I never did completely understand it. Dr. Paquette, I suggest you just go on to the next page and continue the steps in order. He performed these next reactions over in that corner, and he checked the purity of the distillate with that spectrophotometer."

Paquette nodded and moved around the slate workbench to the area Zimmermann had indicated. The Omnicenter director was neither biochemist nor genius, but he had observed his father at work enough to be able to oversee each step of the synthesis. And oversee he had—each maneuver and each microdrop of the way.

The laboratory was quite remarkable. Hidden behind a virtually invisible, electronically controlled door, it had no less than three sophisticated spectrophotometers, each programmed to assess the consistency of the hormone at various stages of its synthesis and, through feedback mechanisms, to adjust automatically the chemical reaction where needed. It was a small area, perhaps fifteen feet by thirty, but its designer had paid meticulous attention to the maximum use of space.

"Did your father design all this?" Paquette asked.

"Be careful, Doctor, your reagent is beginning to overheat," Zimmermann said, ignoring the question as he had most others about his father. "Excuse me, but are you timing a reaction I don't know about?"

"No, why?"

"That's the third time you've looked at your watch in the past ten minutes."

"Oh, that." Paquette hoped his laugh did not sound too nervous. Out of the corner of his eye, he saw Nunes, seated on a tall stool at the end of the lab bench, adjust his position to hear better. "A habit dating back to high school, perhaps beyond, that's all."

He had made up his mind that there was no way he would complete the Estronate synthesis and turn the three notebooks over to Nunes. That act, he suspected, would be his last. He and Zimmermann were not scripted to leave the laboratory alive. The more the evening had worn on, the more certain he had become of that. He glanced at the metal hand plate to the right of the entrance. Though unmarked, it had to be the means of opening the door.

There were less than thirty minutes to go. If Kate Bennett had gotten his message, and if she had taken it seriously, she would be waiting, with help, in the storage area outside the laboratory.

Paquette's plan was simple. At eight thirty-five, allowing five minutes for any delay on Bennett's part, he would announce the need to use the men's room. They had passed one a floor above on their way in. With surprise on their side, whatever muscle Bennett had brought with her should have a decent chance at overpowering Nunes. If there was no one in the storage room when the door slid open, he would have to improvise. There was one thing of which he was sure: once outside the laboratory, he was not going back in. God, but he wished he had a drink.

Traffic into the city was inordinately light for a Friday evening, and it was clear to Jared that barring any monstrous delays, he would make it to Metro with time to spare. Still, he used his horn and high beams to clear his way down Route 1.

Risks. Bring help. There may be trouble. With each mile, Arlen Paquette's warning grew in his thoughts. He had made a mistake in not calling the Boston police before he left Essex. He could see that now. Still, what would he have said? How lengthy an explanation would have been required? His father, he knew, could pick up the phone and with no explanation whatsoever have half a dozen officers waiting for him at the front door to the Omnicenter. Answers. Paquette had promised answers. Perhaps for Kate's sake it was worth swallowing his pride and anger and calling Winfield. Then he realized that the issue went far deeper than pride and anger. The man could not be trusted. Not now, not ever again.

Bring help. Jared pulled off the highway and skidded to a stop by a bank of pay phones. It was seven forty-five. He was twenty minutes, twenty-five at the most, from the Omnicenter. There was still time to do something, but what? With no clear idea of what he was going to say, he called the Boston Police Department.

"I'd—ah—I'd like to speak to Detective Finn, please," he heard his own voice say. "Yes, that's right, Martin Finn. I'm sorry, I don't know what district. Four, maybe."

Finn. The thought, Jared saw now, had been in the back of his mind all along. Tough but fair: that's how his father had described the man. If that was the case, then it would take only the promise of some answers to get him to the Omnicenter.

Finn was not at his desk.

"Has he gone home for the night?" Jared asked of the officer who answered Finn's phone. "Well, does anyone know?" . . . "Samuels. Jared Samuels. I'm a lawyer.

Detective Finn knows me. What is your name?" . . . "Well, please Sergeant, this is very urgent and there isn't much time. Could you see if you could get a message to Lieutenant Finn to meet me at eight-fifteen at the front entrance to the Omnicenter at Metropolitan Hospital?" . . . "That's right, in half an hour. And Sergeant, if you can't locate him, could you or some other officer meet me instead?" . . . "I don't know if it's a matter of life or death or not. Listen, I don't have time to explain. Please, just try."

Jared hurried back to the Volvo, wishing he had more of an idea of who Arlen Paquette was or at least of what was awaiting him at the Omnicenter. It was exactly eight o'clock when he sped over the crest of a long upgrade and saw, ahead and to his right, the glittering tiara of Boston at night.

Perhaps it was the tension of the moment, perhaps the six hours since his last drink; whatever the reason, Arlen Paquette felt his hands beginning to shake and his concentration beginning to waver. He pulled a gnarled handkerchief from his back pocket and dabbed at the cold sweat on his forehead and upper lip. It was only ten minutes past the hour. The hormone synthesis, which had proceeded flawlessly, was well over half completed.

"Are you all right?" Zimmermann asked.

"Fine, I'm fine," Paquette said, clutching a beaker of ice water with two hands to keep its contents from sloshing about. "I . . . I'd like to talk with Mr. Nunes for a moment. Privately."

"Why?" Zimmermann asked with a defensiveness in his voice. "There's no problem with the procedure up to now. I assure you of that. You are doing an excellent job of following my father's notes. Just keep going."

"It's not that. Listen, I'll be right back. Nunes," he whispered, his back turned to Zimmermann, "I need a drink."

"No booze until you finish this work. Mr. Redding's orders." As Nunes leaned forward to respond, the coat of his perfectly tailored suit fell away just enough for Paquette to see the holstered revolver beneath his left arm. Any doubt he harbored regarding his fate once the formulas were verified vanished.

"Nunes, have a heart."

The gunman's only response was an impatient nod in the direction of the incomplete experiment.

"Any problem?" Zimmermann called out.

"No problem," Nunes said as Paquette shuffled back. "Say, Dr. Zimmermann, where's the nearest john?"

Paquette slowed and listened. In less than twenty minutes he planned to ask the same question and wait for Nunes to open the door for him. Then an unexpected push from behind, and the man would be in the arms of the police. It was perfect, provided, of course, that Kate Bennett had gotten his message.

William Zimmermann pointed to the wall behind the gunman. "See that recessed handle in the wall right under that shelf? Just twist it and pull."

Nunes did as he was instructed, and a three-foot-wide block of shelves pulled away from the wall, revealing a fairly large bathroom and stall shower.

"Father had this obsession about hidden doorways and the like," Zimmermann said.

His next sentence, if there was to be one, was cut off by the beaker of ice water, which slipped from Paquette's hands and shattered on the tile floor.

Save for the security light in the front lobby, the Omnicenter was completely dark. Jared parked across the street and was beginning a walking inspection of the outside of the building when a blue and white patrol car pulled up. Martin Finn stepped out, looking in the gloom like a large block of granite with a homberg perched on top. Even at a distance, Jared could sense the man's impatience and irritation.

"I got your message," Finn said, with no more greeting than that. "What's going on?" Behind him, a uniformed officer remained at the wheel of the cruiser. The engine was still running.

"Thanks for coming so quickly," Jared said. "I . . . didn't know whom to call."

"Well?"

Jared checked the time. There were thirteen minutes. "My wife is in Henderson Hospital. Someone tried to run her down with a car earlier today while she was jogging." Finn said nothing. "She's had to have surgery, but she's going to be okay." Still nothing. "She couldn't speak much, but she said it was Dr. Zimmermann, the head of the Omnicenter, who tried to run her down and then chased her with a tire wrench."

"William Zimmermann?"

"Yes. Do you know him?"

Finn looked at him icily. "He delivered my daughter."

Inwardly, Jared groaned. "Well, he was involved in something illegal, possibly in connection with one of the big pharmaceutical houses. Kate discovered what was going on, so he tried to kill her."

"But he missed." There was neither warmth nor the slightest hint of belief in the man's voice.

"Yes, he missed." Jared swallowed back his mounting anger. There was far too much at stake and hardly time for an argument. "When I returned home from the hospital a short while ago, there was a message on our answering machine for Kate from a man named Arlen Paquette. I think he works for the drug house. He asked that she meet him here, in the subbasement of this building, and that she bring help. That's why I called you. I suspect that Zimmermann is in the middle of all this and that he's in there right now."

"In there?" Finn gestured at the darkened building.

"He said the *subbasement*."

"Mr. Samuels, Dr. Zimmermann's office is on the third floor. On the corner, right up there. I've been there several times. Now what on earth would he be doing in the subbasement?"

"I . . . I don't know." There were eleven minutes. "Look, Lieutenant, the man said exactly eight-thirty. There isn't much time."

"So you want me to go busting into a locked hospital building, looking to nail my wife's obstetrician, because you got some mysterious message on your telephone answering machine?"

"If the doors are all locked, we can get in through the tunnels. We don't have to break in. Dammit, Lieutenant, my wife was almost killed today. Do you think she's lying about the broken bones and the punctured lung?"

"No," Finn said. "Only about everything else. Mr. Samuels, I had a chance to do some checking up on your wife. She's in hot water with just about everyone in the city, it seems. Word has it she's just been fired for screwing up here at the hospital, too. Face it, counselor, you've got a sick woman on your hands. You need help, all right, but not the kind I can give."

"Then you won't come with me?" Jared could feel himself losing control.

"Mr. Samuels, because of your wife, I still have enough egg on my face to make a fucking omelet. I'll file a report if you want me to, and even get a warrant if you can give me some hard facts to justify that. But no commando stuff. Now if I were you, I'd just go on home and see about lining up some professional help for your woman."

Before he could even weigh the consequences, Jared hit the man—a roundhouse punch that landed squarely on the side of Finn's face and sent him spinning down into a pile of plowed snow. Instantly, the uniformed officer was out of the cruiser, his hand on the butt of his service revolver. Finn, a trickle of blood forming at the corner of his mouth, waved him off.

"No, Jackie," he said. "It's all right. The counselor,

here, felt he had a score to settle with me, and he just settled it." He pushed himself to his feet, still shaking off the effects of the blow. "Now, counselor, you just get the fuck out of my sight. If I hear of any trouble involving you tonight, I'm going to bust your ass from here to Toledo. Clear?"

Jared glared at the detective. "You're wrong, Finn. About my wife, about refusing to help me, about everything. You don't know how goddamn wrong you are."

He glanced at his watch, then turned and raced down the block toward the main entrance to the hospital and the stairway that would lead to the Omnicenter tunnel. There were less than five minutes left.

Visiting hours had ended. The hospital was quiet. Jared crossed the lobby as quickly as he dared without calling attention to himself and hurried down the nearest staircase. Although he used the dreary tunnels infrequently, he distinctly remembered seeing a sign indicating that the Omnicenter had been tacked onto the system. But where?

The tunnel was deserted, and it seemed even less well lighted than usual. A caravan of stretchers lined one wall, interspersed with empty, canvas industrial laundry hampers. On the wall opposite was a wooden sign with arrows indicating the direction to various buildings. The bottom three names, almost certainly including the Omnicenter, were obscured by a mixture of grime and graffiti. Kate had once told him that it took a special kind of character to love working at Metro, intimating that the spirit of the hospital staff and the loyalty of many of its patients were somehow bound to the physical shortcomings of the place. The concept, like so much else about his wife, was something Jared realized he would have to work a little harder at understanding.

His often far from dependable sense of direction urged him toward the right. There was no time to question the impulse. His footsteps echoing off the cement floor and walls, Jared raced that way, instinctively casting about for something he could use as a weapon, and at the same time, cursing his failure to obtain help.

His sense, this time at least, was on the mark. The spur leading to the Omnicenter was fifty yards away.

It was exactly eight-thirty. The darkened passageway was illuminated only by the dim glow from the main tunnel. Sprinting head down, Jared caught a glimpse of the metal security gate only an instant before he hit it. The gate, an expanded version of the sort used to child-proof stairways, was pulled across the tunnel and bolted to the opposite wall. Stunned, he dropped to one knee, pawing at the spot just above his right eye that had absorbed most of the impact. Then he sank to all fours. If timing was as critical as Arlen Paquette's message had made it sound, he was beaten. The gate, with no space below, and less than a foot on top, was solid.

Exhausted and exasperated, Jared hauled himself up, grabbed the metal slats, and like a caged animal, rattled them mercilessly. *I'm sorry, Katey,* was all he could think. *I'm sorry I fucked up everything so badly.*

"Just hold it right there, son, and turn around very slowly." Jared froze, his hands still tight around the gate. "I've got a gun pointed in your general direction, so don't you go getting too rattled or too adventurous."

Jared did as he was told. Thirty or forty feet away, silhouetted by the light from behind him, was a night watchman.

"Who are you? What are you doin' down here?" the man demanded.

"Please, you've got to help me!" Jared took a few steps forward.

"That'll be far enough. Now how can I go about helpin' you, young man, if I don't even know who in the hell you are?"

Jared forced himself to calm down. "My name is Samuels. My wife is a doctor on the staff here. Dr. Bennett. Dr. Kathryn Bennett. Do you know her?"

The night watchman lowered his revolver. "You the lawyer?"

"Yes. Yes, I am. Listen, you've got to help me." He approached the watchman, who this time made no attempt to stop him.

"Do I, now," the man said. His khaki uniform appeared a size, perhaps two, too big for him. A shock of gray hair protruded from beneath his cap. Even with the revolver, he was hardly a menacing figure.

"Please, Mister—"

"MacFarlane. Walter MacFarlane. Known your wife for years—even before you were married to her."

"Well, Mr. MacFarlane, my wife's in a hospital on the North Shore right now. Someone tried to run her down. We know who, but not why. A few hours ago, a man called and promised me answers if I would meet him in the Omnicenter subbasement right now."

"Subbasement?"

"Yes. He said to bring help because there might be trouble, but there just wasn't enough time for me to get any."

"You sure it's the subbasement? That's the level beneath this one. Ain't nothin' down there but a bunch of cartons and spare cylinders of oxygen."

"All I know is what he said. Please. It's already past time."

"That Kate has been gettin' herself into some kinds of trouble lately."

"I know. Please, Mr. Mac—"

"People talk and talk. You know how it is. Well I'll tell you something, mister. They have their thoughts and I have mine. Ten years I've walked that woman to her car when she stayed until late at night. Ten years. She's class, I tell you. Pure class."

"Then you'll help me?"

Walter MacFarlane sorted a key out from the huge ring on his belt and opened the security gate. "If it'll help straighten things out for Dr. Bennett, count me in," he said.

Arlen Paquette was terrified. There was no way out of the laboratory except past the killer, Nunes, and yet to stay, to complete the Estronate synthesis meant, he was convinced, to die. It was twenty-five minutes to nine. As yet there had not been even the faintest sound from beyond the electronically controlled door. Kate Bennett either had not received his message or had disregarded it. Either way, he was on his own.

Desperately, he tried to sort out the situation and his options. There was no way he could buy time by claiming the procedure was inaccurate. Zimmermann was watching his every step. Could he somehow enlist Zimmermann's help in overpowering Nunes? Doubtful. No, worse than doubtful: impossible. Nunes had already shown him the money, packed neatly in a briefcase that now rested on the benchtop. Zimmermann's expression had been that of a starving wolf discovering a trapped hare.

"Anything the matter?" Zimmermann asked, indicating that once again Paquette was dawdling.

"No!" Paquette snapped. "And I want you off my back. It's my responsibility to verify these formulas, and I'll take all the time I need to do the job right."

At the far end of the lab, Nunes adjusted his position to keep a better eye on the two of them. Suddenly he waved to get their attention and placed a silencing finger over his lips. With his other hand, he pointed to the door. Someone was outside. With the sure, fluid movements of a professional, he slid the revolver from its holster and flattened himself against the wall beside the door.

Paquette decided that he had but one option—and not a very appealing one. He had been a wrestler during his freshman and sophomore years in high school, but had never been that good and, in fact, had been grateful when a neck injury forced him to quit. Since that time, he had never had a fight in any physical sense with anyone. Nunes was taller than he by perhaps two inches and certainly more experienced, but he had surprise and desperation on his side.

Separated from the gunman by one of the spectrophotometers and a tangle of sophisticated glass distillation tubing, Paquette eased his way along the slate-topped work bench until he was no more than ten feet from him. For several seconds, all was quiet. Then he heard muffled voices, at least two of them, from the storage room beyond the door. He strained to pick up their conversation, but could make out only small snatches. Nunes, that much closer, was probably hearing more. Paquette wondered if those outside the door had mentioned his name. If so, and if Nunes had heard, it was the final nail in his coffin.

The voices grew less distinct. Had they just moved away, or were they leaving, Paquette wondered. Even if they were to discover the door—and that was most unlikely—there was no way they could locate and activate the coded electronic key.

Carefully, Paquette slid the final few feet to the end of the laboratory bench. Zimmermann was a good twenty-five feet away—far enough to keep him from interfering. Paquette gauged the distance and then focused on his two objectives: Nunes's gun and the electronic plate on the right side of the door. A single step, and he hurled himself at the man, grasping his gun arm at the wrist with both his hands and spinning against the metal plate.

The door slid open, and Paquette caught a glimpse of a uniformed man fumbling for the pistol holstered at his hip. There was a second figure behind the man, whom he recognized as Kate Bennett's husband. In that moment, Nunes freed his hand and whipped Paquette viciously across the face with the barrel of his revolver. Paquette dropped to his knees, clutching at the pain and at the blood spurting from his cheek and temple.

"All right, mister, drop it! Right now, right there!"

Walter MacFarlane stood in the doorway, his heavy

service revolver leveled at Nunes, whose own gun was a foot or so out of position. Nunes froze, his head turned, ever so slightly, toward the intruder.

From his position four feet behind and to the left of MacFarlane, Jared could see the gunman's expression clearly. He seemed placid, composed, and totally confident.

Back up! Get away from him! Before Jared could verbalize the warning, the gunman was in action. He flicked his revolver far enough away to draw MacFarlane's eyes and then lunged out of the watchman's line of fire and up beneath his arm. MacFarlane's revolver discharged with a sharp report.

The bullet splintered several glass beakers, ricocheted off a wall, and then impacted with a large can of ether on the shelf behind William Zimmermann. The can exploded, the blast shattering most of the glassware in the room. Jared watched in horror as Zimmermann's hair and the skin on the back of his scalp were instantly seared away, his clothes set ablaze.

"Help!" he shrieked, reeling away from the wall. "Oh, God, someone help me!"

He flailed impotently at the tongues of flame that were darting upward through the crotch of his trousers and igniting his shirt. His struggles sent a shelf of chemicals crashing to the floor. There was a second explosion. Zimmermann's right arm disappeared at the elbow. Still, he stayed on his feet, lurching in purposeless circles, staring at the bloody remains of his upper arm, and screaming again and again. A third blast, from just to his left, sent his body, now more corpse than man, hurtling across the slate tabletop, through what remained of the glassware.

Zimmermann's screeching ended abruptly as he toppled over the edge of the table and onto Arlen Paquette. The chemist, though shielded from the force of the explosion by the counter, was far too dazed from the blow he had absorbed to react.

MacFarlane and Nunes both went down before the blast of heat and flying glass. Jared, still outside the laboratory door, was knocked backward, but managed to keep his feet. He stumbled to the doorway, trying frantically to assess the situation.

Intensely colored flames were breaking out along the benchtops, filling the air with thick, fetid smoke. To his right, Walter MacFarlane and the gunman lay amidst shards of glass. The side of the watchman's face looked as if it had been mauled by a tiger. Both men were moving, though without much purpose. To his left there was also movement. The man he assumed was Arlen Paquette was trying, ineffectually, to extricate himself from beneath the charred body of William Zimmermann.

Crawling to avoid the billows of toxic smoke, Jared made his way to Zimmermann, grabbed the corpse by its belt and the front of its smoldering shirt and heaved it onto its back.

"Paquette?" Jared gasped. "Are you Paquette?"

The man nodded weakly and pawed at the blood—his and Zimmermann's—that was obscuring his vision. "Notebooks," he said. "Get the notebooks."

Jared batted at the few spots on Paquette's clothing that were still burning, pulled him to a sitting position, and leaned him against the wall. The fumes and smoke were worsening around them.

"I've got to get you out of here. Can you understand that?"

Paquette's head lolled back. "Notebooks," he said again.

Jared glanced about. On the floor beneath Zimmermann's heel was a black looseleaf notebook. He tucked the book under his arm and then began dragging Paquette toward the doorway. Several times, glass cut through Jared's pants and into his leg. Once he slipped, slicing a flap of skin off the edge of his hand. The wooden cabinets and shelves had begun to blaze, making the room unbearably hot.

Paquette was making the task of moving him from the

room harder by clawing at Jared, at one point getting his hand entangled in Jared's parka pocket.

"For Christ's sake, let go of me, Paquette," Jared shouted. "I'm trying to get you out of here. Can you understand that? I'm trying to get you out."

The smoke was blinding. His eyes tearing and nearly closed, Jared hunched low, breathed through his parka, and with great effort, pulled Paquette's arm over his shoulder, hauling the man to his feet. Together they staggered from the lab. Jared was about to set Paquette down against a wall in order to return for MacFarlane when he remembered the oxygen. There were thirty or forty large green cylinders bunched in the far corner of the storage area. They possessed, he suspected, enough explosive potential to level a good portion of the building.

"Paquette," he hollered, "I'm going to help you up the stairs. Then you've got to get down the tunnel and as far away from here as possible. Do you understand?" Paquette nodded. "Can you support any more of your own weight?"

"I can try." Paquette, his face a mask of blood, forced the words out between coughs.

One arduous step at a time, the two made their way up to the landing on the basement level. Acrid chemical smoke, which had largely filled the storage area below, drifted up the stairway around them.

"Okay, we're here," Jared said loudly. "I've got to go back down there. You head that way, through the tunnel. Understand? Good. Here, take your book with you and just keep going." He shoved the notebook into the man's hands.

At that instant, from below, there was a sharp explosion. Then another. Jared watched as Paquette lurched away from him and then pitched heavily to the floor, blood pouring from a wound on the side of his neck.

Jared dropped to one knee beside the man, surprised and confused by what was happening. "Paquette!"

"Notebook . . . Kate . . ." were all Paquette could

manage before a torrent of blood sealed his words and closed his eyes.

It was then Jared realized the man had been shot, that the explosions he had heard were from a gun, not from the lab. He turned at the moment Nunes fired at him from the base of the stairs. The bullet tore through his right thigh and caromed off the floor and wall behind him. The man, blackened by smoke and bleeding from cuts about his face, leveled the revolver for another shot.

Distracted by the burning pain in his leg, Jared barely reacted in time to drop out of the line of fire. Behind him and from the mouth of the tunnel, alarms had begun to wail. Below him, the man had started up the stairs through the billowing smoke.

Notebook . . . Kate . . . Jared plucked the black notebook from beside Arlen Paquette's body, tucked it under his arm like a football, and in a gait that was half hop and half sprint, raced down the tunnel toward the main hospital. Zimmermann, Paquette, and probably Walter MacFarlane as well: all dead, quite possibly because he had gone to the subbasement rendezvous without enough help. The distressing thought took his mind off the pain as he pushed on past the security gate. Paquette had promised answers for Kate, and now he was dead. Silently, Jared cursed himself.

A gunshot echoed through the tunnel. Hunching over to diminish himself as a target, Jared limped on, weaving from side to side across the tunnel, and wondering if the evasive maneuver was worth the ground he was losing. The main tunnel was less than thirty yards away. There would be people there—help—if only he could make it. Another shot rang out, louder than the last. The bullet, fired, Jared realized now, from MacFarlane's heavy service revolver, snapped through the sleeve of his parka and clattered off the cement floor. He stumbled, nearly falling, and slammed into the far wall of the main tunnel.

"Help," he screamed. "Somebody help!" The dim tunnel was deserted.

A moment later he was shot again, the bullet impacting just above his left buttock, spinning him a full three hundred and sixty degrees, and sending white pain lancing down his leg and up toward his shoulder blade. He tumbled to one knee, but just as quickly pulled himself up again, clutching the notebook to his chest and rolling along the wall of the tunnel. Somewhere in the distance he could hear another series of alarms, then sirens, and finally a muffled explosion.

He was, for the moment at least, out of the killer's line of fire, stumbling in the direction away from the main hospital and toward the boiler room and laundry. Despite the pain in his leg and back, he was determined that nothing short of a killing shot was going to bring him down. With Paquette and Zimmermann dead, the black notebook, whatever it was, might well represent Kate's only chance.

The gunman, crouching low and poised to fire, slid around the corner of the Omnicenter tunnel just as Jared reached the spur to the laundry. Jared sensed the man about to shoot, but there was no explosion, no noise. Or was there? As he pushed on into the darkened laundry, he could swear he had heard a sound of some sort. Then he understood. The killer *had* fired. MacFarlane's revolver was out of bullets, tapped dry. Now, even wounded, he had a chance.

The room he had entered was filled with dozens of rolling industrial hampers, some empty, some piled high with linen. Beyond the crowded hamper lot, Jared could just discern the outlines of rows of huge steam pressers. He gave momentary consideration to diving into one of the hampers, but rejected the notion, partly because of the helpless, passive situation in which he would be and partly because his pursuer had already turned into the tunnel and was making his way, though cautiously, toward the laundry.

Ignoring the pain in his back, Jared dropped to all fours and inched his way between two rows of hampers toward the enormous, cluttered hall housing the laundry itself. Pressers, washers, dryers, shelves and stacks of linens, more hampers—if he could make it, there would be dozens of places to hide . . . *if* he could make it.

There were twenty feet separating the last of the canvas hampers from the first of the steam pressers. Twenty open feet. He had to cross them unnoticed. Kneeling in the darkness, he listened. There was not a sound—not a breath, not the shuffle of a footstep, nothing. Where in hell was the man? Was the chance of catching a glimpse of him worth the risk of looking? The aching in his back was in crescendo, dulling his concentration and his judgment. Again he listened. Again there was nothing. Slowly, he brought his head up and turned.

The killer, moving with the control and feline calm of a professional, was less than five feet away, preparing to hammer him with the butt of MacFarlane's heavy revolver. Jared spun away, but still absorbed a glancing blow just above his left ear. Stunned, he stumbled backward, pulling first one, then another hamper between him and the man, who paused to pick up the notebook and set it on the corner of a hamper before matter-of-factly advancing on him again.

"It's no use, pal," he said, shoving the hampers aside as quickly as Jared could pull them in his way, "but go ahead and make it interesting if you want."

Jared, needing the hampers as much for support as for protection, knew the man was right. Wounded and without a weapon, Jared had no chance against him.

"Who are you?" he asked.

Nunes smiled and shrugged. "Just a man doing a job," he said.

"You work for Redding Pharmaceuticals, don't you."

"I think this little dance of ours has gone on long enough, pal. Don't you?"

In that instant, Jared thought about Kate and all she had been through; he thought about Paquette and the aging watchman, MacFarlane. If he was going to die, then, dammit, it wouldn't be while backing away. With no more plan in mind than that, he grabbed another hamper, feigned pulling it in front of him, and instead drove it forward as hard as he could, catching the surprised gunman just below the waist. Nunes lurched backward, colliding with another hamper and very nearly going down.

Jared moved as quickly as he could, but the advantage he had gained with surprise was lost in the breathtaking pain of trying to push off his left foot. The killer, his expression one of placid amusement, parried the lunge with one hand, and with the other, brought the barrel of the revolver slicing across Jared's head, opening a gash just above his temple. Jared staggered backward a step, then came on again, this time leading with a kick which connected, though not powerfully, with the man's groin.

Again Nunes lashed out with the gun, landing a solid blow to Jared's forearm and then another to the back of his neck. Jared dropped to one knee. As he did, Nunes stepped behind him and locked one arm expertly beneath his chin.

"Sorry, pal," he said, tightening his grip.

Jared flailed with his arms and shoulders and tried to stand, but the man's leverage was far too good. The pressure against his larynx was excruciating. His chest throbbed with the futile effort of trying to breathe. Blood pounded in his head and the killer's grunting breaths grew louder in his ear. Then the sound began to fade. Jared knew he was dying. Every ounce of his strength vanished, and he felt the warmth of his bladder letting go. *I'm sorry, Kate. I'm sorry.* The words tumbled over and over in his mind. *I'm sorry.*

Through closed eyes, he sensed, more than saw, a bright, blue-white light. From far, far away, he heard a muffled explosion. Then another.

Suddenly the pressure against his neck diminished. The killer's forearm shook uncontrollably and then slid away. Jared fell to one side, but looked up in time to see the man totter and then, in grotesque slow motion, topple over into a hamper.

Jared struggled to sort out what was happening. The first thing he saw clearly was that the overhead lights had been turned on; the second thing was the stubbled, slightly jowled face of Martin Finn.

"I was halfway back to the station when I decided there was no way you would have chanced popping me like you did unless the situation was really desperate," Finn said. "How bad are you hurt?"

Jared coughed twice and wasn't sure he was able to speak until he heard his own voice. "I've been shot twice," he rasped, "once just above my butt and once in my thigh. My legs are all cut up from broken glass. That lunatic beat the shit out of me with his gun."

"The emergency people are on their way," Finn said, kneeling down. "It may be a few minutes. As you might guess, there's a lot of commotion going on around here right now. Is Zimmermann dead?"

Jared nodded. Then he remembered MacFarlane. "Finn," he said urgently, "there's a man, MacFarlane, a night watchman. He was—"

"You mean him?" The detective motioned to his left.

Walter MacFarlane, one eye swollen shut and the side of his face a mass of dried and oozing blood, stood braced against a hamper.

"Thank God," Jared whispered.

"We would never have known what direction to go in without him," Finn explained.

At that moment a team of nurses and residents arrived with two stretchers. They helped MacFarlane onto one and then gingerly hoisted Jared onto the other.

"As soon as these people get you fixed up, Counselor, you're going to have a little explaining to do. You know that, don't you?"

"I know. I'll tell you as much as I can. And Finn . . . I appreciate your coming back."

"I think I might owe you an apology, but I'll save it until someone explains to me what the fuck has been going on around here."

"Okay," one of the residents announced. "We're all set."

"Wait. Please," Jared said. "Finn, there's a notebook around here somewhere. A black, looseleaf notebook."

The detective searched for a few moments and then brought it over. "Yours?" he asked.

"Actually, no." Jared tucked the notebook beneath his arm. Then he smiled. "It belongs to my wife."

16

Saturday 22 December

"Mr. Samuels, I'm here to take you up to your room. Mr. Samuels?"

Jared's eyes opened from a dreamless sleep. He was on a litter, staring at the chipped, flaking ceiling of the emergency ward where a team of surgical residents had worked on his wounds. His last clear memory was of one of the doctors, a baby-faced woman with rheumy eyes behind horn-rimmed glasses, announcing that she was about to give him a "little something" so that his wounds could be explored, cleaned, and repaired.

"I'm Cary Dunleavy, one of the nurses from Berenson Six," the man's voice said from somewhere at the head of the litter.

Jared tried to crane his neck toward the nurse, but was prevented by a thick felt cervical collar and a broad leather restraining belt across his chest. He ached in a dozen different places, and he sensed that he was seeing little or nothing through his left eye.

Dunleavy took several seconds to appreciate his patient's predicament. Then he muttered an apology and moved to a spot by Jared's right hand. "Welcome to the land of the living," he said. His voice was kind, but his eyes were sunken and tired. "You've been out for quite a while. Apparently they overestimated how much analgesia to give you."

Jared brought his left hand up and gingerly touched the area about his left eye.

"It's swollen shut," the nurse announced. "You look like you've been kicked by a mule."

Jared felt his senses begin to focus, and he struggled to reconstruct the hazy events following the explosion in the Omnicenter. His first clear image was of William Zimmermann spinning wildly about, his clothes ablaze, the skin on one side of his face hideously scorched. That one was for you, Katey, he thought savagely. An I'm-sorry-for-not-believing-you present from your husband. "What time is it?" he asked.

"Almost four."

"In the morning?"

The nurse nodded. "According to the report I got from the ER nurses, you've been out for about three hours since they finished working on you. We've been too busy on the floor for anyone to come and get you until now. Sorry."

"I need to get out of here," Jared said, fumbling at the restraining strap with his left hand. His right hand, with an intravenous line taped in place, was secured to the railing of the litter.

"Hey, partner," the nurse said, setting a hand on his shoulder. "Easy does it."

"I've got to see my wife. I've—" Suddenly, he remembered the notebook. "My things. Where are my things?"

"We've got 'em, Mr. Samuels. They're put away safe awaiting the moment when we read a legitimate order from your doctor discharging you. Rounds are usually at seven. Until then, if you go, you go in a Johnny."

Jared glared at the man. *I'm a lawyer,* he wanted to shout. I can sue you and this whole hospital for violating my civil rights, and win. Instead, he assessed his situation. In just three hours or so his physicians would make rounds and he could explain to them his need to leave. Three hours. Almost certainly, Kate would be sleeping through them anyhow, under the effects of her anesthesia. He sank back on the litter. "You win," he said.

The nurse said silent thanks with a skyward look and started maneuvering the litter out of the small examining room.

"Just one thing," Jared said.

The man stopped short and again walked around to make eye contact. "I'll listen, but no promises." His tired voice was less good-natured than he intended.

"I had a notebook. A black, looseleaf notebook. It should be in with my things. Get me that, and I promise to be a model patient."

Cary Dunleavy hesitated, but then withdrew the notebook from the patient's belongings bag, which was stashed on the litter beneath Jared. "I'm taking you at your word, Mr. Samuels. Model patient. I'm nearing the end of a double. That's over sixteen straight hours of nursing on a floor that would fit right in at the Franklin Zoo. It's been one hell of a long night, and my usual overabundance of the milk of human kindness is just about dried up. So don't cross me."

Jared smiled, made a feeble peace sign with his bandaged left hand, and tucked the notebook between his arm and his side.

The exhausted nurse returned to the head of the litter and resumed the slow trek through the tunnels to the Berenson Building.

The doors to one of the Berenson elevators opened as they approached, and a patient was wheeled out by two nurses. Jared saw the two bags of blood draining into two separate IVs, and a woman's tousled black hair, but little else, as Cary Dunleavy stopped and spoke to the nurses.

"What gives?" Dunleavy asked.

"GI bleeding. Getting worse. She's going to the OR for gastroscopy. The team's already up there waiting."

"Good luck. Let me know how it goes."

"Will do," the nurse said. The stretchers glided past

one another. "Sorry for the delay, Mrs. Sandler," she continued. "We'll be there in just a minute or two."

Mrs. Sandler. Several seconds passed before the name registered for Jared. "Ellen!" he called out, struggling once again against the leather strap.

Dunleavy stopped. "Hey, what're you doing?"

Jared forced himself to calm down. Ellen was on her way to the operating room, hemorrhaging. The option of waiting for seven o'clock rounds no longer existed. Kate had to see the notebook as quickly as possible. Even if the odds were one in a million against finding an answer for Ellen, she had to see it.

"Dunleavy, I've got to talk to you," he said with exaggerated reason. "Please."

Wearily, the nurse again walked to where he could be seen.

"Dunleavy, you care. I can see it in your face. You're tired and wasted, but you still care."

"So?"

"That woman who just went past here on the litter is Ellen Sandler, a friend of my wife's and mine. Dunleavy, she's bleeding—maybe bleeding to death. There's a chance the answer to her bleeding problem may be in this notebook, but it's written half in German and half in English, and it's technical as hell."

"So?"

"My wife is Kate Bennett, a pathologist here. Do you know her?" Dunleavy's acknowledging expression suggested that he might actually know too much. "Well, she speaks some German, and she knows what's been going on with that woman who just passed us. I've got to get this to her. She's a patient at Henderson Hospital in Essex."

"Mr. Samuels, I can't—"

"Dunleavy, please. There's no time to fuck around. Undo this strap and help me get to a cab. I can move all my extremities, see? I'll be fine."

"I—"

"Dammit, man, look at me! That woman is dying and

we might be able to help her. Get me an against-medical-advice paper and I'll sign it. I'll sign whatever the hell you want. But, please, do it now!"

The nurse hesitated.

"That woman needs us, my friend," Jared said. "Right this minute she needs us both."

Dunleavy reached down and undid the restraint. "It's my ass unless you come back and talk to the nursing office. Probably my ass anyway."

"I'll speak to them. I promise. So will my wife."

Dunleavy's eyes narrowed. "Please, Mr. Samuels," he said. "Don't do me any favors."

Even through the analgesic mist of Demerol and the distracting pain in her chest, Kate Bennett could sense the change in her husband. Bandaged, bruised, and needing a crutch to navigate, he had made a wonderful theatrical entrance into her room, sweeping through the doorway past a protesting night supervisor and announcing loudly, "The fucker's dead, Katey. Dead. He won't ever hurt you again." Then he had crossed to the bed, kissed her on the lips, and firmly but politely dismissed the supervisor and the special duty nurse.

Now he sat on a low chair by her left hand, mindless of his own discomfort, watching intently as she opened the black notebook—the sole useful vestige of the fire, pain, and death in the Omnicenter. There was a strength about the man, an assuredness, she had never sensed before. *The fucker's dead, Katey. He won't ever hurt you again.*

The words on the first page landed like hammer blows. *Studies in Estronate 250, Volume III of III*. Kate's heart sank.

"Jared," she said, swallowing at the sandpaper in her mouth and painfully adjusting the plastic tube that was draining bloody fluid from her chest, "have you looked at this?"

"Just to flip through. Why? Too much German? We'll find someone to translate."

"No. Actually, there's not that much. . . . Honey, it says here volume three of three."

"What?" He shifted forward and read the page. "Damn. I never saw any other books. There might have been others, but there was so much smoke. Everything was happening so fast. . . . Paquette could have explained everything if he had made it."

Kate searched her husband's face as he spoke. It was not an excuse, not an apology, but a statement of fact. Paquette had held the key to a deadly mystery. But Paquette was dead. And Jared, battered, bruised, clearly in great pain, was alive. If she could unlock the answers, it would be because he had risked his life for her. "We'll do the best we can with what we have," Kate said, turning to the first page of what appeared to be a series of clinical tests on a substance called Estronate 250. "I'm still foggy as hell from the anesthetic and that last shot, so bear with me."

There were, all told, one hundred and twenty carefully numbered pages. Paquette, or whoever had conducted this research, had been meticulous and precise. Stability studies; dosage modification studies; administration experiments in milk, in water, in solid food; investigation of side effects. Kate plodded through thirty years of terse German and English explanations and lengthy lists of test subjects, first from the state mental hospital at Wickford and in more recent years, from the Omnicenter. *Thirty years*. Arlen Paquette had not sounded that old over the phone, but perhaps he had taken over the Estronate research from someone else.

Ten minutes passed; then twenty. Jared shifted anxiously in his seat, and stared outside at the sterile, gray dawn. "How long does a gastroscopy take?" he asked.

Kate, unwilling to break her fragile concentration, glanced over at him momentarily. "That depends on what they find, and on what they choose to do about it. Jared,

I'm close to figuring out some things. I need a few more minutes."

"You look pretty washed out. Stop if you need to."

"I'm okay."

"Here. Here's some water."

She took a sip and then moistened her cracked, bleeding lips; then she returned her attention to the notebook. Another ten minutes passed before she looked up. Despite the pain and the drugs, her eyes were sparkling.

"Jared," she said, "I think I understand. I think I know what Estronate Two-fifty is."

"Well?"

"This is amazing. Assuming he's the one who conducted this research—or at least completed it—the late Dr. Paquette was worth his weight in gold to Redding Pharmaceuticals. Estronate Two-fifty is an oral antifertility drug that causes irreversible sterilization. It can be given to a woman by pill or even secretly in a glass of milk."

"Irreversible?"

Kate nodded vigorously, wincing at the jab of pain from her side. "Exactly. Think of it. No more tubal ligations, fewer vasectomies, help for third-world countries battling overpopulation."

"Then the scarred ovaries weren't a mistake?"

"Hardly. If I'm right, the microsclerosis was the desired result, not a side effect."

"But what about the bleeding? What about Ellen?"

Kate motioned him to wait. She was scanning a column marked *Nebenwirkung*.

"Look, Jared," she said excitedly. "See this word? It means side effects. All these women were apparently given this Estronate and monitored for side effects. Jesus, they're crazy. Paquette, Zimmermann, Horner—all of them. Absolutely insane. They used hundreds of people as guinea pigs."

"E. Sandler," Jared said.

"What?"

"E. Sandler. There it is right at the bottom of the page."

Kate groaned. "I may be even worse off than I think I am. Twice over the page and I missed it completely. Bless you, Jared."

Ellen's name was next to last in a column of perhaps three dozen. Halfway down a similar list on the following page, Kate found the names B. Vitale and G. Rittenhouse. She pointed them out to Jared and then continued a careful line-by-line check of the rest of the column and yet another page of subjects.

"I thought those were all the bleeding problems you know about," he said.

"They are."

"Well, whose name are you looking for?"

She looked up and for a moment held his eyes with hers. "Mine," she said.

She checked the pages once and then again before she felt certain. "I'm not here, Jared. I may be in some notebook marked anthranilic acid, but I'm not here."

"Thank God," he whispered. "At least volume three's given us that much."

Kate did not respond. She was again immersed in the columns of data, turning from one page to another, and then back. From where he sat, Jared studied her face: the intensity in her eyes, the determination that had taken her through twelve years of the most demanding education and training. At that moment, more so than at any other time in their marriage, he felt pride in her—as a physician, as a person, as his wife.

"Jared," she said breathlessly, her attention still focused on the notebook, "I think you did it. I think it's here."

"Show me."

"See these two words: *Thrombocytopenie* and *Hypofibrinogenamie*? Well, they mean low platelets and low fibrinogen. Just what Ellen is bleeding from. There's a notation here referring to Omnicenter Study Four B. Modification of *Thrombocytopenie* and *Hypofibrinogenamie* Using a Combination of Nicotinic Acid and Delta Amino Caproic Acid."

"I've heard of nicotinic acid. Isn't that a vitamin?"

"Exactly—another name for niacin. The other is a variant of a drug called epsilon amino caproic acid, which is used to reverse certain bleeding disorders. See, look here. All together, seven women on these three pages developed problems with their blood. They were picked up early, on routine blood tests in the Omnicenter."

"But Ellen and the other two aren't listed as having problems with their blood. There's nothing written next to their names in the side effects column."

She nodded excitedly. "That's the point, Jared. That's the key. Ellen and the two women who died were never diagnosed. Maybe they just didn't have Omnicenter appointments at the right time."

"The others were treated?"

Kate nodded. "That's what this Study Four B is all about. They got high doses of nicotinic acid and the other drug, and all of them apparently recovered. Their follow-up blood counts are listed right here. I think you did it. I think this is the answer. I just hope it's not too late and that somebody at Metro can get hold of the delta form of this medication. If not, maybe they can try the epsilon."

Jared handed her the receiver of the bedside telephone. "Just tell me what to dial," he said.

Kate's hand was shaking visibly as she set the receiver down. "Ellen's still in the operating room. Nearly three hours now."

"Who was that you were talking to?"

"Tom Engleson. He's a resident on the Ashburton Service. In fact, he's the one who called— Never mind. That's not important. Anyhow, he's been up to the operating room several times to check how it's going. The gastroscopist has found a bleeding ulcer. They've tried a number of different tricks to get it to stop, but so far no dice. They've had to call in a surgical team."

"They're going to operate?"

Kate shook her head. "Not if they can't do something with her clotting disorder."

"And?"

"Tom's gone to round up the hematologist on call and the hospital pharmacist. I'm sure they can come up with the nicotinic acid. It's that delta version of the EACA I'm not sure of. Goddamn Redding Pharmaceuticals. I'm going to nail them, Jared. If it's the last thing I do, I'm going to nail them for what they've done."

"I know a pretty sharp lawyer who's anxious to help," he said.

"I'm afraid even you may not be that sharp, honey."

"What do you mean?"

"Well, we've got this notebook and your word that it belongs to Paquette, but beyond that all we have is me, and I'm afraid my word isn't worth too much right now."

"It will be when they see this."

"Maybe."

"Either way, we're going to try. I mean somebody's going to have to come up with a logical explanation for all this that doesn't involve Redding Pharmaceuticals, and I really don't think that's possible. Do you?"

"I hope not."

"How long do you think it will take before we hear from this resident—what's his name?"

Kate suddenly recalled a gentle, snowy evening high above Boston Harbor and felt herself blush. "Tom. Tom Engleson." Did her voice break as she said his name? "I don't know. It shouldn't be long." It had better not be, she thought.

They waited in silence. Finally, Jared adjusted his cervical collar and rubbed at his open eye with the back of his hand. "Kate, there's something else, something I have to tell you," he said. "It has a good deal to do with what you were saying before about your word not being worth too much."

She looked at him queerly.

He held her hand tightly in his. "Kate, yesterday morning I spoke to Lisa."

Kate sat in the still light of dawn, stroking Jared's forehead and feeling little joy in the realization that, in his eyes at least, she had been vindicated. Nearly fourteen years that he might have shared in some way with his daughter had been stolen. Fourteen years. His hatred of Win Samuels was almost palpable. To her, the man was pitiful—not worth hating.

She had tried her best to make Jared see that and to convince him that whatever the circumstances, no matter how much time had gone by, he had a right to be a father to his daughter. He had listened, but it was clear to her that his pain and anger were too acute for any rational planning. There would be time, she had said, as much to herself as to him. If nothing else, there would be time.

The telephone rang, startling Jared from a near sleep.

Kate had the receiver in her hand well before the first ring was complete. For several minutes, she listened, nodding understanding and speaking only as needed to encourage the caller to continue.

Jared searched her expression for a clue to Ellen's status, but saw only intense concentration.

Finally, she hung up and turned to him. "That was the hematologist," she said. "They've started her on the drugs."

"Both of them?"

Kate nodded. "Reluctantly. They wanted more of a biologic rationale than Tom was able to give them, but in the end, her condition had deteriorated so much that they abandoned the mental gymnastics. They have her on high doses of both."

"And?"

She shrugged. "And they'll let us know as soon as

there's any change . . . one way or the other. She's still in the OR."

"She's going to make it," Jared murmured, his head sinking again to the spot beside her hand.

Less than ten minutes later, the phone rang again.

"Yes?" Kate answered anxiously. Then, "Jared, it's for you. Someone named Dunleavy. Do you know who that is?"

Bewildered, Jared nodded and took the receiver. "Dunleavy? It's Jared Samuels."

"Mr. Samuels. I'm glad you made it all right."

"Are you in trouble for letting me go?"

"Nothing I can't handle. That's not why I'm calling."

Jared glanced at his watch. Seven-fifty. Dunleavy's sixteen-hour double shift had ended almost an hour before. "Go on."

"I'm at the nurses' station in the OR, Mr. Samuels. They've just started operating on Mrs. Sandler. I think they're going to try and oversew her bleeding ulcer."

Jared put his hand over the mouthpiece. "Kate, this is the nurse who took care of me at Metro. They're operating on Ellen." He released the mouthpiece. "Thank you, Cary. Thank you for staying and calling to tell me that."

"That's only one of the reasons I called. There are two others."

"Oh?"

"I wanted you and Dr. Bennett to know I'm going to stay on and special Mrs. Sandler after she gets out of surgery."

"But you've been up for—"

"Please. I was a corpsman in Nam. I know my limitations. I feel part of all this and . . . well, I just want to stay part of it for a while longer. I'll sign off if it gets too much for me."

"Thank you," Jared said, aware that the words were not adequate.

But Dunleavy had something more to say. "I . . . I also wanted to apologize for that last crack I made about your wife." He went on, "It was uncalled for, especially since I only know what I know second or third hand. I'm sorry."

"Apology accepted," Jared said. "For what it's worth, she didn't do any of the things people are saying she did, and no matter how long it takes, we're going to prove it."

"I hope you do," Cary Dunleavy said.

"That was a curious little exchange," Kate said after Jared had replaced the phone on the bedside table. "At least the half I got to hear."

Jared recounted his conversation with the nurse for her.

"They've gone ahead with the surgery. That's great," she said, deliberately ignoring the reference to her situation. "Ellen's bleeding must have slowed enough to chance it. . . ."

Her words trailed off and Jared knew that she was thinking about her own situation. "Katey," he said. "Listen to me. Zimmermann is dead and Ellen isn't and you're not, and I'm not. And as far as I'm concerned that's cause for celebration. And I meant what I said to Dunleavy. You are innocent—of everything. And we're going to prove it. Together." He leaned over and kissed her gently. Then he straightened and said, "Rest. I'll wait with you until we hear from Metro." Kate settled back on the pillow.

A moment later, as if on cue, the day supervisor and another nurse strode into the room.

"Dr. Bennett," the supervisor said, "Dr. Jordan is in the hospital. She'll be furious if she finds out we haven't even done morning signs on her prize patient, let alone any other nursing care."

"Don't mind me," Jared said. "Nurse away."

The supervisor eyed him sternly. "There are vending machines with coffee and danish just down the hall. Miss Austin will come and get you as soon as we're through."

Jared looked over at Kate, who nodded. "I'll send for you if they call," she said.

"Very well, coffee it is." He rose and swung his parka

over his shoulder with a flourish. As he did, something fell from one of its pockets and clattered to the floor by the supervisor's feet.

The woman knelt and came up holding a miniature tape cassette.

"Did that fall from my parka?" Jared asked, examining the cassette, which had no label.

"Absolutely," the supervisor said. "Isn't it yours?"

Jared looked over at Kate, the muscles in his face suddenly drawn and tense. "I've never seen that tape before." His mind was picturing smoke and flames and blood . . . and a hand desperately clawing at the pocket of his parka. "Kate, we've got to play this tape. Now." He turned to the nurses. "I'm sorry. Go do whatever else you need to do. Right now we've got to find a machine and play this."

The supervisor started to protest, but was stopped by the look in Jared's eyes. "I have a machine in my office that will hold that, if it's that important," she said.

Again, Jared saw the hand pulling at him, holding him back. *For Christ's sake, Paquette, let go of me. I'm trying to get you out of here. Let go!* "It just might be," he said. "It just might be."

"So, Norton, first that brilliant letter to the newspapers about the ballplayer and now this biopsy thing. We asked you for something creative to stop Bennett, and you certainly delivered."

The entire tape, a conversation between Arlen Paquette and Norton Reese, lasted less than fifteen minutes. Still, for the battered audience of two in room 201 of Henderson Hospital, it was more than enough.

"It was my pleasure, Doctor. Really. The woman's been a thorn in my side from the day she first got here. She's as impudent as they come. A do-gooder, always on some goddamn crusade or other. Know what I mean?"

For Kate and Jared, the excitement of Reese's disclosures was tempered by an eerie melancholy. Paquette's conscience had surfaced, but too late for him. The man whose smooth, easy voice was playing the Metro administrator like a master angler was dead—beaten, burned, and then most violently murdered.

"You know what amazes me, Norton? What amazes me is how quickly and completely you were able to eliminate her as a factor. We asked, you did. Simple as that. It was as if you were on top of her case all the time."

"In a manner of speaking I was. Actually, I was on top of her chief technician—in every sense of the word, if ya know what I mean."

"Sheila." Kate hissed the word. "You know, I tried to believe she was the one who had set me up, but I just couldn't."

"Easy, boots. If you squeeze my hand any tighter, it's going to fall off."

"Jared, a woman lost her breast. Her breast!"

"You must be some lover, sir, to command that kind of loyalty. Maybe you can give me a few pointers some time."

Maybe I can, Arlen. Actually, it wasn't that tough to get Sheila to switch biopsy specimens. She had a bone of her own to pick with our dear, lamented, soon-to-be-ex pathologist. I just sweetened the pot by letting her pick on my *bone for a while beforehand.*

Norton Reese's laughter reverberated through the silent hospital room, while Kate pantomimed her visceral reaction to the man.

"I wonder," Jared mused, "how the lovely Ms. Pierce is going to respond when a prosecutor from the DA's office plays this for her and asks for a statement. I bet she'll try to save herself by turning State's evidence."

"She can try anything she wants, but she's still going to lose her license. She'll never work in a hospital again."

"Well, you really stuck it to her, Norton. With that chemist from the state lab in our pocket, Bennett's father-in-law doing what he can to discredit her even more, and now this biopsy coup, I doubt she'll ever be in a position

to cause us trouble at the Omnicenter again. Our friend is going to be very impressed."

"And very grateful, I would hope."

"You can't even begin to imagine the things in store for you because of what you've done, Nort. Good show. That's all I can say. Damn good show."

"We aim to please."

The tape ran through a few parting formalities before going dead.

Jared snapped off the machine and sat, looking at his wife in absolute wonder. "I would have broken," he said.

"Pardon?"

"If those things had come down on me like they did on you, I would have cracked—killed someone, maybe killed myself. I don't know what, but I know I would have gone under. It makes me sick just to think of how isolated you were, how totally alone."

"That's where you're wrong. You see, you may have had doubts about me, and justifiably so, but I never had doubts about you; so I wasn't really as alone as you might think."

"Never?"

Kate took her husband's hand and smiled. "What's a doubt or two between friends, anyway?" she asked.

EPILOGUE

Friday 9 August

Though it was barely eight-thirty in the morning, the humidity was close to saturation and the temperature was in the mideighties. August in DC. It might have been central Africa.

Silently, Kate and Jared crossed the mall toward the Hubert H. Humphrey building and what was likely to be the final session regarding her petition to the FDA for action against Redding Pharmaceuticals.

The hearings had been emotional, draining for all concerned. Terry Moreland, a law-school classmate whom Jared had recruited to represent them, had been doing superb work, overcoming one setback after another against a phalanx of opposition lawyers and a surprisingly unsympathetic three-man panel. One moment their charges against the pharmaceutical giant would seem as irrefutable as they were terrifying, and the next, the same allegations were made to sound vindictive, capricious, and unsubstantiated. Now the end of the hearings was at hand—all that remained were brief closing statements by each side, a recess, and finally a decision.

"Yo, Kate! Jared!" Stan Willoughby, mindless of the sultry morning, trotted toward them carrying his briefcase and wearing a tweed jacket that was precisely six months out of phase with the season. He had attended all the sessions and had testified at some length as to Kate's character and qualifications. "So, this is going to be it, yes?" he said, kissing Kate on the cheek and shaking Jared's hand warmly.

Over the months that had followed the arrest and resignation of Sheila Pierce and Norton Reese, the two men, Willoughby and Jared, had formed a friendship based on more than superficial mutual respect. In fact, it had been Jared who suggested a year or two of cochairpersons for the department of pathology, and who had then cooked the dinner over which Willoughby and Kate had come up with a working arrangement for dividing administrative responsibilities.

"We can't think of anything else that could go wrong—I mean go on—this morning," Jared said.

"You were more correct the first time," said Kate. "Most of this has been pretty brutal. First, all the threads connecting that animal Nunes to Redding Pharmaceuticals evaporate like morning dew. Then, suddenly, Carl Horner gets admitted to Darlington Hospital with chest pains and gets a medical dispensation not to testify. I don't know. I just don't know."

"We still have the notebook and the tape," Jared said.

Kate laughed sardonically. "The notebook, the tape, and—you neglect to add—a dozen earnest barristers asking over and over again where the name Cyrus Redding or Redding Pharmaceuticals is mentioned even once."

"Come, come, child," Willoughby chided. "Where's that Bennett spirit? We've made points. Plenty of them. Trust this old war horse. We may not have nailed them, but we've sure stuck 'em with a bunch of tacks."

"I hope you're right," she said, as they spotted Terry Moreland waiting for them by the steps to the Humphrey building.

The gray under Moreland's eyes and the tense set of his face spoke of the difficult week just past and of the ruling that was perhaps only an hour or two away.

"How're your vibes?" Kate asked after they had exchanged greetings and words of encouragement.

Moreland shook his head. "No way to tell," he said. "Emotionally, what with your testimony and Ellen's account of her ordeal, I think we've beaten the pants off them. Unfortunately, it doesn't seem as if we have a very emotionally oriented panel. When that fat one blew his nose in the middle of the most agonizing part of Ellen's testimony, I swear, I almost hauled off and popped him one. Watching the indifference creep across his face again and again, I couldn't help wondering if he hadn't already made up his mind."

"Or had it made up for him," Jared added.

"Absolutely," Moreland said as they pushed into the air-conditioned comfort of the office building and headed up to the second floor. "That sort of thing doesn't happen too often, I don't think, but it does happen. And all you have to do is look across the room to realize what we're up against. Hell, they could buy off St. Francis of Assisi with a fraction of what those legal fees alone come to."

The hearing room, modern in decor, stark in atmosphere, was largely empty, due in part to the surprisingly scant media coverage of the proceedings. Moreland had called the dearth of press a tribute to the power of Cyrus Redding and the skill of his PR people.

Redding's battery of lawyers was present, as were two stenographers and the counsel for the Bureau of Drugs. The seats for the three hearing officers, behind individual tables on a raised dais, were still empty.

Moreland and Stan Willoughby led the way into the chamber. Kate and Jared paused by the door. Through the windows to the north, they could see the American flag hanging limply over the Senate wing of the Capitol.

"I don't know which is scarier," Kate said, "the pharmaceutical industry controlling itself or the government doing it for them. I doubt Cyrus Redding's tactics would make it very far in the Soviet Union."

"I wouldn't bet on that, Dr. Bennett."

Startled, they turned. Cyrus Redding was less than five feet from them, wheeled in his chair by a blond buck who looked like a weightlifter. The words were the first they had heard the man say since the hearings had begun.

"I have many friends—and many business interests—in the USSR," he continued. "Believe me, businessmen are businessmen the world over."

"That's wonderfully reassuring," Kate said icily. "Perhaps I'd better submit an article to the Russian medical literature on the reversal of the bleeding complications of Estronate Two-fifty."

"I assure you, Doctor, that all I know of such matters, you have taught me at these hearings. If you have a moment, I was wondering if I might speak with you."

Kate looked at Jared, who gestured that he would meet her inside and then entered the hall.

Redding motioned his young bodyguard to a bench by the far wall.

"I suspect our hearing to end this morning," he said.

"Perhaps."

"I just want you to know what high regard I have for you. You are a most remarkable, a most tenacious, young woman."

"Mr. Redding, I hope you don't expect a thank you. I appreciate compliments only from people I respect."

Redding smiled patiently. "You are still quite young and most certainly naive about certain facts."

"Such as?"

"Such as the *fact* that it costs an average of sixty million dollars just to get a new drug on the market; often, quite a bit more."

"Not impressed. Mr. Redding, because of you and your policies, people have suffered and died unnecessarily. Doesn't that weigh on you?"

"Because of me and my policies, dozens of so-called orphan drugs have found their way to those who need them, usually without cost. Because of me and my policies, millions have had the quality of their lives improved and countless more their lives saved altogether. The greatest good for the most people at the least cost."

"I guess if you didn't believe that, you'd have a tough time looking at yourself in the mirror. Maybe you do anyway. I mean, a person's denial mechanism can carry him only so far."

Redding's eyes flashed, but his demeanor remained calm. "Considering the hardship my late employee has put you through, I can understand your anger," he said. "However, soon this hearing will be over, and soon we both must go on with our lives. I would like very much to have you visit me in Darlington, so that we might discuss a mutually beneficial joint endeavor. You are a survivor, Dr. Bennett, a woman who knows better than to subvert her needs in response to petty pressures from others. That makes you a winner. And it makes me interested in doing business with you."

"Mr. Redding," she said incredulously, "you seem to be ignoring the fact that the reason we're here is so that I can put you *out* of business."

Redding's smile was painfully patronizing. "Here's my card. The number on it will always get through to me. If you succeed in putting Redding Pharmaceuticals out of business, you don't have to call."

Kate glared at him. He was too smug, too confident. Was Terry Moreland's fear about some sort of payoff justified? "We're going to win," she said, with too little conviction. She turned and, disregarding the proffered card, entered the hearing room.

"What did Dr. Strangelove want?" Jared asked as she slid in between him and Terry Moreland.

Kate shook her head disparagingly. "The man is absolutely certifiable," she said. "He told me how little understanding I had for the difficulty, trials, and tribulations of being a multimillion-dollar pharmaceutical industry tycoon, and then he offered me a job."

"A job?"

"A mutually beneficial endeavor, I think he called it."

"Lord."

At that moment, without ceremony, the door to the right of the dais opened, and the three hearing officers shuffled into their seats, their expressions suggesting that there were any number of places they would rather have been. Before he sat down, the overweight, disheveled chairman pulled a well-used handkerchief from his pocket and blew his bulbous nose.

Kate and Jared stood by the stairway, apart from the groups of lawyers, reporters, and others who filled the corridor outside the hearing room. The recess was into its second hour, and with each passing minute, the tension had grown.

If over the previous four days the Redding forces had held the upper hand, the brilliant summation and indictment by Terry Moreland had placed the final verdict very much in doubt.

Of all those in the hallway, only Cyrus Redding seemed totally composed and at ease.

"I have this ugly feeling he knows something we don't," Kate said, gesturing toward the man.

"I don't see how the panel can ignore the points Terry made in there, boots. He's even better now than he was in law school, and he was a miniature Clarence Darrow then. But I will admit that Strangelove over there looks pretty relaxed. Say, that reminds me. You never said what your response was to his offer of a job."

Kate smiled. "I thought you were never going to ask. The truth is, I told him I would be unsuitable for employment in his firm because the first thing I'd have to do is take maternity leave."

Jared stared at her. "Slide that past me one more time."

"I was saving the news until after the verdict, but what the heck. We're due in April. Jared, I'm very excited and very happy. . . . Honey, are you all right? You look a little pale."

"This is for real, right?"

Kate nodded. "You sure you're okay? I can see where going from having no children to having a fourteen-year-old daughter and a pregnant wife might be a bit, how should I say, trying."

Jared held her tightly. "I keep thinking I should say something witty, but all that wants to come out is thanks. Thank you for this and for helping me reconnect with Stacy."

"Thanks accepted, but I expect something witty from you as soon as the business in this chamber is over. And please, don't make it sound like I've done something altruistic. I'm as excited about Stacy's visit as you are."

Jared's daughter would be in Boston in just ten days. Her first trip east. It was a journey that would include visits to Cape Cod and Bunker Hill, to Gloucester and the swan boats and the Old North Church. But there would be no visit to Win Samuels. Not now, and if Jared had his way, not ever.

"Hey, you two, they're coming in," Terry Moreland called from the doorway.

"What's the worst thing the panel could do to Redding?" Kate asked, grateful that Jared had chosen not to distract his friend with the news of her pregnancy.

"I guess turning the case over to the Justice Department for further investigation and prosecution would be the biggest victory for us. A hedge might be the referral of the whole matter to administrative channels within the FDA, in order to gather more information prior to a follow-up hearing." They settled into their seats. "Either way," Moreland added, "we'll know in a minute."

Kate slid the black notebook off the table before them, and held it tightly in her lap.

"Ladies and gentleman," the chairman announced, shuffling through a sheaf of papers and then extracting one sheet to read, "this panel has reached a unanimous decision regarding the charges brought by Dr. Kathryn Bennett against Redding Pharmaceuticals, Incorporated, of

Darlington, Kentucky. It is our feeling that the late Dr. Arlen Paquette did, in fact, conduct illegal and dangerous human research on the synthetic hormone Estronate Two-fifty and that he may well have also experimented illegally with other unproven substances. However, all available evidence indicates that the man, though in the employ of Redding Pharmaceuticals, was acting on his own and for his own personal gain. There is insufficient evidence to demonstrate prior knowledge of Dr. Paquette's criminal activities by Mr. Cyrus Redding or any other director of Redding Pharmaceuticals.

"Therefore, it is our recommendation that no further action be taken on this matter, and that all charges against Redding Pharmaceuticals be considered dealt with in a fair and just manner. Thank you all for your cooperation."

Without another word, the panel rose and marched from the chamber.

Kate and the three men with her sat in stunned disbelief, while across the room, lawyers were congratulating one another boisterously.

"I don't believe it," she said. "Not a recommendation for further study, not a reprimand for hiring someone as unprincipled as Arlen Paquette, nothing."

She glanced to one side, and almost immediately her eyes locked with Cyrus Redding's. The man favored her with another of his patronizing grins, and a shrug that said, "You have to expect such things when you play hardball with the big boys, young lady."

Kate glared at him. The battle may be over, Cyrus, she was thinking, but not the war. Somewhere out there is a noose so tight that even you won't be able to wriggle free—and I'm going to find it. Reese, Horner, Sheila Pierce. Somewhere, somehow, someone's going to come forward with proof of what you've done.

Jared took her hand, and together, they walked from the hearing room. "I'm sorry," he said softly.

"Me, too. But mostly, Jared, I'm frightened."

"Frightened? I don't think they'd dare try and hurt you."

She laughed sardonically. "You heard the verdict in there. I'm sure they don't even think I'm worth bothering to hurt."

"Then what?"

"It's the damn drugs, Jared. Starting with Estronate. Think of how many human guinea pigs there are in this one notebook. We contacted as many of the women as we could find, but there are others we just couldn't locate—and, I'm sure, other drugs. How many women out there are just starting to bruise? How many people—men and women—are developing weird tumors from medications they are trusting to make them well or keep them healthy?"

Jared gestured helplessly. "Kate, there are injustices all around. You've done what you could do."

"It's not enough. Jared, these drugs are like time bombs—unpredictable little time bombs capable of exploding inside anyone. I've got to keep after Redding. I've got to find some way to turn some heads around here, and if not here, then publicly. Somewhere, there's got to be a way. There's—"

"What is it, Kate?"

"What about an ad?"

"An ad?"

"In *The Globe*, *The Herald*, all the Boston and suburban papers—a classified ad asking women to search through their medicine cabinets for Omnicenter medications we can analyze. Maybe that's where the rope is to hang that bastard and put the other companies on notice. Right in those medicine cabinets. If enough Redding products were found contaminating enough Omnicenter medications, even the FDA panel wouldn't be able to ignore the company's involvement. I'm going to do it, Jared. As soon as we get back to Boston, I'm going to do it. And if it doesn't work, I'll try something else."

She glanced back down the corridor just as Redding was wheeled into the elevator. That sound you keep hearing in your ears is my footsteps, Cyrus, she was thinking. You had better get used to it.

About the Author

Michael Palmer, M.D., is the author of *Silent Treatment, Natural Causes, Extreme Measures, Flashback, Side Effects,* and *The Sisterhood.* A graduate of Wesleyan University and Case Western Reserve University School of Medicine, he trained in internal medicine at Boston City Hospital and Massachusetts General Hospital. Dr. Palmer is currently on the emergency-room staff of Falmouth Hospital. He lives with his wife and three sons on Cape Cod.

In this excerpt from Michael Palmer's new novel, *Silent Treatment*, you will meet Dr. Harry Corbett—and his mysterious nemesis, a skilled healer whose diabolical prescription is: murder.

SILENT TREATMENT

Available now in hardcover

CHAPTER 1

The indoor track, a balcony just under an eighth of a mile around, was on the top floor of the Grey Building of the Manhattan Medical Center. Ten feet below it was a modestly equipped gym with weights, the usual machines, heavy bags, and some mats. The fitness center, unique in the city, was exclusively for the hospital staff and employees. It had been created through the legacy of Dr. George Pollock, a cardiologist who had twice swum the English Channel. Pollock's death, at age ninety, had resulted from his falling off a ladder while cleaning the gutters of his country home.

Harry Corbett was on his fifteenth lap around the track when he first sensed the pain in his chest. At that moment of awareness, he was actually thinking about Pollock and about what it would be like to live until ninety. He slowed a bit and rotated his shoulders. The pain persisted. It wasn't much—maybe two on the scale of one to ten that physicians used. But it was there. Reluctant to stop running, Harry swallowed and massaged his upper abdomen. The discomfort was impossible to localize. One moment it seemed to be beneath his breastbone, the next in the middle of his back. He slowed a bit more, down from an eight-minute-per-mile pace to about ten-and-a-half. The ache was in his left chest now . . . no, it was gone . . . no, not gone, somewhere between his right nipple and clavicle.

He slowed still more. Then, finally, he stopped. He bent forward, his hands on his thighs. It wasn't angina, he told himself. Nothing about the character of the pain said cardiac. He understood his body, and he certainly understood pain. This pain was no big deal. And if it wasn't his heart, he really didn't give a damn where it was coming from.

Harry knew his logic was flawed—diagnostic deduction he would never, ever apply to a patient. But as with most physicians who experienced physical symptoms, his denial was more powerful than any logic.

Steve Josephson, jogging in the opposite direction, lumbered toward him.

"Hey, you okay?" he asked.

Still staring down at the banked cork track, Harry took a deep breath. The pain was gone, just like that. Gone. He waited a few seconds to be sure. Nothing. The smidgen of remaining doubt disappeared. *Definitely not the ticker,* he told himself again.

"Yeah. Yeah, I'm fine, Steve," he said. "You go ahead and finish."

"Hey, you're the zealot who goaded me into this jogging nonsense in the first place," Josephson said. "I'll take any excuse I can get to stop."

He was sweating more profusely than Harry, although he had probably run half as far. Like Harry, Josephson was a general practitioner—"family medicine specialists," the bureaucrats had decided to name them. However, a task force had recently been charged with determining whether or not to reduce the privileges of GPs in the hospital in favor of specialists, and they were almost ready to present their findings. From the rumors Harry had tapped into, the recommendations of the committee, headed by cardiac surgeon Caspar Sidonis, would be harsh—the professional equivalent of castration.

"We've been running together three or four times a week for almost a year," Josephson said, "and I've never seen you stop before your five miles was up."

"Well, Stephen, it just goes to show that there's a first time for everything." Harry studied his friend's concerned face and softened. "Listen, pal, I'd tell you if it was anything. Believe me I would. I just don't feel like running today. I've got too much on my mind."

"I understand. Is Evie going in tomorrow?"

"The day after. Ben Dunleavy's her neurosurgeon. He talks about clipping her cerebral aneurysm as if he was removing a wart or something. But I guess it's what he does."

They moved off the track as the only other runners in the gym approached.

"How's she holding up?" Josephson asked.

Harry shrugged. "All things considered, she seems pretty calm about it. But she can be pretty closed in about her feelings."

Closed in. The understatement of the week, Harry mused ruefully. He couldn't recall the last time Evie had shared feelings of any consequence with him.

"Well, tell her Cindy and I wish her well, and that I'll stop by to see her as soon as that berry is clipped."

"Thanks," Harry said. "I'm sure she'll appreciate hearing that."

In fact, he doubted that she would. As warm, bright, and caring as Steve Josephson was, Evie could never get past his obesity.

"Did you ever listen to him breathe?" she had once asked as Harry was extolling his virtues as a physician. "I felt like I was trying to converse with a bull in heat. And those white, narrow-strapped tees he wears beneath his white dress shirts—pul-lease. . . ."

"So, then," Josephson said as they entered the locker room, "before we shower, why don't you tell me what *really* happened out there."

"I already—"

"Harry, I was halfway around the track from

you and I could see the color drain from your face."

"It was nothing."

"You know, I spent years learning how to ask nonleading questions. Don't make me regress."

For the purpose of insurance application forms or the occasional prescription, Harry and Josephson served as one another's physician. And although each persistently urged the other to schedule a complete physical, neither of them had. The closest they had come was an agreement made just after Harry's forty-ninth birthday. Harry, already obsessive about diet and exercise, had promised to get a checkup and a cardiac stress test. Steve, six years younger but fifty pounds heavier, had agreed to have a physical, start jogging, and join Weight Watchers. But except for Josephson's grudging sessions on the track, neither had followed through.

"I had a little indigestion," Harry conceded. "That's all. It came. It bothered me for a minute. It left."

"Indigestion, huh? By indigestion do you perhaps mean chest pain?"

"Steve, I'd tell you if I had chest pain. You know I would."

"Slight correction. I know you *wouldn't*. How many men did you lug back to that chopper?"

Although Harry rarely talked about it, over the years almost everyone at the hospital had heard some version of Na Trang, or had actually composed one themselves. In the stories, the number of wounded he had saved before being severely wounded himself had ranged from three—which was in fact the number for which he had been decorated—to twenty. He once overheard a patient boast that his doctor had killed a hundred Viet Cong while rescuing an equal number of GIs.

"Stephen, I am no hero. Far from it. If I thought the pain was anything, anything at all, I'd tell you."

Josephson was unconvinced.

"You owe me a stress test. When do you turn fifty?"

"Two weeks."

"And when's the date of that family curse?"

"Oh, come on."

"Harry, you're the one who told me about it. Now, when is it?"

"September. September first."

"You've got four weeks."

"I . . . Okay, okay. As soon as Evie's situation is straightened out I'll set one up with the exercise lab. Promise."

"I'm serious."

"You know, in spite of what everyone says about you, I always thought that."

Harry stripped and headed for the showers. He knew that Steve, in spite of himself, was staring at the patchwork of scars on his back. Thirty-one pieces of shrapnel, half a kidney and a rib. The design left by their removal would have blended into the pages of a Rand-McNally Road Atlas. Harry flashed on the incredible sensation of Evie's breasts gliding slowing over the healed wounds in what she used to call her patriotic duty to an old war hero. *When was the last time?* That, he acknowledged sadly, he couldn't remember.

He cranked up the hot water until he was enveloped in steam. Two weeks until fifty. *Fifty!* He had never experienced any sort of midlife crisis that he could think of. But maybe the deep funk he had been in lately was it. By now the pieces of his life should have fallen into place. Instead, the choices he had made seemed to be under almost constant attack. And crumbling.

He thought about the day halfway through his convalescence when he had made the decision to withdraw from his residency in surgery and devote his professional life to general practice. Something had happened to him over his year and a half in Nam. He no longer had any desire to be center stage. Not that he minded the drama and intensity of the operating room. In fact, even now he truly enjoyed his time there. But in the end, he realized, he simply wanted to be a family doc. *Simply.* If there was one word most descriptive of the life Harry had chosen for himself, "simply" might well be it. Get up in the morning, do what seems right, try to help a few people along the way, develop an interest or two outside of work, and sooner or later, things would make sense. Sooner or later, the big questions would be answered.

Well, lately things weren't making much sense at all. The big answers were just as elusive as ever.

More so. His marriage was shaky. The kids he had always wanted to have just never happened. The financial security that he had expected would gradually develop over the years was tied to a brand of medicine he was not willing to practice. So he never allowed his office to become a medical mill. He never sent a collection agency after anyone. He never refused anyone care because they couldn't pay. He never moved to the suburbs. He never went back for the training that would have made him a subspecialist. The result was a car that was seven years old, and a retirement fund that would last indefinitely—as long as he didn't try to retire.

Now his professional stature was being hauled up on the block, his wife was facing a neurosurgeon's scalpel, and just four weeks from the first day of the ninth month of his fifty-first year, he had experienced pain in his chest.

* * *

After twenty-one admissions to Parkside Hospital, Joe Bevins could close his eyes and tell time by the sounds and smells coming from the hallway outside his room. He even knew some of the nurses and aides by their footsteps—especially on Pavilion 5. More often than not, he was able to get the admissions people to send him there. The staff on that floor was the kindest in the hospital and knew the most about caring for chronic renal-failure patients who were on dialysis. He also liked the rooms on the south end of the floor best of any in the hospital—the rooms with views of the park and, in the distance, the Empire State Building.

It wasn't a great life, having to get plugged in at the dialysis center three times a week, and having to be rushed to Parkside every time his circulation broke down, or an infection developed, or his blood sugar got too far out of whack, or his heart rhythm became irregular, or his prostate gland swelled up so that he couldn't pee. But at seventy-one, with diabetes and nonfunctioning kidneys, it was a case of beggars can't be choosers.

Outside his door, two litters rattled by, returning patients from physical therapy. One of them, a lonely old gal with no family, had lost both her legs to gangrene. Now they were just keeping her around until a nursing-home bed became available. *It could be worse,* Joe reminded himself. *Much worse.* At least he had Joe Jr., and Alice, and the kids. At least he had visitors. He glanced over at the other bed in his room. The guy in that bed, twenty years younger than he was, was down having an operation on his intestines—a goddamn cancer operation.

Oh, yes, Joe thought. No matter how bad it got for him, he never wanted to forget that it could always be worse.

He sensed the presence at his door even before he heard the man clear his throat. When he turned, a white-coated lab tech was standing there, adjusting the stoppered tubes in his square, metal basket.

"You must be new here," Joe said.

"I am. But don't worry. I've been doing this sort of work for a long time."

The man, somewhere in his forties, smiled at him. He had a nice enough face, Joe decided—not a face he took to all that much, but not one that looked burnt out or callous either.

"What are you here to draw?" he asked.

Joe's doctors almost always told him what tests they had ordered. They knew he liked to know. All three specialists had been by on rounds that morning, and none had said anything about blood work.

"This is an HTB-R29 antibody titer," the man said matter-of-factly, setting his basket on the bedside table. "There's an infection going around the hospital. Everyone with kidney or lung problems is being tested."

"Oh." The technician had an accent of some sort. It wasn't very marked, and it wasn't one Joe could place. But it was there. "Where're you from?" he asked.

The man smiled over at him as he prepared his tubes and needle. The blue plastic name tag pinned on his coat read: G. TURNER, PHLEBOTOMIST. Trying not to be obvious, Joe looked down at his clip-on identification badge. It was twisted around so that it was impossible to read.

"You mean originally?" the man responded. "Australia originally. But I've been here in the U.S. since I was a child. You have a very astute ear, Mr. Bevins."

"I taught English before I got sick."

"Ah-ha. I see," Turner said, glancing minutely at the door, which he had partially closed on his way in. "Well, then, shall we get on with this?"

"Just be careful of my shunt."

Turner lifted Joe's right forearm and gently ran his fingers over the dialysis shunt—the firm, distended vessel created by joining an artery and vein. His fingers were long and finely manicured, and Joe had the passing thought that the man played piano, and played it well.

"We'll use your other arm," Turner said. He tightened a latex tourniquet three inches above Joe's elbow, and took much less time than most technicians did to locate a suitable vein. "You seem to take all this in stride. I like that," he said as he gloved, then swabbed the skin over the vein with alcohol.

"All those doctors don't keep me alive," Joe said. "My attitude does."

"I believe you. I'm going to use a small butterfly IV needle. It's much gentler on your vein."

Before Joe could respond, the fine needle, attached to a thin, clear plastic catheter, was in. Blood pushed into the catheter. Turner attached a syringe to the end of the catheter and injected a small amount of clear liquid.

"This is just to clear the line," he said.

He waited, perhaps fifteen seconds. Then he drew a syringeful of blood, pulled the tiny needle out, and held the small puncture site firmly.

"Perfect. Just perfect," he said. "Are you okay?"

I'm fine.

Joe was certain he said the words, but he heard nothing. The man standing beside his bed kept smiling down at him benevolently, all the while keeping pressure on the spot where the butterfly needle had been.

I'm fine, Joe tried again.

Turner released his arm and placed the used needle and tube in the metal basket.

"Good day, Mr. Bevins," he said. "You've been most cooperative."

With the first icy fingers of panic beginning to take hold, Joe watched as the man turned and left the room. He felt strange, detached, floating. The air in the room was becoming thick and heavy. Something was happening to him. Something horrible. He called out for help, but again there was no sound. He tried to turn his head, to find the call button. From the corner of his eye, he could see the cord hanging down toward the floor. He was paralyzed—unable to move or even to take in a breath. The call button was no more than three feet away. He strained to move his hand toward it, but his arm was lifeless. The air grew heavier still, and Joe felt his consciousness beginning to go. He was dying; drowning in air. And there was absolutely nothing he could do about it. Nothing at all.

The pattern on the drop ceiling blurred, then

darkened, then faded to black. And with the deepening darkness, Joe's panic began to fade.

From beyond the nearly closed door to his room, he heard the sound of the cart from dietary being wheeled to the kitchen at the far end of the hallway. Next he caught the aroma of food.

And after twenty-one hospitalizations at Parkside, most of them on Pavilion 5, he knew that it was exactly eleven-fifteen.